THE STORY OF YOU

Published by Green Crow Publishing, LLC
www.greencrowpublishing.com

ISBN: 978-1-967309-05-4 (ebook)
ISBN: 978-1-967309-06-1 (paperback)

First Edition: November 18, 2025

0 9 8 7 6 5 4 3 2 1

I0563329

# THE STORY OF YOU

DANIEL MAUNZ

*Of course this book is for you, Patrick.*
*We couldn't be any prouder of you.*

# PROLOGUE

The world only made sense to me upon recognizing my inherent resistance to joy.

For much of my existence I plodded through the paces of life, naively assuming others shared my spirit of apathy even if, like me, they sought to hide it by putting on their best faces out in the world. Throughout high school, I learned to mask my indifference with a variety of veneers, such as a contemplative frown as I listened to other students discuss an assigned reading in English class or an intense furrowing of my brow while absorbing a pep talk before a basketball game. But beneath that window dressing, there was a well of pure disinterest. Moreover, I believed concealing that detachment was simply an expectation placed on all adults.

Despite my suspicions that the world at large was also wearing forced smiles, some deep-seated instinct drove me to make my own artificial grin as authentic as possible. In fact, so strong was my need to project a sense of normalcy that it motivated me to thrive in areas where I felt nothing but cold dispassion. When I started high school, I was recruited into the world of football due solely to my size, and my playing career soon became a dance of contradictions: I spent the summer silently praying for the school budget vote to fail so the upcoming season would be canceled, only to flourish on the field in autumn after my wishes were denied. To my annoyance, I achieved such success as a lineman that I earned a scholarship to a college I otherwise couldn't have afforded. And so, after graduating, I numbly accepted that my sentence as an athlete would be extended for an additional four years, not that I ever outwardly expressed anything other than unmitigated delight at the prospect.

At college, I found myself surrounded by enthusiastic jocks, passionate in their vain efforts for our subpar team. Maintaining the strategies developed in high school, I outwardly matched their bravado, joining their pregame chants with vigor while hiding my lack of regard for the outcome of the actual games. I continued to suspect at least some of my teammates were also going through the motions, even if there was no tangible evidence to support my theory.

Only in my senior year of college did I appreciate how off the mark my hypothesis was: as bad as our team was, my teammates collectively delighted in spending our Augusts running wind sprints in ninety-degree heat while wearing pounds of equipment. In November, they were ecstatic to play games in subfreezing temperatures, when every play invited the possibility of chunks of flesh being ripped out of our appendages, and the frozen ground made it feel as if we were playing tackle football on asphalt. My teammates were not torturing themselves solely to maintain the illusion of normalcy. Their happiness was genuine.

I was the anomaly. And I realized then that would be the case for the rest of my life.

With that insight in hand, I began embracing my strangeness and stopped presenting as anything other than my true self. And so, once I went to law school—a decision I made for no reason other than to kick the can of choosing a career another three years down the road—there was no panache to my existence as a student: I went to class, listened to the lectures, and did whatever assignments were asked of me. There were times I witnessed other students vigorously debate each other on some assignment, and a part of me would mourn, if only for a moment, my inability to muster any similar enthusiasm, but such instances were easy to shake off. That passion simply wasn't there, and I felt no desire at that stage of my life to feign it.

My first job as an attorney was for a midsized litigation firm on Long Island, where I once again performed the tasks assigned to me to the best of my ability with no emotional connection to the work itself. Even though by that point I'd recognized the unique nature of my internal deadness, I couldn't help but feel bewildered at how different my view of being an attorney was from that of my colleagues.

There was one occasion, after I went out to a mandatory lunch with my litigation unit, I heard a coworker proclaim how much fun it had been. I responded with a sharp look, seeking to discern whether the comment had been sarcastic in nature. But it seemed sincere, prompting me to replay the lunch in my mind—small talk about our plans for the summer, an anecdote about a quirky client. Running through it all, I couldn't find anything that even arguably fell within the scope of "fun"—only the inherent loneliness in realizing others enjoyed what I did not, although I was well used to that by then.

Once I learned to stop regretting how different I was from my colleagues, my focus turned to how I could make the most out of my situation. It didn't take long to formulate a strategy to live my best life: don't waste time pursuing happiness and, instead, concentrate on minimizing annoyances.

It was undoubtedly the mindset of a grump, but I was comfortable enough in my own skin not to care. Still, maintaining even that modest tinkering to my mindset was a trickier proposition than one might think. For example, while I rarely desired to accept an invitation to dinner with old friends, it was sometimes worth the three hours of boredom to avoid the days of drama that would follow if I were to decline the invite outright. I often had to engage in complicated computations in making those day-to-day decisions, but they all boiled down to one question: which choice would cause the least amount of pain or annoyance? The possibility of *enjoying* something was never a factor in that analysis. So you can imagine my surprise when a path to happiness—a conduit to joy—entered my life.

But that is precisely what happened when I met your mother.

A secretary named Joan at my firm sought to introduce us, thinking we would hit it off.

"She loves to laugh, and you have such a great sense of humor!" Joan told me. I tried to resist, explaining in earnest I wasn't dating material by virtue of being dead on the inside. But Joan only laughed. "See, there's that sense of humor of yours!"

I still didn't give in, but Joan was relentless in her efforts. It reached a point where I realized the annoyance of being badgered about going on a date eclipsed the discomfort of spending an hour meeting someone new. Once I secured a promise from Joan never to bother me again about my personal life if I went on that one date, I reluctantly agreed to it.

A few days later, I met your mother for drinks after work. Even though I'd seen a picture of her, I wasn't confident in my ability to find her in a crowded bar, given my lack of facial recognition skills. It wasn't uncommon for me to go to court and introduce myself to an attorney I had already met countless times, simply because I didn't recognize them with their hair pulled back in a ponytail. But I was fairly certain that Joan had also sent a picture of me to your mother, and I hoped she'd be able to spot me as I wandered about the bar aimlessly.

My optimism was rewarded when I felt a timid tap at my shoulder.

"Excuse me, are you Will Banfield? I'm Anne."

I turned to face your mother, who looked much as she had in the picture I'd seen of her. Her sparkling blue eyes seemed especially bright when contrasted with her fair features, and her smile didn't seem forced at all—it radiated genuine warmth. Right away, I could sense your mother's kind spirit, but that didn't bring me any comfort in that moment. It merely made me feel bad about wasting her time as I went through with the motions of our date.

There were no nerves on my part—I felt zero pressure whatsoever to impress her. It was a foregone conclusion to me that nothing would come of our meeting, and I wasn't inclined to be anything other than my flawed self from the outset. Part of me hoped that operating without a filter could speed things along by scaring her off, ending the night early and allowing us both to get home at a reasonable hour.

But the strange thing is, it didn't.

I was myself that night, and against all odds, your mother wasn't repulsed. In fact, she seemed attracted to whatever energy I was putting out there. I've spent a long time wondering what she saw in me that night to keep her from making an excuse to leave. The best I can say about myself is that I was honest to a fault. But in a world that's so often filled with phoniness, I suppose that's not nothing.

It didn't take long for your mother to confirm I was right in my assessment of her gentle nature. She listened wide-eyed as I told her about myself and my unique view of the world, and my difficulties in enjoying things the way others did. After sensing her genuine interest in what I had to say, I tried to gauge her perception of life, and she delighted in giving thoughtful responses to my odd questions. She laughed hard when I asked, with complete sincerity, whether she felt anything positive after receiving a Christmas card in the mail, and that laugh triggered something deep, and nearly unrecognizable, within me.

*Joy.*

While I couldn't generate that spark for myself, I was astounded to discover that I could experience it vicariously through your mother. But the source was irrelevant—joy was joy. Her bliss resonated with me, and her tremendous heart made me sure that devoting my existence to ensuring her happiness was a noble pursuit, with the added benefit of also being personally fulfilling.

Several hours later, as I sensed our date wrapping up, I asked your mother if she would like to get together again, and she readily agreed. Several nights later, the two of us drove out to Long Beach and walked along the boardwalk, learning more about each other in the process. When we finished our walk, I ventured, with some trepidation, "That was fun, right?" I think your mother interpreted it as a rhetorical question, but it wasn't. Only once she confirmed her enjoyment of our stroll was I able to feel that joy myself.

No longer did I feel dead inside, and your mother seemed more than content with my presence in her life. A year after we met, we were engaged, and six months after that, we were married. It was one year into our marriage when your mother told me she was pregnant.

Pregnant with you.

I felt like a third wheel as your mother marveled at your residency inside her. The love in her voice was unmissable when she described feeling you rest during the day while she was out and about, only to swim around when she lay down for the night. I was glad for it—your mother was as happy as I'd ever seen her. And that, in turn, made me happy.

In the third trimester of the pregnancy, your mother started complaining about a feeling of itchiness on her extremities. She scratched at her skin despite herself, leaving her legs and arms constantly raw. But when she voiced her concern to her doctors, they laughed away her complaints. "That's just part of the process of being pregnant!" the doctors told her. "I went through that myself!" a physician's assistant added at one point. Your mother accepted these explanations without protest, but she couldn't shake the feeling something was off.

As the due date approached, your mother once again articulated her worries to the doctors. They agreed, if only to appease her, to run some tests. Her blood was drawn and your mother spent two days anxiously awaiting confirmation that she was being silly and that everything was proceeding just as it should.

Two days later, in the early evening, your mother finally heard back from one of her doctors. The test results had come back—she had cholestasis of pregnancy, a relatively rare condition that impacts the flow of bile from the liver. You and your mother were both at risk, and she was told that they would have to induce labor immediately, even though the due date was over a week away. Getting you out as soon as possible became the number one priority.

I raced your mother to the hospital on a snowy Friday evening across icy roads that were thankfully devoid of traffic. When we got there, the hospital assigned your mother a bed, and I sat uselessly at her side while doctors and nurses filtered in and out to implement various procedures to induce labor. But although the labor pains were quick to come, you were not.

Your mother spent over fifty hours in labor, carefully monitored by a rotating team of nurses who realized early on that whenever she rested on her right side, your heart rate would drop. The nurses took to buttressing your mother with pillows to ensure that she remained perched on her left until she was ready to deliver. All the while, I sat next to the bed, offering nothing but lame encouragement and feeling guilty about my increasing exhaustion, knowing it was a minuscule fraction of what your mother was experiencing.

Shortly after midnight on Monday, a doctor examined your mother and declared she was still not dilated enough to give birth. "I think we need to consider an abdominal delivery," the doctor told us. Noting my confused look, the doctor added, "A cesarean." Your mother, beyond exhausted, readily agreed.

From there, a team of doctors and nurses prepped her for surgery while I donned my own set of scrubs so that I could be present for the birth. After your mother was wheeled away, a nurse escorted me to a small waiting room, empty except for a chair and a muted television affixed to the wall, playing CNN. The nurse let me know before leaving that someone would come for me once they were ready to start the procedure. She further advised me to keep my eyes down when they brought me into the operating room until I was safely behind a curtain.

After what seemed like an inordinate amount of time, I was finally summoned and escorted to the operating room. I instantly forgot the nurse's earlier warning and glanced at your mother, laying on her back with a team of medical professionals surrounding her. I noticed she had already been cut open, and I averted my eyes at the sight of all the blood. A curtain had been set up across her shoulders to ensure she couldn't see what was being done to her body. But I knew she could feel it, despite the anesthesia.

Your mother offered me a tired smile when I joined her behind the curtain, and I brushed a few strands of hair out of her eyes. Otherwise, I didn't know what I should be doing, so I just stood there, occasionally stroking her head, and focused on hiding my own anxiety. The medical team spoke quietly amongst each other, but even the words I could make out were gibberish to me, and I soon began to tune them out. I detected movement behind the curtain, but I could only guess at what was transpiring.

A few minutes later, a new sound pierced the room: a baby's cry. Before I could process what was happening, a nurse darted out from the other side of the curtain, whisking a bundle to a corner of the room where a pediatrician was waiting to run some routine tests. I squeezed your mother's shoulder and mouthed at her, "Great job." She was too tired to respond, but she angled her head toward me in silent acknowledgment.

A nurse approached me and said in a soft tone, "Come,

meet your son." I glanced at your mother, feeling guilty that I'd meet you before she could, but I nonetheless followed the nurse across the room. She pointed toward a small bassinet and I peered in, seeing you for the first time.

You lay stretched out on a thin blanket, with your eyes closed. I was taken aback at how long and pink you were, with your head full of light-colored hair. Another surprise to me was that you were no longer crying and, in fact, appeared to be sleeping, which I couldn't fathom after the journey you had just taken. They had put an identification tag around your right ankle and attached a plastic contraption to what remained of your umbilical cord, but you were otherwise completely naked. I felt inexplicably shy and uncertain of how to interact with you and so, not knowing what else to do, I took a light hold of your right foot, which felt impossibly small in my hand, and gently shook it.

"Hello, Quince," I murmured as I held your foot. The nurse gave me a side glance.

"Kwince?" the nurse asked. "With a K?"

"With a Q," I corrected her. "It's the name of a character in *A Midsummer Night's Dream*. My wife loved that name ever since she stumbled across it in high school, and she vowed to use it the first chance she could. I was worried that people would constantly mispronounce the name by giving it an extra syllable and say it like the Spanish fifteen, but those concerns were laughed away."

"It's a beautiful name," the nurse said, and it wasn't clear if she meant it or if that was just something she had been trained to say after every birth. She gathered you up, taking care to support your head with one of her hands as she did, before adding, "Let's go introduce Quince to his mommy."

The nurse then carried you over to your mother, with me shuffling behind.

"Hi there!" your mother said to you, beaming at our approach. Her shoulders twitched, only to stop once she remembered she didn't have access to her arms, which were pinned at her sides. Instead, she resorted to caressing you with her exhausted eyes, pouring out waves of unadulterated love. The nurse lowered you next to your mother's face, and your tiny hand, flailing in the air, briefly found your mother's cheek. I snapped myself out of my reverie quick enough to find my phone and take a photo of the moment. I thought about asking the nurse to take a picture of the three of us, but she was busy holding you, and everyone else in the room seemed occupied.

*There will be time enough for family pictures later,* I remember thinking.

Wondering how long it would be until your mother was free to hold you herself, I forced myself to start paying attention to what was transpiring on the other side of the curtain in case I could divine any clues. I had expected tuning in to sounds conveying the routine matter of putting your mother back together, but that wasn't what I heard. There was an urgency in those muffled voices that made my blood run cold. Even though that was my first time in an operating room for a C-section, I could sense from the energy in the room we weren't dealing with business as usual.

Something was wrong.

A surgical attendant glided around the curtain and whispered to the nurse holding you, prompting her to leave abruptly, carrying you away from us. Another nurse approached me and said in a soft but firm voice, "We need to take you out of here."

"What's happening?" I asked, as I allowed myself to be led out. I glanced back at your mother just before the curtain hid her face from my view, and she looked back at me with tired, unfocused eyes. I blew her a kiss, trying to convey that everything was fine.

"We can't talk here," the nurse said with increased forcefulness. There was nothing I could do to help with whatever was happening, other than be as compliant as possible, so I didn't argue and instead kept pace with the nurse as she exited the room. I slowed down to look back one last time upon reaching the doors. The curtain obscured your mother's face, but a medical team buzzed around her, completely ignoring my exit.

There were many voices speaking at once, making it impossible to tell what was happening, but then one voice cut through the tumult: "Heart rate down to thirty-nine."

"Oh God," I whispered, stopping in my tracks, but the nurse gently pushed me through the doorway with a firm hand on my back. She led me back to the waiting room I had occupied before the procedure and sat me down before letting out a long breath. The nurse studied me, registering the anxiety on my face, and I could see her expression soften somewhat. She took a moment to reflect on what information she was free to share before speaking.

"I don't know exactly what's happening," she admitted. "Your wife's heart rate was dropping, which raised some concerns that are being addressed. That's all I know right now. I'm sorry I can't tell you more. Someone will be in shortly to give you a more meaningful update."

With one last sympathetic look, the nurse exited the room, leaving me alone once again with the muted CNN. Some time later, a doctor who I recognized as your mother's obstetrician joined me in the room and gave me the promised update.

And that was how I learned that your mother passed away shortly after your birth.

The doctor explained what had transpired and reassured me that your mother didn't experience any pain in her final moments. I tried to focus on everything she explained after that initial pronouncement, but her words washed over me as I processed this loss. I knew the tears would come eventually, once the shock passed, but all I remember in that immediate aftermath was trying to recalibrate what the world would look like without your mother in it. I thought of all the people who would grieve for her and feel the pain of her absence, and I started to mourn for them.

I mourned for your mother's parents and her sister. Once I married your mother, they had entrusted me with the responsibility of keeping her safe and happy. It was my most important job, but one in which I ultimately failed.

I mourned for you. Throughout the pregnancy, I often reflected on how lucky you were to be born to the kindest person I had ever known. A person destined to be a fabulous mother. But through a cruel twist of fate, you'd be stuck with me, and only me. I would do my best, of course—that was the one command your mother undoubtedly would have given me before her passing, had there been an opportunity. But I also knew my "best" would fall woefully short of what your mother would have provided, and that your life would be the poorer for it.

I mourned for your mother. Her happiness only grew during her pregnancy, culminating with that brief moment where she got to meet you face-to-face. I suspect your mother, with her eternal optimism, would have expressed how thankful she was to have been gifted that moment at all, but to me it seemed terribly unfair she'd only been given that brief tease. She, of all people, deserved more than that. She deserved a life with you.

And finally, as selfish as it was, I mourned for myself.

Right away, I recognized that your mother's passing would strip me of my access to joy. It was only through her that I could experience happiness, and I slowly became resigned to resuming a life focused on the avoidance of pain.

It would be years before I realized I was wrong. Joy would not be unattainable, even after your mother's death, though it would take me some time to discover this. But I'd come to find another conduit through which I could experience joy, and even love, notwithstanding my general resistance to such things, and that is the story I'd like to tell you now.

This is the story of you.

# PART I

*The Things You Saw*

**1**

The days following your entry into the world and your mother's departure from it were a chaotic blur. Family from all directions descended upon us for your mother's funeral and to meet you for the first time. There was no shortage of people willing to watch you in those days while I struggled to process your mother's loss. Too out of sorts to put up a resistance, I numbly accepted their help, although I would have welcomed the distraction of caring for a newborn. It also felt like a dereliction of my duty, outsourcing your care at such an early stage, even though I can see with hindsight that I needed that time to grieve.

But the family tornado eventually died down, leaving just the two of us. I knew it would take a lifetime to work through your mother's unexpected passing, but one thing was clear at the outset: your mother would have wanted me to be as perfect a father to you as I could manage.

And that is what I was determined to do.

There is a cliché—or perhaps "trope" is a better word—in stories about a father holding onto a lifelong resentment of a child after his wife dies in childbirth. Having gone through that experience myself, I can attest that I never came close to harboring any negative feelings toward you regarding your mother's fate. I was, in fact, relieved to have you in my life at that time, since caring for you represented a well-defined task for me to carry out as a way to honor your mother. Without you, I would've been devoid of purpose. It scares me to think about what I would have done without you during that time.

And so, I assumed the role of a single parent with energy and focus. When you had a diaper that had to be changed, I leaped at the opportunity. When you were hungry, I was ready with a warm bottle of formula. I learned to sleep above the covers to buy myself an extra second to reach you when you cried out during the night.

I did nothing for myself during those early months. There were no babysitters to watch you while I went on a fishing trip with friends. There were no television shows I snuck in while you were sleeping. I slept when you slept, and when you were awake, you were my focus. I thought this dedicated attention to you would've made your mother proud of me.

It took a long time to realize that despite my efforts, there were many ways in which I was failing you. By ensuring that you were constantly clean, fed, and warm, I thought I was checking off all the boxes of caring for an infant. But, of course, there was more to it than that. There were many intangibles I was failing to deliver while carrying out my responsibilities with precision, if not heart.

It would be some time before I learned the cost of my failures.

~

In fact, I only started to question my parental skills a few months after your fourth birthday, when your preschool called me in for a meeting in April.

I had received a vague email from your teacher, Ms. Natalie, asking if I was available to come in one morning to speak with her. She suggested dropping you off at school early to allow us to talk while her assistant, Ms. Alex, watched you along with the other students whose parents had arranged for early drop off. I fired off a quick response agreeing to that plan, although I wasn't particularly curious about the meeting. The school had hosted parent-teacher conferences in the fall, and I assumed this was nothing more than the spring iteration.

Both of us were dragging on the morning of the meeting. You had called out for me three times over the course of the night after being awoken by nightmares, and on each of those occasions it took some time to console you and lull you back to sleep, and then even more time to fall back asleep myself, only to be awoken again by you shortly thereafter. I had hoped you'd sleep in because of your restless night, but the opposite proved to be true: you woke up at 4:30 that morning, about two hours before sunrise.

There were bags under your eyes from your poor night of sleep, but I knew it would be impossible to convince you to sleep a bit more. Instead, I allowed you to lead me downstairs, where you quickly located your tablet and beelined to the couch to play one of your peaceful video games—the kind that didn't seem to entail anything more than dragging a cartoon animal around a screen to interact with other characters. With my eyes barely open, I started brewing a pot of coffee for myself and made my way back to you, holding a box of Cheerios in one hand and a box of Rice Krispies in the other. Your eyes flicked up at my approach, and after a moment's thought, you pointed at the Cheerios and returned to your tablet. I poured the selected cereal into a bowl and placed it at your side on the couch. You didn't look up, but I knew you'd pick at your breakfast while you played.

After pouring a cup of coffee, I opened the living room curtains and took a seat on the opposite end of the couch. There wasn't much to see out the window—just a streetlight barely illuminating the house across the road. Small forested areas flanked our front yard on both sides, giving a tunnel vision vibe to the view outside from our living room.

I spotted some movement in the dark near our free-standing bird feeder, but it seemed too small to be a bear, or even a deer. *Raccoon*, I speculated. *Or maybe a possum.* Even though it had been over two years since we'd moved upstate to the town of Blue Bank, located two hours north of Manhattan, I still hadn't gotten used to the amount of life surrounding our home at all hours of the day. Or night. After growing up in suburban Long Island, I remained amazed at seeing anything through the window that was more exotic than a squirrel or mourning dove. The thought of ever becoming jaded at the sight of a family of deer, no matter how common an occurrence that was in our region, was unimaginable to me.

The darkness outside, contrasting with our illuminated living room, conveyed a reflective quality upon the window, and I took a moment to appreciate the image of the two of us sitting together on opposite ends of the couch. Although our poses were identical, each with our left leg folded over the right, we otherwise couldn't have looked more different from each other. I was tall and bulky—my weight was the same as my old football days, even if the ratio of muscle to fat had unpleasantly shifted over the past twenty years—with dark hair and scruff on my face that I intended to shave before meeting your teacher. By contrast, you were skinny and pale, and your fair features could have only come from your mother's side of the family. I took solace, not for the first time, that you seemed to have more of your mother in you than me.

We didn't speak while you remained engrossed in your tablet, occasionally picking at some Cheerios, and I tried to shake the cobwebs out through a combination of willpower and caffeine. Once I woke myself up a bit more, I contemplated asking about your rough night of sleep, but decided against it. I thought you would probably get annoyed at my interruption, and I didn't want to agitate you while you were in a state of calm.

*If he has these nightmares again tonight, we'll definitely have a talk*, I promised myself.

The sky was showing hints of life by the time I polished off the entire pot of coffee, and I went upstairs to shower and shave in anticipation of my meeting. I left the bathroom door open while I bathed in case you called out for me, but you didn't appear to even register my absence. When I returned downstairs, clean and fully dressed, the sun had fully risen and you remained affixed to the couch, intent on your tablet.

"We'll have to leave soon," I said. "We're going to school earlier than usual today." But if you heard me, you gave no acknowledgement.

You didn't resist once I announced it was time to get ready for school, and you wordlessly started your before school ritual with me hovering along beside you: brush the teeth, go to the bathroom, get dressed. Bundle up in a winter coat and hat to deal with the forty-two-degree weather outside. Head out to the car, which was hopefully sufficiently warmed up via the remote starter. By eight o'clock, we were on the road, driving due east toward your school.

"Look, Quince," I said at one point, trying to make eye

contact with you in the back seat through the rearview mirror. "All the kids who are usually out here waiting for the school bus aren't here yet. That's because we're leaving earlier than usual." I always made a point of explaining the obvious to you when we drove around, believing my bland narrations to be good for your development.

You were engrossed in your tablet, but you paused to look up and out the window, only to refocus again on the game you were playing. The lack of a response was disheartening, but I couldn't blame you. My observation hadn't been particularly interesting.

After ten minutes of driving, we reached your school, which was a solitary building surrounded by farmland in all directions. There were often children being led outside to the playground around the time I normally dropped you off, but on that morning, there was no activity around the school, and the parking lot was empty except for a few parked cars belonging to the staff who worked the early shift.

Once I parked, I exited the car and circled around to let you out of your booster seat in the back. You made a small noise of protest as I took your tablet out of your hands, but I knew it wouldn't lead to a breakdown—this was a ritual we went through every morning in those days.

"You can play with your tablet again after school," I promised. With some token reluctance, you let me lift you out of the car, place you on the ground, and take your hand to walk across the lot. As we made our way to the building, a chilly wind hit us, and I wondered whether you were dressed warmly enough. I often forgot that as a four-year-old, your tolerance for the cold was lower than mine.

Upon reaching the school, I was surprised to discover

that the door where I usually dropped you off was locked. Normally, I would let you inside and wait for someone in the administrative office to escort you to your classroom. Not wanting to be obnoxious by immediately ringing the doorbell, I waited a moment, hoping someone had heard our arrival and was coming to let us in. But after a few moments, you shivered, and I decided to risk rudeness and be proactive by pressing the button next to the door.

A few seconds later, an older woman I didn't recognize came to the door and peered at me through a small window.

"Yes?" she asked, her voice muffled through the glass.

"Umm...." I felt embarrassed articulating the obvious. "Can you let us in?"

She studied me again, and I was cognizant of the fact my size made me an imposing figure. The woman then repositioned herself to look down at you through the window, and I thought that would be enough to satisfy her. But she still didn't open the door.

"Who are you?" she asked through the glass. I was growing annoyed that we were having this conversation while you and I were stuck out in the cold.

"I'm Will Banfield. This is my son, Quince." I quickly rubbed my hands up and down the side of your arms to warm you up, hoping the woman would take the hint, and added, "Ms. Natalie asked me to come in early today to speak with her."

The woman merely frowned. I was on the verge of pulling out my driver's license to prove my identity when another face—one that I recognized—appeared at the door. The school's administrator, Ms. Leona, whispered to the other woman as she opened the door for us with a smile.

"Please, come in," Ms. Leona said, before squatting

down in front of you. "And good morning, Quince! It's so lovely to see you today." You didn't respond, but merely lowered your head while shielding yourself behind my legs.

Ms. Leona didn't seem insulted by your nonresponse as she stood back up. Turning to the woman who had barred our entry, she asked, "Would you mind escorting Quince here to Ms. Natalie's room?"

The woman held out a hand for you and, after a moment's hesitation, you took it and allowed yourself to be led down the hallway. Ms. Leona watched you depart before showing me to a small conference room near the school's entrance.

"Please, come in here. Ms. Natalie will be with us shortly." She lowered herself into a chair in front of a metal table and gestured to a line of chairs on the other side. "Sit anywhere you like."

All the chairs, except for one, were sized for toddlers, so I settled into the regular-sized seat and waited.

"I'm sorry about the difficulty you had getting in this morning," Ms. Leona said. "Everyone here has been extra vigilant after what happened in Greenfield last week."

"Ah, of course," I said. I spent little time watching the news, but some local events rose to a level that reached even the willfully ignorant like myself. The week before, a nine-year-old boy in the next town over was waiting at the foot of his driveway for his school bus to arrive, only to disappear without a trace before the bus showed up. The apparent abduction had shaken the community to its core, and parents and schools were all operating on high alert in case that kidnapping was the start of something bigger.

"It's terrible what happened to that boy," I added, if only to say something. Ms. Leona offered me a sad smile, but she didn't look as if she had any inclination to leave.

"Please don't feel you have to keep me company," I said after a few awkward moments. Ms. Leona frowned, looking confused. "I'm happy to wait here until Ms. Natalie arrives," I added.

But before Ms. Leona could respond, Ms. Natalie entered the room carrying a thin manilla folder with papers poking out of the sides. She was young and petite and perhaps because of her own relative lack of experience generally seemed much more comfortable around the children than their parents. During drop-offs and pickups, I tried to respect her shyness by engaging with her as little as possible, in contrast to some of the other parents who demanded a full debriefing from her each day.

"Good morning, Mr. Banfield," Ms. Natalie said in her quiet voice. "I passed Quince on the way here. He's looking tired today."

"Yeah, he had a rough night of sleep," I said with a small grimace. "He's been having nightmares lately. Plus, he's started waking up pretty early again. He was good for a while, but it's been 4:30 or earlier the past few days. Maybe he's going through another sleep regression? I don't know."

"They say that sleep regressions typically stop around the age of two," Ms. Natalie said. She sounded timid, as if she feared challenging my hypothesis. Ms. Leona nodded in support of her teacher.

"That's what they say," Ms. Leona agreed. "Although I wonder sometimes. I've read that sleep regressions can be a side effect of children's brains developing as they grow, but aren't our brains still developing into adulthood? It never made much sense to me that the experts claim sleep regressions stop so early in childhood."

I, of course, had no real insight into the subject and regretted bringing it up at all.

"Well, regardless," I said. "Sleep hasn't been easy the past week for either of us. But that's all it is. Nothing to worry about."

Ms. Leona and Ms. Natalie both nodded, more a signal they were ready to move on than a sign that they agreed with me. I waited for Ms. Leona to excuse herself so we could start our conference, but I was surprised when Ms. Natalie closed the door behind her and settled into another chair next to Ms. Leona. I realized I'd been called for something more serious than a routine check-in.

Looking back and forth between the two women, I said, "I assumed this was just a standard parent-teacher conference, but it seems I'm mistaken."

Ms. Leona glanced at Ms. Natalie, who blushed. I guessed that Ms. Natalie had been assigned the task of preparing me for this meeting but had neglected to do so. Ms. Leona seemed to decide that wasn't an issue worth hashing out just then and reapplied her focus on me.

"Ms. Natalie has advised me of certain... behaviors of Quince's that we wanted to discuss with you. Really, just some things we hoped to put on your radar to the extent they require further addressing."

I frowned, confused by the vagueness of her explanation. Ms. Leona glanced at Ms. Natalie once again, who picked up on that cue.

"Quince is a very sweet boy," Ms. Natalie started in a soft voice, not looking directly at me. "He plays very well with others, and he loves to help around the classroom when given a task." She stopped, gathering her thoughts.

"But...," I said, prompting her.

"Well, it's just there are some areas of his development that have given us cause for concern." She opened her folder and removed a checklist. "This is a list of skills and behaviors we expect to see in four-year-olds like Quince. Throughout the year, we monitor each student in the hope of confirming they have these skills. And although Quince is age appropriate for most of these, he is lacking in some ways. Mostly related to language."

"Language?" I blinked.

"Yes, language." Ms. Natalie consulted her sheet. "Four-year-olds can typically speak in sentences of four words or more, but I've never heard a sentence out of Quince. The most I get is a one- or two-word answer to a direct question. 'Yes.' 'No.' 'That one.' That's the extent of his language, from what I can see."

She paused, giving me an opportunity to ask questions, but I was rendered speechless. *He's not talking at all in school?* I wondered. *How is it I'm only hearing about this now?* But I decided against giving voice to that accusatory thought.

"Thank you for sharing this with me," I said in a measured tone. "I have to say, though, this is not at all consistent with my experience with Quince at home."

But as soon as the words were out of my mouth, I wondered if they were true. *Have I ever heard Quince speak in full sentences?* There were times you would repeat something you had seen in a video or heard in a song, which could be a long string of words, but I struggled to think of a time you constructed a complex sentence as an independent thought.

"I can only report on what I've seen," Ms. Natalie said, as diplomatically as possible. "So, of course, if he is behaving differently at home, we should work on figuring out why that is the case."

"Are you suggesting that Quince isn't comfortable around Ms. Natalie?" Ms. Leona asked with a frown, looking mildly offended. "That seems unlikely to me. Ms. Natalie is a sweetheart!"

I didn't see any benefit to engaging in a debate on that issue, so I opted to take a different tack.

"Look, I know Quince is on the quiet side," I said. "I think part of that is being raised by me—I'm not usually one to waste words, and I guess that must've rubbed off on him to a degree. But we are also just emerging from a pandemic. Could it be possible that he's a little delayed speech-wise because he's been locked up at home for the past two years?"

"That could certainly account for some of his issues, yes," Ms. Natalie conceded. "But even compared to his class-mates, who struggled through the pandemic in the same way as Quince—"

"But if they have brothers and sisters at home, they would still have more experience communicating," I pressed. "Even if they only have a set of parents, they'd still be more exposed to language on the regular. It's just me and Quince at home—it's a quiet house for the most part."

Ms. Leona placed a hand on Ms. Natalie's arm to keep her from responding before saying, "Regardless of the cause of Quince's apparent speech delays, I think the more impor-tant issue is getting him the help he needs to catch up. If that's what he needs."

With a long exhale, I closed my eyes and rubbed at my temples, struggling to collect myself. After a moment, I looked up again and asked, "What do you mean 'if that's what he needs?' I thought you just said he needs help."

"We are only reporting what we are seeing," Ms. Natalie said. "So that you can address it as warranted. Whether that involves seeking a speech therapist, or even a developmental pediatrician—"

"A developmental pediatrician?" I interjected. "Do you think Quince is on the spectrum?" My head swiveled back and forth between Ms. Leona and Ms. Natalie, begging either of them to answer, but they each looked away, uncomfortable with my direct question. It was obvious they both came into the meeting intent on not doing anything that could be construed as an assessment.

Plenty of armchair physicians had diagnosed me as being neurodivergent over the course of my adult life, although I hadn't ever been curious enough to go through the steps of being assessed by a trained professional. In my mind, I was what I was, and I was comfortable enough with whatever that might be. So, my visceral reaction to that mild hint you might be on the autism spectrum didn't stem from a fear of you being different, but from a fear of the unknown. I didn't know exactly what it would mean for me or, more importantly, you, if an expert evaluated you as being neurodivergent. I was barely holding it together as it was—I didn't know whether I could properly handle any more complications.

Once the silence in the room reached the point of being uncomfortable, Ms. Leona finally spoke.

"Again, we are merely flagging some observations for you that may warrant early intervention," she said, making it clear that they had done their part, and the ball was squarely in my court.

I must've looked lost and overwhelmed because I could see both Ms. Leona and Ms. Natalie soften as they shared a look. It seemed as if they were both frustrated that they couldn't be more helpful. With a small shrug, Ms. Natalie opened her folder once again and extracted a piece of paper.

"Even though Quince hasn't started kindergarten, he could be entitled to services through the school district if they determine he qualifies," Ms. Natalie said. "You should reach out to them and consider having Quince formally assessed."

She slid the paper across the table to me, and I glanced at it, recognizing it as a list of contacts in the district.

"Well, thank you for this," I said, folding up the paper and tucking it into my pants pocket. "And thank you for bringing this to my attention. I'll certainly look into this."

As I stood up, I added, "I assume there are no other issues we need to discuss?"

Ms. Leona and Ms. Natalie exchanged a long glance, silently communicating with one another. I took the hint and sat back down.

"There is... one other thing," Ms. Natalie said meekly. "And it might be nothing. But I wanted to make you aware of it."

Ms. Leona and I both gestured at her to continue.

"Quince, despite being on the quiet side, is usually remarkably well-behaved. He follows directions very well and is always so eager to be a helper in the classroom. And, perhaps because of his calm nature, his classmates all love to play with him—he is very easygoing and a wonderful listener." I tensed, bracing myself for the inevitable *but*.

"But," she added, "there was an incident last week that was very out of character for him. You may remember we had a field trip last Thursday to Miller Farm?"

I nodded, vaguely remembering an email from a few weeks earlier discussing that trip. The class was going to a farm to pick asparagus, or something along those lines. The school expected parents to chaperone their own children on field trips, but I had made arrangements with your teachers so you could attend without me. They were usually very accommodating of requests like that, given that I was a working single parent.

"Well, Quince was fine that morning," Ms. Natalie said. "He seemed very happy as we drove out to the farm, and he was excited to explore it all. But as soon as we approached the barn where all the parents and students were meeting up, something changed in him. He started crying, which was odd to see since he's usually so calm, although it isn't that uncommon for a four-year-old. There have been plenty of times where one of Quince's classmates broke out in tears, only to stop and start playing again a few minutes later as if nothing happened. But Quince was inconsolable that day. I spent fifteen minutes trying to calm him down enough to get a sense of what was bothering him, but it was impossible. His anguish got worse and worse as he stood there, and he was outright wailing as we removed him from the scene altogether. Only once Ms. Alex took him back to our car did he start to calm down. After he had settled, Ms. Alex tried to have Quince rejoin the class, but he broke down again the second they went back onto the farm. When we tried to talk to him about it, he just shook his head without saying a word."

*That doesn't sound like Quince at all*, I thought. But it wasn't entirely clear to me why they had shared that story. "Well, like you said, he's four," I said. "Kids have tantrums sometimes, right?"

Ms. Natalie shook her head. "Children can tantrum. But that wasn't what this was. He didn't seem to be acting out. He didn't even seem sad or hurt." She thought for a moment, trying to find the right word, before blurting out, "He looked terrified. *Terrified.*"

I stared at her, trying to make sense of what she was saying. *Terrified of what?*

"You know," I said, not quite keeping the irritation out of my voice. "Had I known about this incident when it happened, I could have spoken with Quince about it at home. Tried to get some sense of what was bothering him. It's not easy to revisit something like that with him days later."

"We had planned on bringing this to your attention at the end of the school day," Ms. Natalie replied, sounding affronted. "But you were late for pickup, and I couldn't wait for you. Ms. Alex had to stay with Quince until you showed up, and she didn't think it was her place to bring this up with you. I knew you and I would be meeting this morning, so I figured there would be no harm in waiting a few extra days to discuss this—when you had time to listen."

My face flushed, and I looked away to hide it. *Damn it, she's right.* My workday that Thursday had ended with a court-ordered mediation that I attended virtually. A judge spent a half hour speaking with me at the end of the session, and I found it impossible to get a word in to excuse myself, which kept me from picking you up at the normal time. By the time I freed myself to rush over to the school, it was already 5:25—twenty-five minutes past the scheduled pickup.

"I remember," I said in a conciliatory tone. "And I'm sorry about that. It was...." I trailed off, realizing no one was interested in hearing my excuses. "I don't mean to blame anyone. This is just a lot to take in all at once. I'm struggling to process it."

Both women nodded in understanding.

But then a thought occurred to me. *That incident happened last Thursday?* I remembered your struggles with nightmares over the past few days, trying to recall when they started. *It might have been last Thursday.*

"Are you certain Quince saw nothing that day that could

have traumatized him somehow?" I asked, but Ms. Natalie shook her head.

"No, nothing. And all the kids were in that area the entire time, and no one else was bothered. We were truly at a loss for what set him off."

"Maybe the incident at the farm is nothing," Ms. Leona said, trying to get things back on track. "It is very possibly an anomaly. But again, we wanted to bring it to your attention in case—well if it happens again, we wanted you to have that context. And in the unlikely event it develops into a pattern, perhaps it is worth bringing up to a child psychiatrist."

*Great. I'll add it to the list*, I thought with some bitterness. This was a lot to take in, and I wasn't at all prepared for the information dump.

"Thank you both for speaking with me about these issues," I said as kindly as I could manage, reminding myself not to punish the messengers for this unwelcome news. "I appreciate the communication, truly. And I will definitely act upon everything you said. Is there anything else?" This time, I waited for them to shake their heads before rising out of my chair. With a nod of thanks to each of the women, I exited the room and made my way back outside to the parking lot.

As I walked back to the car, I spotted Ms. Alex leading your class to the playground in a more or less straight line, which was the norm on days when the weather was cooperating. Several of your classmates recognized me as they shuffled along and called out.

"It's Quince's daddy!" one girl shrieked.

"My birthday is next month!" another boy called out to me.

"My cousins are visiting my house tomorrow!" yet another girl yelled.

Amid that chaos, you trudged along in the middle of the line. You remained unfazed by the other students calling out to me, but it was hard to tell if their antics amused you. Your face was unreadable and offered no clue what was happening in that head of yours.

And, of course, you were silent.

## 2

In 2019, shortly before you turned two, I tried to escape the life of a litigator, realizing the long hours and unrealistic billing requirements were not conducive to being a single parent. Or, at least, not conducive to being a good parent.

Out of pure desperation, I applied for a job as in-house counsel at a fairly new business centered on the manufacturing of sports equipment. I wasn't a particularly good fit for the position, but I thought it was worth a shot, and it seemed like a promising place to work. The company had only come into existence about ten years prior, but it had grown to a point where it was looking to hire its own internal attorney.

I interviewed with the company's owner, a bombastic man named Andrew Harris. He explained that the position I was applying for had just been created, and they had no proper sense of what their in-house counsel would do on a day-to-day basis. As such, his first interview question to me was how I would define the role if hired. After some thought, I answered, "I'd view my primary responsibility as keeping crap from reaching your desk."

He hired me right on the spot.

Andrew made it clear he was looking to interact with me as

*little as possible once I started working, and that I would have no one else in my department. With that in mind, I broached the possibility of working remotely. Andrew was reluctant at first, but his resistance faded once I pointed out it would save him the trouble of finding me an office. His only request was that I live somewhere within arm's reach of Putnam County, where the business operations were located, in case my physical presence in the office was ever needed. I agreed, and you and I resettled upstate to a small home in Dutchess County in the town of Blue Bank, a quiet community sitting on the Hudson River that was home primarily to farmers and individuals working at the local liberal arts college. My in-laws, who were largely scattered around Long Island, were chagrined by our relocation or, more specifically, your relocation. But I reassured them as best I could that we'd only be a few hours away and that you would remain very much in their lives.*

*That fresh start gave me hope I might recapture the ability to raise you properly. When I was a litigator, there were long stretches where I wasn't able to pick you up from daycare until after you had already fallen asleep for the night. We only saw each other for an hour or two each day during that time, and I hardly felt like a father to you at all. Working from home would give me the luxury of interacting with you in the morning and after work, although I'd still need someone to watch you during the day. It was a wonderful arrangement. At least, it was for a few months.*

*But then the COVID-19 pandemic happened.*

*It's often said that it takes a village to raise a child. But I would come to learn there are circumstances where even that necessity becomes an impossibility, such as when there is a global pandemic.*

*In that case, you're on your own.*

*Businesses other than those deemed essential were ordered to* close once the initial wave of the virus hit, and that included the daycare you were enrolled in at the time. In the early days of the pandemic, I took some time off from work to keep you entertained, hoping that everything would be back to normal in a week or two. Once it became clear that wasn't going to happen, I resumed working while juggling my responsibilities to you. Drafting a memo for work while keeping you in my line of sight became the norm, and I barely did enough at my job to keep my head above water.

Until that point, I had been following the advice of professionals regarding screen time for toddlers. But once the pandemic reached its second month, I realized the state of the world had made it so that the simple goal of survival trumped ideal parenting. Against my better judgment, but realizing I had no viable alternatives, I ordered a tablet off the internet that was filled with videos and games to keep you busy and entertained over the course of the day while I worked on a laptop a few feet away from you. Most of the games you played seemed educational, encouraging the learning of letters, basic counting, and colors, so I hoped the disruption to our lives was not causing you too much developmental damage. And, if nothing else, the arrangement helped us both to get through the day, which was laudable enough back then.

I didn't know how long we would continue with the routine of me trying to work while you were engrossed in your tablet. A few months into the pandemic I heard someone on the news speculate that the summer would prove to be the end of the virus as people spent more time outdoors, making the disease harder to spread, and in June 2020, there were enough dips in the number of reported cases to tease that an end might be in sight. Unfortunately, those numbers only seemed to rise again as soon as the temperature dropped in the fall.

Despite my sanity being tested during that year, you

appeared unaffected by the state of the world. It was all you knew, and days filled with sitting on the couch while you navigated your tablet had become your new norm. But even when I pulled myself away from work, there wasn't much for us to do. Back then, you refused to wear a mask, and I was afraid to take you to venues where you might be exposed to the virus. By November, it was too cold to spend more than a half hour outside, so even our opportunities to stroll quiet nature paths together, bundled up as best as we could manage, were short-lived. I also questioned whether you enjoyed those brisk walks—you seemed relieved once those hikes ended, and you were once again free to snuggle up on the couch with your tablet.

Every day there was a new report about the number of infections and updated death toll numbers. And those numbers scared me. So focused was I on keeping you safe that I became blind to the harm that prolonged period of isolation was doing to you. And to the extent I recognized your growth was being inhibited, I took some solace in assuming that other children your age would be in similar boats. If you came out of the pandemic having to catch up, so would others.

The world had settled enough by the summer of 2021 to enroll you in a new preschool program. You were about three-and-a-half years old, and at that age you could be persuaded to wear a mask, which the school required for its three- to four-year-old program. Every morning starting that September, I took you to school and lined up in the cold with other masked parents and their children, waiting for someone from the administration office to escort each child to their classroom. At the end of each day, I waited outside for someone from the school to collect you and pass you back into my care.

The administrators and teachers tried to minimize the risk of outbreaks as much as possible by having the children play outdoors on the playground whenever the temperature crept *above freezing, and on those occasions, I sometimes spotted you happily chasing your classmates up and down slides and running in circles around the swing set.* The worst is behind us, I would think, watching you bound about, full of joy. *That sentiment only grew after a few months, when the school announced it was relaxing its mask-wearing policy. Granted, life still wasn't quite normal, but it finally felt like things were heading back in that direction.*

*But that meeting in April with Ms. Leona and Ms. Natalie to address your speech delays extinguished any flicker of optimism I felt around that time. The worst wasn't in our past after all, I realized. We were still stuck in it, even if the challenges confronting you and me had evolved. Yet, I would learn even that assessment was inaccurate.*

*The worst wasn't behind us, nor were we mired in it.*

*And that, I'd soon realize, was because the worst was yet to come.*

MUSCLE MEMORY alone guided me back to our house as I drove home after the meeting at your school, lost in my head. Even once I was back and settled at my desk, logged into my work computer, I found it impossible to concentrate on anything other than you and the dilemma that had unexpectedly dropped in my lap. I forced myself to eyeball the roughly forty unread work emails that waited for me, flagging those that I'd have to follow up on at some point, but even as I did, I still couldn't shake visions of you wordlessly navigating eight hours of preschool, constantly bombarded by the din of your boisterous classmates. Replaying the morning's meeting in my mind slowly expanded to revisiting the last two years, and I lost count of all the critical points where I had failed you as a father during that time.

*That's in the past,* I told myself. *There's nothing to be gained by beating myself up.* But the guilt was impossible to cast away, as was the worry I felt about what you were going through at that moment.

One trick I had developed in my career—for those times when I was so overwhelmed with the amount of work in front of me that I didn't even know where to start—was simply writing out a to-do list. Laying out all the tasks to be done on a single piece of paper, rather than letting them swirl around in the chaos of my head, somehow made it all become well-defined and attainable. I realized going through that exercise regarding you might likewise bring me some peace.

But I found myself at a loss almost immediately upon starting that list. The one clearly-defined assignment in front of me was to contact the school district to have you evaluated. There would undoubtedly be more tasks to follow, but it seemed like everything would flow from that initial step. With that in mind, I found the paper I had received earlier that morning and located a number for your district. Under normal circumstances, I'd have been more comfortable emailing than placing a call, but my anxiety required immediate satisfaction—I couldn't risk ending up in a position where I was waiting days for a response.

And so, pushing my social anxiety aside, I called the district. After being transferred several times, a kind-sounding woman in the Committee on Preschool Special Education informed me that my first step would be to get you registered, after which they would contact me about having you evaluated for special education services.

"But to be perfectly honest with you," the woman told

me, "given that we're already in April, and things slow down at the end of the school year, it's possible your son won't be evaluated until the end of the summer, if not later. You should definitely register him now to get that ball rolling, but... well, I just want to manage your expectations."

That was less than welcome news, although I didn't see any point in arguing with her about it. After getting off the phone, I went through the legwork of having you registered in the district, if for no other purpose than to trick myself into thinking I was taking proactive steps to help you. But even after completing my navigation of the online registration system, I remained disquieted by the possibility that it might be months before you received the help you needed. Too much time had already been lost, and I couldn't bear to let your development languish for another four months, if not longer. Kindergarten was a little more than a year away, and I wanted you to have the best chance you could get to catch up before then, to the extent you were able.

I rarely spent money on myself, but that wasn't a product of any inherent cheapness on my part; rather, it was a recognition that I wouldn't derive any happiness from buying anything beyond the essentials. In this case, however, I wasn't afraid to throw money around for your benefit. And given the choice of waiting months for free services from the school or paying out of pocket to get you immediate help... well, the decision was obvious to me.

Ignoring the work emails that were filtering in, I searched for speech therapists in our area. To my surprise, I could only find one: a woman named Nora Glaspie. Her website described her as a licensed speech-language pathologist (or SLP), with an office about thirty minutes away in the small city of Poughkeepsie. I could request an appointment for a speech evaluation through her website, and it took some time to fill in the various fields asking for information about you and your development history. Less than a half-hour after hitting submit, I received an email confirming our appointment for that upcoming Saturday. *Five days away*, I calculated. I hated to even let that much time go to waste, but I accepted I'd done all I could for the moment.

Still, I remained in a state of restlessness for the remainder of the week, feeling time slipping away while I could be helping you, but not knowing what to do. Every now and then I tried to engage you by broaching what your teacher told me, but my clumsy efforts only seemed to aggravate you.

"No!" you snapped at one point, after I asked if you were comfortable vocalizing questions at school. "We are not talking about that now!"

*That sentence was seven words*, I noted after the outburst. *Perhaps there's more language in Quince than I realize?* But other than that defiant proclamation, you said little that week. *Be patient*, I reminded myself on more than one occasion. *Wait for the SLP to give her assessment.*

The week crawled by at a snail's pace. Each day was full of worry and anxiety, leading to a night disturbed by your continued nightmares, which culminated in a cruelly early wake-up call. And then repeat. It felt like a minor miracle once Saturday finally arrived, and the process of getting you whatever help you needed could finally begin in earnest. Throughout the week, I had tried to prepare you for the evaluation, but it was never clear to me how much you were listening, or understood.

As we drove south for our appointment that Saturday morning, I made one last effort to prepare you.

"Now, Quince," I said as I drove, glancing at you in the

rearview mirror. "We are going to go see a nice woman named Ms. Nora. She will want to play with you for a little bit, so all you have to do is listen and do what she says. Okay?"

Silence. I checked on you again and saw that you were focused on your tablet.

"Quince!" I said in a louder tone, and you snapped out of your reverie.

"What?" you responded, annoyed, as you looked up at me. But then something out the window caught your eye and you stared, transfixed.

"What's that?" you asked, not taking your eyes off the side of the road up ahead.

I stole a peek to see where you were looking and followed your gaze, although I saw nothing of note at first. But then I spotted something, even though it wasn't all that remarkable: a small cross with flowers placed in the ground next to a tree—a monument to a fatal accident, I assumed. As we passed the tree, your head swiveled to follow it.

"That was a cross," I explained. "Sometimes people put them in the ground if someone they loved was hurt in a car accident."

"No," you said, irritated. "Not a cross."

I shrugged—I didn't want to get drawn into a debate with you—and kept driving. A few minutes later, I looked back to find you gently snoring, your head angled in a way that looked quite uncomfortable, and I tried to assess that development. *This nap will either take the edge off for this evaluation*, I thought, *or there might be some grumpiness.* But it was what it was, and I drove the rest of the way with your gentle snores serving as the soundtrack for the ride.

We arrived at Nora's office ten minutes before our scheduled time. As soon as the car was turned off, you stirred and started mumbling incoherently. I was relieved to see you stayed dry throughout that nap since I had neglected to bring you a spare outfit.

"Quince, Quince," I said, reaching into the back seat to rub your arm. "We're here to play with Ms. Nora."

"No," you responded. "I'm not playing with Ms. Nora today."

*His language seems to be at its best when he's being willful*, I noted. Once again, I felt a glimmer of hope that your struggles were more about finding your voice than a lack of tools, but that was for Nora to explore.

"Please," I said in a pleading tone. "Just come inside with me. It'll be fun." I got out of the car and made my way to your door.

With your grogginess fading, you reluctantly allowed me to pick you up and place you on your feet in the parking lot. You didn't move at first, and I wondered whether I'd have to physically carry you inside. After a moment, however, you let me guide you by the hand into the office building.

Once inside, I paused, uncertain where to go. We found ourselves in a small, cramped foyer, empty except for a single wooden bench that looked uncomfortable, which opened to a hallway flanked on both sides by a series of closed wooden doors, with no hint as to which one might be hiding Nora. You sensed my hesitancy and pulled at my hand to keep going, and I let you lead me deeper into the musty building, if only because I had no other ideas myself.

My steps were timid as we proceeded, the warped wooden floors creaking our arrival. You kept tugging me forward, walking as if you knew exactly where you were heading. Once we traversed the entire hallway, you pointed with triumph at a door marked "Exit" that I assumed led outside to the back of the building.

"I don't think that's it, Quince," I said, taking out my phone to call Nora for some guidance.

But just as I pulled up her phone number, a Black woman, perhaps a few years younger than I, opened a door in the hallway and stuck her head out, scanning back and forth before settling on us. She was dressed comfortably in jeans and a blouse, with her dark hair pulled back.

"Do you happen to be Will?" she asked. At my nod, the woman added, "And this must be Quince! It's so wonderful to meet you. I'm Nora. Please, come on in."

She stepped out into the hallway, holding the door wide to allow us entry. Your shyness had resurfaced at Nora's arrival, and you clutched my leg, forcing me to half-drag you as I limped into the office. Nora closed the door behind her as she joined us, and she didn't seem at all put off by the fact that you were using my body to shield yourself from her.

Nora, in exaggerated fashion, leaned to her side to get a direct look at you hovering behind me.

"Hello, Quince!" she said brightly. I felt you burrow your face into the back of my pants when she addressed you by name.

"You can say 'hi,' Quince," I prodded, trying to turn so Nora could see you. When that proved to be unsuccessful, I added, "He's a bit shy."

Nora laughed, her brown eyes twinkling.

"Oh, that's okay!" she exclaimed, before crouching down to be at your eye level, where she whispered to you in a conspiratorial tone, "I can be shy, too."

I didn't particularly believe her, but I appreciated her attempt to establish some semblance of camaraderie with you.

"Oh, Quince!" Nora exclaimed as she stood up, sounding as if a thought had struck her. "I just remembered something! I have some toys in here. Would you like to play with them?"

Nora gestured around the small unkempt office, and I noticed a dollhouse with some figures inside, a few toy trucks, and a couple of puzzles. You stuck your head out from behind me to see for yourself, and after a beat, you cautiously emerged to take a few tentative steps toward one of the vehicles. You glanced at me for approval, and only at my nod of encouragement did you pick up the toy cement mixer to study it. While Nora watched you play, I found a chair in the corner, hoping to make myself as invisible as possible to allow Nora to get to work.

"Can I show you something really cool about that truck?" Nora asked you. You nodded and she held out a hand so you could pass the toy to her. You handed it over and stepped back, watching Nora as she placed the truck on a desk and revved it backwards a few times before releasing it. The cement mixer sped forward on its own and flew off the desk onto the floor.

"Oh, no!" Nora cried in a playful tone. "What a bad driver!"

You giggled and bobbed in place. "What a bad driver!" you agreed. Nora glanced at me, and I remembered admitting in my initial request for an assessment being uncertain whether you had a tendency to engage in echolalia.

I was uncertain whether this play was part of the evaluation or simply a means of acclimating you to Nora. But after a few minutes of exploring toys with you, Nora confirmed that the formal assessment hadn't yet started by taking out a flip book with various illustrations on each page.

"Quince," she said, getting your attention. "I have some pictures here," she added, setting the book of pictures on a desk. You stopped playing with a doll you had snatched to peer at the displayed illustrations. "Can you sit with me for a little bit and look at these pictures with me?"

You turned to me, seeking reassurance. I gave you a quick nod of approval and lumbered up to hold out a small chair for you to sit in across from Nora. After you settled into your seat, I scurried back to my spot in the corner, trying once again to minimize my presence.

"Now, Quince," Nora said, pointing to the page. "Can you find the boat?" I arched my neck and saw Nora had opened the book to a simplistic picture of a car next to a small ship. You hesitated a moment before pointing at the boat.

"Excellent!" Nora exclaimed, jotting down a note on a piece of paper. You beamed at her reaction and bounced in your seat, ready to show off again. Nora flipped the page to reveal a new illustration. "Can you point to the dog on this one?"

You and Nora continued to go through the book, and you proved adept at identifying various noun words that were posed to you. But the questions got harder as you progressed, and you didn't try to hide your frustration when confronted with words you didn't recognize, or concepts you didn't fully understand.

"Can you point to the picture where the boy is *over* the dog?" Nora asked you at one point. The page had two pictures: One with a boy sitting on a bench with a dog beneath it, and another with the opposite arrangement. You stared at the page without answering, and I fought the urge to blurt out anything that could constitute a hint.

"If you don't know, you can just say 'I don't know,'" Nora prompted, but you didn't accept her advice.

"No!" you announced, hopping out of your seat. "The book is closed!" You found me in the corner and grabbed my hand, trying to pull me out of my seat. "Let's go!"

"He fell asleep in the car on the way here," I explained to Nora as you tugged at my arm. "He may be a little cranky."

"I'm not cranky!" you insisted, still trying to yank me up. Uncomfortable with the tug-of-war that had broken out, I threw Nora a look that begged for a lifeline. After a beat, she opened a desk drawer and extracted a small toy dog on a leash, which she placed on the ground.

"Quince, can you help me feed this puppy?" she asked. You didn't look up, so she inserted a small plastic treat into the dog's mouth, which prompted it to make some chomping noises. On registering that sound, you stopped tugging on me to stare at the dog.

"Uh oh!" Nora said. "I think now he has to go potty!" She pushed down on the leash, which caused the dog to sit back and make a small pooping noise. When the dog stood up again, the treat was on the ground, having emerged from its bottom. Your eyes were wide as saucers while you processed what you'd just seen.

"He went potty!" you squealed before getting down on the ground to study the toy up close.

"Would you like to try?" Nora asked, offering you a handful of plastic treats.

Without speaking, you reached out to take the offering from her and set out to feed the dog, giggling each time the toy let out a gentle fart noise and expelled a treat out the opposite end.

"I think Quince just needs a hard reset," Nora told me in a soft voice, not that you were paying us any attention. "We'll just let him play for a bit and try again."

I nodded, feeling somewhat embarrassed at your outburst. "I think this is just a lot for him," I said, but Nora waved me off.

"He's doing great!" she said. I figured she either was

being polite or was referring to your overall demeanor. It was already obvious to me you weren't exactly dominating the speech evaluation.

After a few minutes, Nora kneeled next to you, watching you play. The toy dog let out yet another fart, prompting Nora to pretend to fall backwards onto her hands.

"Wow!" she said, panting slightly in her prone position "That was a big one!"

You laughed hard. "That was a big one!" you exclaimed. and I wondered again if echolalia was an issue I simply hadn't noticed until that point.

Nora stood up and dusted herself off. "Now Quince, can we try a few more pages of the book?" she asked. You started to object, so she added, "You can play with the pooping dog some more when we're done. I promise. Let's just do a few more, okay?"

She was patient while you mulled over her offer, and only once you gave a meek nod of acquiescence did she take the toy away and settle back in her chair. You threw me a nervous look before trudging back to your seat.

And then the evaluation continued.

The form of the questions shifted as you advanced. As much as you struggled with the early questions that asked you to point to a picture as a response, you did even worse once the questions sought to elicit a verbal response from you. When shown a picture of a dog and asked to identify it, all you could offer was "I don't know" and a shrug. You seemed to think that was an adequate response and, in fact, looked almost proud at having taken and fully embraced Nora's earlier advice. As you continued to resist giving substantive verbal responses to those inquiries, I refrained from speaking, making sure not to provide any improper help.

Finally, the evaluation was mercifully completed, and Nora, true to her word, dug out the toy dog and handed it back to you. You resumed playing on the floor, and Nora gestured at me to join her at her desk.

"He did great," she said again with a smile, and I appreciated the white lie. She spoke in a hushed voice, and I surmised she didn't want you to hear us talking about you. "It will take me about a week to write up the evaluation and then I'll email it to you, and if you have any questions—"

"Can you work with him?" I cut in, and Nora blinked. "While I understand you haven't written up your evaluation yet, it's clear to me he needs help. I'd like to get that going as quickly as possible. If you're available, that is. I don't know how to help him myself."

Nora frowned, thrown off by my eagerness, and I pressed my case.

"It's been hard for us, especially since the pandemic. I'm coming to realize I haven't been as good of a parent to Quince as he's deserved, and I need to make that right. I mean, I make a point of reading to him every night, and we regularly do puzzles together on weekends. I know he's had way too much screen time in the past few weeks, but he's been sleeping terribly and I've just been so tired every morning...."

I trailed off, not knowing what else I could say. Nora studied me, looking curious.

"What is Quince's support system at home?" she asked, and I cocked my head, confused.

"It's just me," I said, wondering what she was getting at. I had already advised Nora through the intake forms I submitted that your mother died shortly after your birth. "And that's the issue: I'm not really a talkative person by nature, so I'm sure I've been a terrible role model for him."

"I understand it's just you and Quince at home," Nora said, "but what other adults are in his life? Are there grandparents, or aunts or uncles, who help watch him?"

"No," I said. 'My side of the family either lives down south or out west, with my in-laws mostly on Long Island. Quince has an aunt named Veronica—although she goes by Ronnie—who is my wife's sister. She's divorced and has three children that are slightly older than Quince. They've been trying to get together with us for some time, but...." I paused. *But I've been blowing off those invitations*, I thought, knowing I couldn't say that. "But it's been hard for the extended family to get together since the pandemic hit," I concluded.

Nora frowned. "So what happens if, for example, you come down with the flu?"

I shrugged. "When I'm sick, I load up on medicine and do what I have to do. Those days tend to suck." I wasn't sure where she was going with this line of questioning. "I mean, he's not only exposed to me. He goes to a preschool during the day while I'm at work, although he doesn't seem to be doing much talking there, which is what led me to request this evaluation."

Nora, looking thoughtful, turned to watch you playing by yourself, and I tried to imagine what was going through her head as she studied you. I thought I detected a hint of pity on her face. *Does she feel sympathy for Quince's delayed speech?* I wondered. *Or is her sympathy premised on the fact that he's stuck with me as his father?*

Nora turned back to me, looking like she had made a decision. "Okay," she said. "We can start off with one hour a week and go from there. Would the same time next Saturday be convenient for you?"

"Of course," I said. "And I'm grateful for your willingness

to work with him. But I hate to put all of this off for another week. Is there a way for you to see him earlier than that?"

Nora gave me a reassuring look that I recognized as meant to ease my anxiety.

"I don't think waiting a week will harm Quince," she said. "And it will give me a chance to write up my evaluation for you beforehand, which will be a roadmap for the things we need to work on," Nora said. "In any event, there are things *you* can do to help Quince develop his language right away. You don't have to wait to see me again."

"Like what?" I asked.

"Play with him. Grab some toys and act out little stories. Give him scenarios that force him to express himself. You can also go out and show him the world—expose him to new things and expand his language. Eventually he'll be so excited at everything he is learning, language may just pour out of him. It's amazing how quickly children can find their voices once they receive the proper motivation."

I nodded, appreciating the advice. "Okay. Got it. And it's funny you say that, because all week I was thinking about how I suspect there's more language in Quince than he lets on. There are times he seems to forget himself and he releases these articulate sentences. But most other times, he just seems to clam up."

"Selective mutism exists," Nora said and then paused, as if struck by a thought. She looked back at me with a quizzical look on her face and asked, "Has Quince under-gone any major life changes recently? Or been exposed to anything that could have been emotionally traumatizing?"

I thought of your breakdown on your field trip last week, and Ms. Natalie's assessment that you had looked utterly terrified. *But how do I explain that to Nora?* I wondered, and I chose not to say anything. "No," I said. "Not that I can think of."

Nora shrugged. "It was just a thought. But I suspect I'll develop a better sense of what is causing any speech delays once I get to working with him."

"Fair enough," I said. "And I promise I'll be diligent as far as playing with Quince and taking road trips."

Nora smiled at my dumbing down of her earlier advice and extended a hand.

"It was great to meet you both," she said as we shook. "I'll get you that evaluation as soon as I can." She then lowered herself to your eye level, and you looked up at her from the toy dog you were still studying. "Goodbye, Quince, and thank you for helping my dog. Maybe next week you can come back to feed him again?"

You replied with a solemn nod and returned the toy to her. I held out a hand, which you took, and we made our way back to the car.

On the drive home, you stared out the window in silence. At one point I thought you had fallen asleep, and I jumped when you abruptly called out, "Look! Look!"

You were pointing out the left side of the car, although there was nothing that was particularly noteworthy. The only thing I saw was a small cross against a tree on the far side of the road, and I realized we were in the same spot where you had spoken out on the drive earlier that morning.

"Yes, it's the cross again," I said. In the rearview mirror, I could see you staring at it, transfixed. *What's so special about that cross?* I wondered.

"What do you see, Quince?" I asked aloud. When you didn't respond, I added in a louder tone, "What are you looking at, buddy?"

But you just continued to stare out the window, leaving me to speculate on what was happening in your head.

## 3

As you struggled through your speech evaluation, I couldn't help but wonder what your life would have looked like had your mother survived. Or, alternatively, if it had been me who'd died instead of her. It was a mental exercise I often fell into whenever I had to watch you grapple with an obstacle that would have likely been avoided but for my failures as a parent. The bottom line is that I knew, beyond a doubt, that your life would have been immeasurably better if you had your mother in place of me.

My default setting is quiet and introspective—by contrast, your mother was upbeat and bubbly, her inner joy pouring out through her words and actions. While your days with me had largely been spent with you lost in your tablet as I soberly worked on a laptop beside you, I imagined your mother in my shoes, filling the house with music so the two of you could spend hours together singing, dancing, and laughing. And even though I made a point of reading you a book or two each night before bed, your mother would have undoubtedly injected more love and life into that task—perhaps acting out the tales she read with puppets and slowly encouraging you to claim them as your own to create your own stories.

*You undoubtedly had the unfortunate luck of being stuck with the lesser of your two parents. My inherent nature put me at a decided disadvantage as a father, and in those early years of your life I accepted that as an unfortunate, albeit immutable, fact. The very notion of changing my character seemed as unattainable as willing myself to become taller.*

Be yourself. *That is a lesson instilled early on, and it takes many of us, myself included, years to buy into the notion. But there is a danger in that advice, a danger to which I succumbed. The hazard lies in thinking that upon attaining your true self, there is no longer any need to grow. That is, of course, a fallacy, but a particularly grievous one to maintain upon becoming a parent. At that point, it's more necessary than ever to grow, and specifically, to grow into whatever it is your child needs. And that, I realized during your speech evaluation, is where I came up short: I failed to evolve into the father that you needed.*

*But I took some comfort in the fact that it wasn't too late to start.*

THE NIGHT after your evaluation was another restless one for both of us. You seemed unable to go more than an hour without waking up from a nightmare, a problem that didn't get much better even after I grabbed a pillow so I could sleep on the floor of your room to keep you company for the rest of the night. I vainly hoped my presence by the side of your bed would comfort you, but the nightmares persisted. You awoke again at 4:15 in the morning, and it was obvious you were up for the day, no matter how exhausted you looked.

Even after that horrid night of sleep, I didn't bemoan the early wake-up. I was excited to start the day—I had decided that it would be the day things would start turning around for you. For us.

As was our usual morning routine, we made our way downstairs together, but on reaching the ground level, we parted ways: you headed to the couch to find your tablet while I veered off into the kitchen to brew a strong pot of coffee. Given my ambitious plans and lack of sleep, I was heavily relying on caffeine to fuel me through the day.

Once I made the coffee, I poured it into the largest cup I owned—a twenty-ounce mug featuring an image of a kitten riding a unicorn, which your mother had gifted to me for Christmas the year before you were born. After adding a splash of soy milk that I didn't bother to stir in, I took a long sip and imagined the caffeine spreading throughout my body, kicking each of my cells awake, one by one. One more sip and I felt almost hyper, even if it was just a placebo effect. In any event, I was at last ready to get started, and I made my way to the living room, where I found you sprawled on the couch with your tablet.

*Play and road trips*, I thought as I approached you. Road trips were off the table at the moment, since we were still two hours away from any hint of sunlight. Which left....

"Hey, Quince," I said. "Would you like to play with me?"

Your eyes flicked up toward me at my question, only to resettle on your tablet. I was prepared for the non-reaction, and I shrugged as if I couldn't care less.

"Okay, fine," I said. "I'll play by myself."

You didn't respond to that pronouncement, and I could only hope my words were reaching you at all. Scanning the living room, I spotted some random toys thrown unceremoniously in the corner: a few cars of varying sizes, a small plastic princess, and a felt fox.

There were plenty of times we played together before

then, when I had the energy and you were in the mood, but those occasions tended to be silent affairs, whether it be quietly working on a puzzle or working in tandem to stack blocks to form various towers. It wasn't my style to grab a doll and act out a scene in a funny voice. But Nora helped me realize the necessity of breaking the confines of my nature. Or at least expanding them a bit.

I gathered the toys and carried them to our kitchen table, which was still in your line of sight from the couch. While spreading them out on the table, I peeked back at the living room, but you didn't seem at all curious about what I was doing.

After lining up the toys, I tried to figure out how to actually play with them in a way that at least approximated "fun." Not knowing where else to start, I took one thumb-sized car, dragged it backwards, and was relieved when it sped forward upon being released.

"Whoa!" I exclaimed as the car raced forward and fell off the table, and I didn't bother to check to see whether my feigned enthusiasm drew any attention from you. "That car is fast!"

The next car was larger but lacked the windup capabilities of the first. But after poking at it, I discovered its doors could open to allow another small toy to be inserted into the driver's seat.

"Hmm," I murmured, loud enough for you to hear. "I wonder who should drive this car? The princess or the fox? I think... the fox!" The fox was pliable enough to jam in the driver's seat and maintain a position that vaguely suggested it was operating the vehicle.

The one remaining toy vehicle was a dump truck with no notable features other than a mounted bed that could be lifted and lowered. I placed the plastic princess in the back of the truck and continued my narration, beginning to feel more than a bit absurd.

"I think the princess will ride in this truck!" I announced, fighting the urge to glance at you. Playing hard to get was the only way I thought I could entice you to engage.

*Okay, now what?* I thought. I reminded myself that you were only four years old—there was no reason to overthink this.

"Hello, Mr. Fox!" I sang out in a princess-like voice.

"Good morning, Princess Marshmallow!" I had the fox reply in a deeper tone.

"Would you like to have a race?" Princess Marshmallow asked.

"Why, that would be lovely!" the fox answered.

I took the vehicles in my hands and gave them each a push, but the princess's truck veered into the fox's car, knocking it off of the table.

"Ahh!" the fox shrieked as he fell to the floor.

"I'm so sorry!" the princess called out. "I'm not a very good driver!"

"It's okay!" the fox yelled out from the floor. "I'm not hurt. It was just an accident!"

As I crouched down to recover the fallen toys, I subtly glanced into the living room and was surprised to see the couch was empty other than your abandoned tablet. Startled, I stood up and looked around to see where you had gone, only to discover you standing directly behind me, studying the remaining toys on the table. You looked deep in thought, like you were digesting the scene you had just witnessed. Your eyes were twinkling as a shy smile spread across your face before you looked up at me to issue a command.

"Do it again!"

WE SPENT the next few hours playing together, with nominal breaks for coffee refills, as the sun gradually rose into the sky and flooded our kitchen with morning light. You weren't an active participant as we played—not yet—but it didn't take you long to settle into the role of director, instructing me on what you wanted to see through hand gestures and the occasional vocal prompt. Most of your cues encouraged me to continue with the car accident theme I stumbled upon by chance. That type of play was probably overly violent for our purposes, but when I tried to steer the role-playing away from crashes, you were quick to get me back on point.

"Now have this car crash there," you requested at one point, pointing to a table leg. I was so pleased to see you craft such a long sentence, I happily agreed.

"Is the princess hurt?" you asked after the resulting collision, sounding genuinely concerned.

"Hmm, let's see." I put on a thoughtful face and pulled the princess out of the car, having her stagger about with a hand on her head.

"Oh, my head hurts!" I had the princess moan, and you giggled. "I feel so woozy!"

You repeatedly instructed me to recreate that crash several times, always seeking reassurance afterward that the princess had not been harmed. It made little sense to me, but you seemed to loosen up after each of those role-plays, as if a tension was exiting your body.

Upon reaching my point of exhaustion, I announced it

was time for breakfast, and you groaned at the interruption in our play.

"Let's just eat something, and then we'll go somewhere special," I said. That cut off your whining, and you blinked several times, digesting my proposal.

"Somewhere *special*?" you repeated.

"It's a surprise."

"Is it new?" you pressed.

"It is new to you," I said. "So let's just eat some Cheerios and then we will check it out."

You processed this and then, with a start, sprinted for a box of Cheerios on the counter and poured it into a bowl before I could reach you to assist. Only about twenty percent of the cereal hit its intended target, as the rest scattered across the counter or onto the floor.

"I'm sorry!" you said, although I thought I detected a hint of amusement in your voice.

"It's fine," I said, too pleased with our progress that morning to even feel a tinge of annoyance. "It was an accident. Just eat while I clean this up."

You attacked your breakfast with reckless abandon, shoving fistfuls of Cheerios into your mouth while I tried to find everything that missed your bowl. Just as I finished cleaning up, you announced you were done and held up your empty bowl as proof.

"That was quick!" I said, and you giggled.

"That was quick!" you repeated, leaving me to wonder if you were being agreeable or exhibiting echolalia again.

"Alright, you held up your end of the bargain," I said. "Let's go take a ride."

It took some time to brush our teeth and otherwise get ready, but then we were in the car driving west across the Hudson River. A few minutes into the trip, I realized I'd forgotten to take your tablet, but you didn't complain, and I wrote it off as an inadvertent blessing. You quietly looked out the window as we drove, and even though I occasionally tried to engage you in conversation, I gave up upon accepting you weren't in a talkative mood and were only going to keep ignoring me.

After about twenty minutes of driving, we reached a fairly congested area of Kingston I thought of as being its downtown, even though the locals called it "Uptown" for whatever reason.

"I see a church!" you remarked, as I searched for a spot to park on the street. There were a few churches in the vicinity, so I glanced in the rearview mirror to find out what exactly you were looking at.

"Yes, that's a big church," I said. "That's called the Old Dutch Church."

"The Old Dutch Church," you repeated slowly, as if trying to memorize the name.

"Should we go look at it?" I asked, and you nodded your head with great enthusiasm.

There was a good amount of traffic in the area, and it occurred to me that it was Easter Sunday—a holiday that often snuck up on me since I wasn't particularly religious. The traffic congestion was undoubtedly caused by those churchgoers who only show up for the high holidays. Fortunately, I came across a car pulling out of a spot and waited to seize it for myself. Once I parked, we exited to the sidewalk where you stood, back arched to look up at the church's steeple.

"That's a really big church!" you observed.

"It sure is," I agreed. I tapped you on the shoulder and pointed across the street. "And look, I see another church. And another church."

You took a second to admire those other, smaller churches and murmured, "Yes, I see." But then you turned back to study the Old Dutch Church.

"Look at all the people!" you said, pointing at its main doors, and I frowned, confused. There was undoubtedly an Easter service going on inside, so the building was almost certainly full of attendants, but no one was actually standing in front of the church at that moment.

"Where are the people, Quince?" I asked, trying to figure out whether this was a language mishap. "Do you mean inside the church?"

But you stamped your foot in frustration.

"No! Not inside!" You stabbed the air with an extended finger, pointing at the doors. "Those people!"

"Oh, okay," I said, merely to placate you. I didn't want to deal with a breakdown in public. "I'm sorry, I didn't see them at first."

You gave me an odd look, as if wondering how I could be so stupid, but you let the matter go. You continued to stare at the doors, and my curiosity got the better of me.

"What are the people doing, Quince?" I asked. When you didn't respond, I added, "Are they sad? Are they happy?"

"Umm," you said, squinting at the church. "I think they are happy."

"Oh, good. I'm glad."

It wasn't easy getting you to stop studying the church, but after a few minutes, I convinced you to wander further down the street, until we came across a vegan bakery, which was open despite the religious holiday. There was no one inside other than a woman behind the counter, but her presence was enough to trigger your shyness, and you hid behind my legs as soon as she greeted us. I ordered a brownie and an iced coffee for myself before gently guiding you out from behind me.

"Would you like a treat, Quince?" I asked. At your nod, I picked you up so you could see the options behind the glass window. You stared, overwhelmed by the possibilities, even though I suspected you wouldn't care for most of the treats. Finally, just to move things along, I suggested a marzipan cookie, and you bobbed your head in agreement without taking your eyes off the goodie. As I went to pay, you suddenly pointed at a blue macaron covered in sprinkles.

"I don't think you'll like that, buddy," I said, but you pointed at it again, this time with greater emphasis.

"Alright, fine." I nodded at the woman to add that to our dessert box. *It's good exposure to new experiences*, I thought, trying to justify what would likely be a waste of money.

After I paid, we found a small table on the street and got to work on our dessert. As I suspected, you took one nibble of your colorful macaron, put it back in the box with a curt command for me to "save it," and then took the marzipan cookie which, after one bite, proved to be more to your liking. I sipped at my coffee and noticed you looking back toward the steeple of the church, piercing the sky about a block away.

"That's a beautiful church, right?" I asked, trying to draw some language out of you. But you only nodded in response.

"Are you having fun?" I asked as another prompt, but again, all I received in return was a brief nod.

*I'm not good at this*, I thought. I was used to people struggling to draw *me* into conversations; it was uncomfortable being on the other end.

"Look, Quince," I said, and something in my voice must have conveyed I was getting serious because you turned away from the church to face me. "I know you're on the quiet side, and that's okay. I'm quiet, too, most of the time. But sometimes, in order to learn about the world, we have to use our voice and ask questions. So please never be shy about asking me things, no matter what. Okay?"

You nodded, and I could only guess whether I had gotten through to you in any meaningful way.

Once we finished eating, we continued to wander down the street, which was lined with colorful buildings, and crossed a rainbow crosswalk. The brisk air felt almost pleasant in the sun, and I realized that the weather was probably the best one could hope for in the Hudson Valley in mid-April. Most stores were closed on account of it being Easter Sunday, but a handful of restaurants were open. You took in all the sights with great enthusiasm, pausing occasionally to study some piece of window art or another. There were some other people meandering along the street as well, although they didn't seem to draw your interest. But I was surprised when you suddenly stopped at an unremarkable empty doorway and stared at it, completely enthralled.

"Are you okay?" I asked once it became clear you wouldn't move without prompting.

"Why is the girl sad?" you asked, ignoring my question. I looked back at the door, which appeared to be an entry for an apartment building, and I still didn't have any idea what you meant by "the girl." Even after looking up and down the street, I had no clue what you were referencing.

"I don't know," was all I said in response, remembering you getting upset earlier at my confusion regarding what you saw at the church. "Why do you think she's sad?"

You frowned, deep in concentration, before answering

"I think she is sad because the man is yelling at her." You spoke in halting fashion—it seemed as if forming that

sentence had pushed the limits of your language capabilities.

"Oh," I said. "That isn't kind of the man."

You bobbed your head in agreement before allowing me
to lead you further along the street, and as we walked, I tried
to work through my confusion. The concept of imaginary
friends to a four-year-old was familiar to me, but nothing I
read ever suggested imaginary *strangers* could also be an
issue. But I couldn't think of a way to delve deeper into what
you saw, or thought you saw, without upsetting you, so I let
the matter be for the moment.

We circled around the block and made our way past the
rear of the church, heading toward our parked car. You
arched your neck to enjoy one last look at the steeple before
hopping into the back seat. Our busy morning seemed to
have exhausted you, and I wasn't surprised when, minutes
into the drive home, I noticed you sound asleep, snoring out
of your open mouth. I figured you had earned the rest, so
when we pulled into our driveway, I waited in the idling car
until you woke up of your own accord. After about forty
minutes, you began to stir, and a few minutes later you were
awake enough to stagger inside with me to have some lunch.
From there, we spent a few more hours simulating accidents
with your toy cars.

We were both spent by day's end, and you went to bed
on the early side despite your earlier nap. I shared your
exhaustion, but it was a satisfied weariness. The day had
gone as well as I could've hoped, and I suspected my efforts
—and yours—would pay dividends before long. Our hours
of play, broken up by a trip to Kingston, had produced
exchanges that approached conversations, and I suspected
there was plenty more language waiting to pour out of you.

We merely had to tap it.

And so, the next morning also involved hours of play before school started. You didn't tire of the car crash theme, and you were delighted when I took you into the basement to retrieve some other vehicular toys we had long forgotten. We spread various cars and trucks across the kitchen floor, only to speed them into each other while I narrated the action as best as I could. I constantly assured you that the drivers of the vehicles were unharmed after each accident (other than perhaps feeling a bit woozy), and on those occasions where I forgot to give an explicit reassurance, you reminded me to do so with a gentle tap. Otherwise, you were mostly a silent spectator, aside from an occasional hand gesture signaling what I should do with the toys, but I hoped you'd soon grow bored with your passive role and push me aside to take over as the generator of the action.

This trend continued through the rest of the week. Again, I felt like I was on the right track, and I got some confirmation in that regard when I noticed your nights were becoming more and more restful and less interrupted by nightmares. It was a positive development, albeit one I did not fully understand. Perhaps our play was just leaving you too tired to dream at night.

Another positive sign was your abrupt disinterest in your tablet. Our new routine seemed to scratch an itch your tablet couldn't satisfy, and your first request after waking up each morning was to go downstairs to play. After a few days, I stuffed your tablet into the back of a closet, hoping that "out of sight, out of mind" would prevent any future relapse.

Toward the end of the week, I received an email from Nora with her formal speech and language evaluation attached. I braced for the worst when I opened the document, and I wasn't far off in my prediction. Nora stated in the report that your articulation skills were difficult to judge because of your shyness and lack of responses, which hurt to read, even though I knew it was accurate. A table in the report labeled "CASL-2 Score Summary" laid out scores for your receptive and expressive vocabulary, sentence expression and comprehension, and additional rows for inference and pragmatic language. I wasn't clear on what each of those categories meant, but the bottom line was clear: your percentile rank in each row sat somewhere between two and twelve percent, which the table identified as either "deficient" or "below average." The tail end of the report recommended that you receive speech and language therapy to improve your overall language and play skills.

*Well, at least I didn't make a mistake in setting him up for speech therapy right away*, I thought, but it was a minor consolation.

Some part of me must've been hoping I'd been wrong in my assessment of your language, and that everything was actually fine, because I felt a renewed sense of hurt and frustration as I skimmed the report, written in cold clinical language that seemed at odds with Nora's outgoing personality. But I pushed aside any resentment that I might've naturally felt—I understood Nora was merely fulfilling her duties to the best of her abilities, just as I had done the previous week when Nora entrusted me with the responsibility of teaching you language through play.

While your evaluation report felt like a blow, I took solace in your openness to speech therapy. In fact, you seemed downright excited by the prospect of working with Nora again when I brought it up.

"Nora is very nice, right?" I asked you on Saturday morning before we had to leave to meet with her for your first session.

"Yes," you said, before adding, "Nora has dark skin."

"She does," I agreed, mildly uncomfortable with the turn in the conversation. "But that's okay. We're all different. Some people have light skin, some people have dark skin. Some people are tall, and some people are short. What matters is that she's a kind person, right?" You nodded in agreement. *There's probably a more nuanced conversation about race to be had at some point*, I thought. *But hopefully that's a good enough explanation for a four-year-old.*

You didn't put up any resistance once it was time to leave to see Nora again, cooperating as I secured you in your booster seat. Once we were on the road, you were content to stare out the window as we made that journey south.

"Look!" you blurted out around the halfway point of the drive, and I realized we were coming up on the section of the road with the cross that had consumed your attention the last time we made the trip.

"What is it, Quince?" I asked, concentrating on the road.

"Look!" you repeated with greater urgency. And then, as we approached the cross on the side of the road, you said, "That's a pretty bad car accident!"

"What?" Startled, I took my eyes off the road to scan around us, but there was no activity whatsoever.

"Look at that car accident!" you marveled before adding, "Just like Princess Marshmallow!"

As we drove past the cross, your head swiveled to remain focused on that area alongside the road, and I tried to fathom what you were imagining.

"What do you see, Quince?" But you didn't respond to the open-ended question. I tried to think of an easier question for you to handle.

"What color is the car in the accident?" I asked.

"Umm...." You thought hard. "I think it is red. You don't think it is red?"

"I think you're right," I said, not wanting to upset you. "Is the car big or small?"

You thought it over once again. "Umm... pretty small." You paused before laughing. "The car is missing the top!"

*Missing the top?* I wondered if you were connecting the story you'd created in your mind to the cross. Perhaps you learned the meaning of a roadside memorial at some point. Or maybe it was a mere coincidence, and you were laying out a scenario that mirrored our play throughout the week. It could've also simply been a complete language mishap. In any event, it seemed odd enough to warrant reporting to Nora, and I made a mental note to bring that up to her.

A few minutes later, we reached Nora's office. She greeted you warmly upon opening her office door for us before lowering herself to your level to speak with you.

"Would you like to play some games with me, Quince?" she asked, her brown eyes dancing with excitement. You glanced at me for approval, and at my small encouraging nod, you bobbed your head in agreement.

"That's awesome!" Nora said. "Now, do you mind if your daddy waits outside while we play? He will be very close if you need him."

She threw me a hopeful look I interpreted as suggesting it would be easier for her to work with you if I wasn't around. I didn't take offense at being kicked out of the room.

"It's okay, Quince. I'll wait for you right in that hallway," I said. You seemed reluctant but didn't protest when I slowly exited the room.

"There are a few things I'd like to talk to you about later," I muttered to Nora as I left.

"Sure," she replied in a soft voice. "We can chat afterwards."

Nora closed the door after me once I was back in the

hallway, and I found a wooden bench to settle upon for the duration of my hour-long exile. *What am I going to tell her?* I wondered, trying to gather my thoughts. I mentally ran through the past week, sifting through the limited conversations you and I had. It seemed like you'd made progress, but I wasn't sure if that was misplaced optimism on my part.

I couldn't help but think about some of the strange things you'd said throughout the week, and I pondered over how much I should disclose to Nora. The happy people only you could see at the church. The sad girl on the streets of uptown Kingston. The car crash on the road to Poughkeepsie involving a red car with a missing top.

I feared sharing those anecdotes with Nora would only cause her to shrug her shoulders and refer you to a child psychiatrist. But, I reminded myself, it would be selfish not to be forthcoming simply to avoid an unpleasant diagnosis —if that's the help you needed, then so be it. With that in mind, I resolved to give Nora a full account of our week and trust that whatever came of it would be in your best interest.

I took out my phone to check the time and sighed upon seeing I still had another fifty minutes to kill on that hard bench. *Now what?* I thought again about your description of the imaginary accident we passed on the way to Nora's office, with the odd details you included, and my curiosity got the better of me.

A search on my phone for car accidents in the region generated an uncountable number of results. *What exactly am I looking for?* I wondered as I scrolled through them. But I stopped upon reaching a color picture of a totaled car, accompanied by text identifying the photo as being the aftermath of a car crash from two months earlier.

Specifically, the area around the pictured car tickled my memory, and I could place it as the section of road that always caught your attention on the drive to Poughkeepsie. I skimmed the text, which explained how a young man speeding at dusk swerved off the road to avoid a deer, only to wrap his car around a tree. The man died on impact, but it wasn't the description of the accident that made my blood run cold. No, it was the picture of the car itself that froze me to my core, coupled with my memory of how you described the vehicle in the accident: a fairly small, red car that was missing the top. I zoomed in on the picture to make sure my eyes weren't deceiving me, but the larger image only confirmed what I had seen.

The pictured car, wrapped around a tree in a gruesome fashion, was a red convertible.

**4**

During your mother's pregnancy, I had mentally prepared for the many trials we would undoubtedly face as parents.

I knew there would be sleepless nights and days of exhaustion. I knew that however well I planned, there would be times I was under-equipped to deal with a diaper explosion in a public setting. I knew that regardless of how well-behaved you were as a toddler, there would be occasions where I'd have to throw dignity out the window, pick you up, and carry you screaming and crying out of a store. And when those challenges ultimately came to pass, I set my jaw and dealt with them, having already lived through those scenarios in my mind countless times.

But there was one thing that caught me completely off guard in my new role as a father. And that was the fear.

Fear was an enemy I rarely encountered for most of my existence, given that it is the opposite of apathy, which is the realm where I spent most of my adult life. As such, I had few occasions to face fear head-on. But that all changed once you were born. At that point, fear marched in and suffused every essence of my being.

On the first night after bringing you home from the hospital you slept in fits and starts in a bassinet a mere arm's reach away from the bed where I lay in a sleepless daze. Every time I was close to passing out, you would stir, causing me to bolt upright, terrified of ignoring some early SIDS warning or uselessly dozing as you somehow suffocated yourself.

Several months later, you were sick for the first time, and I rushed you to the pediatrician, convinced by your watery cough that you were dying of pneumonia. The doctor listened to your lungs with a stethoscope and chuckled at my paranoia, asking me if that was the first time I'd ever heard a baby cough. He explained that babies' airways are so narrow that their coughs often sound ghastly. I nearly wept with relief at my misplaced anxiety.

I remained a prisoner of fear even once you became a toddler, as I couldn't help but imagine the worst whenever you were out of my line of sight for more than a few seconds. And when COVID-19 swept through the world, a wave of anxiety was triggered within me after any outing.

It was only around the time you turned four that the fear in me subsided, and I recognized that it was largely because of your growing abilities to communicate. When you were feeling ill, you could let me know what specific part of your body was hurting. On those occasions when you woke up scared in the middle of the night, you could often identify the source of your worry and give me a chance to remedy it. If you were angry or frustrated, you had the ability to tell me it was simply because you were hungry, if that's all it was.

And thus, once your ability to articulate your needs developed, I thought my fear was a thing of the past. Discovering the picture of the totaled red convertible that matched your description was only a seed—the smallest of inklings you might see things that were invisible to the rest of us—but that was enough to rekindle my fear. Even worse, I suspected your dark visions were too complex for you to explain in your limited language.

You had become more of a mystery to me than ever, only unlike the incident with your cough, there was no doctor available to reassure me it would all be okay.

I WAS SO ENGROSSED in conducting research on my phone, jotting down notes and intersection locales on a scrap of paper, that I didn't notice when Nora opened her office door at the end of your session. Only once she cleared her throat did I look up, and I hastily pocketed my notes before entering her office.

You seemed content as you played with Nora's farting dog, only giving me the briefest of glances upon my reentry before turning your attention back to the toy. Nora strode to her desk and sat in her chair, gesturing for me to do the same in the seat facing her.

"We spent most of the day playing," she explained in a low tone, as I settled into my seat. "I want Quince to feel comfortable working with me, so today was largely about building trust. We touched upon some speech issues, but our true work will start next week."

"Sure. That makes sense." I stood, and Nora frowned.

"Wasn't there something you wanted to discuss with me?" she asked.

*Oh, right,* I thought. *I was going to tell her about those visions.* That had been the plan before I started wondering whether there was more of an issue there than mere errant speech. I was no longer comfortable being so forthcoming —at least, not while my understanding of what you were going through remained fragmented at best.

"Oh, that. I just wanted to let you know I took your advice from last week," I said. "Quince and I spent the entire week playing, and we visited some cool places. You're right —I saw how all of those experiences helped foster speech, so I'll be sure to keep it up."

I tried to smile, but it surely came off as inauthentic because Nora's brow furrowed as she studied me, a puzzled expression on her face.

"I'm glad to hear it," she said in a measured tone. She glanced at Quince and added, "He's really a sweet boy. I'm looking forward to working with him more."

"Thank you. That means a lot."

It took a few minutes to pry you away from the pooping puppy, but then we said our goodbyes to Nora and were back in the car, driving north in the general direction of our home.

"When can I play with Ms. Nora again?" you asked from the back seat.

"Next week," I said. "Was it fun?"

You didn't give a verbal answer, but I saw you nod through the rearview mirror.

"I'm so glad," I said. "She seems really nice, and she said she had so much fun playing with you, too."

After about fifteen minutes, we approached the roadside cross that always drew your interest. But before reaching that point in the road, I turned right onto a side street, and you registered the detour.

"Where are we going?" you asked.

"I want to show you something," I said.

"I want to go home." You sounded irritable.

"Let's just look at a few things." I took my eyes off the road for a moment to look back at you before adding, "And after, we'll go out and get you an iced tea."

Iced tea was your favorite drink, and it was a card I only played when I really needed to bribe you into doing something. At my invocation of that specific beverage, you settled back into your seat and exhaled loudly.

"Fine," you said in a pained voice, and I could all but hear your eyes roll.

After ten more minutes of driving, I slowed down as we approached a t-intersection, which was actually my first planned stop. It was another accident site I'd found on my phone earlier while you were working with Nora. Specifically, a fatal car accident that had taken place at that spot about four months earlier, when a drunk driver fell asleep at the wheel and hit a signpost at full speed, dying on impact. I was curious whether this location would similarly induce you to visualize the car accident. But you didn't comment as we approached the intersection, even though you appeared to be looking out the window in the general vicinity of where the accident had occurred.

"Do you see that?" I asked, trying to prompt you. But you only look confused.

"What?" you asked, looking back and forth out the windows.

*He doesn't see anything*, I realized. Out loud, just to answer your question, I said, "Oh, just that pretty cloud up there."

You looked underwhelmed as you pressed your face to the window and arched your neck to peer upwards at the sky. "Yes, I see it," you reported, sounding bored.

I continued to drive.

*Is there something special about that area with the cross Quince always talks about?* I wondered. *Or maybe he sees nothing because this accident happened longer ago than the other*

*one? Or am I being completely irrational, and he didn't actually
see anything at all?*

I had a lot of questions. Fortunately, my notes included
additional spots to visit on our winding journey home, and I
hoped your reactions to those other locales would provide
some insight into what you were experiencing.

The next car accident site I found was about fifteen
minutes away, and it had happened less than two weeks
before. If your inability to see anything relating to the first
accident site stemmed from how long ago it happened, I
thought a more recent one might shed some light on the
rules regarding what you could see. If you were perceiving
things unique to you—which was still very much an open
question in my mind—I assumed there would be some logic
dictating when those visions were activated. It was simply a
matter of gathering enough data points to establish a
pattern. But before I could even reach the next destination,
you called out, "Look!"

You pointed excitedly out your window. There was
nothing on the side of the back road we were heading down,
other than a steep ditch separating the road from an abut-
ting forest.

"What is it, Quince?"

"You don't see it? You don't see the bus?"

I was caught off guard—this wasn't on my list of regional
car accidents. But my research had been rushed, and I
undoubtedly missed a great deal in the forty-something
minutes I had to search for car crashes earlier. And, of
course, there are countless accidents that aren't noteworthy
enough to find their way onto the internet. As such, I had no
real reason to doubt what you claimed to be seeing.

"It's hard for me to look while I'm driving, buddy," I said.
"Why don't you tell me what you're looking at?"

You looked hard at the ditch, your head swiveling as we passed some unremarkable point.

"Umm, the bus is upside down."

"Is it a school bus?"

"I think so."

"Is anyone hurt?"

Silence. I tried again.

"Can you see children on the bus?"

"I think so. I think the children are scared."

"I don't blame them, with the bus being upside down and all." I made a mental note of where we were so I could thoroughly research any incidents involving a flipped bus later. "But I'm sure they'll be okay."

"I think so," you agreed, although you sounded more hopeful than confident.

A few minutes later, we reached the next spot on my list, which was the site of where a car had spun off the road after hitting a patch of black ice and crashed into a tree. The couple in the car sustained injuries—the driver getting the worst of it—but they both survived. I was curious what your reaction, if any, would be to that one given the absence of any fatalities, but you confirmed viewing that incident as well once we reached the location, when you looked out your window and marveled, "Look at that car spinning!" You sounded amused, and I was left with the impression you didn't fully appreciate the nature of whatever it was you saw.

Our next stop required us to visit the nearby town of Mossville, and it was a sad one: a car running a red light struck a mother and her six-year-old daughter while they were crossing the street on foot. The mother survived, notwithstanding the severe injuries she sustained, but her daughter died shortly after the accident. This incident happened over a year earlier, and I hoped it might clarify one way or another, the extent to which your apparent visions were limited to recent events.

I drove slowly as I entered the town and crawled to a snail's pace upon reaching the traffic light where the fatal mishap had occurred. Glancing in the rearview mirror, I saw you looking down, on the verge of falling asleep.

"Quince," I said, and when you didn't stir, I repeated your name again, louder. "Quince!"

Startled, you looked up, but then something outside the window immediately captured your attention. You stared hard at the intersection with wide eyes, only to suddenly and violently turn away.

"No!" you yelled. "No!" You started to cry in the back seat, and it didn't take long for those cries to evolve into sobs. "I want to go home! I want to go home now!"

"What do you see, Quince?" I pressed as gently as I could. But you didn't respond—you just kept bawling.

*I'm traumatizing him*, I realized with a start, and a sick feeling crept into my stomach.

I had been so curious about what you could see that I failed to appreciate the toll those visions took on you. Granted, I tried to justify it as a necessary exercise to understand what you were going through, making me better positioned to help you, and there may have been truth to that as well. But it didn't alter the fact that my actions had hurt you, and I felt awful for it.

"Do you want to go get that iced tea?" I hoped to distract you from your anguish, but you wouldn't allow it.

"No," you snapped. "I want to go home. Can we please go home?"

"Okay," I said, feeling defeated. "We'll go home now."

Once we arrived back at our house, you beelined for the couch and sat at its far end, hugging your knees and staring into nothing. I hovered at the entry to the living room, wondering what I could do to make you feel better. You rejected a snack when offered and immediately resumed your stare into empty space, and I assumed you were struggling to process whatever you had seen earlier. It was torture seeing you suffer in isolation like that, but I couldn't think of how to start up a conversation without agitating you even further. I retreated to the kitchen to give you some space, resolving to talk with you once you had settled down. But when I checked back in on you a few minutes later, you were fast asleep, your head propped up by the armrest of the couch.

You were still wearing your shoes and jacket so, taking care not to disturb you, I removed them and gently reset your legs on the couch. After covering you with a blanket, I took a seat at the kitchen table and tried to think.

*That was a pretty big meltdown*, I thought, mentally stating the obvious. Other four-year-olds were undoubtedly prone to such outbursts, but it was out of character for you

I struggled to recall the last time you had been so upset, and I came up empty. But then I remembered my meeting with your teacher earlier in the month where she described a similar atypical explosion from you. After digging through my emails, I found the information relating to the site of the field trip where that breakdown had occurred: Miller Farm.

*What did he see there that day?* I wondered, tapping another Google search into my phone.

It didn't take long to find an answer. Nearly ten years earlier, when the property was under different ownership, a drunken fight broke out between two farmhands based on a rumor that one had been having something of an affair with the other's wife. Things got out of hand, leading to one taking an ax to the back of the other's head, killing him instantly, and leading to the arrest and incarceration of the assailant. The Miller family purchased the farm several years later, and that gruesome incident was, to my knowledge, largely forgotten by the community.

Forgotten, but apparently reawakened in your eyes, at least.

*Jesus Christ*, I thought, tossing my phone aside and letting my head drop into my hands. *How many nightmares has this poor kid seen?* I couldn't shake the thought you had likely experienced several traumatic scenes throughout your life, and I had been oblivious. Worse, even upon recognizing the problem, I didn't know how to address it going forward. It seemed as if you had been unfairly sentenced to a lifetime of visions centered on violence, hate, and fear. Far too much weight to ask any four-year-old to carry.

A noise bubbled in my throat as I tried to hold back the tears, but my resistance lasted only a moment before I was quietly sobbing into my hands. Raising you as a single parent pushed me to my limits in the best of times, and I felt ill-equipped to help you navigate this utterly unfamiliar terrain. My bumbling parenting style, imperfect as it was, might have given you a chance at a normal life in the absence of these complexities, but in that moment, it fully hit me that you were going through a crisis, and I didn't know how to do a damn thing to help you.

I wept alone in the kitchen for some time, keeping my anguish at a low enough volume so as not to disturb your rest. It was unclear how long you would sleep—you looked exhausted at the time you nodded off.

I was surprised when I felt your small hand rest on my shoulder.

"Are you okay, Daddy?"

I looked up and subtly wiped the tears from my eyes

with my upper arm—I had a tendency to try to maintain a strong front for you. But I could see from your face I wasn't tricking you at all. You saw my pain.

"I'm okay, buddy," I said. "I was just a little sad."

You nodded, thoughtful.

"Are you sad because of the girl?" you asked. It wasn't hard to guess what you were referencing.

"The girl who was hit by the car?"

"Yes."

"I'm sad about a lot of things," I said. "But that girl getting hurt was definitely sad." I hesitated before adding a lie: "I'm sure she'll be okay."

You looked doubtful at first, but then you seized onto my optimistic assessment. "I think so," you agreed, as if trying to convince yourself.

I didn't know if my dishonesty would help you at all—at best, it might serve as a Band-Aid for your damaged psyche —but it seemed to brighten your disposition at least a bit. You reached up toward my head with both arms extended, and I shifted in my seat to lift you. Once you were eye level with me, you wrapped your arms around my neck and gave a tight squeeze. I closed my eyes, holding you close until I felt you loosen your hold, at which point I lowered you back to the floor.

"There," you said, looking satisfied. "I gave you a hug. Now you feel better."

A smile touched my lips as I realized you weren't wrong. I had often been on the other end of similar exchanges when you fell or banged your head into something, and it was comforting to know that a well-timed hug could, in fact, be powerful enough to drive the pain away.

"You're right," I said. "I do. I feel better."

You beamed at me, but then after a moment you grew

serious, as if struck by a sudden thought. A frown spread across your face while you scanned the kitchen, seemingly looking for something.

"Hey," you said, continuing to eyeball the room. "What happened to my iced tea?"

WE WENT for another car ride for the promised iced tea and then returned home to spend the afternoon building various towers out of some toy blocks we dug out of the basement, challenging ourselves to construct the tallest tower possible without it collapsing. At one point I had the bright idea to grab a measuring tape, and you delighted in announcing the height of each stack of blocks.

"Sixty-six inches!" you called out at one point. "That's the tallest one yet!"

Language seemed to flow out of you more easily when you were motivated by sights and activities to discuss, just as Nora had predicted. Every day I felt more confident you'd find your voice eventually, even if there was plenty of work left to be done to get you to that point. You still seemed shy to the point of muteness around everyone other than me, but I was glad you were working regularly with Nora—it could only benefit you to work on communications with another adult.

You were happy enough, but tired, when it came time to put you to bed that night. Just after I finished tucking you in, you asked, "Was the girl naughty?"

"What's that, Quince?"

"Was the girl naughty for being in the street?"

"Oh, no. It wasn't the girl's fault. She didn't do anything

wrong." I thought it over as I walked to turn off the lights. "It's sad, but sometimes bad things just happen."

As you digested that nugget of profundity, I flicked the lights off and left, closing your bedroom door behind me, and headed to my room, where I flopped on the bed and opened my laptop. I wanted to document all your visions, or those instances where you inexplicably didn't seem to have a vision, while that information was fresh in my mind. There had to be a pattern there, one I couldn't see just yet, and cracking that code seemed to be the key to getting you whatever help you needed.

I opened a blank Excel spreadsheet and stopped, trying to decide the best way to package the data I'd accumulated so far. After a moment's thought, I labeled the first column of the spreadsheet, "Description of Incident," which I planned on using as a field to input everything I knew about a particular event you viewed. Next, I added a column titled, "Quince's Observations" to memorialize anything note-worthy you said about a particular incident. The next two columns I labeled, "Date of Incident" and, "Date of Viewing." It remained unclear to me just how far back in time you were able to see, and I hoped having those dates laid out in a single chart might be revealing.

Once I set those column headings, I took to filling in the spreadsheet with what I knew, which wasn't much.

The first entry was for the car accident that started it all—the roadside cross on the drive down to Poughkeepsie, serving as a monument to the man who died after swerving off the road. I added another entry for the school bus that had flipped into the ditch, although I didn't have any information regarding the details of that incident, aside from what you told me, including when that incident happened—my internet search for that accident had been fruitless. I included another row in the spreadsheet for the couple you saw who spun off the road and survived the resulting crash, and I made an entry for the girl who was struck by the car in Mossville. After a moment's thought, I inserted the murder at Miller Farm, even though you hadn't actually described that one to me.

Those examples, which painted such a conclusive picture in my head, seemed sparse when laid out on a computer screen. *What else?* I thought, before remembering our trip to Kingston the week prior, and your comments about the girl who was "sad" because a man was yelling at her. There wasn't a lot to go on for that one—it would probably be impossible ever to decipher the details of the incident generating that vision—but I added it to the list, nonetheless.

As I was contemplating what else to add to the spreadsheet, I heard a muffled cry coming from down the hall. Casting my computer aside, I strode to your room and opened your door, where you were sitting up in bed, tears streaming down your face. You said nothing when I came in but held your arms out for me to lift you.

I obliged, and we didn't speak as you sobbed into my shoulder. Some time later, after you calmed down a bit, I wiped your face clean with a tissue and placed you on your bed, where you remained sitting up.

"Did you have a nightmare?" I asked, and you nodded, your lips pressed together.

"Was it about the girl?" I asked.

"I think so. I don't remember." You looked like you were on the verge of tears again.

"Look, Quince," I said, rubbing at the back of my head. "I don't know what happened to that girl who got hurt." I continued to believe it would be unhelpful to be completely forthcoming about that girl's fate. "But you shouldn't be afraid of what you saw because it can't hurt you. I'm your daddy, and it is my job to love you and keep you safe. And that is what I am going to do. Okay?"

You nodded, although your face still showed fear.

"Would you feel safer if I stayed in here tonight while you slept?" I asked. "There's nothing to be afraid of, but if that will help...."

"Yes, please," you responded in a small voice.

"Okay. Just give me a minute."

I went back to my room and changed out of my t-shirt, caked with your tears and snot, and grabbed a pillow off the bed before returning to your bedroom. Once there, I tucked you back into bed and then sprawled out on the floor with my pillow. It didn't take long to hear your muffled snores, but I was determined to stay in your room all night in case you woke again and needed a comforting presence.

I had learned a great deal that day, not that I knew what to do with the information I'd gathered. But the intel had come at a cost. My series of trials had assaulted your mental wellbeing, and I questioned whether I was doing you more harm than good. And yet, I knew you would inevitably suffer through future traumatic visions if I did nothing. There was no obvious course of action since whatever I did, or didn't do, would ultimately hurt you.

I laid awake for some time, wrestling with my uncertainties and the fact that any decisions I might make would only lead to pain. As much as I wished to have the clarity to come up with a viable game plan, I knew the best I could offer you, at least in the short term, was well-intentioned floundering, and there was no rational basis to suspect that would lead anywhere useful. But I knew I'd do it anyway, if only because the only other option was to give up.

And that was a nonstarter.

## 5

As much as I knew I'd never give up on trying to help you, I equally knew my efforts were bound to bring you pain. That caused me to question my actions, but eventually, with the benefit of the wisdom that so often comes with the gift of hindsight, I realized I was wrong for doubting myself on that front.

And that is because I would come to learn that a common mistake parents make is proceeding under the assumption that the goal of being a parent is to have your children love you.

It's surprisingly easy to generate smiles from children. Simply plying them with candy, ice cream, and all the television they could ever wish for will put a parent in their child's good graces. But like most easy solutions, it isn't the correct one.

Sometimes it's necessary to take action that will anger your child, or even hurt them, when it is in their best interest, which isn't an easy thing to do when a child is too young to appreciate the "'why" behind the parent's actions. Whether it be taking a child to the dentist to have a cavity filled, or forcing them to bathe over their protestations, or putting them down to bed even when they want to stay up and play, parenting is full of choices that *could end up incurring the short-term wrath of a child. But that doesn't mean those decisions were wrong.*

*As I grew into the role of a father, I discovered the goal of being a parent wasn't to inspire the love of a child, even though it's normal to hope for that. The purpose of being a parent isn't to be loved—it is to give love. It is giving your children whatever they need.*

*In order to help you, I had to continue investigating what you were experiencing. I knew that wouldn't be an easy road for you, but that didn't mean it was the wrong one—it was a journey you had to take for there to be any hope of you attaining peace. As much as it troubled me, I came to accept that fate, for whatever reason, had decreed that your path go straight through hell.*

*But if I couldn't save you from that experience, at the very least I could make sure you didn't take that trip alone.*

THE NEXT MORNING was a rare instance where I woke up before you did. I was achy from my night on the floor, but I had somehow slept well otherwise. After rubbing the blurriness out of my eyes, I checked my phone for the time: 6:06, which was much later than your normal wake-up time.

*Poor kid is exhausted from yesterday*, I thought. You continued to snore face down in your bed and showed no signs of stirring. I was intent on being there when you finally woke up—the last thing I wanted was for you to think I'd abandoned you in the middle of the night—so I carefully tiptoed down the hall to retrieve my laptop before returning to your room.

I settled on the floor, reopening the spreadsheet I'd started the night before, and resumed looking for patterns in your visions. As I scanned the computer screen, my mind wandered to the choices I'd made up to that point. It was hard to avoid the conclusion that I'd been proceeding like a fool. After I started questioning the nature of your visions during your last session with Nora, I should've headed home and taken time to reflect on what I knew in order to develop a plan of action. Instead, I hastily mapped out a tour of car accident sites to satisfy my curiosity, and likely traumatized you in the process.

What was done was done, but I knew I had to be smarter going forward. And so, while I studied the Excel spreadsheet, I did what I should have done from the outset: I gathered myself and confronted the problem logically.

*What do I know at this point?* The answer didn't amount to much: *Quince sees things, and these things often bother him.* There were two ways of dealing with that problem. The first was to keep you locked up, or at least confined to confirmed "safe" areas, in an attempt to avoid your troubling visions entirely. And, perhaps, a few years down the road, you might become mature enough to comprehend the nature of what you were seeing and be better equipped to process those visions.

But I knew that wasn't the answer. I had experienced firsthand the effects of you being locked away during the pandemic—however necessary it may have been at the time —and how that isolation negatively impacted your development. Sequestering you might temporarily solve the problem of your uncontrolled visions, but it would only open the door to a host of others. That was not a road I wanted to go down.

As such, the only viable option I saw was what I clumsily attempted yesterday: work to understand the nature of what you were seeing and go from there. And do my best not to damage you too severely in the process.

My eyes continued to run up and down the list of entries on my computer. It was a bleak list, to be sure. Plenty of death, including a murder. The only nonviolent incident appeared to be some sort of verbal abuse. *Is that the pattern?* I wondered. *Does Quince only see pain and death?*

But it couldn't be that simple. I recalled another fatal car accident we had passed involving a drunk driver who fell asleep at the wheel, which you didn't seem to see. *What was different about that one?* The answer to that question seemed to hold a big clue for deciphering the mystery of your visions, but it continued to elude me.

And still, there was more. *The church.* You saw a mob of people there, although I spent little effort questioning you about it at the time. Typing as quietly as I could so I wouldn't disturb you, I added the church viewing to the bottom of the spreadsheet, and in the column labeled, "Quince's Observations," I wrote, "The people look happy." Seeing that addition to the table marginally lifted my spirits. It seemed to eviscerate any notion that you only saw misery and fatalities. But it only made me even more confused about what triggered your visions and what didn't.

*I need more information*, I thought again. But after the emotional toll on you yesterday, I knew it would be unfair to subject you to further death and destruction, so car accidents and murder sites were off the table. You already had more than your share of trauma for a weekend—you deserved a peaceful Sunday.

And then it hit me.

It was Sunday.

What better day to go to church?

∿

You woke up shortly after 7:30—the culmination of a twelve-hour sleep that confirmed the previous day had pushed you to your limits. But you seemed refreshed and upbeat after bouncing out of bed, and you excitedly asked what we were doing that day—a far cry from the days when you numbly accepted a day puttering about the house.

"Do you remember the really big church we saw last week?" I asked.

You nodded. "The Old Dutch Church?"

"Yes, that's it." I was surprised you remembered the name. "I thought today we could try to look for other churches. Maybe the churches we have here in town."

"Do you mean churches we never saw before?" you asked, sounding intrigued.

"That's right. Does that sound fun?"

You thought it over for a moment before jumping up and down, squealing.

"Yes, please!" you yelled as you continued to bound about, and I marveled at how easy it was to make you happy sometimes.

A short while later, we drove into the heart of Blue Bank, which I knew had three churches near one another. One of those was about to start a nine o'clock service and had a mob of people wandering in, so I guided you toward the other two churches situated next to each other.

"What do you think, Quince?" I asked, as we faced the two of them from the sidewalk.

You looked back and forth between the churches, trying to decide which to investigate first. One church was made of red brick, and the other was a white Catholic church with a tall steeple. With a decisive point of your finger, you selected the Catholic church and ran toward its front doors. I could hear the muffled sounds of an organ coming from within—a service seemed to be in session—but otherwise, all was quiet outside.

"What do you think?" I asked again, trying to prompt some clue as to what you were seeing.

"It's beautiful!" you exclaimed, spinning around and looking up to take it all in.

"Do you see any people?" I asked and immediately regretted the leading nature of the inquiry. You threw me a suspicious look, one that wondered why I was asking such a silly question, but you didn't respond.

"There are people inside the church," I explained. "That's what the music is. They are having a ceremony and singing."

Your wariness dissolved—you appeared to appreciate the intel.

"The people are inside *and* outside," you said, correcting me.

"Oh, right," I said, looking around at the emptiness surrounding us. "I forgot about the outside people. Do you think they are happy?"

"Hmm." You studied the empty air around you before reaching your conclusion. "Yes, very happy. But the girls in the white dresses look sad."

*White dresses?* I wondered, then it suddenly made sense to me. *Ah, weddings. Of course.*

"Why do you think the girls in the white dresses are sad?" I asked.

"They are crying. But the other people look happy." You paused, thoughtful. "That isn't kind of them to laugh at the crying girls."

"Well, sometimes people are so happy that they cry," I explained. "When people are super happy, they might cry.

But other times, people are sad when they cry. Crying can mean different things."

"Are the girls in white crying because they are happy?"

I shrugged. "Maybe. I hope so."

You processed this in silence before announcing, "I want to see the other church!"

We walked down the block to the brick church and on arriving, you again commented about a happy mob that I couldn't see, sprinkled with crying women in white dresses. *Car accidents and weddings*, I wondered. *What do they have in common?* It was easy to imagine a hacky dad joke answer to the question, but I remained stumped. Still, I was glad to have made some progress in deciphering the nature of your visions.

"Now let's look at more churches!" you called out.

You seemed at peace for once with the visions you were experiencing at these churches, so I was more than happy to agree to your request. We hopped into the car and made the ten-minute drive to the town of Rhinebeck, which I knew had at least a few churches for you to check out.

Religious services were in full swing once we arrived, making it impossible to park near the churches I had in mind, so I had to settle for a spot on the far side of town. You grumbled at the walk as we made our way through the heart of the village, but you otherwise still seemed to be in good spirits. The main street running through town was fairly quiet, with most of the local shops closed—other than those dealing in coffee or breakfast—so the sidewalks were pretty much empty.

"Is that man sad?" you asked as we approached the other end of town, and I tensed, preparing to deal with another vision of yours. But I was surprised when I looked up and actually saw the person you were referencing.

The man, who looked to be in his early forties, clutched a handful of fliers in one hand and a stapler in the other. Bags under his eyes suggested he hadn't slept well in some time, and he didn't look at us as we walked by despite your loud question about him. His forlorn face remained focused on his task, which was posting a flier to a wooden bulletin board erected near the street. I gave you a slight tug to keep moving, but you pulled back, transfixed by what the man was doing. The man set a flier in place with four quick staples and then stoically proceeded down the street, searching for the next place to display his papers.

Once the man departed, I allowed you to yank me toward the newly affixed bulletin. The page was dominated by a picture of a young boy in a red jacket, smiling up at the camera from what looked to be his driveway. The page displayed the word, "MISSING" prominently at the top in capital letters. Below, on the right side of the sheet, was the boy's name—Connor Callaghan—followed by a recitation of Connor's height, weight, and eye color. The poster indicated the boy was last seen on April 5, 2022—nearly three weeks earlier—at his home at 28 Pine Grove Road in the nearby town of Greenfield.

*That's the boy who was kidnapped a few weeks ago while waiting for his school bus*, I realized. And, I assumed, the man we had passed was the boy's father, putting up his fliers wherever he could in a desperate attempt to locate his son. *Has he been doing that for the last three weeks?* I wondered. I questioned whether the father's work would make a difference, but I could certainly understand and appreciate the need to do *something*, even if only to create the illusion of being helpful, when confronted with a seemingly hopeless situation.

Empathy isn't a particularly strong suit of mine, but my

heart went out to the father as he made his way down the street, wordlessly posting his fliers. I was barely holding it together as I struggled to deal with your visions and the extent to which they had traumatized you, but at least I knew you were otherwise safe. If you were ever taken from me, being subjected to God only knew what....

I simply couldn't comprehend that degree of pain.

"Who is that boy?" you asked, pointing at the picture on the flier.

"That boy is lost. The man is the boy's daddy, and he's trying to find his son."

"Oh." You pondered this information in silence and reached up to hold my hand. "That is very sad. We should help that man."

I gave your hand a brief squeeze and sighed. "I wish we could, but...."

I trailed off, prompting you to look up at me with a confused look on your face.

"But what?" you asked. I didn't answer right away—the gears were turning in my head.

"Nothing," I finally said, making a decision. "Let's take a ride. I promise we can come back to the churches later."

We turned to head back to our car, but after a few steps, I raced back to the flier to snap a picture of it on my phone before turning back to rejoin you.

"Where are we going?" you asked once we were back in the car and driving out of Rhinebeck. You sounded more curious than annoyed that we were leaving before visiting the churches.

"I just want to show you something," I said as I drove, following my phone's directions for the address I had plugged in.

Twenty minutes later, we arrived in the town of Greerfield, which looked similar to many of the towns on our side of the Hudson River: a small main street with shops and restaurants surrounded by homes and, beyond those, fields dedicated to farming. I drove through the center of town and turned off onto a side street, which eventually turned into Pine Grove Road.

It was a fairly affluent part of the town, with various houses spread apart from one another, sitting at varying elevations on the hilly terrain. Long driveways meandered from those houses to the street, making it easy to imagine how a child waiting alone for a school bus in the morning could be taken with no one seeing anything suspicious. I drove at a snail's pace down the road, and I slowed even more upon reaching a mailbox with the number, "28" affixed to its side.

*Please see something, Quince*, I prayed, holding my breath as I passed by the house.

"Look!" you cried out, and I released my breath all at once.

"What do you see, Quince?" I asked, trying not to sound too eager.

"Do you see it?" you asked, pointing out the window. "Look at the bird!"

A red cardinal stood on the ground next to the driveway, casting nervous looks in all directions before pecking at seeds that had spilled out of a bird feeder hanging from a tree above.

"I see the cardinal," I said, continuing to drive as slowly as I could. "It is beautiful. But do you see anything else?"

You didn't respond, and soon the house was behind us. *Damn it*, I thought. After making a three-point turn, I went back past the house again, but the cardinal was gone. You remained silent.

A sense of defeat settled in me. *I truly expected that to work,* I thought, although I was unsure what success would have even looked like. What would have happened if you had been gifted some vision of the abduction itself? Would you have been able to recite a license plate number or describe the person who snatched the boy? It was a moot point, of course, since that kidnapping was inexplicably one of those things you couldn't see, much to my dismay. It was the first time I could imagine something positive coming out of your visions, and I felt crushed that your ability eluded you when it was most needed.

"Can we go back to the churches?" you asked, sounding bored.

"Sure." I felt empty inside, but I did the best I could to mask my disappointment.

I'm not a religious person by any means, but I tend to believe that many things in life happen for a reason. There is nothing I wouldn't have given for the ability to take your cruel visions away from you and spare you those nightmares, but it would have been an easier pill to swallow had I known your suffering served some higher purpose. As heartbroken as I was that we couldn't help Connor and his family, it also burned to suspect everything you were going through was completely arbitrary and served no purpose other than to cause you pain. It hurt to think life could be so cruel.

But that didn't change the fact it so often is.

## 6

*To what extent did my shortcomings as a father stem from pride?*

*After your mother's death, I was determined to raise you to the best of my ability. Other than those first few days following your birth, I politely declined any offers from family members to watch you, operating under the belief that accepting any help would be an abdication of my responsibilities to you. That stubborn commitment to raise you entirely on my own surely contributed to my later decision to relocate to the Hudson Valley, where there would be no family or friends within a two-hour radius of us. Only when it was impossible for me to watch you, such as sending you to preschool while I was working, would I allow anyone else to step in and assist with your care.*

*For a long time, I thought my commitment to you was a testament to my worth as a parent. It took a long time to understand that most of my decisions stemmed from arrogance rather than an honest assessment of what was in your best interests. I pushed myself to the point of exhaustion and wore the near constant bags under my eyes as a badge of honor, never asking myself whether you would have been better served had I accepted the help so often offered to me by members of our extended family* or others. Just as a person lifting weights doesn't want a spotter to assist them on their final rep, I deluded myself into thinking I had to care for you by myself every step of the way in order for my work as a father to have meaning.

In short, I made it all about me when it should have been entirely about you. You undoubtedly would have benefited from other adults in your life, rather than being isolated with me, but I didn't make that part of my calculations. And so, I wrestled with wondering how much of your developmental delays were tied to my selfishness.

The struggle to help you deal with your visions was a humbling experience. It made me realize I didn't have all the answers, or even any answers. Our inability to help the kidnapped boy only compounded that humility. These failures gradually stripped away my ego and forced me to contend with a single question, which happened to be the only question that matters:

What was best for you?

The answer to that inquiry manifested as two realizations—two truths that seemed nearly contradictory.

The first was that I still wasn't doing enough for you. I had to do more.

The second realization was that, whatever that something "more" was, I needed help to achieve it.

It wasn't something I could do alone.

EVEN THOUGH THE weekend had been an emotional rollercoaster, I felt sad when it came to an end, bringing us back to our respective routines of preschool and work. You woke up early again on that Monday, and I savored the few hours we'd have together before dropping you off at school.

But once 8:30 came, we had to stop building churches, put your colorful blocks away, and head out to preschool.

I had developed mixed feelings about your school. On the one hand, it was a place that didn't seem to trigger your visions, and it was a small comfort knowing you weren't being traumatized over the course of the day. And yet, it was unsettling that you were spending your entire day in an environment where you were too uncomfortable to use your voice.

I didn't want to pull you from school completely—there was surely a benefit to you spending time with children your own age. And ending your enrollment wasn't an option —not without quitting my job, which would only lead to a new swarm of problems. Still, I couldn't shake the persistent and unnerving feeling that came from knowing we would only have a few scant hours after work each day to eat dinner before I put you to bed. I didn't want to wait until the following weekend to resume our work, given all the progress we had made.

After dropping you off at school, I returned home and shot off an email to Andrew Harris, the head of my company, asking if we could talk. It was a rare request, as I took great pride in not bothering him on the daily. Andrew called me back within a minute, as I knew he would.

"What's going on, Will?" he asked, not bothering to waste time with greetings after I took his call. "How's your lawsuit going?"

Andrew and I rarely engaged in small talk, but on those occasions when our paths crossed, he never failed to ask about the wrongful death lawsuit I had filed against the hospital and doctors involved in the procedure that led to your mother's passing. That litigation always fascinated

Andrew, even though it was a slog I tried not to think about unless I had to. Your mother's side of the family pressured me into bringing that lawsuit against my better instincts—I was personally of the opinion that no one did anything wrong, and your mother's death was just one of those sad things that life occasionally throws at us. But your mother's parents and sister were persistent, so to appease them, I hired an attorney to file suit on my behalf shortly before the statute of limitations was set to expire. The case progressed slowly, primarily because of delays in the court's calendar in the wake of the COVID outbreak, but discovery was finally winding down, suggesting that the end might finally be in sight. Still, I believed our case was weak, notwithstanding my attorney's repeated assurances it had a high settlement value.

From a broader perspective, Andrew seemed both mystified by and terrified of the litigation process, which I always found somewhat endearing when contrasted with my never-ending weariness of the judicial system. I had cashed in on Andrew's strange phobia of litigation by earning goodwill through taking care of almost all our company's legal matters without his involvement. As far as he was concerned, I was a magical fairy that simply made legal problems disappear.

But as much as he feared becoming a target in litigation, Andrew's fascination with it peaked when he could observe it from the sidelines, having no personal stakes in the game. Such was the case with my wrongful death lawsuit, and I knew indulging Andrew's curiosity was a small price to pay for the long leash he kept me on.

"Hi, Andrew," I said. "The lawsuit is dragging. I was deposed a few weeks ago, not that I had anything of substance to say. I think there's a mediation scheduled for this summer, although the date of that escapes me right now."

"Wow," Andrew said, breathless at my bland update. I wondered whether Andrew was a fan of John Grisham—if he was titillated by my non-news, I couldn't imagine how he'd respond to a legitimate legal thriller.

"Anyway," I said. "Thanks for getting on the phone with me, and I'm sorry to bother you. Something's come up that I wanted to talk to you about."

"Alright," he said, and I could tell from his voice he was bracing for bad news.

"My son, Quince—who is just about four-and-a-half— he's been going through some stuff." I didn't want to divulge the full truth, of course, but I thought my sales pitch had a better chance of landing if I sprinkled in a few flavorful details. "There are issues with delays in his speech," I added, "and we're trying to get him caught up."

"Okay," Andrew said, and I could hear relief in his voice that my issue was at least not directly related to his company. "I'm sorry to hear that."

"Yeah, thanks. The thing is, I've been working with him a lot lately, whenever I'm able, and I can already see it's making a big difference. Quince also started working with a speech therapist, and she seems great, although that's still early in the process. My concern is that Quince spends his days at school, where he's apparently not talking at all. I'm nervous that whatever progress we're making on the weekends is lost by the time the work week rolls around. It would be great if I could work with him on a more consistent basis. That's why I was hoping to adjust my schedule to allow me more time with him during the week."

After a long pause, I checked my phone to make sure we hadn't been disconnected.

"What do you mean 'adjust your schedule?'" Andrew finally asked, sounding less than thrilled with the proposal.

"Well, right now, Quince is in school from nine to five which is when I'm working. By the time I get him, he barely has enough energy to eat some dinner before heading off to bed. But if I could shift my hours—say, put in four hours in the morning and four hours after he goes to sleep at night—I'd be able to take advantage of the afternoon and keep working with him. At this point, I seem to be the only person in his life he's comfortable talking to, and I'm afraid that if I'm not available for him, his development will stagnate."

Andrew started to respond, but I quickly added, "And I recalled that talk you gave a few weeks ago where you stressed the importance of flexible work arrangements, so...." I hadn't been paying much attention to Andrew's annual address to the company, which I watched online via Zoom, but I at least retained that one nugget.

"To be honest," Andrew said, "when I said that, I was really thinking of positions where we have enough people to fill in any gaps that arise from someone's absence. But you're our only in-house counsel. If you're not around, we are attorney-less."

Fortunately, I was ready for that rejoinder.

"Look, most of my work involves working with outside counsel," I said, which was true. "And those attorneys are spread all around the country, covering four time zones." Also true. "So if I split my work over the course of a day, I'll be better equipped to deal with our east coast attorneys in the morning and our west coast attorneys in the evenings."

That last part was stretching the truth a bit, but I hoped Andrew wouldn't challenge it out of a concern of exposing his lack of understanding of what I did day-to-day.

"I don't know, Will...."

"Let me put it this way," I said. "When you hired me, I swore I'd do my best to keep legal matters from reaching your desk, and I think I've delivered on that promise. And I'm telling you now that what I'm proposing will not impact the quality of my work one bit. Of course, if I'm wrong, you can easily throw me back into my current arrangement, and you won't hear a peep from me. But I'm confident that if you let me shift my hours like this, you won't see any difference in my work, and it will mean a lot to me. And to my son."

There was no response, but I didn't know what more I could say to make my case, so I waited. When I heard a loud sigh come through the phone, I knew I'd won this battle.

"Alright," Andrew said. "We'll give this a try, for now. But I reserve the right to change my mind if this arrangement presents any issues. Just how long do you see this going on for?"

"I don't know. As long as it takes? That's all I can really say besides thank you."

"You're welcome," Andrew said, sounding as if he was already having second thoughts. *That's fine*, I thought. *I'll make sure he doesn't regret this.* "Is there anything else?" he added.

"No, that was it. And seriously, thank you so much. This means everything to me."

"Yeah, yeah," Andrew grumbled. "Alright. Anyway, good luck with your lawsuit. Let me know how your mediation goes." And then he hung up.

I felt a weight lift from my chest. No longer would I have to wait until the weekend to take you out into the world to develop my understanding of what you were going through. Now, I only needed to dedicate a few hours each morning to work before picking you up at lunch, at which time we could continue to spend more time together in the hope of coaxing additional language out of you. Granted, I'd have to put in a few hours of work each night after you went to bed but that was no particular hardship. I wasn't doing anything interesting during that time, anyway.

I was on the verge of calling your school to inform them of this new arrangement when my phone vibrated. The displayed number had a local area code, suggesting the call wasn't spam, so I took it.

"Hi, Will." I recognized Nora's voice immediately. She seemed caught off guard by how quickly I answered her call. "How's it going? I was just calling about Quince's session for this weekend. I wanted to see if it would be possible to do it remotely via Zoom?"

"Remotely?" I repeated dumbly.

"Yes. I'm sorry, but I'll be going down to the city this weekend to visit my in-laws. My husband is a professor at Harp College, which I think is actually right by where you live. Anyway, he just canceled his Friday classes so we could visit his family in Manhattan for his mother's birthday. I can still make time to see Quince, but an in-person meeting just won't be possible this week."

*Damn it*, I thought. I had decided to let Nora in on your secret, even though I was still working on how to convince her that my fanciful story was truthful. But I knew that wasn't a conversation to be had over the phone, or even over the computer. There was probably no harm in waiting another week to discuss it with her, although my anxiety about your predicament seemed to increase every day. It was getting harder and harder to be patient when it came to dealing with your visions, but it appeared as if I'd have to be.

"Well, yes, that would work," I conceded. But then an idea struck me, and I added, "Could you possibly make some time to see us in person on Saturday? We can come down to the city to meet you—I won't even need a full hour. I realize this is an odd request, but there's something we really need to show you relating to Quince's development."

"Umm...."

But before Nora could refuse, I continued, "I promise I wouldn't even ask this if we weren't dealing with something important. And I don't mean to pull you away from your family, but we only need a few minutes. We can meet you near wherever you're staying to make it as convenient for you as possible."

"And you can't tell me what this is all about now?" Nora asked, her voice revealing a hint of curiosity.

"It's not an issue that can be easily put into words. But it's important, and I'm afraid I'm not properly addressing this problem, so it's gnawing at me. That's why, if it's possible for you to step away and see us for a bit, it would mean the world to me." My voice broke, and I took a second to collect myself before adding, "We really need your help."

And for the second time in ten minutes, I listened to silence through my phone while the other end weighed a proposal.

"Okay," Nora finally said. "I can't imagine what this is about, but I'll make myself available if it's that important. I'm staying with my in-laws in downtown Manhattan, near Fulton Street. My husband is a lovely man, but... well, let's just say I'm not averse to an opportunity to step away from his family for a spell. Would you be able to get down there on Saturday?"

"Downtown?" I thought hard. "Can you meet us at the Fulton Street subway station, by the 2 and 3 line?" I asked, pushing my knowledge of New York City's subway system to its limits. "You tell me what time and we'll meet you there."

"That's only about two blocks from where we're staying, so that works for me," Nora said. "How about noon?"

"Noon it is," I said. "Thank you. And I know this is a really strange request, but... well, you'll see."

YOU WERE PLEASANTLY surprised when I took you out of school at lunchtime, and you were outright ecstatic upon learning the early pickup was not a one-time deal. As the week progressed, it became clear our new arrangement was a substantial improvement—well worth the effort of the late nights I'd have to put in at work after putting you to bed. With my afternoons open, it didn't take long for us to fall into a routine: a quick lunch before heading out to explore the Hudson Valley, finding new towns to wander aimlessly and discuss.

Those afternoons were peaceful and transformative for both of us. You peppered me with questions about various things I took for granted and probably wouldn't have even noticed had you not been with me, and I answered those queries to the best of my ability—the meaning of blinking pedestrian signs, the purpose behind truncated domes popping out of the ground at intersections, what was happening inside various ant hills you stumbled across. I could only hope my explanations were feeding your appreciation for what life had to offer.

Your development was everything I could've hoped for More surprising, however, was the impact your questions had on my view of the world. It felt as if a hazy filter was being lifted from my eyes as I learned to look about with discernment for anything you might find interesting and worthy of discussion. The architectural contrast between a ranch home and a colonial. The difference between pine and deciduous trees. A squirrel burying an acorn under a bush. There were countless items to point out to you to pique your interest, and I marveled at everything I had missed until then.

As enjoyable as those afternoons were, we couldn't completely avoid sobering reminders of the overarching challenges we faced. During our wanderings, it wasn't uncommon for you to report on new visions, whether it be another brutal car crash or someone apparently throwing themself off the bridge leading to Kingston, and I steadfastly added each of those incidents to my spreadsheet. Yet even as that data continued to accumulate, I remained unable to decipher the puzzle behind your visions.

When Saturday rolled around, you were excited to learn that we'd be taking a ride into New York City, and it dawned on me that it would be your first train ride. I tried to describe for you what New York City would be like—I assumed you had no memories of our earlier time living in Queens, making Kingston the largest city you'd remember seeing—but I could tell you didn't fully understand my descriptions of Manhattan. Even pictures I pulled up from the internet failed to convey the scope of that metropolis. A huge, sprawling city is probably just something one has to experience in order to comprehend it.

I had been worried about how you would handle being confined in an Amtrak train car for the trip to New York, but you quickly put my concerns to rest shortly after we boarded. You were perfectly content for the duration of the ride, kneeling on a seat to stare out the window at the constantly evolving scenery, watching it gradually transform from rural to urban over the course of a few hours.

As with any situation where you were taken into a new

environment, I fretted at whether you would see anything that triggered you, but nothing on the train ride set you off. Manhattan itself was even more worrisome, given how much violence it had seen over the course of its history, but again, nothing disturbed you once we disembarked at Penn Station. It was possible that the volume of people buzzing about the station simply obstructed any visions you might have otherwise had, but I could only speculate in that regard.

You marveled at the size of Penn Station, and it was difficult to snap you out of your reverie as you took it all in. Only when I mentioned we had to get to a subway—or as I put it, "a train that moves underground"—were you incentivized to keep moving.

We hopped on the Number 2 train, which was crowded for a Saturday, although nowhere near as packed as it would've been at rush hour during the work week. Again, nothing on the train seemed to bother you—the speed at which we were traveling underground simply entranced you. At one point, a kindly old woman earnestly told you how beautiful your eyes were, prompting you to scurry behind my legs out of shyness, and I mumbled a "thank you" while I tried to draw you out from behind me. Otherwise, the ride was uneventful, and after a few minutes, we reached the Fulton Street station and exited onto the platform.

I had timed our arrival so we'd get to the station about fifteen minutes before noon—I didn't want to keep Nora waiting for us—but I spotted her almost immediately, sitting on a bench, idly looking at her phone. You also saw her and ran toward her with a huge grin on your face, only to pull up short as your shyness reasserted itself. Nora looked up from her phone at your approach, and her face brightened.

"Quince!" she exclaimed. "It's so wonderful to see you!" She looked around the subway station. "Isn't this exciting?"

You nodded and then wordlessly pointed at the train we had just exited as it sped away into a dark tunnel. Nora watched the train vanish, visibly matching your excitement.

"That is amazing!" she said to you. "I can't believe how fast these trains can go. Is this your first time in New York City?"

You thought it over for a moment before nodding your head vigorously.

"Oh, that's wonderful! I love it here—I hope you love it, too." Turning to me, she said, "Hi, Will. I hope you had an easy trip in." I was relieved to see she didn't seem at all put out by stepping away from her family to see us.

"It went as smoothly as it could have," I told her. "Thanks for meeting us like this." I looked around the station, gathering my bearings. "I don't want to waste any more of your time than I already am, so let me show you what I'm concerned about."

I took you by the hand and led you toward a set of stairs that would take us back to street level. Nora fell in on my other side as we walked.

"So," I said to Nora, speaking quietly so you couldn't overhear. "I don't know how to put this exactly, but I've learned in the past week that Quince has a tendency to see things."

Nora frowned as she kept pace with me. "What kinds of things? Imaginary friends?"

"That's what I was thinking at first, too, but...." I trailed off. "It's more than that. And that's really what I wanted to show you."

"Okay." Skepticism in Nora's voice made it clear she was reserving judgment, not that I could blame her. Despite looking both confused and intrigued, Nora held her tongue as we continued to walk.

We found the exit and went up the stairs to Fulton Street. You stopped once we emerged on the sidewalk, stunned by the towering skyscrapers surrounding us, and I had to nudge you aside to keep you from blocking the exit to those people coming up behind us.

"Wow," you muttered, looking up and around as I led us down the street, heading northwest. "It's so big."

A sense of dread settled in me as we walked. All week I had tried to avoid thinking about this moment, but now that we were so close, the possibilities of what might transpire assailed my thoughts. If nothing happened, I'd feel embarrassed about wasting Nora's time, but that wasn't the source of my anxiety. No, the sick feeling in my stomach stemmed from the possibility that *something* would happen, and I could only hope it wouldn't hurt you. Or, at least, not hurt you too badly—this was one of those instances where I thought you might have to endure some hardship for a greater purpose. Still, I tried to minimize any potential harm to you by arranging for us to ascend to the street at a sufficient distance from what I wanted you to see—I hoped that would protect you from the worst of it.

*This must be done*, I reminded myself, yet again. *I can't help him alone, and this is something Nora has to see for herself, with no room to doubt what Quince can see.*

We reached Gold Street, where Fulton Street curved slightly to the left, and you froze in place at the revelation of the new view before us. I didn't prod you, and Nora, startled, threw me a confused glance at our sudden stop. But I barely registered her look—I was focused solely on you.

You stared up into the sky ahead, and I could tell from your face you were trying to make sense of what you were seeing. I felt tears come to my eyes, which I tried to blink away. For once, I had no doubts about the nature of your vision, and memories I tried to avoid for two decades rose to the surface.

"Is the building on fire?" you asked in a small voice. "There's a lot of smoke." Nora's head swiveled to you, and then up to me. I didn't take my eyes off you, and I held up a finger to Nora, asking her for patience.

"It is," I said.

You continued to watch, motionless. Some pedestrians gave us annoyed looks as they scurried around us, but you didn't notice them. Instead, you continued to stare at the expanse before us.

Suddenly, you gasped. "Is that a plane?" you asked, your eyes wide, and Nora's head jolted again.

"Will, what's going on?" she asked, no longer able to hold her tongue. She sounded alarmed. I forced myself to take my eyes off you and mouthed to her, "Just watch."

"Yes. I think that was a plane," I murmured as you continued to stare ahead. *This must be done*, I told myself again, trying to shake the guilt I felt at subjecting you to this.

Minutes crept by, and you continued to stare, entranced, until you flinched violently.

"It fell," you muttered, amazed. You looked up at me, looking more confused than horrified. "Why did it fall?"

Nora stared at you, her mouth agape.

"The fire melted the building," I said, simplifying it as best as I could, and you nodded in understanding. But a moment later you jumped again, wildly looking around.

"Why are the people running, Daddy?" you asked. Your body was tense, as if you were wondering whether we should be sprinting ourselves.

"They are scared. But we will be okay." I reached for

your hand and gave it a tight squeeze. "I promise." You looked skeptical, but you trusted me enough to resist the urge to bolt.

I glanced at Nora, who was still staring at you in shock. She felt my look, and her wide eyes found mine. Her mouth moved wordlessly, as if trying to catch one of the countless questions bouncing around her skull, and I knew she didn't need any further convincing. The scene you were watching was far from finished, but I didn't want to expose you to any more of it than was strictly necessary.

"Come on, Quince," I said. "We can leave now."

After one last lingering look down the way, you let me turn you around and lead you back toward the subway station from which we'd come. Nora hesitated a beat before joining us, and the three of us headed southeast on Fulton Street, lost in our respective thoughts, as we walked away from the World Trade Center.

# PART II

*The Lives We Saved*

## 7

I missed your mother in more ways than I could count, and for most of those, she was simply irreplaceable. Yet others could conceivably fill at least some of those holes resulting from your mother's passing.

I have a tendency to internalize the things that trouble me, which takes its toll. As much as I would deny it, I share the same need to vent as most people do, and I am likewise no less susceptible to tunnel vision than anyone else. I wasn't interested in finding a new wife, and it would be impossible to replace your mother, but what I needed was much simpler than that.

I simply needed someone to talk to. And more specifically, someone to talk to about you.

That wasn't my intent when I first let Nora in on your secret. I chose her because she seemed to be the only other adult you were even mildly comfortable speaking with, and I hoped she could make some sense of the secrets lurking within you by drawing out your language. What I didn't count on, however, was the extent to which having Nora on our team would lessen my burden. Merely having someone available to listen to my frus-

*trations and offer ideas and a fresh perspective in response was something I didn't realize I needed. But it absolutely was.*

*Your problems were enormous, and I was only on the verge of understanding just how big they were. The weight couldn't be lightened, which was a lesson I had learned the hard way. But I discovered something after bringing Nora into the fold and filling her in on the secret of your visions:*

*The weight is easier to bear with someone else there to help carry it.*

THERE WASN'T adequate time for a full debriefing after we met Nora in downtown Manhattan. She asked me a few questions to reassure herself she had witnessed something authentic, such as inquiring whether you had ever been to New York City before or if there was some other way you could have learned about the September 11th attacks prior to that day. Her skepticism didn't offend me, and I patiently answered all of her questions. Nora looked both troubled and thoughtful when she parted ways with us that afternoon, but before she did, we made plans to meet at her office in a few days to discuss where to go from there.

That Monday, I picked you up from school at lunchtime and drove straight down to Nora's office, taking an indirect route in order to avoid any known sites of prior car accidents. You were content in the back seat picking at the snacks I brought along to hold you over until we had time to eat a proper lunch. When we were about ten minutes away from Nora's office, you registered where we were heading and perked up.

"Am I playing with Miss Nora today?" you asked, sounding hopeful.

"Maybe for a little bit," I said. "But first I have to talk with her, so you can play with her toys when we get there."

"Can I play with her pooping dog?"

"Yeah, sure."

Once we arrived and made our way into her office, I studied Nora carefully to see how she received you. I wondered whether there would be any change in her demeanor—any suggestion she was afraid of you or viewed you as some sort of freak. But she greeted you with her usual warmth, crouching down to speak at your level.

"Can I play with your pooping dog?" you asked. Nora's face split open in a wide grin as she revealed the toy she'd been hiding behind her back.

"Somehow, I knew you would ask about this guy!" she said brightly. You wordlessly seized the dog and settled with it on the floor. Nora and I watched you for a moment before she took me to a seat by her desk.

We stared at one another, not sure exactly where to start.

"So," Nora said.

"So."

We sat in silence, each hoping the other would start speaking. Nora gave in first.

"I had some time this weekend to think about what you showed me," she said. "And rest assured, I did not tell a soul about that. Not even my husband."

I nodded my thanks, although I hadn't been particularly concerned about Nora being a blabbermouth.

"It's still not entirely clear to me what I saw," she admitted. "And, to be honest, I'm a little confused about why you showed that to *me*."

"Quince isn't comfortable talking around many people," I explained. "He's been opening up to me lately, but other than that, there's no one he's willing to speak with. But even though he's only seen you a few times, I can already tell he likes you and is comfortable with you. I hoped that by working with him, you might gather some insight into what he's experiencing. Because my understanding probably isn't that much greater than yours at this point."

"Fair enough," Nora said, glancing at Quince before turning back to me. "At the risk of stating the obvious: you realize that what you showed me on Saturday isn't exactly in the scope of my professional expertise?"

I chuckled despite all the anxiety I was feeling. "Well, I'd be happy to consider any referrals you might make to someone more qualified to deal with this."

"Point taken," Nora said. "But what *are* we dealing with?" Before I could respond, Nora added, "I know you said you don't know much. What *do* you know?"

"Quince... sees things." It was hard to articulate, and I spoke slowly, carefully choosing my words. "Events from the past. They often seem to be car accidents or wedding ceremonies at churches, with some miscellaneous stuff thrown in. He seems to see troubling stuff more often than good things, for what that's worth. But there were some car crash sites I found—fairly recent ones, too—where Quince couldn't see anything. So, the pattern of what Quince views, or doesn't view, continues to elude me." I shook my head. "To be honest, I wasn't even sure he would see anything on Saturday. It was an educated guess, at best."

"How does Quince usually respond to what he sees?" Nora asked.

"He likes the wedding visions," I said. "I think he feels like he's crashing multiple parties at once when he sees those. The car crashes and violence, though.... Some of it he might've gotten used to, but a lot of it definitely bothers him.

Sometimes I wonder whether he's suffering emotional trauma from those visions."

I paused as a thought occurred to me.

"Do you think that could tie into his speech delays?" I asked. "Trauma sustained by these horrific things he's seeing?"

Nora looked away, thoughtful.

"Emotional trauma can, of course, derail developmental trajectories, including speech," she said. "I've worked with children who went through a traumatic experience and subsequently experienced delays in their expressive language. In those cases, I refer the parents to a psychologist who can work on the trauma issues. But I realize that may not be an option here, for obvious reasons."

Nora pressed her lips together, deep in thought.

"This is somewhat outside my wheelhouse," she continued, "but I've absorbed some information about trauma over the years. It's a physiological reaction—alterations in the brain and nervous system caused by the storing of unresolved emotions."

"Do you think that's what Quince is experiencing?" I asked.

"I don't know," she said with a small shrug. "What is traumatic to one child might not be to another. But I think it's fair to say that Quince's visions are negatively impacting him, even if the extent of that harm remains an open question. It would be helpful to have a better idea of what he's seeing and how he experiences it. I assume he's not just seeing a replay of an event in real time—it appears to be compressed in some way."

"Why do you say that?" I asked, confused.

"That vision Quince had on Saturday of the September 11 attacks; he described a plane hitting a tower and then a tower collapsing, even though we were only there for a few minutes," Nora explained. "But there was nearly an hour between those events when they happened in 2001, so it appears he's seeing a truncated version of the actual event. As his language develops, Quince should be able to give us some deeper insight into the nature of his visions. In the interim, we'll have to just keep trying to decipher clues."

Nora's insight impressed me, even though she had limited exposure to your visions, and I knew I had made the right choice in involving her.

"That makes sense," I said. "I never really gave that much thought. But I've been trying to track everything I've learned so far." I handed Nora a document I made a point of printing out for our meeting—the spreadsheet I had created to track your visions. "I'm trying to document the things Quince has seen. When I can find information about an incident tied to a vision, I add it to this table, but Quince has seen some stuff I just can't account for. There's only so much you can find on the internet, I guess. And on the flip side, as I said earlier, there are some locations where I knew a car accident had taken place, yet Quince did not seem to see anything when we went to the site. If there's a pattern there, I'm just not seeing it."

Nora took to studying the spreadsheet silently. Her hazel eyes bounced around the page as she read, and reread, each of the entries, and her intense focus reminded me of someone engrossed in a challenging crossword puzzle. You seemed perfectly content feeding Nora's toy dog on the floor, so I sat back and waited for Nora to finish reviewing the document.

"*Happy* people at a wedding. *Sad* woman in Kingston. *Scared* people running on 9/11," she muttered, stressing each adjective as she read them aloud. "There are a lot of emotions in these descriptions."

"Isn't that just how four-year-olds talk?" I asked.

"Maybe," Nora said, absently stroking her chin. "But I think there's a nuance here that Quince couldn't convey in his limited language. This is more than just *happy*, *sad*, and *scared*. People—well, some people at least—feel outright joy when they get married. The people Quince saw running down the street in downtown Manhattan weren't simply scared—they were *terrified*. Quince's developing language may water down the descriptions somewhat, but these are more than basic emotions. He's seeing the heavy stuff, good or bad."

Suddenly Nora looked up, eyes wide.

"Strong emotions," she said. "It's strong emotions."

"Come again?"

"These things he sees—they are tied to intense emotions. Terror. Joy. Anguish. That's the pattern. That's it."

I frowned, assessing her conclusion and trying to find holes to poke in it.

"But he doesn't see every car accident," I said. "For example, he didn't see the one—"

I trailed off as the answer came to me, and Nora shared a small smile in recognition of my gained understanding.

"He didn't see the accident where the driver fell asleep," she said. "There was no emotion there at the time of impact. Just a quick and sudden death. It still fits the pattern."

"Wow. Emotions." I shook my head, trying to fathom the import of this development. *Can emotions be so strong they leave a psychic residue? Is that truly what these viewings relate to?* "That wasn't on my radar. At all." With a snort, I added, "Probably because emotions are so alien to me."

Nora rolled her eyes. "Oh, stop it. Almost every time we talk, you're sick with worry. You wouldn't have pressured me into meeting up with you in the city this past weekend if emotions were truly so foreign to you."

"Okay," I said. "Fair enough." I had considered myself dead on the inside for so long, it never occurred to me that my self-diagnosis might warrant a reevaluation.

But then a thought occurred to me.

"There was a kidnapping last month in our area. Apparently, someone abducted a young boy while he was waiting for the school bus at his home. Quince and I actually ran into the boy's father last week while he was putting up fliers about his missing son. Quince said he wanted to help, so I drove us out to where the boy was snatched, but Quince didn't see a thing. I didn't know why, but if your theory is correct, that means someone took the boy without him being terrified. So perhaps he was lured somehow, maybe by someone he knew...."

I was digging for a clue, but there still wasn't much to go on.

"There are a lot of potential explanations for why Quince couldn't see that one," Nora said, her gentle tone implicitly recognizing my frustration. "But it was very kind of you both to try and help that family." She smiled at you on the floor as you peered inside the pooping dog's mouth, trying to figure out how its digestive system worked. "He's a great kid. We'll figure out how to get him whatever help he needs."

"That's really all I want," I said. "To help him. Where do we go from here?"

"That's the ten-thousand-dollar question, isn't it?" Nora took a deep breath as she mulled it over.

"Last year, I worked with a three-year-old boy who was

struggling with his speech, particularly his ability to enunciate," Nora finally said. "He couldn't pronounce sounds such as *s*, *sh*, and *t*. I tried to work with him in a variety of ways, but we made little progress. Finally, his parents took my advice—which I had offered at the outset—and had the child's hearing tested. It turned out he had a mild hearing impairment, which made it very difficult for him to register, and accordingly replicate, certain sounds. But once we identified the problem, addressing it became fairly straightforward."

"Okay," I said, confused by the non sequitur.

"What I'm saying is that it's nearly impossible to fix something you don't understand. And there seems to be a lot about Quince's ability that remains a mystery. How far back can he see? What exactly does he see when he has one of his visions? What happens if he has multiple visions at the same time—can he focus on one, or turn them off entirely? Does Quince have any understanding that his visions aren't actually happening in real time? These are all questions we should try to answer."

"How do we do that?"

"Part of it is to just keep doing what you're doing: take Quince out in the world, keep track of how he acts, and try to decipher those clues. But maybe the most important component will be Quince himself, and his development. As his language grows, he'll have a better ability to share with you what he's seeing and how he's perceiving everything. And there'll be a point when you'll probably have to talk with him about it and explain how he's different from the rest of us. He's seeing a lot of scary stuff right now, but it will only help him when he's able to learn those visions aren't real. Or at least, aren't real at the present time."

"Alright," I said. "In the interim, if he's being traumatized by his visions—do you have any advice on that front?"

Nora grimaced, and I could sense her frustration at having limited knowledge of that topic as compared to speech and language.

"Nothing concrete," she admitted. "Just do your best to make him feel safe. I've seen psychologists work with children through play—reenacting traumatic scenes to help them process those emotions they're struggling to release. Maybe you can try that?"

"Oh," I said. "I think I may have accidentally done that already."

I remembered how adamant you were about recreating car crashes when we started regularly playing with toys a few weeks earlier, and how you found comfort in seeing the dolls involved in those crashes walk away with no injuries graver than feeling somewhat woozy. I explained all of that to Nora, and she smiled in approval.

"Well, there you go!" she said. "And that goes to a larger point: don't discount your instincts. If you think you're doing something that's comforting Quince, or bothering him, listen to your gut. You're better positioned than anyone to help Quince. And don't get me wrong, I'll help as much as I can." Nora paused. "Maybe we can switch to two sessions a week?" she asked after a moment. "That will give me more time to work with Quince and see if I can gain any insight into his perception of the world. But it'll also allow you and me to have a chance every few days to compare notes on whatever we've learned."

"Sounds good," I said. "Thank you. You've already helped a ton. I know this is an odd case for you, and I really appreciate you not running away from us."

Nora inclined her head in acknowledgement. "Of course. That's why I get paid the big bucks!" she said with a quiet laugh.

"Alright, I'll step out so you and Quince can get to work with whatever time we have left. You gave me a lot of good advice just now, but.... Well, I can't help but think there's still more I should be doing for him. I'll give that some thought while the two of you are doing your thing."

I started to stand, and Nora reached out, placing her hand on mine to keep me in my seat.

"Look, Will," she said as she withdrew her hand. "I have two girls myself, ages eight and ten. We live up in Tivoli, which I think is pretty close to where you live, if I'm remembering correctly. We settled there a few years ago when my husband took a job at Harp College. As you undoubtedly know, our area is predominantly white, which was no surprise to me—I understood that would be the case when we settled there. But when my oldest, Alaina, was Quince's age, she started pre-K, and some of the other children in her class made comments to her about her skin color. I'm sure a lot of it was only curiosity about seeing a Black girl, although at least a couple of those kids seemed to be repeating vile things they heard from their parents. But regardless, Alaina started regularly coming home from school upset over the way the other children talked to her. And that made me livid. I met with Alaina's teachers multiple times to discuss the situation, and I tracked down as many of those other parents as I could to fill them in on what was going on. Of course, I did my best to explain to Alaina why those children were acting as they were. Eventually, I reached a point where I had done everything I could to fix things for my daughter, and I resigned myself to the fact that there comes a time as a parent where you have done everything possible, and there is only one thing left to do."

"What's that?" I asked, and Nora gave a sad shrug.

"In the end, all you can do is love your kids to the best of your ability and hope for the best."

# 8

An interesting side effect of exploring the mystery of your visions was unwrapping the mystery of you—specifically, who you were as a person.

It's tempting to say your personality blossomed during those afternoons we spent together, but that's not quite accurate. A soul always resided inside your body, even if it remained mostly hidden from outside eyes until you were able to communicate. But once it did, your essence radiated, and I was proud of who you revealed yourself to be.

I'd be lying if I said I wasn't preoccupied with your visions during that time, as they appeared to hold the key to understanding any developmental delays you were experiencing. But you were, of course, more than those visions. You were a four-and-a-half-year-old boy on the verge of discovering his voice, which was just as fascinating, if not more so, than your unique ability to see emotional residues.

As we spent more and more time together, I was pleased to receive further confirmation that you had much more of your mother in you than you had of me. Granted, I recognized from the beginning how much you physically resembled her, with your light-colored hair and fair skin tone. But it took longer to fully appreciate that your mother's gentle nature also lived on in you, even after your prolonged exposure to me as your sole caregiver.

As far as I could tell, the only attribute of mine that had carried over to you was my tendency not to waste words. Everything else appeared to derive from your mother, whether it be your love of animals and nature, your kind disposition, or your love of books. When your mother died, I mourned for your lost opportunity to learn from her and bask in her love, so I took great comfort in learning much of her essence lived on through you. I was relieved to discover that my ability to lead you astray through blundering parenting was limited. More importantly, your mother shining through you helped to maintain a sense that she was still with us.

One afternoon, you and I traversed an area called "Poet's Walk," which was a paved pathway near our home that meandered through forested hills before opening up to an expansive view of the Hudson River. Along the way, you stopped to study a caterpillar on the path I hadn't even noticed until you crouched down beside it. You wordlessly found a twig and held it low to the ground, patiently waiting for that caterpillar to climb aboard. Once it did, you slowly moved the bug to a grassy area about six feet off the path. "No one can step on it there," you explained, and I recalled a similar incident five years earlier when your mother had similarly made me help her collect various caterpillars from a sidewalk and move them onto the grass. Both you and your mother effortlessly performed that same act of kindness—one that I would have never thought of doing if left to my own devices.

At first, I wondered whether your inherent goodness stemmed from a need to please others, but that suspicion didn't last long. You, like your mother, would have spent however much time it took to save those caterpillars, even if there was no one there to *witness your actions. No, you were not driven by a desire to please.*

*You simply wanted to help those who needed it.*

NORA ADVISED me at our first meeting to take you out in our community to stimulate your mind and motivate you to discuss things you found of interest, hoping to coax language out of you. Several weeks later, in the wake of learning about your visions, Nora had offered similar counsel, only this time geared toward the goal of getting a better understanding of what you were experiencing with your visions. I have more than my share of dumb moments, but I'm usually smart enough to recognize valuable advice when I hear it, so in the weeks following our trip to Manhattan, I once again embraced her suggestions with gusto.

One weekend, I drove us north to visit Saratoga National Historical Park which was the site of a major Revolutionary War battle in 1777. There's no shortage of powerful emotions on a battlefield—certainly ones strong enough to cast a lasting resonance—yet you didn't seem to see anything of note when we visited. *There's some sort of time limit regarding how far back Quince can see,* I concluded. After mentally filing that bit of gained intel, I could concentrate on simply having a fun day with you in Saratoga.

When we went out during the week, we stayed within about forty minutes of our home, but on weekends, that radius widened significantly and covered a great deal of New York State. I did my best to avoid major highways on those trips, as those seemed to host a greater percentage of fatal car accidents than side roads. Taking as many precautions as possible, I even set up a Google alert system to notify me via email when a new accident happened—one that was newsworthy, at least—so I could be sure to avoid the area afterward. Of course, it was impossible to shield you completely from your visions. There remained plenty of occasions during our drives when you would unexpectedly jump in your seat and comment upon some collision or another. But they didn't seem to bother you as much as they once did, which I attributed, in part, to my non-reaction to those incidents. If your visions of accidents didn't bother me, perhaps that made it easier for you to accept they shouldn't trouble you either. Your nightmares also decreased in frequency, giving me some semblance of hope you were coming to terms with your visions in your own way.

I relied heavily on churches as I continued to investigate the nature of your visions. Churches were the one venue that consistently elicited meaningful viewings, and you seemed to enjoy the positive energy those visions brought.

"How many women in white dresses do you see, Quince?" I asked on one occasion when we revisited a church in our town. Your finger bounced around in the air, counting, before you gave up and dropped your hand.

"I'm not sure," you finally told me.

"More than five?" I pressed.

"Oh, yes! Definitely more than five."

"More than ten?"

More counting on your part, but then you stopped again.

"I don't know."

But I didn't need a precise number—it was enough knowing you were simultaneously seeing multiple weddings, or at least the jubilant exit from the church following a ceremony.

"All of those happy people you see are part of something

called 'weddings,'" I explained to you. "It's a ceremony where two people who love each other promise to stay together forever. When a man marries a woman, the woman will often wear a white dress for the wedding. But there can also be weddings between two men or two women."

"Weddings." you repeated, testing out the word.

"Do you like watching weddings?" I asked, and you responded with an earnest nod.

"When you see these weddings," I added, "do they look funny?"

"They aren't funny," you answered, sounding offended, and I gave some more thought to the best way to frame my question.

"I don't mean funny 'ha ha,'" I explained. "But if I touch you, my hand stops. See?"

I rested a hand on your shoulder to illustrate my point.

"But what do you see if I walk over here?" I sauntered toward the doors of the church, assuming I was trampling through multiple invisible celebrations. "Nothing is stopping me, but what do you see?"

"Umm...." You thought hard, searching for words, but I thought you at least understood my question. "You walk through them like they are clouds."

*Like they are clouds?* I surmised you meant they were flowing around me in some fashion. But I thought I understood what you were getting at.

"Like ghosts?" I assumed you had some exposure to the basic concept of ghosts.

"Yes," you said. "Kinda like ghosts."

"Do I look funny when I walk through the people?" I asked, wandering about, and you giggled, seeming to appreciate for the first time the absurdity of the show I was putting on.

"Yes, it is funny!" You giggled once more. "Do it again!"

I dutifully twirled in front of the church, and you laughed hysterically at my antics. Your laughter only spurred me on, and I became so engrossed in my dance that I didn't immediately notice when a priest emerged from the church. I was in the middle of a dramatic spin when I caught his disapproving glare, bringing an abrupt end to my routine. Embarrassed, I shuffled away with you, but that momentary humiliation soon gave way to elation.

*That's progress*, I thought. *Quince seems to understand there's a difference between reality and these visions of his.* It was a good start, one that might lay the groundwork for having a conversation with you down the road about what you were seeing. In the interim, I planned to keep highlighting for you the differences between the real world and what you saw through your visions. Churches seemed like the best place to continue that work, and I continually sought new ones in the Hudson Valley for us to visit.

Later that week, we found ourselves in the town of Saugerties, which sat north of Kingston on the west side of the Hudson River, to investigate its selection of churches. After you completed your review of the last church in the area, I tried to lead you back to the car.

"Can we walk for a little bit?" you asked. It wasn't an uncommon request—you enjoyed wandering around towns when you had the energy. Granted, it occasionally led to you tiring out and needing to be carried back to our car, but I didn't mind. Those walks were beneficial to you, even if the possibility of accidentally stumbling across some horrific vision was a constant source of anxiety for me.

"Sure, we can walk," I said. "Lead the way."

You hopped up and down, excited at the prospect of directing our route, before setting off down the street with me at your side. There was no discernible pattern to your path, other than that you seemed more inclined to turn at intersections than continue straight. After a few minutes, we were on a block filled with weatherworn colonials—the kind of homes that would be adorable with some TLC but looked as if they had been neglected for some time, like the owners had given up on repairing the damage suffered through every savage winter. I checked the map on my phone and was pleasantly surprised to discover that our meandering walk had somehow brought us back in the general direction of our car, which was only about two blocks away.

"How about that way?" I asked, pointing down a street that was the most direct route back to the car. You accepted my prompt and led me down a beaten sidewalk. But after a few houses you stopped, a confused expression on your face.

"Is that boy scared?" you asked, looking away from me, and I sighed. *Here we go again.* I hoped whatever you were seeing wouldn't be too traumatic.

I followed your gaze and noticed you staring into an open garage affixed to the side of an unkempt home. There was no activity around the house. The mostly empty garage had enough space to store a large vehicle, even though none was parked there at the moment.

"Why do you think the boy is scared?" I asked, looking into the garage with you.

"I don't know. He just looks scared." You frowned, looking thoughtful, before adding, "The man is being too rough."

*That poor kid*, I thought. *Sounds like he has an asshole for a father.* I was uncomfortable lingering in front of the house, so I gave you a gentle tug to prompt you to keep walking.

But as we turned back toward the sidewalk, a dark gray van rolling down the street suddenly sped up, only to park abruptly a few feet from where we were standing.

"Come on, Quince," I muttered with some urgency, but you remained cemented to the spot.

A man with a graying beard emerged from the van and strode toward us, his dark eyes flashing anger. *Damn it, Quince*, I thought, dreading what seemed to be an inevitable confrontation.

"You got a problem?" the man said to me without preamble, stepping just a little too close to us for my comfort.

"No problem," I said, trying to sound unbothered. "Just taking a walk with my son."

I hoped that would be the end of it, but the man continued to study me.

"There a reason you're looking at my house like that?"

He rolled his shoulders, as if he was loosening up for a fight. Even in the best of circumstances, I would've been less than thrilled with this development, but the absolute last thing I wanted was to get drawn into a brawl in front of you. I looked up and down the street, but other than the three of us, no one was around.

"I'm sorry about that," I said, still trying to defuse the tension. "My son thought he saw something over there. A rabbit, I think. That's all we were looking at."

Perhaps it was my imagination, but I thought my white lie accomplished its intended goal, because the man seemed to loosen up slightly.

And then you chimed in.

"No, Daddy!" you said. "Not a rabbit. A boy! I saw a boy!" And then you looked directly at the man standing in my face, and added, "And *he* was the one who—"

"Quince!" I said sharply, cutting you off. I glanced back at the bearded man to see how he was responding to your outburst, and his reaction surprised me.

The man didn't look confused or angry at what you said. Instead, there was a brief widening of his eyes at your pronouncement suggesting something else: panic. He quickly looked back toward his house, as if checking for something. I instinctively followed his look, and I noticed a detail about the house that had escaped me until then: narrow basement windows, nearly touching the ground, were uniformly boarded up, making it impossible to look into his basement. Or, presumably, out of it.

The man turned back to me, having regained his composure somewhat, and I forced myself to look him in the eyes.

"There's no boy," he spat at me, sounding overly defensive.

Now it was my turn to control my face. A suspicion was settling in, and the mere possibility it might be true was enough to make me want to pick you up right there and sprint down the street as fast as I could. As I struggled to process the gravity of what we had wandered into, one thing was apparent right away: we were in danger. And I knew our best chance of getting out of it depended entirely upon my ability to maintain a convincing poker face.

"I don't know what he's talking about," I said with a small, forced chuckle and a nonchalant shrug. "He makes up these stories sometimes."

The man looked down at you, and I was disturbed by how long he held that gaze. *Get your sick eyes off of him!* I wanted to scream, but I knew I had to hold my tongue. I feared you would speak up again to contradict my lies, but your shyness reasserted itself once the man stared directly at you, and you clammed up entirely.

"Anyway," I said. "I'm sorry to have encroached upon your privacy like that. We'll just be on our way."

The man didn't respond, and I wasn't sure how he would react if I turned my back on him. As calmly as I could manage, I picked you up and walked down the street, fighting the urge to look back. I could sense you staring back at the man over my shoulder, and I hoped you'd at least give me some warning if we were being followed. But you remained silent as I whisked you away.

"Is the man following us?" I finally whispered to you, after a minute of walking. But you didn't respond.

After turning at the intersection and being certain we were no longer in that man's line of sight, I lowered you to the ground. Still, I was on edge, waiting for a gray van to speed out and turn onto our street.

"I don't like that man, Daddy," you said, looking shaken.

"I didn't either. But we're okay." I hoped that was true.

*What the hell do I do?* I was frozen with indecision, but standing on a sidewalk with you made me feel too exposed. I didn't yet know what the plan of action should be, other than getting back to our car.

Thankfully, we had an uneventful five-minute walk back to where the car was parked, and I felt profound relief once we were buckled in with the doors locked.

"Quince," I said, turning back to you from the driver's seat. "The scared boy you saw in the garage. Do you remember what he was wearing?"

"Umm. I think it was a red coat."

I took out my phone and searched through my photos for the missing child poster I had photographed several weeks earlier in Rhinebeck.

Once I located it, I saw that the boy pictured on the flier, who was named Connor, was wearing a bright red jacket.

Still, I was uncertain. It was suspicious as hell, but I questioned whether I had enough to act upon.

"Okay, Quince," I said, turning back to you again. "Do you remember seeing that daddy a few weeks ago, who was putting up papers because he was looking for his missing son?"

You thought for a moment before giving a dubious nod.

"And do you remember how you said you wanted to help that daddy?"

Another nod, this time with more certainty behind it.

"I think we might be able to help that man and his son after all, but first I have to ask you a very important question. Are you ready?"

Yet another nod.

I showed you my phone, displaying the picture of the flier, zoomed in and centered on the face of the missing boy.

"Is that the same boy that you saw in the garage before?"

You thought hard as you stared at my phone, and I wasn't sure if your delay in answering was indecision on your part or just a byproduct of you taking the question seriously. But after a few beats, you looked back up at me, and I didn't see any hint of doubt in your eyes.

"Yes," you said. "That's the boy."

"Thank you, Quince."

I tried to piece together what had happened, based on my limited knowledge of how your visions worked. When Connor was picked up, he wasn't scared—whether it was because he was in shock or otherwise—but by the time he reached his abductor's house, terror must have been pouring out of him. The abductor roughly removed the boy from the van while it was parked in the garage, presumably with the garage door lowered—you had only been able to witness that exchange through your vision because the door was raised when we walked by earlier. From there, the boy was locked away in the basement, for God only knew what purpose.

It all seemed to fit. But the question remained: what was I going to do about it?

A solo rescue mission was off the table for a variety of reasons, not the least of which was that caring for you remained my priority, no matter what. There was no way I was going to leave you behind while I tried to break into that house myself. An alternative was to call the police and come clean about your vision, but it was unlikely anyone would believe me. The attorney in me also noted that even if I could somehow convince the police about your ability, they'd still lack probable cause to get a warrant to investigate the home.

*Ah*, I thought. *That's the answer. All I have to do is commit perjury.*

The missing child poster on my phone listed a number for the police, for anyone with relevant information to call. I took a minute to craft a story in my head that was simple and consistent with my earlier exchange with the apparent kidnapper. My fictional narrative was imperfect, and possibly wouldn't survive deep scrutiny, but I couldn't see how those flaws could be discovered until after the police investigated the house and, in a perfect world, saved Connor.

I took one last look at you in the back seat, reflecting on just how much trust I was placing in you, and then called the number from the poster. A woman answered, who transferred me to a gruff-sounding detective after I explained the purpose of my call.

"This is Detective Hughes. You're calling about Connor Callaghan?" the man asked.

"Yes," I said. "I was just out for a walk with my four-year-old son, and we passed by a house where I had something of a confrontation with the man living there. He was agitated because we had stopped to look at his home, and he was very defensive and upset after my son mentioned seeing a boy inside. But then, as we were talking, I spotted someone through a window myself. I'm nearly certain it was Connor, who I recognized from a missing child poster I saw in town. So I called it in right away."

You were listening intently in the back seat—I think you picked up on the serious nature of the conversation.

"Just how good of a look did you get at this kid?" the detective asked.

"It was a good look. I couldn't have been more than thirty feet away." My mind wandered, thinking about what would happen to me if I was completely off base, but I caught myself and refocused on the conversation.

"Do you have the address for this house?"

I gave the information to the detective and waited while I heard him type away at a computer. Whatever he found in looking up the address seemed to be meaningful because he let out a long exhale before coming back to me.

"I'll need you to come in and sign a statement," Detective Hughes said, and I picked up on a hint of excitement in his voice. "We should be able to get a search warrant, but this is time-sensitive so—"

"I'll be right there."

You were excited when I said we were going to the police station, and under the circumstances, I was, too. Once we arrived, we didn't spend much time there—I was pleasantly surprised by how efficiently they dealt with me. After conducting a quick interview, the police officers reduced my statement to writing for me to sign, and then they sent us on our way. We arrived back home around dinnertime, and I wondered whether my lies would save a life, or if they would only land me in hot water.

The next day I received my answer by way of the local news. The man who had confronted me—whose name, I came to learn, was Adam Bagshaw—had been an uncle of Connor Callaghan by marriage until Connor's aunt left Bagshaw several years earlier. Shortly after I left the station the previous day, the police executed a search warrant on Bagshaw's residence "based on a tip the child was being held at that location," as the news reported it, and almost immediately located a makeshift cell in the basement where Connor had been confined for the past several months. The police arrested Bagshaw and took Connor in for evaluation and treatment. The news segment featured a brief clip of Connor's parents on their front lawn, sobbing with relief and thanking God and the police for bringing their son home to them.

You wandered into the living room while I watched the news and emphatically pointed when the TV flashed a photo of Connor—the same picture of him in the red jacket that was on his missing poster.

"That's the boy!" you shouted. "Did his daddy find him?"

"He did," I said, prompting you to jump up and down, cheering. I started to cry softly, although I can't say whether those tears stemmed from relief for Connor's family, or whether they were for Connor's ordeal and the scars it would leave upon him for the rest of his life. Or perhaps the tears related to pride and the knowledge, which only I possessed, that you had saved Connor and his family. Probably all the above.

As relieved as I was that we could help Connor, I couldn't help but worry about the trauma he undoubtedly sustained, and the work he and his family would have to go through to regain some sense of normalcy. *Kids can be resilient*, I reminded myself, thinking of the progress you made over the past two months. *It's amazing what they can do with proper love and support.* I thought back to Connor's father, whose path we briefly crossed weeks earlier in Rhinebeck, and the pain etched into his face while putting up his missing posters to allow him to maintain the illusion of hope, and I felt confident Connor was returning to a loving family that would do everything they could for him. *Connor will be okay*, I thought. *It may take time, but he'll be okay.*

That night you went to bed easily and fell asleep before I could even leave the room, gently snoring with a small, self-satisfied smile on your face. And for once, I felt confident that you'd be okay, too.

# 9

*One odd quirk of being a parent to a young child is dealing with a constantly changing landscape. Just a few months into becoming a parent, after a prolonged period of sleepless nights, you might think you finally have your infant on a workable sleep routine, only to realize you're back at square one after some rewiring in your baby's brain triggers a sleep regression. Later, after your child becomes a toddler, you may finally convince them to eat a banana, and they will happily do so every day until there is an abrupt and inexplicable change in their appetite prompting them to push away any proffered fruit with utter disgust. It doesn't take long to realize that any structure you build as a parent sits on a foundation of shifting sand, and it's just a matter of time before the framework collapses and you're forced to begin anew.*

*And despite this, parents cling to optimism as their child grows because, despite the occasional missteps, there is almost always unmistakable progress and growth. For every step backwards, there will be two or three steps forward, and you learn to accept minor setbacks for what they are and focus on the big picture: ideally, a winding path that leads to a happy and well-developed child.*

*I went through a similar journey with you, but particularly regarding your visions. There were bumps in the road, to be sure, but as my understanding of what you were experiencing grew, so did my hope that an avenue for you to have a normal-ish life was revealing itself. After we helped save Connor Callaghan, I felt confident that we were heading in the right direction. Hell, I was flying high with pride, and even found myself wondering at times what else the two of us could accomplish together.*

*I was a fool to relinquish my fear, even by a little. Hope is a wonderful thing, but optimism, if not properly handled, can be disastrous. And yet, in the wake of helping to save Connor, that's exactly what I was: optimistic, confident, and excited about our future together.*

*In other words, I was perfectly positioned to be knocked back on my ass.*

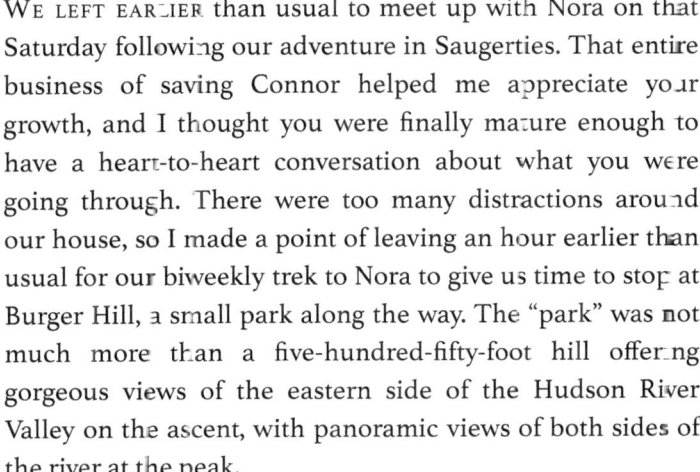

WE LEFT EARLIER than usual to meet up with Nora on that Saturday following our adventure in Saugerties. That entire business of saving Connor helped me appreciate your growth, and I thought you were finally mature enough to have a heart-to-heart conversation about what you were going through. There were too many distractions around our house, so I made a point of leaving an hour earlier than usual for our biweekly trek to Nora to give us time to stop at Burger Hill, a small park along the way. The "park" was not much more than a five-hundred-fifty-foot hill offering gorgeous views of the eastern side of the Hudson River Valley on the ascent, with panoramic views of both sides of the river at the peak.

You were confused when I stopped at the parking lot

next to the hill, looking around as if trying to remember whether you had ever been there before.

"Where are we going?" you asked. "Are we going to Ms. Nora?"

"We are," I said. "But I thought it'd be fun to stop at this park on the way there."

"A park?" you asked, brightening. "Does it have a playground?"

"I'm sorry, but I don't think there's a playground. But there's an enormous hill we can climb, and that should be fun." Feeling guilty about getting your hopes up, I made a mental note to research new playgrounds in the area for us to visit when we had some time.

Fortunately, you didn't seem all that disappointed.

"A hill?" you asked. "Is it really big?"

"Yes."

"Is it really, *really* big?"

"It's right there!" I said, pointing out the window. "You can see how big it is, but let's go get a better look."

Once I let you out of the car, you let out a squeal and darted to the only path leading out of the parking lot, which wound up and down over smaller mounds before reaching the base of Burger Hill itself. The uneven terrain made it difficult to keep you in my line of sight while you scurried ahead of me, but whenever you escaped my view, I hollered out your name, and you would hustle back, eager for me to pick up my pace. After a few minutes of walking, we reached the base of the hill and started our climb upwards.

You tirelessly sprinted up the hill a few yards before stopping, at which point you took great joy in turning to run back to me with gravity speeding you along, only to climb back up again and repeat the process. I only had enough energy to trudge up the hill, step by step, and once we were halfway to the top, I paused to collect my breath.

"Look at the view, Quince!" I exclaimed, gesturing all around us at the acres of forested lands that were visible in the distance.

"I see," you muttered, sounding impressed, and then you looked off to your left at a lone oak tree sitting on the hill. "Look!"

You hurried toward the tree and I followed at a more reasonable pace, stopping to watch once you reached it. Your eyes were wide and reverential as you studied the great oak, circling with your head tilted back so you could study it from all angles.

"It's beautiful," you breathed before approaching the trunk with your arms extended to give it a hug, and I inwardly smiled at your love of nature. I took a seat on a bench positioned directly under the leafy branches, feeling grateful for the shade. Once you finished your embrace, you scampered over and sat on the bench next to me, idly kicking your legs under you.

"I'd like to talk to you, Quince," I said, and you immediately assumed a defensive look.

"What?" you asked, sounding sullen, while you gazed at the scenery surrounding us. I wondered whether it would be possible to get you to focus.

"You know how you sometimes see things like car accidents, or weddings at churches?" I asked, and you nodded as you continued to apprise the tree.

"Well," I continued. "I can't see those things."

You stopped kicking your legs under the bench and frowned.

"I can't see them now either," you said, and I knew you had missed my point.

"No," I said. "I mean, even when I'm at a church, I don't see all the people outside like you do."

"Why can't you see them?"

I shrugged. "Sometimes people see different things." I was careful in my explanation—I didn't want you to feel like a freak of nature. "I think you can just see some things that are invisible to me."

"What is 'invisible?'" you asked, carefully reiterating that new word.

"It just means something you can't see. So there are some things you see that I can't, or maybe other people can't see either."

"Are those the things you can go through like ghosts?" you asked, and I nodded.

"Yes! Exactly! Those things are invisible to many people, like me. Do you understand?"

You were silent for a while, taking this all in, before saying, "I think so."

"Good." I paused, wondering if that was enough progress for the day. But we had time, and you were in a listening mood despite my earlier trepidations so I pushed a bit further.

"These ghost-things you see—I think they are things that happened a long time ago."

"Like dinosaurs?"

"Well, not exactly." At least, I was reasonably certain you couldn't see dinosaurs. I added, "But if we are at a church and you see a wedding I can walk through—that isn't a wedding happening right then, when we are there, but it may have happened a week ago. Or a month ago. Or a year ago. Does that make sense?"

But I must've pushed too hard because you abruptly hopped off the bench, ignoring my question.

"I'm sorry," you announced, sounding firm yet polite. "I don't want to talk about this now."

"Okay." I stood with a sigh, hoping I'd at least managed to lay the groundwork for another conversation down the road. "We can talk about this more later."

We left the tree and resumed climbing the rest of the hill. The ascent had apparently sapped most of your energy, because you no longer darted up and down as we made our way to the top. Instead, you settled in next to me, panting slightly, looking down at your feet to focus on each difficult step. But then the slope leveled, and we finally found ourselves alone at the crest.

Chiseled stone carvings centered on the summit identified all the mountain peaks across the Hudson River that were visible from our vantage point. After you scampered about from carving to carving, examining each, you pointed out every mountain you could spot in the distance with a huge smile spread across your face. Sentimentality isn't usually my thing, but it was such a beautiful moment for the two of us I couldn't resist the urge to document it.

"Let's get a picture, Quince," I said, and you were more than willing, allowing me to pick you up and hold you in my left arm while I took a selfie of the two of us, grinning with our heads pressed together, with the Catskill Mountains serving as a distant backdrop. After taking that photo, I let you explore the area for a few more minutes before summoning you so we could start heading back. The descent tested the limits of my shoddy knees, but it was otherwise smoother going than the way up had been, and in minutes we were back at our car. After checking us both for ticks, we were back on the road, continuing our drive south toward Poughkeepsie.

A few minutes into our ride, we passed the cross on the

side of the road, but you didn't immediately comment on it. Instead, you looked thoughtful as you gazed out the window.

"Was that crash real?" you asked once the cross was well behind us, and I could only assume you were still reflecting upon our talk from the hill.

"There was no crash now," I explained. "The crash we just passed happened a long time ago, but you're able to see it now, even though I can't."

You still looked confused, so when we stopped at the next red light, I took out my phone, bringing up the picture of the two of us from the top of the hill that I took earlier, and held it up for you to see.

"It's like this picture," I said. "This photo shows us up on the hill, even though we aren't there right now. It's the same thing with the car accident: you can see it, even though it happened months ago. Does that make sense?"

You nodded slowly, and I could detect some hint of understanding on your face, even though I could still see the gears turning in your head. But that was okay—I never thought getting you to understand your visions would be easy or quick.

A short time later, we parked in the lot outside of Nora's building. After making our way to her office, I was surprised when you greeted her with a hug—an embrace that Nora happily returned before handing you her pooping dog toy. You happily settled on the floor with it, laughing to yourself after every bowel movement. *He may get sick of that toy one day,* I noted, *but it's not today.*

"Did you hear?" Nora asked me in a hushed tone as we sat at her desk.

I blinked. "Hear what?"

"I saw on the news that the police found that child who

was kidnapped! It sounds like it was the boy you and Quince tried to help a few weeks ago. You must've heard about that, right?"

"Yes, we heard. We're so happy for the boy and his family." I paused. "Can you keep a secret?"

Nora frowned, cocking her head and looking somewhat affronted. "Given that I'm already keeping a pretty big one, you know I can."

"Yes, of course. It was more of a rhetorical...." I paused, catching myself before I went off on a tangent, then said, "Not only did we hear about that boy being saved, but the reason the police found him was—"

I jerked my head in your direction, and Nora's eyes widened.

"Quince? But I thought you told me he couldn't see anything at the boy's home?"

"That's right, he couldn't," I said. "But he had a vision while we were wandering around aimlessly in Saugerties and somehow ended up right in front of the kidnapper's house." I filled Nora in on the details of that day, culminating with my perjured statement to the police that led to the search warrant.

"Oh, my goodness." Nora paused, dumbstruck. "That is unbelievable."

"We got so lucky," I said. "Not only did we accidentally take a path that took us past that house, but we did it when the garage door was open. If not for that, we would've just continued walking, oblivious to anything being wrong, and that boy would still be stuck in the basement."

"You were probably due some good luck," Nora said, still looking stunned at my revelation. "I'm glad you're finally getting it."

"It's been a pretty good week," I agreed. "And not only

that business with the kidnapping." I proceeded to detail to Nora my efforts to teach you the nature of your visions, and the progress you made in coming to understand them.

"That's great!" Nora said, bobbing her head in approval. "And I appreciate you sharing all of that intel—that's super helpful for me to know. I'll be sure to keep all of that in mind while I'm working with him."

"Okay," I said, taking that as my cue that Nora was ready to get started with you. "I'll leave you to it. If you need me, I'll be out in the hall."

I took a few steps toward the door and stopped as a thought came to me.

"Actually," I said, "if you don't mind, I'm going to head out and walk down the street for a bit. It's a pretty nice day."

Nora's lips twitched—she looked as if she was fighting the urge to laugh at me.

"As far as I'm concerned," she said in a measured tone as she checked her watch, "the next forty-eight minutes are yours to do with as you will. Go try and have fun."

With a solemn nod, I left you and Nora and exited the front of the building and, after a moment of indecision, started walking west in the general direction of the Hudson River. I figured I'd just wander that way for twenty minutes and then turn around, which would give me ample time to get back before you finished up with Nora.

Ten minutes into my walk, I passed by a cute café and contemplated buying a drink. *Maybe I should get one for Nora as well?* I wondered, although I had no idea what her beverage of choice might be. As I was mulling over that minor dilemma, my phone vibrated with an incoming email. One quick glance revealed it to be nothing more than an automatic email generated by the Google alert notification I had set up some time earlier, which informed me whenever a new article popped up involving a car accident in our region. I scanned the email and felt satisfied once I confirmed the site of the accident was not on any of our normal routes, making it unlikely you'd ever have occasion to view that incident.

But after a moment, my brain kicked alive, and I returned to the email, studying it more intently. I skimmed it once and then forced myself to read it again at a much slower pace. And then I read it a third time.

"Oh my God." My pulse was racing, and I felt the need to do *something*, although I did not know what. With my phone in hand, I marched back toward Nora's office, but after a few strides, my impatience got the better of me and I quickened my pace to an all-out run.

I was panting and sweating from the half-mile sprint when I arrived back at Nora's office a few minutes later, but I didn't bother to compose myself before knocking on her closed office door. Without waiting for an invite, I burst in, and you and Nora each looked up at me in surprise at my sudden unexpected reappearance. I spotted the pooping dog toy behind Nora and wordlessly pointed at it. She understood my meaning and handed it to you.

"Let's take a little break, Quince, okay?" she said, throwing me a worried look.

"Okay," you said, cheerfully taking the dog before sitting on the ground to play. Nora took me by the arm and gently pulled me to a back corner of the office, and I numbly allowed myself to be led.

"Will, are you okay?" Nora asked. When I didn't answer, she added, "You look ill."

I tried to find the words and came up short.

"It's not just the past," was all I could spit out. Nora blinked, utterly confused. I forced myself to take a few deep breaths, and only once I'd regained some control did I try to speak again.

"You know how I'm tracking Quince's visions?" I said in a measured voice, trying hard not to ramble. "Every vision he reports to me, I add to my spreadsheet. For most of those entries, I could tie the vision to something in the news, but there were exceptions. I figured that was just a natural result of my shoddy research, or Quince seeing things that weren't newsworthy for whatever reason."

"Okay," Nora said, sounding a touch impatient for me to get to the point.

"For example," I continued, "a few weeks ago, Quince told me he saw a school bus filled with children that went off the road and tumbled into an embankment. I couldn't find anything about that incident on the internet, but I otherwise thought little about it. It seemed strange I couldn't find any reports of that one—it sounded like a story that would've generated some news coverage. But I shrugged it off."

Nora continued to frown, waiting for my point.

"I regularly receive emails with news alerts regarding car accidents in the area, which I set up with the goal of keeping Quince clear of scenes that would be horrific for him to view. And when I was out walking just now, I received another alert about an accident that happened yesterday after school: a school bus that drove off the road and rolled into a ditch. In the exact location where Quince, several weeks ago, had experienced that exact vision. Don't you see?"

Nora's mouth opened, but she didn't speak. I could see

she was still processing this development, so I proceeded to connect the dots for her.

"Quince isn't only seeing the past. He's also seeing the future."

## 10

*My relationship with the future was constantly evolving.*

*For most of my life, in those days before I met your mother, I hardly thought about the future at all. My focus was on avoiding discomfort and that, mostly, didn't require substantial planning. I simply aspired to live a painless existence, with no grand plans to start a family, climb a corporate ladder, or anything else that might show up on someone's five-year plan. I limited my concerns about the future to figuring out what I needed to pick up at the supermarket to get through the week, but not much beyond that.*

*Only after I fell in love with your mother did I have any reason to think about what was in store for us, but even those thoughts mostly focused on figuring out what needed to be done for your mother to achieve her vision of a perfect future. She often talked of her wish to one day live in a white colonial with two or three children and a small menagerie of cats, dogs, and whatever other cute animals were on her mind at the time. Wanting nothing more than to make her happy, I often reflected on what I needed to do to breathe life into her dreams. And yet, your mother's happiness aside, I remained fairly apathetic to the future as it related to me personally.*

*The first time I developed any sort of genuine curiosity about what the future might hold was after you were born. From the earliest days of your infancy, I wondered what kind of person you would grow into with me as your sole caretaker. But even those musings about the future were nothing more than idle curiosity. There were a billion different directions life could take you, and I didn't see the point in looking too closely at any specific hypothetical route you might traverse. Instead, as you grew into yourself, I took comfort knowing that whatever the future had in store for you, your kind heart would enable you to make the most of it.*

*Understanding the true nature of your visions, and realizing they weren't limited to past events, compelled me to take a harder look at the future. In this process, I experienced, for the first time, an appreciation of what the future truly was—an unexplored wilderness filled with unimaginable dangers that I couldn't possibly shield you from.*

*And it terrified me.*

~

NORA STARED INTO SPACE, trying to make sense of my revelation.

"You believe he's seeing the future?" she finally asked, a hint of skepticism in her voice.

"That bus flipped in the exact way Quince described it at the precise location where he saw it," I explained. "It's too specific to be a coincidence." Nora still looked as if she needed further convincing, so I added, "You saw firsthand how he can see the past. Why is it so impossible to believe he can see events in the future?"

"It's not that I don't believe you, but—" Nora paused. "The past has already happened, so that is set in stone in my mind. But the future is—" She trailed off, at a loss for words. "It just seems like a different beast entirely," she finally said.

"I know," I said. "I can't explain it. Maybe these emotional resonances aren't bound by the same rules of time and space that we're accustomed to? I'm not equipped to answer that. All I can tell you is I'm nearly certain Quince is seeing the future as well."

"Let me put it this way," Nora said. "Suppose you knew last week Quince's vision of that bus toppling into a ditch was a vision of the future, and you labored to fill in the ditch before the accident happened. Then what? Could you have undone that vision?"

"It's a fair question," I said. "But I don't know. That's something else we'll have to figure out." My pulse was racing, and I took a deep breath to calm myself before continuing. "Just when I thought I was getting a handle on all of this, there's a new component that is completely alien to me. I truly don't know what the rules are. At all."

Nora watched you play as she worked through the issue in her head. It was hard to tell if she believed what I was saying, but she at least appeared open to the possibility that I was correct. Our demonstration to Nora in Manhattan had opened her mind to things she would have thought were impossible, and I hoped she could go along with this additional piece of the puzzle without firsthand proof, which would be much more difficult to arrange than the business with the World Trade Center.

"Let's say you're right, and Quince can also see events with strong emotional ties that take place in the future," Nora finally said. "What does that change for you?"

"What does that change?" I repeated thoughtfully. It was a good question, and I needed a moment to formulate a response. "For starters, I can steer Quince away from a lot of bad imagery that is out there by doing some research before we visit a new place. But now I see that's impossible—I can't research events that have yet to happen."

"But that was never a foolproof plan anyway," Nora replied. "It's impossible to catch everything, and Quince sees some bad stuff no matter what you do, right?"

I nodded—it was true. When we went out, you often reported seeing gruesome events, but it remained unclear whether those visions were related to future events or past incidents that I simply couldn't catch through my research. But Nora's point was well-taken: there were too many scary happenings in the past to learn about all of them, no matter how hard I tried.

"So what else is really scaring you about this development?" Nora asked.

Not for the first time, I was thankful for bringing Nora into our circle, as I valued her ability to get to the heart of matters. I glanced at you to confirm you weren't listening to us, but continued in a hushed tone out of an abundance of caution.

"On the way here, I stopped at a park and had a short heart-to-heart with Quince about his visions. And I thought he was understanding, to some extent, and I felt more optimistic than I had in a long time. It's demoralizing to realize this is so much more complicated than I thought it was, and it's going to be that much harder to have any of this make sense to him."

Nora could tell that wasn't all of it. "Okay. What else?"

"Well... when we thought he was just seeing things in the past, there didn't seem to be any implications beyond how those visions were impacting Quince: is he being traumatized by his visions? Are they negatively impacting his development in some way? Granted, his view of the past helped solve that kidnapping case, but that was more of a fluke than anything else. Generally speaking, I thought since Quince was seeing events that had already happened, any harm stemming from those incidents had already been done. But if he's seeing things that haven't occurred yet... that comes with some real responsibilities, right? A few weeks ago, we went to downtown Manhattan and Quince saw a replay of 9/11. What happens if he's out somewhere and sees a vision of another terrorist attack, only one that takes place in the future? What are we supposed to do with that?"

"Quince is four years old," Nora said, blunt as ever. "I don't think it's fair to expect him to be a savior. Maybe one day he'll be positioned to make things better, but that's not something to worry about now. Your job isn't to save the world. Your job is *him*." Nora cocked her head in your direction with a meaningful look.

"Of course it's about him," I said. "But if he sees something—"

"If he sees something that can be fixed, worry about it then," Nora cut in. "But there's no point in stressing about it now. That spreadsheet you have of his visions—do you really think you can spend the rest of your life monitoring accident sites that *might* relate to future visions in a desperate attempt to keep those crashes from happening?"

I hadn't thought about it, but of course she was right. It would be impossible in most cases to avoid a tragedy scheduled to take place at some indeterminate time in the future.

"Bad things happen," Nora said in a softer tone. "You and Quince are allowed to live your lives without feeling guilt about future incidents that he viewed. My suggestion is to just keep at what you have been doing—helping Quince grow and gain some appreciation for how he's different from the rest of us—and not lose sleep over how his visions might allow you to fix the future. Because you certainly have enough other stuff on your plate."

"Fair enough," I muttered, although I thought what she was saying would be easier said than done. And despite her assurances that this development didn't mean anything had to be different, I knew in my gut that the landscape had changed. We undoubtedly would have to deal with a new set of trials, even if I couldn't then foresee exactly what those challenges would be.

Or the danger we would find ourselves in.

MY HEIGHTENED ANXIETY NOTWITHSTANDING, the rest of the week went smoothly, and I noticed you were commenting less and less about your visions. There were times we drove around together where I could see you staring intently out the window, and I assumed your visions were becoming somewhat routine for you, and thus not as comment-worthy as they had once been. This was a mixed blessing in my mind: as much as it worried me to hear about your troubling visions, it was even worse being in the dark about what you were seeing.

While I remained fixated on the implications of what I had learned concerning your limited abilities to see the future, your focus was on your preschool graduation ceremony, which was held at the end of that week. In the days leading up to the event, you repeatedly asked if I'd be there, and I reassured you that I was taking off from work that Friday for the sole purpose of attending. Once that day finally arrived, you bounced around with excitement until it

was time for both of us to head to your school for the
ceremony.

They held the event outside under a canopy that
covered several rows of folding chairs arranged for the
parents. The chairs faced another line of seats at the front
for your class to sit in. I arrived early and grabbed a spot in
the first row to ensure you'd see me once you emerged with
your classmates. After the assorted families were settled,
your class exited the school in a single line, with your
teachers gently prodding all of you along. You trudged at
the rear of that formation, looking lost in your own head,
but your face brightened upon seeing me in the crowd. Your
right hand, hovering waist-high at your side, threw me a
quick wave as you marched with the other preschoolers to
your seats.

There wasn't much to the ceremony itself, although it
was cute enough. Your class kicked off the proceedings by
singing the A-B-C song, with some boisterous boys belting it
loudly and out of tune. You dutifully mouthed the lyrics,
even though I didn't get the impression any noise was actually coming out of you. The teachers then played a CD with
a song that I assumed was called "Shake the Sillies Out"
because the singers kept repeating that sentiment to music
as the class laughed and wiggled their extremities. After
that, the class sang one last song together—something
about new friendships and adventures—before the students
were called up one by one to receive a completion certificate. Your classmates each ran up and gave enthusiastic
hugs to your teachers after being summoned, but on
hearing your name, you walked up, silent and stoic, to
receive your certificate. Your teachers, not wanting to
encroach on your boundaries, each held up a hand at your
approach, and you solemnly gave both of them a quick high

five instead of a hug before taking your certificate and shuffling back to your seat.

You and I spent a lot of time together, but I rarely had the occasion to see you alongside other children your own age, and I tried to gauge whether your demeanor, so different from the other kids in your class, was a positive, a negative, or just a neutral personality quirk. I thought it was fairly evident you weren't comfortable with your teachers or your school in general, which was troubling. I had signed you up for summer camp at that preschool, with another year of pre-K starting in September, but I found myself questioning that plan.

You had made great strides in opening up around me, and even with Nora, but you still appeared to be mostly mute in the setting of your school.

*Maybe he needs a fresh start?* I wondered. I couldn't imagine you coming out of your shell at that school after having already spent so much time there engaged in a ritual of silence. Granted, the school was better than nothing, but I made a mental note to look into other options for the fall.

At the end of the ceremony, your teacher directed the children to toss their caps, made with black construction paper and a few well-placed staples, and everyone, including you, was more than happy to do so. In fact, all the other kids had so much fun throwing their caps that they immediately tracked them down once they landed to hurl them again. But you were the lone exception. After flinging your cap, you watched it flutter to the ground in front of you before looking up at me, a broad smile painted on your face, to confirm I had seen all the action. I gave you a wave to let you know I was watching, and you subtly bounced in place, excited but otherwise quiet.

Once the other children tired of throwing their caps

around, they were led to a blow-up castle that had been erected behind the school. A flurry of excited squeals at seeing the structure led to shoes being kicked off and small bodies throwing themselves into the bowels of the castle. You took your time removing your Velcro sneakers, but I was pleased when you ran into the castle to play with the other children. I lurked outside, occasionally peering in through a netted window to check on you, knowing full well I was helicopter parenting but not really caring, while other parents clustered together to make small talk. I could hear excited voices from inside the castle as the kids bounced around, but I never heard yours. During moments of relative quiet, though, I could make out your distinct giggle, and I knew you were doing just fine in there.

After about ten minutes of play, a girl emerged, looking slightly dizzy, and spotted the school's playground, which was completely empty. She quickly put on her shoes and ran to the swing set. Shortly after, the rest of the class exited the bounce castle to join her. When you emerged, you located your sneakers and handed them to me, pointing at your feet in a silent instruction to put them back on you. *He's reverting to muteness in this environment*, I noted again as I strapped your shoes back on you. Once I finished, I gave you a quick pat on the back and you darted away to the playground, where the other children were chasing each other up and down various slides.

A few minutes later, the school's administrator, Ms. Leona, emerged to thank the parents for coming out before politely asking everyone to leave so they could set up the graduation ceremony for the pre-K class that was scheduled to start in about an hour. It took some time for the parents to coax their respective children off the playground, but soon everyone was heading back to the parking lot.

"Where are we going now?" you asked once we were back in our car, and I felt relief at hearing your voice again.

"I was planning on heading home," I admitted. "But is there somewhere else you'd like to go?"

You thought it over for a moment.

"Can we go to a *new* playground?" you asked, and I assumed that brief taste at the school had whetted your appetite. *Although*, I recalled, *you were also asking about playgrounds last weekend.* It seemed like an itch you legitimately needed to scratch.

"Okay, fine," I answered with a sigh. Truth be told, I didn't particularly love taking you to playgrounds for several reasons. They were germy—a concern that was only heightened following the COVID outbreak. I also worried about bigger kids inadvertently, or even intentionally, knocking you around. Another problem was that on those rare occasions where we had visited playgrounds in the past, you lost interest almost immediately in the area designed for toddlers, at which point you'd wander toward the section intended for children aged five or older. Any attempt I made to guide you away from those more dangerous areas inevitably led to tears, and it was all downhill from there.

But you were a year older than the last time we went to a playground, and you had shown tremendous growth over the past two months alone. Maybe you were ready to handle that experience without making it terrifying for me. Of course, I worried about what you might see at a playground —past, present, or future—but that was an ever-present concern and no reason to keep you from one.

I drove to the rec center in the next town over, which I recalled had two playgrounds sitting amid various playing fields and basketball courts. After parking, I steered you toward the smaller playground, designed for children aged two to five, and there were only a handful of toddlers running about while their mothers played with their phones on the outskirts of the play area. You eyeballed the other children, as if weighing whether you wanted to engage them, before heading off by yourself to an unoccupied slide. I assumed the playground had some history of children falling and getting hurt, but you didn't seem to experience any visions in that regard. *Maybe those emotions weren't strong enough to leave an imprint?* I wondered.

"Wheeeeee!" you cried as you slid down the slide, arms raised in the air. I held out my hand for a high-five at the bottom, which you gave with great enthusiasm before racing back up to do it again.

After repeatedly conquering that slide and exploring the rest of the area, testing out all the other tame rides it offered, you returned to me with a bored expression on your face. As you gazed across a grass field toward the other playground, I knew what was coming, and I tried to nip it in the bud.

"That's a playground for the big kids," I explained. "Maybe next year you can go on it."

"I just want to look at it," you said, and I frowned.

"If you look at it, you're going to want to play on it," I said. "But it's not for four-year-olds."

"I won't play on it!" you insisted. "I just want to look!"

I didn't respond right away, which you apparently interpreted as a "yes" because you sprinted toward the other playground without waiting for me. Stifling a groan, I jogged after you, and as I got closer to the other playground I fully appreciated, for the first time, the extent to which it wasn't intended for younger kids.

Most of the attractions in the area were larger versions of what was available on the toddler playground: bigger swings, a larger seesaw, and a more elaborate rope net to climb. But the centerpiece of the playground was an elaborate tower connecting to three monstrous slides: a twisting tunnel, a straight slide, and another bumpy slide.

There was a cluster of kids, maybe ten years old, navigating their way up to the top of the tower via a metal ladder, but otherwise, the playground was empty. Some adults—presumably the older children's parents—sat on benches scattered on the periphery of the playground area. I wasn't entirely sure why those other children weren't in school. *Homeschooled perhaps?* I thought, but I spent little energy worrying about it.

You stared up at the enormous tower as you approached and inadvertently kicked an empty beer can lying on the ground. I placed my hand on your shoulder to stop you before you could pick it up to examine it.

"That's garbage." I explained. "We don't want to touch that."

"It's those damn kids who come here at night," a middle-aged man sitting on a nearby bench piped in. "It's bad enough they use this spot to drink, but they have to leave their shit behind as well. Buncha assholes."

I gave the man a tight smile and nod, hoping you hadn't been paying enough attention to learn any new words from him. However, your attention was focused solely on the tower, and I couldn't tell if you were mesmerized by the size of those slides or if you were perceiving something else entirely.

"Can you see the boy and the girl?" you asked after a moment, and given that there were no girls on the playground, I knew you were experiencing a vision.

"No, I can't," I answered. "What are they doing?"

"They are hurt. The girl's arm looks like this." You traced a zigzag shape in the air with your finger. "That was a big fall." You shuddered, processing what you had seen, before adding, "I don't want to go on those slides."

*Well, at least it doesn't sound like those kids died*, I thought, wondering if this was a past vision or something that had not yet happened. It was a perplexing vision, in any event. It wasn't hard to imagine a scenario where a child could get hurt falling off the tower, or even falling off a slide. But two kids at once....

I walked closer to the structure, studying it.

"Daddy, don't get too close," you warned. "You could get hurt."

"I promise to be careful." I studied the base of the tower —nothing seemed amiss.

"Where did they fall, Quince?" I called back over my shoulder. You pointed up at the very top of the tower, which was about twenty feet off the ground.

"Right there," you said. "I think it broke."

"*It* broke? What was it that broke?" I maneuvered to the area directly under where you were pointing and looked up —I still saw nothing out of order. *Maybe this was something that happened years ago*, I thought. But the possibility that it wasn't kept me rooted to the spot.

I shuffled along, searching for anything out of the ordinary up above, but everything seemed to be as it should. After a few minutes of looking up, my neck began aching, and I rolled my head around to stretch some life back into those muscles. As I tilted my head down toward the ground, a glint of something buried amongst the wood chips caught my eye. I kicked a few chips away before finding what I had glimpsed: a slightly rusted, irregular-shaped nut.

"What's that?" you asked, cautiously approaching as I picked it up.

"It's hardware," I said. "They use these, and bolts, to hold everything on the playground together. I'm not sure what this is doing down here."

I kept searching the ground, scattering wood chips around in case anything else was obscured, but I couldn't locate any additional nuts or bolts. I couldn't imagine a single dislodged nut giving rise to a safety hazard, but I was paranoid in light of your vision.

"Stay here,' I told you, and I waited for your nod of agreement before lumbering into the structure. The tower was designed for children, and I felt like a jackass as I made my way up a metal set of stairs into a small room filled with various levers and gears for children to play with. After sticking my head out a window to check on you, I clambered up a ladder to the top of the tower. The boys I had spotted earlier were milling about up there, and they gave me odd looks as I emerged, but otherwise stayed clear. It took me a second to orient myself, but I soon located the side of the tower you had been pointing at earlier.

Nothing seemed defective at first glance, but then I noticed something: the section of the wall circling the top of the tower was only being kept in place by large nut-less bolts that were protruding at the joints. A simple push of my finger could drive any of them out of their holes with nothing there to hold them in place. *Someone removed all of the nuts*, I realized. I quickly counted the bolts that had been tampered with—there were at least a dozen—and concluded this was an intentional act of vandalism. There was no sign of the removed nuts themselves, other than the one I found on the ground, and I assumed that whoever was responsible had attempted to remove the evidence.

"Hey, kids," I called out to the children on the platform. I felt creepy and uncomfortable as they looked at me, confused about what I was doing up there at all. "It locks like this wall over here is broken, so you should stay away from it," I warned them. "Okay?"

They nodded, but I could see they were curious about the damage. I planned on speaking with their parents as soon as I got back on the ground—I didn't feel authorized to order them out of the tower myself—and I hoped those kids' curiosity didn't get them into trouble in the time it took me to descend. After peering out to check on you, I climbed back down as fast as I could manage and took you with me as I worked my way around the playground area to explain the situation to all the parents.

"Are you telling me those assholes tampered with the playground?" said the man who had complained earlier about teens coming to the park at night, after he overheard me speaking with a mother. "Pieces of shit!"

I ignored him, hoping you were doing the same, and continued my task of speaking with the adults in the area. Thankfully, those parents took action and summoned their children off of the tower. Within a few minutes, they cleared out the entire structure.

*Now what?* I looked around the park and spotted a man in the distance, wearing a navy uniform and emptying a garbage can into bins arranged on the back of a pickup truck. Assuming the man was a park employee who could address the situation, or at least direct me to the right person to speak with, I headed off in his direction.

At least, that's what I tried to do. I frowned, confused, upon realizing I hadn't actually taken a step despite my intent to do so. Instead, I remained rooted to the spot. Once more I tried to walk to the man, and I again found it nearly impossible to compel my legs to take that first step.

*What the hell is this?* I wondered, looking down at my suddenly useless legs. *Am I having a stroke?* I had a vague recollection of learning at some point that stroke victims can have trouble controlling their extremities.

I concentrated hard on my right foot, willing it to lift off the ground. It moved slowly—as if I was ensnared in quicksand—but inch by inch, I raised my right foot, extended it forward a few inches, before placing it back on the ground. By the time I was done, I was panting from the exertion of that single step. *What is going on?* I wondered again, mentally preparing for another similar struggle with my next step. But that first one proved to be the hardest, as I could walk in normal fashion thereafter. By the time I reached the park worker, I was already wondering whether I had imagined that weirdness with my leg.

"Excuse me?" I said as I approached the man.

"Yeah?" the worker asked in a bored tone, looking up at me.

"I noticed that the tower on that playground over there has been tampered with. Many of the nuts were removed at the top, and it looks like at least one wall up there is barely holding on at this point. I found this nut on the ground." I handed over the hardware I had previously located, and the man peered at it. As he did, I looked back to check on you, and you seemed fine—you stood with your back to me, preoccupied with studying the tower, and seemingly disinterested in what I was up to.

"How the hell did someone get this off?" the worker wondered aloud. "You see this shape? This requires a special tool to remove it."

"I don't know," I admitted. "But those nuts are off, however they did it." The man didn't respond, and I wasn't sure he appreciated the gravity of the situation. "So you'll take care of this, right? Seems pretty dangerous to me."

The man shook his head, coming out of his reverie. "What? Oh, yeah, we'll take care of it from here."

He took out his phone and called someone as he walked away, without a word of thanks. *Whatever*, I thought. *As long as they address it somehow.*

I jogged back and found you continuing to study the structure.

"Quince?" I said upon reaching you, and you turned toward me at the sound of my voice.

"Oh!" I blurted out upon seeing your face and immediately followed up with a sharp intake of breath through my clenched teeth. Blood freely ran out your nose, painting the bottom half of your face a dark red, with some droplets falling to the ground from your chin. You seemed oblivious to the mess, and you looked confused at my shocked reaction.

"What is it?" you asked. I fished in my pockets and found a tissue, wrinkled but otherwise clean. You flinched away from me as I tried to dab at your face. "What is it?" you repeated.

"Your nose," I said. "It's bleeding."

You put a tentative hand up to your face and drew it away upon feeling that wetness, studying the blood on your fingertips. That curiosity gave way to fear, and you started bawling.

"It's okay," I said, wiping your face as best I could. I found a few more tissues in my pocket and got most of the blood off, but a good amount of it had smeared across your face, leaving a pinkish hue in its wake. "Sometimes we get bloody noses when the air is dry. Here." I found another tissue and handed it to you. "Hold this under your nose until the bleeding stops."

You followed my instructions and stopped wailing, although tears continued to stream out of your eyes.

"Am I still bleeding?" you asked, your voice muffled by the tissue covering the lower half of your face.

"I can't tell. It will stop soon. But we should get home and clean you up."

We walked together back to the parking lot, but you paused partway to glance back at the playground.

"The boy and the girl are gone," you noted, looking at the tower in the distance. "Where did they go?"

"I don't know," I said, but my mind was racing. *Did I change that future event, at least?* I wondered. *Is that why the vision went away?*

Thankfully, your nosebleed stopped by the time we got home, and after a long bath, there was no evidence it had ever happened.

We returned to the park the following day. I wanted to confirm my warnings about the vandalized tower were being heeded, and I was relieved to see cautionary tape around the structure with signs saying it was closed for repair.

"Are the boy and the girl who fell still gone?" I asked, and you nodded.

"I can't see them," you said.

"That's good," I said, believing it was, in fact, a positive sign.

"Why is that good?" you asked, and I hesitated. I didn't think you were quite ready to hear that some of your visions were tied to the future, but I didn't want to lie to you.

"Maybe you can't see the boy and the girl because they aren't hurt anymore," was all I said. "And that would be good, right?"

You nodded. "Yes. That would be good."

And why wouldn't it be? You and I had harnessed your ability, once again, to remove some pain from the world, even if it was only helping a pair of children avoid a few broken bones down the road. *Maybe there'll be other opportunities to make more meaningful contributions at some point*, I even dared to think. *Other opportunities to fix the future.*

*How could that be anything* but *good?* The question was rhetorical, but in time I learned it had an answer.

An answer for which I was completely unprepared.

# 11

*For most of my life, I had no desire or occasion to reflect upon my childhood, but that changed around the time you turned four. My earliest memories started close to that same age, and I returned to them for insight into how you were perceiving the world. It was an imprecise exercise to be sure—I can't imagine any two people think exactly alike or see things in the same light. But there were still lessons to be learned from revisiting the recesses of my mind, and one such lesson was that good memories tend to fade much easier than the bad*

*I have a vague recollection of spending time as a child roller-skating up and down our street, but I don't remember any of those specific experiences. Still, I recall with crystal clarity being seven years old and falling while roller-skating, breaking my wrist and mangling it so that it could only be reset through surgery. I remember my mother settling in to sit by the side of my hospital bed, prepared to comfort me after the operation, only to be driven away by the cruel laughter of my father, who mocked her for babying me and insisting there was no point in staying since the anesthesia would knock me out until morning. My father's scorn forced my mother to leave, reluctantly, but he was wrong in his assessment. I awoke after the surgery shortly before 2:00 a.m., alone on my side of a dark and unfamiliar room with my right arm in a cast. Across the room I could barely make out another boy, roughly my age, laying in bed, surrounded by his family, napping on whatever chairs they could find. The night crawled slowly, and the absence of a clock made it impossible to gauge the passage of time. Desperate to know how long I had to wait until sunrise, when I could expect my family to return, I repeatedly summoned the increasingly annoyed nursing staff to give me an update on the time. I'll never forget the relief I felt at seeing the first hint of the sun peek through the window, confirming that impossibly long night was finally behind me.*

*Even my most vivid memories of being a teenager are those where I was hurt. I played football each fall, but I have no recollection of any specific win, or any sack I made, or any fumble I recovered. But I remember a practice in August of my junior year of high school when the head coach, in a misguided effort to toughen me up, led the team in a chant of "wuss, wuss, wuss..." as they watched me conduct a downfield blocking drill alone against the biggest and strongest member of our team—an inside linebacker named Joe Romano. I recall struggling to tune out those taunts as I endured hit after hit from Joe, and only releasing the tears I'd been holding back after practice, when I was safe in the sanctity of my bedroom. I'll never lose the memory of sobbing into my pillow to hide my pain from the rest of my family, all while wishing I could quit, but knowing that doing so would not only trigger the wrath of my father, but would also effectively confirm the truth of the chants levied against me earlier in the day.*

*My point is that the bad stuff sticks to us more than the good ever could. And even though you made progress in understanding your visions, I could never fully protect you from the horrors that only you could see. I knew the pain and violence you saw would*

*solidify as memories you'd never be able to shake. No matter how*
*much light I introduced into your life, it would only serve, at best,*
*as a distraction from the darkness.*

*It would never be enough to cancel it out entirely.*

EVEN SO, a distraction is better than nothing, so I decided to
take you to the water park on a hot Tuesday in early July.

In theory, there was no meaningful change to our daily
routine after your "graduation" since you immediately
started summer camp at the same school and with the same
hours, but the oppressive heat in the afternoons made it
more and more difficult for us to spend time outside for any
longer than a few minutes. We kept ourselves occupied, but
we mainly directed our energy at playing indoors where we
could enjoy the comfort of central air-conditioning. In the
span of a few weeks, our house became filled with an assort-
ment of marble runs, pillow forts, and giant robots made of
cardboard and duct tape. Sure, the house was a wreck, but I
didn't mind. You were happy, so it was all good.

Still, I started feeling restless from spending so much time
indoors, and I imagined you felt the same. We didn't have a
pool, and there were no beaches near us, so cooling off was a
bit of a challenge. But then I got wind of a brand new water
park that had opened a few weeks earlier over Memorial Day
weekend on the other side of the Hudson River, about an
hour's drive away, and I thought it was worth a visit. It looked
to be on the small side, with only a few attractions, but I
figured it was probably more than enough to blow your four-
year-old mind. I also questioned how long the park could
operate—I couldn't imagine that a water park in the Hudson
Valley, which has, at most, three months of hot weather over

the course of a year, could remain open for long, so I felt particularly motivated to visit it before it went out of business.

Guilt also partially motivated the timing of our trip. A mediation was scheduled for Thursday of that week in my wrongful death lawsuit relating to your mother's passing. I wasn't looking forward to it—the litigation remained an albatross around my neck—but the mediation also meant I'd have to head down to Manhattan for a full day, which involved making arrangements to get you into school early that morning and keep you there until 6:00 p.m. It wouldn't be a fun day for you, and that inspired me to balance the scales at least somewhat by giving you a dose of enjoyment earlier in the week.

Since the water park was only a few weeks old, I hoped it wouldn't host any gruesome visions of the past to haunt you. Of course, even if that assumption was correct, there was always the possibility of you seeing something that hadn't yet happened, but I accepted that as an unavoidable risk that came with going anywhere new.

A more practical complication stemmed from the fact that you couldn't swim. Early in your life, I tried to expose you to water by signing us up for "Mommy & Me" swim lessons (they let me in, despite being a daddy), and I think that early experience helped you become somewhat comfortable in a pool, but I didn't stick with those classes long enough for you to gain any real swim expertise. That was an issue I hoped to rectify at some point via swim lessons, but in the short term, I purchased a small blue swim vest for you to wear at the park to keep you from sinking in the event you escaped my line of sight for more than a second.

We left for the water park early that Tuesday, in part

because we were both awake at the crack of dawn anyway, but also because I wanted to be there at its opening and hopefully beat the worst of the crowds. You had a poor night's sleep, troubled by nightmares—a rarer occurrence in recent weeks, but still a problem that hadn't completely disappeared—and you fell asleep shortly after we started driving. I was perfectly fine with you passing out in the car —not only would you catch up on some sleep, but I wouldn't have to worry about you spotting anything troubling on the ride.

You awoke immediately once I shut off the car in the water park's lot, and you were thrilled and amazed to discover we were already there. Families carrying towels and beach bags filtered across the parking lot toward the entrance, and once we exited the car you tugged at my hand, impatient to join them. I applied sunscreen to each of us as quickly as I could, realizing full well I was probably looking ghostlike because of my rushed work, before allowing you to lead me into the park.

After paying the entrance fee, a teenage girl working the entrance measured your height—forty-five inches—and wrapped a red paper bracelet around your wrist to mark you for the rides you could go on alone and those you had to go on with me. But, as the girl explained, since you were over forty-two inches, there were no rides you would be barred from completely.

"I can go on all the rides?" you asked afterward in a hopeful tone while I stuffed our towels into a rented locker. In doing so, I realized that although I had remembered to bring a change of clothes for you, I failed to anticipate my own needs—I'd have to endure the hour-long ride home later in a wet bathing suit.

"Yes, you can go on anything here you like!" I said aloud to you. "Where do you want to start?"

It turned out you wanted to go on the first attraction you saw: a set of enclosed slides requiring the use of either a single or dual rider tube. We took a double tube and climbed a set of wooden stairs until we stopped at the end of an already long line. In fact, the entire park was already more crowded than I had expected—it seemed not as many people had returned to work after the long Fourth of July weekend as I had hoped would. *Oh well*, I thought. *I'm not doing this for me. As long as Quince is having fun....* And all early indications suggested you were.

As we waited in line, an embarrassed-looking father and a crying young boy descended past us, the boy apparently having second thoughts upon reaching the top. I wondered whether you might respond similarly once we reached the front of the line.

"Is this scary?" I asked, trying to get a sense of how you were feeling.

"Umm, a little bit," you admitted. "But it is mostly fun."

A few minutes later, we reached the top and followed the lifeguard's instructions to sit in the figure-eight shaped tube with you positioned in the front, me in the rear. You studiously heeded each of the lifeguard's directives as you settled into the tube. Once you were in position with a firm grip on the handles, the lifeguard used his foot to push our vessel toward the mouth of the slide, and then we were flying.

Even though the climb up felt as if we had ascended hundreds of feet, the ride down lasted but a few seconds. We rocked back and forth as we navigated the slide's curves, accelerating all the way down. I let out a tentative "wheeeee," but you didn't feel compelled to follow along;

you remained silent the entire way down. After we came out of one particularly sharp curve, I spotted the end of our ride —a large open pool at the foot of the slide—and I tightened up in anticipation of the impact.

We lurched forward upon exiting the slide and hitting the open water, and then we gently floated toward the pool's exit steps, which were flanked by a pair of bored-looking lifeguards. After struggling to get out of our double tube, much to the annoyance of the lifeguards, I surrendered my dignity by simply falling backwards into the water. That sudden loss of weight disturbed the tube, causing you also to spill in next to me. You must have accidentally inhaled some pool water in the process because you were coughing and sputtering when your head popped up again, your vest keeping you afloat. But then we found the steps and clambered out, dragging our tube behind us. Once we were back on land, you paused, processing the experience, and your blank face revealed nothing of what you were feeling.

"How was that, Quince?" I asked, wondering if I had merely found a new way to traumatize you. You gave my question some thought before a shy smile spread across your face.

"Let's do another slide!" you exclaimed, hopping up and down in excitement.

We spent the next hour engaged in a cycle of carrying a tube up wooden stairs, only to turn around and ride it back down. You wanted to try each of the slides multiple times, but eventually the novelty wore off enough for you to want to venture deeper into the park. By that time, the water park was already at nearly full capacity, and families and children filled just about every area.

"What's that?" you asked, pointing at a structure standing in a shallow pool labeled, "Splash Zone." The attraction was a fairly complicated maze of stairways and slides, punctuated by water pouring out of nozzles arrayed at varying heights to spray anyone who dared to enter the vicinity. A half dozen lifeguards in rain gear patrolled the area, although their role appeared to be limited to blowing their whistles at any kids who dared to run on the slippery surfaces.

"I don't know," I answered, figuring you'd have fun exploring it for yourself. "But we can check it out."

As we walked toward the Splash Zone, we passed a large rectangular pool filled with children and their parents. The pool was shallow on one end—ankle-deep, at most—but it gradually deepened to five feet on the far side. A rope divided the shallow area from the deeper end of the pool, which was primarily occupied by older children with strong swimming abilities.

"Look," you said, pointing in the general direction of the pool.

"Yes, that's a nice pool," I said. "We can go in there later, if you want. But maybe not the deep end."

"Why are they pushing on the boy?" you asked, sounding puzzled.

"Umm...." Despite my better instincts, I stopped to look for a boy being knocked around and saw nothing.

"I don't see him," I said. "I think this may be one of those things you can see, but I can't."

"You can't see the boy?"

"No. What's the boy doing?"

"He's just lying there." You shrugged, uncertain how to elaborate. "A lady in red was pushing him. But now she is kissing him."

"She's kissing the boy?" A thought came to me, and I pointed at a nearby lifeguard in a red bathing suit.

"Is that what the woman is wearing?" I asked. You studied the lifeguard and her uniform before nodding your head.

"Yes, I think so," you answered. "Why is she pushing and kissing the boy?"

For once, I was quick to piece together the riddle.

"Sometimes, if people breathe in water, it's called drowning, and they can get hurt. The people in red bathing suits are called lifeguards, and it's their job to keep everyone safe. So if a person drowns, a lifeguard can do things to help them breathe again. There's something called mouth-to-mouth resuscitation, which looks like kissing, and something else called CPR, which involves pushing on someone's chest to get the water out of their lungs and help that person breathe again. So maybe that's what you're seeing?"

You were quiet, and I wondered whether I had adequately explained what you appeared to be viewing. As you continued to study the same area across the pool, my curiosity got the better of me.

"Can you still see the boy?"

"Yes."

"Did he get up?"

"No, he's just laying there. The woman is still pushing and kissing him. Another woman is crying, but a man is holding her."

*Damn*, I thought.

"Is the boy moving at all?"

"No. He's just like...." You froze in place with your arms at your side, imitating a lifeless body.

*It must be a future vision*, I thought, as feelings of helplessness settled in. If there was a drowning death—or even a near-death incident—within the first month of the water park's opening, I was certain I'd have come across that news while vetting the park. Unlike the incident at the play-ground, I didn't see a straightforward way of avoiding the dark outcome you saw, and the guilt tied to that harsh reality weighed upon me.

"Oh," you suddenly said, brightening up. "There's the boy. He's up walking!"

"He is?"

"Yes! He's right there!"

I followed your pointing finger, not really expecting to see anything. And so I was quite surprised when I realized I could also see what you were pointing at: a young boy—maybe eight years old—following along behind a group of older teenagers. Those other kids appeared to be relatives of the boy: brothers, cousins, or a mix of both.

"That's the boy?" I asked. "The same boy you saw over there?" I pointed across the pool.

"Yes." You frowned as you looked back across the pool and then quickly back at the boy as he passed us. "He is over there and over here," you reported, sounding confused as you struggled to process the apparent contradiction.

The version of the boy I could see was wearing bright yellow swimming trunks, so I asked, "The boy across the pool, what color is his bathing suit?"

You peered in that direction. "Umm... I think it is gold."

*Close enough*, I thought. *Now what?* Even if that was the same boy—and I had no reason to doubt you—I wasn't sure what to do. Perhaps the boy and his family had a season pass and planned to come to the water park regularly throughout the summer, and your vision was something that would happen weeks from then.

But then again, it was possible the boy was destined to die that day.

I felt you tug at my hand. "Come on!" you pleaded,

trying to pull me toward the Splash Zone. You didn't seem bothered by your vision, which I hoped was another sign you were getting better at recognizing them as something not necessarily tied to our reality. But I felt troubled, and indecision froze me in place.

I could see the boy in the yellow bathing suit heading off toward the tube slides with his group, away from the area of the park where you spotted the apparent drowning. *He's safe for the moment, at least.* I thought I'd be able to monitor the swimming pool from the periphery of the Splash Zone to see if he returned. With that mild reassurance, I finally allowed you to lead me away.

Most of the parents were resting in lounge chairs set up around the perimeter of the Splash Zone, with children running and shrieking as they navigated the large water playground. I removed your water vest—there was nothing in the area deeper than a foot of water—and let you loose. You were hesitant at first to go off without me, throwing me tentative looks as you shuffled away, but I kept responding with reassuring waves. Soon you were cautiously climbing inside the structure, taking care to steer clear of any wild children who ventured too close to you.

After making sure you were getting by on your own, I turned my attention back to the pool, which remained crowded. There was no sign of the boy in the yellow trunks, and I figured he'd have to cross in front of me to get back from the other end of the park where I'd seen him heading. And once that happened.... Well, I wasn't sure what I would do. But in the interim, I stood vigil on the periphery of the Splash Zone, swiveling my head between you, as you explored the network of water slides, and the pool area to make sure the boy hadn't returned.

After about forty-five minutes of playing, you scooted down a slide and splashed your way over to me.

"I'm all done here!" you announced. "Let's do something else."

"Oh, okay," I said. "How about the pool?" I felt tense from my monitoring, and I reasoned it might be easier to relax somewhat if I positioned myself at the site of the future incident.

"Hmm," you said, sounding thoughtful. "Maybe."

We walked back toward the pool, but along the way you spotted the entrance to the park's lazy river further down.

"I want to go there!" you declared, trying to pull me with you.

"But what about the pool?" I asked.

"I want to do that other one first."

*Damn it.* I remained unsure of what I should be doing. *Am I really expected to track that young boy the entire time I'm here to make sure he's safe?* It was absurd, but it seemed equally insane to potentially put a child's life at risk while floating around a lazy river. *I wish I knew where that kid was,* I thought. It would have made my decision easier if I could confirm he was off eating lunch, or otherwise engaged in something that would keep him far away from the pool for the near future.

I looked around, but there was no sign of the boy or his group, which wasn't that surprising given the size of the park. You pulled again at my hand. "Just a second, Quince," I muttered as I continued scanning the crowd, looking for the boy. My eyes passed over the pool and the mob of people swimming in it, and something caught my eye. The throng of swimmers in the pool had shifted slightly, opening up a previously unavailable line of sight to me, and I spotted the boy in the deep end of the pool, surrounded by his group.

*They must've gotten to the deep end by traversing the length of the pool itself*, I realized. *That's how I missed them.* But my self-chastising transitioned to fear once I recognized what was transpiring.

The boy in the yellow bathing suit was literally in over his head as he struggled to keep afloat amongst his older and larger companions, who all seemed able to stand on the pool floor while keeping their heads above water. They were taking turns batting a beach ball, knocking into each other in their efforts to keep it in the air, and seemingly oblivious to the peril of their smallest companion. I watched, horrified, as that boy went under the water, only to see his face poke out of the surface moments later with a desperate gasp for air. But then one of the larger members of his group knocked into him again, and the boy went back under.

"Hey!" I shouted to a lifeguard seated about ten yards away from me, but he either ignored me or didn't hear me, and instead remained focused on the swimmers. The pool was so crowded I thought it possible the lifeguard simply couldn't see the boy struggling to keep afloat in the deep end.

The boy's head emerged yet again for a sharp intake of air, only this time the beach ball was descending directly above him once he shot out of the water, and three of the larger members of his group knocked into him simultaneously as they went for the ball. He went under once again, only this time the others quickly filled the area he had been occupying. I couldn't see the boy below the surface, but I knew he was down there.

Trapped, somehow.

"Help him!" I screamed again at the lifeguard, who threw me an annoyed look before turning back to the pool, not seeing anything amiss. There wasn't time to press my case to him.

*Damn it.*

"Stay here!" I snapped at you, preparing to jump into the pool myself.

But after a few moments, I was surprised to see that I hadn't moved at all and, in fact, I remained firmly rooted to the spot where I had been standing on the side of the pool.

Once again I found myself unable to move of my own volition—my feet felt as if they were glued to the ground. As panic settled in, I recalled the recent incident at the playground where I underwent a similar inexplicable freezing, yet I had been able to overcome my immobile state then with a focused effort. Letting out a primal scream, I grit my teeth and extracted my foot off of the ground, inch by inch, and found the strength to throw my body forward into the pool. On hitting the water, I felt that hold evaporate, and I once again had full control of my body. I waded as fast as I could toward the boy who had submerged, pushing aside anyone who impeded my path.

"He's drowning!" I shouted as I half-swam, half-ran across the pool. "That boy is drowning!"

Everyone in the vicinity stopped what they were doing and heads started swiveling to locate a drowning child. I ignored them and pressed forward until I reached the cluster of kids who had been playing with the beach ball, and they backed away at my approach. The boy in the yellow bathing suit, floating aimlessly under the water, was easy to spot once those others cleared away. I lifted him out of the water—he was surprisingly light in my arms—and waited for his gasp of breath upon regaining access to the air.

But it didn't come.

*I'm too late*, I thought, forlorn, but I shook off that fatalistic thought and focused on getting the boy out of the water.

As I turned toward the closest side of the pool, I found myself face-to-face with the lifeguard I'd been yelling at moments earlier, who had apparently jumped into the water shortly after I did. That lifeguard wordlessly took the boy from me and repeatedly blew his whistle as he carried him out of the pool toward the side where you had viewed the boy dying earlier. A barrage of whistles from all directions confirmed that multiple lifeguards in the region finally registered what was transpiring and were descending upon us.

One lifeguard—a woman in a red bathing suit—ran to the boy to perform CPR after he was deposited on the ground outside the pool. But the boy didn't stir.

*Is this what you saw, Quince?* I wondered, watching helplessly from the pool. *Did I not change this outcome at all?*

The lifeguard continued to work on the boy, alternating mouth-to-mouth resuscitation with chest compressions. A hushed crowd gathered around the scene, and other lifeguards held them back to give the woman room to operate. I heard a wail, and spotted a woman who looked as if she might be the boy's mother try to run toward him, but a lifeguard likewise held her back.

Over and over again, the lifeguard applied the same pattern of mouth-to-mouth and chest compressions. I was on the verge of losing hope that I had altered that tragic outcome at all when the boy suddenly coughed, water spraying out of his mouth. He was quickly rolled onto his side as he continued to cough more water out of his lungs, and I heard an audible sigh of relief from the crowd.

I likewise offered a silent thank you to the universe as I

contemplated what I had changed, given that it didn't seem as if I did all that much. *Did I somehow shave a few seconds off the time before that boy received CPR?* I wondered. *Was that the difference?*

As I pondered those questions, I waded back to the area of the pool where I had initially jumped in. I wasn't concerned about you wandering off while I was helping the boy, but I felt uncomfortable with you being out of my sight for so long. I assumed you were tracking the drama and would run to me once I exited the pool, and I was surprised when you didn't appear after I climbed out.

"Quince?" I called, hoping you would come find me.

The lifeguards' whistles had drawn curious onlookers from other sections of the park, and the influx of people made it hard to see where you might've wandered off to. As I scanned the crowd, I noticed some onlookers were no longer watching the boy in the yellow bathing suit—they were focused elsewhere. Specifically, they were collectively honed in on a small cluster of people standing in a semi-circle near a corner of the pool. I couldn't make out what was going on through that mass of bodies, and I navigated my way through them to see what was happening.

Everyone in that semicircle was looking down, concerned looks on their faces as they studied something on the ground. I pushed my way through until I could see for myself what had captured their attention. The first thing I saw amid that small crowd was another lifeguard, crouched down as she barked urgent orders into a radio. But then I could make out what she was hovering over, and I froze.

It was you, lying face up on the ground, unconscious, with blood pouring out of your nose and down the sides of your face as if it had no intention of ever stopping.

**12**

*The one question you never want to ask yourself as a parent is, "What have I done?" Yet those four words haunted me after your collapse at the water park.*

*Discovering you in that state left me bewildered and confused, and I struggled to hold myself together in the immediate aftermath. Yet even through that chaos, one truth registered almost immediately. I did that to you. I was the cause. It would take some time to work through exactly what happened, but the details were immaterial. All that mattered was I injured you, and that realization threatened to tear me apart.*

*Following your mother's death, I went through countless rounds of mental gymnastics to identify the various ways in which I failed her, but as time passed, I could accept the irrationality of blaming myself for what happened. But I knew the future held no such reprieve for what I did to you. Simply put, if I had been removed from the picture entirely, you would have been unharmed. But I was there, and by helping the boy in the yellow bathing suit, I placed you in harm's way.*

*I knew it in my bones, even if I didn't understand it.*

*None of my attempted excuses, crafted in the hope of easing my crushing guilt, proved to be sufficient. "I couldn't just let that boy drown!" was my internal rationalization at one point. "I had no idea I was putting Quince in danger!" was another line of thought I tried to embrace. But these excuses were meaningless because they were ultimately irrelevant. My job as a parent wasn't simply to raise you in a nonnegligent manner. I was under an absolute duty to protect you and keep you safe, whatever it took.*

*But I failed.*

*Logically, there was no way I could've known when I leaped to that drowning boy's aid the damage that would result from my intervention. It wasn't remotely on my radar that my actions would push you to the brink of death. But it didn't matter, for one simple reason:*

*Just because something is unforeseeable doesn't mean it can't also be unforgivable.*

∼

*What have I done?*

The question struck again as I sat in a corner of an unfamiliar room in an unfamiliar hospital. You laid unconscious in bed, an arm's reach away, with a ventilator mask covering most of your face. Electronic monitoring equipment surrounded you, but I maneuvered my chair to ensure you'd see me immediately upon regaining consciousness.

Assuming you regained consciousness.

*How long has it been now?* I checked the time on my phone again—a regular habit at that point—and did the math. You had been unconscious for nearly twenty-seven hours. The duration of your coma was long enough that some doctors had already started, as gently as they could, to prepare me for the possibility of brain damage.

If you woke up at all.

*Oh God, what have I done?*

It was a minor blessing you were no longer bleeding out your nose, although that took an inordinate amount of time to stop. Your skin tone in the best of times was fair, but the blood loss had left you at one point looking almost completely white. I thought, as I watched you in bed, that you were regaining some color, which I took as a positive—I was desperate for any hints of recovery.

The doctors had run several tests, which they explained to me in great detail. But as far as I could tell, those tests only left them more confused as to what had happened to you.

*"The CT scan revealed nothing abnormal."*

*"We've ruled out kidney and liver failure."*

*"Nothing remarkable to note after his MRI."*

*"Out of an abundance of caution, we conducted a lumbar puncture, but...."*

*"We're still waiting on the results of his blood test, and...."*

It became harder and harder to focus on what the doctors told me, knowing they were on a wild goose chase, testing for known maladies and not realizing they were contending with something completely alien. If I thought sharing my limited knowledge of your condition with the doctors would help, I would have done so. Yet the doctors couldn't find any physical evidence of what had harmed you, and I was too ashamed to reveal the source of your injuries to them.

It was me.

"What have I done?"

I blinked upon realizing I'd said that one aloud, and I glanced around to make sure no one had come into the room who might've overheard me. Regret for that escaped utterance struck as I recalled what one doctor had told me earlier:

*"Quince can probably hear you in some way. Some studies have concluded that coma patients may experience adverse reactions when negative energy is introduced into the room. So you should talk to him in a positive light while he is unconscious, as much as you can."*

I pushed my guilt and self-loathing aside for the moment, knowing they wouldn't help anything, and thought about what I could say to you. Small talk was never a strong suit of mine.

I took your hand, small and limp in my larger one, and gave it a squeeze.

"Hey, Quince," I said. "It's Daddy. I'm right here. We're going to get you all better, okay?"

You didn't react, and I felt as if I was wasting my breath. But I forced myself to continue.

"I've been here since they brought you in. And I'll be here when you wake up, so don't worry about that. I've just been sitting here waiting for you and thinking. I've been doing a lot of thinking."

I gathered my thoughts—there was no reason to rush that one-sided conversation. Through the door, I could observe constant activity in the hallway, but there was no sign of anyone coming in to check on you.

"Hey, you know how when you work with Ms. Nora, I leave the room to wait for you?" I continued. "I'll let you in on a secret: a few weeks ago, I decided to use that time to go for a walk. Never a long one—I want to make sure I'm there when you and Nora finish. But sometimes I'll venture outside and stroll for a block or two just to get some fresh air. I've really come to enjoy it. On some days, there's this gentle breeze coming off the Hudson River that cools me right off whenever I'm on the verge of sweating. And there's a bakery not that far from Ms. Nora's office—we should visit it when you feel better—and it smells fantastic, although I've never gone inside. I simply stand in front of the glass window of that shop to admire all sorts of colorful cupcakes while savoring the scents for a few minutes. That's enough for me."

I glanced out the window, which revealed a beautiful day. *Perhaps the sun will reposition later so some sunlight comes directly into the room*, I thought, hopeful. *It'd be nice if you could feel some sun while you're stuck in bed.*

"Those walks never struck me as being that big of a deal," I added. "But over the past day I've been sitting here with you, I recognized something. That act of going out by myself and taking a walk solely for pleasure, that's new for me. Your mother and I often went out for walks together, and I enjoyed them because she did. In other words, I did it for her, because her being happy made me happy. Same thing when you and I found a new place to wander around, at least at first. But I realized something's changed."

My throat tightened, and I took a second to collect myself, not wanting you to hear any hint of distress in my voice.

"Since this whole thing started with you in April, all I wanted to do was understand what you were going through, so I could help you," I said, once I regained my composure. "I tried so hard to see the world through your eyes to make sense of it, even though I'm not all that empathetic by nature. But I tried so hard—I really did. And I guess I must've succeeded, at least to some extent, because I can see now that I've changed. In pushing myself to see the world through your eyes, I accidentally learned to see the beauty in it."

I raised my left arm to wipe away my tears with a sleeve while maintaining a hold of your hand.

"But even though you taught me to find that beauty, it's more fun to experience it with you. And that's why you need to get better, buddy. There's still a lot more for us to explore, but we can't do it while you're in a hospital bed. You need to wake up when you're ready, and we'll get back out there. Because there's so much out there waiting for us."

Movement out of the corner of my eye caught my attention, and I was surprised to see Nora hovering at the doorway, unsure if she should enter. I had emailed her earlier that morning to let her know what happened and that we'd miss your next appointment, but I hadn't expected her to show up.

I stood, motioned for her to come in, and immediately set to wondering whether a hug was appropriate. Nora made my indecision a moot point by striding toward me and ensnaring me in a tight embrace.

"It's going to be okay, Will," she murmured in my ear as she held onto me. "I know it."

She pulled back and firmly gripped my arms, staring into my eyes, and only once I nodded in agreement did she relinquish her hold.

"You hear that, Quince?" she said, turning to you on the bed and patting your hand. "You're going to be okay."

I offered her the chair I had been sitting in and dragged another over for myself.

"Thank you for coming," I said as I sat. "You didn't have to do that."

"Of course," she said. "Is it just you or—" She trailed off, but I understood her question.

"My mother- and father-in-law on Long Island said they'd drive up tomorrow to check on him—they are babysitting Quince's cousins and can't make it today. So it's just me for now. When I let them know this morning, they seemed annoyed that I didn't tell them earlier. I tried to explain that there wasn't really a chance to let anyone know what happened until a little while ago, with all the tests and everything." Letting out a deep exhale, I added, "I also had to call my attorney in this litigation I'm involved in to cancel a mediation scheduled for tomorrow, and I could pick up on his irritation, although he tried to hide it. So that's been my morning: just annoying people."

Nora eyed me up and down, giving me a hard look.

"You look exhausted. And are you wearing a bathing suit?"

I glanced down at my swim trunks.

"Yeah, I forgot to bring a change of clothes to the water park, and I've been stuck here, so...." I shrugged, and Nora nodded her understanding.

"How's the little guy doing?" she asked.

"I don't know. He hasn't stirred at all, but he looks peaceful now. Yesterday was rough, with a nosebleed that just wouldn't stop, but at least that's over with."

"Do the doctors have any clue what happened?"

"Nothing came up on their tests, so no. The medical staff is officially stumped." I lowered my voice. "But I know what happened. At least, I think I do."

Nora cocked her head with a questioning look and leaned in to listen.

"Yesterday at the water park, Quince had a vision of a boy drowning and dying," I said. "But then it turned out the boy in his vision was actually there that day—I mean physically present at the park at the same time as us. I made a point of monitoring that kid all morning to ensure he was okay. And then after a while I spotted the boy drowning in the pool, and I jumped in to help him. That boy still needed CPR, but the lifeguards were able to resuscitate him, which differed from what Quince had seen in his vision. And to the best of my knowledge, the moment I jumped into the pool to help that kid was when Quince collapsed."

Nora frowned. "I'm not sure I understand."

"I've thought about this so much since then," I said. "Do you remember when you asked me if it was possible to change one of Quince's future visions? I know the answer now. You can, but it's *hard*. The universe doesn't want things to change, and you have to really fight to cause a deviation. So when I tried to rescue that kid, I could feel reality trying to prevent me. It took all my strength to even move a limb once I decided to jump into the pool to save that boy. But I was able to do it and throw myself in. Only then could I feel that loss of resistance—it was as if I had to exert a ton of energy to push reality onto a different track, but everything was rolling smoothly again once that was done. Only—" I stopped, hesitant to speak a damning truth.

"Only what?" Nora prodded.

"Only that in doing so, I altered Quince's vision of the future." I looked at you, motionless on the bed. "And the act of negating that vision hurt him. It nearly killed him, assuming it doesn't actually—"

I trailed off, looking away, as Nora processed this information.

"You don't know that to be true," she finally said. "It could've just been a coincidence and—" But she stopped when I shook my head.

"No," I said. "A few weeks ago, Quince had another vision of the future. A couple of kids at a playground who fell and injured themselves. I stopped that accident from happening as well, and I felt the same pressure from reality when I tried to change that outcome. Again, it took all of my strength, but I overcame it and fixed things so those children wouldn't be hurt. Quince's nose started bleeding then, too, although I didn't think much of it at the time. You see, that was a minor change, and it only hurt him a little. Yesterday, I significantly altered the future by saving that boy's life, and that change is threatening to kill Quince. I see this now."

Nora was silent for a long time, not knowing what to make of that.

"But why would that be the case?" she finally asked. "Why would changing one of Quince's visions physically hurt him?"

I threw my hands up.

"I don't know. There's no sign of anything physically wrong with him. But—"

"Yes?"

"I have a theory." *Theory* was probably an overstatement, but a picture had manifested in my head while I hovered at your side over the past day.

Nora cocked her head. "Alright, let's hear it."

I took a deep breath.

"Okay. Imagine that our universe is a train making its way down a track. The past is the track behind us, and the future is the track laid out in front. We can only see things based on where the train car is at any given time—that's the *present*."

"Alright," Nora said, letting me know she was with me so far.

"But Quince is different. He can glimpse pieces of the track behind us, as well as portions that lie ahead on this train ride. The *past* and the *future*. His brain is somehow tied to those sections of track. And the past is what it is—there's no changing that. But the future? There's some flexibility there."

I paused when a nurse stuck her head into the room. She looked around, apparently realizing she was in the wrong place, and left. I continued.

"So, like I said, it's possible to change the future. To push the train onto a different track, if you will, although it takes substantial effort to do so. And most of the people on the train won't even recognize that change when it happens— they'll merely feel a smooth train ride. But not Quince. His brain was tied in some fashion to that defunct piece of track, and he feels the tear when he's ripped away from it. And that's how I hurt him: I pushed our reality onto a different track."

Nora processed this in silence, and I wasn't sure if I lost her with my analogy.

"That... is a lot," Nora finally said, and I shrugged.

"It is. And I may be completely off base. All I know for sure is that altering one of Quince's visions of the future hurts him, and if... once Quince wakes up, going forward, whatever he sees about the future, I have to accept that it's meant to be. Because nothing will make me put him through this again."

Nora nodded, looking thoughtful. If she disagreed with anything I was saying, she knew that now wasn't the time to debate it.

"I hear you," she said. "And I know you'll figure all that out once this guy is back on his feet." Nora's face suddenly brightened, as if she had just remembered something. "I'll be right back," she said, abruptly heading out the door.

I didn't know where Nora had gone—I thought it may have just been a quick visit to the women's room—but my curiosity grew when she didn't return after a few minutes.

After twenty minutes went by and Nora still hadn't come back, I wondered whether she had gone home without saying goodbye. But then Nora finally reappeared, about a half hour later, carrying several bags of varying sizes.

"Here are some clothes. I had to guess at your size," she said, handing one bag to me. Inside, I spotted new sweatpants, socks, boxer shorts, and a few T-shirts of various colors.

Before I could thank her, Nora added, "And here's some lunch." As she passed me another plastic bag, she remarked, "Quince told me once that you are both vegetarian. I remember being impressed by him knowing such a large word. So I hope grilled cheese is okay with you?"

"It's perfect," I said, realizing I had eaten nothing in over a day. I salivated at the scent of the sandwich. "Do you mind if I—"

"Of course not," Nora cut in. "Please. Eat."

I scarfed down that food while Nora politely averted her eyes, and after I was done, I went into the small bathroom in the corner of the room to wash up and change into the new clothes Nora had brought me. After I dressed in clean clothes and had some food in my belly, I felt vaguely human once again.

"Thank you so much for all of this," I told Nora, after reemerging in my new clothes. "I'll pay you back for—"

"No, you won't," Nora said firmly. "That was on me."

Not seeing the point in arguing about it, I inclined my head in thanks again and took a seat next to Nora. We watched you together in silence for some time, until a thought occurred to me.

"Hey, how are you holding up?" I asked, turning to Nora.

She blinked before letting out a small chuckle.

"Me?" she said. "I'm worried about you guys, but otherwise I have no complaints."

"Oh, okay. That's good to hear."

I turned back to look at you, but Nora continued to study me, puzzled.

"Why do you ask?" she said. "Should I *not* be okay?"

"Oh. No, it's not that," I said, turning back toward her. "It just struck me that when I see you, all I do is talk about our problems. So I wanted to check in on you."

Nora, looking somewhat amused, rolled her eyes in dramatic fashion.

"Well, yes. We talk about what you and Quince are going through a lot. But that's because you're paying me to help Quince, and I'm doing that to the best of my ability. Granted, this is an odd case that has required me to veer outside of my normal lanes, but you shouldn't feel bad that our conversations are generally focused on you and Quince."

"Fair enough," I said. "And you've been a tremendous help, and you're wonderful at your job. Only...."

"What?"

"Well, you're here now, even though you don't have to be. And at the risk of crossing any inappropriate boundaries, I've come to think of you as a friend to our family. So please don't be shy if there's anything we can do for you, because you've already gone above and beyond for us."

Nora's face was unreadable, and I wondered whether I had inadvertently said something to offend her. I had a propensity for saying the wrong thing, as your mother had often pointed out even if she seemed to find my foot-in-mouth disease somehow endearing.

"That is kind of you to say, Will," Nora finally said. "I appreciate that. But I meant it when I said I was doing okay. I have my share of problems to be sure—I'm no different from anyone else in that regard—but they aren't a drop in the bucket compared to what you two are going through right now."

"What are your problems?" I asked, before quickly adding, "I don't mean to pry, of course, so feel free to ignore that question." But Nora waved off my concern.

"Oh, just little things that pop up now and then," Nora said. "A lot of my drama these days relates to my husband's job. Robert—that's my husband—is contemplating taking a position at a new college, but that will require an out-of-state move, and we aren't quite seeing eye-to-eye on that front yet. I'm not worried for myself—it wouldn't be too difficult for me to reestablish my office elsewhere—but I question what impact such a big move would have on our girls. It would undoubtedly be rough on them."

I felt alarmed that the possibility of Nora moving out of state, away from us, was even a topic of discussion, but I chose not to verbalize that selfish thought. Instead, I gave a sympathetic nod and said, "I'm sure you'll all figure out what's best for your family. And perhaps a move would be hard on your children, but then again, they might surprise you. Kids can be resilient."

"Yes," Nora acknowledged. "They can be."

I started to say something else but stopped upon hearing a new sound in the room. Nora and I both looked toward the door, expecting to see a doctor or nurse coming in, but there was no sign of anyone. After a moment, we heard the sound again—a low groan, nearly inaudible—and we could finally identify the source.

It was you.

~

AND THAT'S how I learned coming out of a coma is not at all like waking up from a nap. It's a slow, gradual process with fits and starts and a great deal of waiting as hints of consciousness teasingly appear, only to slip away. So, even though it wasn't easy or quick, you were finally emerging from your coma.

You remained silent and unconscious after those initial groans, but you showed renewed life an hour later, even if you were still well short of being alert. At one point, you started crying in a sleep-like state, and I was quick to grab your hand and reassure you I was there. Nora couldn't bring herself to leave while you were showing signs of recovery and, after calling her husband to let him know she'd be out longer than expected, she waited in the lobby while the medical staff continued to monitor your progress in regaining consciousness.

It was late afternoon when your eyes finally opened. Upon waking up, you looked confused and scared, and even after I lunged to your side to let you know I was still there, it took some time to calm you down.

"You're in the hospital," I told you, and you blinked.

"The hospital?" you asked, before your eyes closed and you drifted off once again.

I darted out to the lobby to give Nora the update. I spoke as quickly as I could, not wanting to be gone for too long in case you stirred again. Nora was relieved to hear about your progress, but she showed no sign of leaving, even after getting the good news.

"Please, go," I told her. "Thank you so much for coming, and for everything you did, but you should get back to your family. I'll text you whenever I get any news. I think Quince will be okay." And I meant it—it wasn't just wishful thinking on my part.

Nora reluctantly agreed and, after popping back into your room to whisper you a goodbye, left for home. As promised, I sent her regular updates, which all conveyed positive news. My prediction that you would be okay proved to be spot-on as time passed, with increasing signs of a full recovery.

As the hours ticked by, your grip on consciousness became stronger and stronger. Most importantly, there was no sign of any brain damage—you looked to be your old self as you shook off the last remnants of that coma, albeit in a severely weakened state. But that didn't overly concern me —I knew you'd get your strength back in time.

You stayed in the hospital for a few more days to undergo additional neurological tests and general observation. The doctors remained perplexed by what ailed you and insisted on follow-up tests down the road to ensure your episode wouldn't be a recurring issue. But once they ran out of tests to conduct on you, the doctors agreed you could be discharged.

To your delight, you exited the hospital via wheelchair, and you giggled for the duration of that ride. The nurse pushing you seemed to get a kick out of your antics and playfully accommodated you by moving the wheelchair left or right in response to your pantomimed steering. You still looked tired and weak by the time you were loaded in the car, which I had retrieved from the water park a few days earlier while your grandparents kept you company for a few hours. Still, there was a sparkle in your eyes that led me to believe the entire ordeal at the hospital would one day be seen as nothing more than a close call. An extremely close call, at that. But one that wouldn't leave any lasting damage.

To be sure, I counted myself lucky that I was leaving the hospital with the same boy I brought to the water park earlier that week, and I vowed never to put you at risk like that again.

"Are we going home, Daddy?" you asked as I pulled out of the hospital parking lot.

"We are," I said, glancing at you in the rearview mirror.

"Am I sick? Is that why I needed the hospital?"

"You were," I told you. "But you're better now. And we're going to make sure you don't get sick like that ever again."

*Whatever it takes.*

# 13

*Realizing I couldn't act upon your visions of the future was a double-edged sword.*

*On the one hand, no longer would I have to grapple with the uncertainty that manifested whenever you foresaw someone's wretched fate. And since the past was behind us, and the future was untouchable as far as I was concerned, there wasn't much left for me to worry about other than how your visions might impact your personal development. Gone were the days when I'd have to follow a child throughout a water park to ensure his safety, or lose sleep wondering how I could prevent a car crash when nothing was known other than the site of the accident. My inability to act on your premonitions brought a certain degree of peace, given that there was no reason to wrestle with indecision once the ability to make a decision was taken off the table.*

*And yet....*

*I knew there'd be occasions where I'd be required to steel my heart and watch someone obliviously head toward some preordained doom. Perhaps if I was religious, those situations would have been easier to accept, in that I could simply write off those dark outcomes as representing God's will, but that wasn't a luxury I possessed. There would undoubtedly be times that the weight of immeasurable guilt would crush me, but still, I was prepared to accept that shame.*

*At some point—when you were older and had a better understanding of your visions—I knew you'd inherit the strain that comes with consciously allowing bad things to happen, and I dreaded the day when you would share my burden. You would see people hurt, or even die, yet be powerless to help them, and I knew that would run afoul of everything you are. But that was a problem for another day. For the meantime, I was thankful that the impossible load was mine alone to bear, no matter how much it ultimately tore me up inside.*

*It was a price I was willing to pay, no matter the cost.*

THE DAYS FOLLOWING your release from the hospital were a period of healing for you. I took time off work while you regained your strength. You slept upwards of fourteen hours a night, which was quite out of character for you, as your body slowly recovered from your ordeal. When you had sufficient strength to get out of bed or off the couch, we spent our time assembling Lego sets, and you were surprisingly adept at following the illustrated directions that came with each of the kits. There were times you spent hours focused on diligently following instructions as you meticulously crafted some building or vehicle, and I wondered how many other four-year-olds possessed that type of attention span.

After a week at home, I sensed you had recovered enough to return to summer camp at your school, which was only a few hours in the morning. You didn't object upon being taken back there, but I noticed that you'd revert to your semi-mute state upon arriving at your school each morning. I remained troubled by the fact you'd be starting pre-K there in September, since I had been unsuccessful in finding any other viable options.

In mid-August, I finally received something of a break in that regard. After dropping you off at camp one morning, my phone vibrated with a call I normally would've ignored, but the fact that it was coming from a local 845 area code piqued my curiosity.

"Is this Will Banfield?" a pleasant-sounding woman's voice asked once I answered.

"Yes," I replied in a cautious tone, bracing for a donation request.

"Hello!" the woman replied brightly. "This is Michelle from Tiny Toes Preschool! You reached out to me earlier this summer about availability in our program, and I told you at the time that we were all filled up for the year."

"Oh, yes. I remember." Tiny Toes was a small but prestigious preschool in our town that offered morning preschool classes. The school focused on art and I thought it would have been a perfect fit for you given your gentle nature. But when I reached out to that school earlier in the summer, they told me that the class, which they capped at a dozen students, had already filled up.

"Well, it so happens we *just* had a boy drop out of our class for this September. I came across your contact information, and I figured I'd reach out to see if you were still looking for a program for Qu—" She paused, and I sensed she was struggling to pronounce your name.

"It's Quince," I cut in. "One syllable. And yes, we are absolutely still interested in your program." I thought it over for a second and decided maybe a little due diligence was warranted, no matter how badly I wanted you to get a fresh start at a new school. "Well, at least, I think so," I corrected myself. "Would it be possible to show the school to Quince and see how he takes to it?"

"Of course!" Michelle said with a laugh. "I'll actually be at the school all day today if you're available to swing by. I'd love to meet Quince!"

"Sounds great," I said. "Thank you so much. We'll come over this afternoon. I'm sure Quince will love it."

The future felt slightly less scary after that. You desperately needed a change in scenery, and it felt serendipitous to receive that call in response to my prayers. The ordeal at the hospital already seemed as if it was long in the past, with you not showing any hint of long-term effects, and I felt as if I finally knew enough about your visions to avoid putting you in harm's way again. It had been an undeniably bumpy road, but at last the worst truly seemed behind us.

After I picked you up from camp that afternoon, you realized immediately that we weren't driving home.

"Where are we going?" you asked from the back seat.

"We're going to look at a new school," I said. "Maybe a new place for you to go next month. Would you like that?"

But you didn't respond. *Fair enough*, I thought. *I can't blame you for wanting to see the school before you commit.*

Tiny Toes sat on the edge of the business area of our town, and its small parking lot was nearly empty when we arrived. You spotted the school immediately, or, more specifically, a narrow play area in front of the school with several slides and plastic toys scattered in and around a sandbox.

"Can I play there?" you asked.

"Maybe after we meet your teacher," I said, holding your hand and guiding you to the door.

"Why is that girl crying?" you asked, pointing at nothing, and I let out a sigh before stopping.

You followed my lead and stopped as well, staring at an unremarkable area by the front door. Crouching down so I could look you in the eyes, I said, "That is a girl I can't see. And we are going to meet your teacher now, and she probably can't see the girl either. So when we meet Ms. Michelle, if you see any other children, just know they aren't really there, okay?"

You nodded.

"And try not to talk about them. At least not in front of your teacher. You and I can talk about whatever you see afterwards. I don't want to confuse Ms. Michelle."

"Okay, Daddy," you said. I hoped you understood the nature of my request and, more importantly, would remember it while we were visiting the school.

"Anyway. The girl that is crying," I said. "Is she with a mommy or daddy?"

You nodded again. "I think so. I think it's her mommy."

"She's probably someone who went to this school last year and felt scared about going for the first time. Sometimes children are nervous when they have to go to a new school. But you can be brave, right?"

You gave a small bob of your head—a timid "yes."

It surprised me that you only experienced one vision of a child resisting being dropped off at preschool. Come to think of it, I realized you never had that sort of vision at your current school. *Whoever he is seeing must have been utterly terrified for her fears to leave an imprint like that,* I thought. But I knew that was just the nature of taking toddlers to preschool sometimes, and I didn't hold it against Tiny Toes.

We walked together to a glass door, and I gave it a soft knock, which prompted you to hide behind my leg. A moment later, a kind-looking woman appeared at the door, a beatific smile spread across her face as she opened the door for us. She was tall and slender, her graying hair pulled back with a hair clip, and wearing loose-fitting bohemian clothes.

"Hello!" she said by way of greeting. I attempted to walk in but struggled with you clutching my right leg. After gently prying you off, I took you by the hand and tried to coax you inside.

"Hi, I'm Will. And this is Quince," I added, with a nod down toward you. You didn't seem as if you wanted to enter, and Michelle picked up on your anxiety.

"It is wonderful to meet you, Quince," she said, squatting down to your level. Michelle suddenly put her finger to her lips in an exaggerated expression of thoughtfulness. "You know what, Quince? I have some toys inside if you'd like to come look at them."

You thought it over before responding with a tight nod. Michelle held out a hand, and I was caught by surprise when you took it and allowed her to escort you in.

Once inside, your eyes grew wide upon taking in the classroom. The room contained a reading area with a plush circular rug at its center, as well as a small table accompanied by several child-sized chairs. Books, costumes, train sets, blocks, and other worn but usable toys filled the rest of the room.

"What do you see, Quince?" Michelle asked, her hands on her knees. You looked around, not knowing where to start, before running to a cage positioned on top of a bookcase. You pointed at it, looking to Michelle for an explanation.

"Oh, that is our class guinea pig, Charlotte!" Michelle explained. "Do you like guinea pigs?"

I wasn't sure if you'd ever seen a guinea pig, but you bobbed your head with great enthusiasm. Michelle reached into the cage and carefully extracted the large rodent, which squirmed in her grasp.

"It's okay," Michelle told you in a hushed tone. "You can pet her."

You threw me a quick look to confirm that I had no objections before extending a cautious hand to pet Charlotte. You giggled on making contact, and then gave her a few more soft strokes on her back.

"I can tell already that Charlotte loves you, Quince!" Michelle exclaimed as she returned the guinea pig to the cage, prompting you to laugh again.

"Charlotte loves me, Daddy!" you squealed, turning to me.

"She sure does!" I agreed.

Once Charlotte was resettled in her cage, you took to exploring the rest of the room. Michelle followed at a distance, talking in a manner that invited conversation but putting no pressure on you to respond.

"I wonder what that wand does?" she asked at one point when you picked up a plastic stick to study. Michelle suddenly snapped her fingers. "Oh yes! I believe that's the wand that can turn people into frogs. So please be careful with that one, Quince!"

You studied the toy wand with renewed interest and then pointed it at Michelle. Michelle's eyes went wide before she crouched low to the ground, hopping in place.

"Ribbit!" she croaked. "Ribbit!"

"Uh oh!" I said, picking up on the nature of the game. "You better point that at her to turn her back! Quick!"

Startled, you nodded and again thrust the wand in Michelle's direction, this time with greater emphasis. Michelle stood back up, looking relieved.

"Oh, thank goodness!" she said, blinking and stretching

her limbs. "I thought I was going to be a frog forever! Thank you, Quince!"

You cracked a smile, and I knew right then we had found you the right school.

You continued to explore the toys in the room, and after Michelle saw you were comfortable, she came over to me to chat.

"Wow! He seems like a great kid!" she said as she approached.

"Thank you! And yes—he is," I said.

"While we have a minute," she said, "why don't I tell you a bit about our program? It is three hours, from nine to noon, Monday through Friday. We have a small class—our enrollment is currently eleven, with room for one more if you're interested—and our focus is on learning through play. Creativity is very important here, and the children love to put on a play for the parents in the fall. In the spring, we spend several weeks focusing on art, and we dedicate each day to a different artistic style. The children really love Jackson Pollock day, where we put plastic sheets up around the room and really just let them have fun flinging paint around. They will definitely need a bath afterward, but it's well worth it."

"It sounds amazing," I said, speaking the truth. The class she was describing seemed to have a gentle energy that I thought would suit you well.

"We also have a great relationship with the town," Michelle added. "There's a community center across the road that we use a few times throughout the year, including a holiday pageant we put on in December with some other schools in the area. We hold that pageant after work so most parents can usually attend, which is great because it is adorable. The center also allows us to use their space in

June for an art show where we can show off the children's work for the parents and anyone else who may be interested. It adds a formality to the event that the children just love. Are you familiar with the community center?"

"I'm actually not," I admitted. "But we moved here just as the pandemic hit, so we may not have had occasion to see it in full swing."

Michelle nodded in understanding.

"Yes, they've been mostly dormant these past few years," she said. "But I think they're finally restarting again, which I'm so happy to see. It's such a wonderful space for the entire community. We really felt its absence."

Michelle checked her watch.

"I actually finished up my work here today much quicker than I thought I would, so I was going to head home in a few minutes," she said, "but if you and Quince are interested in seeing the community center, I'm happy to walk you over there on my way out. It's just across the road."

"Oh. Sure!" I answered with great enthusiasm, even though I wasn't all that curious about it. But I figured it would be rude to decline Michelle's polite offer.

"Hey, Quince!" I called out, and you looked up from a toy train you were studying. "We are going to go look at something across the street now, okay?"

"What is it?" you asked without getting up.

"It's...." I paused, trying to think of how to describe it. "I don't know exactly. But that's why we should go look at it—so we can figure that out."

You processed this and seemingly accepted my logic because you put the train down and ran back to me, hopping up and down in place.

"Do you need the bathroom?" I asked, noting your pee-pee dance.

"No," you insisted. "I'm okay."

Michelle gave you a moment in case you changed your mind and then shrugged with a smile.

"Okay then!" she said. "Let's go take a walk."

Michelle followed us after we exited, locking the door behind her. You held my hand as we traversed the parking lot, continuing to bounce up and down as you walked. But you stopped once we reached the street and looked back toward the school.

"I have to use the bathroom!" you declared, drawing a sigh out of me.

"Look, Quince!" Michelle jumped in, pointing at a large building diagonally across the road. "That's the community center! They'll have a bathroom in there you can use. Is that okay?"

You nodded and allowed us to continue across the street.

"This is a great space," Michelle commented as we walked. "So much of the town's life runs through here. This center hosts theater groups throughout the year, and they do so much for the children, whether it is hosting Easter egg hunts in the spring or harvest festivals in the fall. There's an open space behind the main building bordering a cornfield owned by a nearby farm, so in the weeks leading up to Halloween they'll work with that farm to build a corn maze that's incorporated into their autumn festivals. It's so much fun!"

"I had no idea this place was even here," I said.

"Well, as I said, it was mostly shut down these past few years. But I understand things are finally starting up again. Knock on wood."

We arrived at the front doors of the center. On the side of the building, there was a small parking lot positioned in front of a tall fence that ran parallel to the lot. Near the building there was an opening in the fence, perhaps ten feet wide, through which I could see a grassy field I assumed was the space behind the building Michelle had alluded to earlier.

Once inside the building, we found ourselves in a large lobby. I was taken aback by the space—it somehow seemed larger than the outside view suggested. Several sets of doors were on the right, and through the open ones, I could make out a small auditorium with a stage area in the front. But I knew we'd have to hold off on checking out that room—the first order of business was finding you a bathroom.

I spotted the men's room at the other end of the lobby and pointed it out to you, but you didn't respond. As I crouched down to get your attention, I noticed you were lost in your own thoughts. You scanned the lobby with wide eyes and an open mouth, and I could tell from your expression that you weren't merely impressed by the architecture.

Something was disturbing you.

I leaned close to you and whispered, "Are you seeing something?"

You nodded, looking perturbed by whatever vision you were experiencing. I was aware of Michelle hovering near us, so I put my mouth right next to your ear.

"We can talk about whatever you're seeing later, okay?" I murmured. "Let's just get you to the bathroom, and then we'll leave."

You absently bobbed your head as it swiveled around, gazing at the floor around you, a troubled expression on your face. I took your hand and gave Michelle a tight smile.

"Excuse us," I said, gesturing toward the men's room.

"Of course!" she responded.

But as we got closer to the bathroom, I spotted a woman inside mopping the floors around the urinal. *Damn it,* I thought. I eyed the women's room, wondering if anyone would object to us going in there, given that the building appeared to be mostly empty. As I was assessing my options, a balding man in a polo shirt entered the lobby and looked us over before diagnosing my dilemma.

"Ah, the never-ending quest for a bathroom!" the man bellowed. A moment later he spotted Michelle, standing at the far end of the lobby, and called out, "Hello, Michelle! What brings you here?"

"Hi Steve! I'm just showing this potential new student the space!" she called back.

"A new student?" Steve said, turning back to us. "Well, in that case, I'll let you in on a little secret: I'm the manager here, and my office is back down that way." He pointed to the hallway from which he'd emerged. "And if you go a little further, past my office, there's another small bathroom you can use."

"Thank you so much," I said. "That would be amazing."

"It's my pleasure!" Steve proclaimed before walking off to chat with Michelle.

I followed the man's directions, and you accompanied me in increasingly halting steps.

"Come on, Quince," I said once you slowed to a near stop. "I thought you had to go potty?"

You didn't look at me—you remained distracted by whatever you were seeing. I took you by the hand to prompt you, and you allowed me to lead you into the hallway. On reaching that passage, you paused, looking puzzled as you stared out a window facing the back area, but then you snapped out of it and continued a few more steps before freezing in your tracks. Your face displayed shock, which then gave way to something else.

Terror.

Pure, abject terror.

"Stop it," you said, not to me but to the open space in front of us. You took a cautious step forward and turned slightly, focused on something invisible to me, before saying with increased urgency, "Stop it!"

*This is new*, I thought, dread settling in. *He's never spoken to a vision before.*

"Quince," I said under my breath. Something bad was happening, and I wanted to leave right away. "Are you okay? Can we just go to the bathroom and get out of here?"

I tried to hold your hand, but you shook me off and took another tentative step forward without looking at me.

"You stop it!" you cried again, your high-pitched voice cracking in its fury. Your words echoed throughout the lobby, and I could hear Steve and Michelle's footsteps as they hurried toward us.

"Is everything okay?" Michelle asked on arriving, but you ignored her. You continued to stare at something unseeable to the rest of us, and you appeared both terrified and angry.

"Stop it! Stop it, stop it, stop it!" you commanded, sounding increasingly frantic, and I could sense Michelle's and Steve's confusion, even though I didn't take my eyes off you.

*What the hell is he seeing?* I wondered. *This is the worst one yet.* So strong was my desire to leave that I contemplated tucking you under my arm and sprinting out of there, consequences be damned.

"Quince," I said, trying once more to recapture your attention without making more of a scene than we already had. But you kept staring straight ahead, and the defiant fury on your face dissolved into a look of helplessness. "Quince, I think we should—"

But you ignored me, and I could see you mentally over-come your despair to resummon your anger, which spilled out of you with a command that shook me to my core.

"Don't do it!" you called out, before gathering your breath to scream again.

"Don't you hurt my daddy!"

My mouth dropped open. *Oh.*

Michelle and Steve looked at one another, each looking for an explanation of what was happening. You continued to stand with your back to us, watching... something. But then you let out a stifled sob, which you caught almost immedi-ately, and continued watching whatever you were viewing. The rest of us stood there, frozen with uncertainty, as you remained transfixed on the scene you were witnessing. After a few moments, you snapped out of your shock and let out an anguished cry, which echoed through the building as you abruptly broke into a run, heading back toward the lobby.

"I...." But I trailed off, my mouth moving wordlessly, before I gave up on trying to explain anything. "I should get him," was all I said.

I walked after you at first, but picked up my pace after realizing you weren't letting up in your run. You sprinted through the lobby and pushed your way out the front door to the area in front of the community center. I caught up to you and grabbed you by your shoulders before you reached the street. Not realizing that it was me who seized you, you flailed in my grasp, but I turned you around to ensnare you in a hug.

"It's okay. It's okay," I murmured, rubbing your back. Your body heaved as you sobbed against my chest, and I didn't rush you as far as letting those emotions out.

"The man hurt you," you said in a small broken voice

once you collected yourself somewhat. You sucked in air through your nose, trying to keep snot from escaping, before repeating in a breathless voice, "The man hurt you."

"What man?" I asked, but you didn't respond.

"How do you know the man hurt me?" I asked. Again, you didn't answer, so I offered a leading question: "Was I bleeding?"

After a moment, you nodded your head.

"A lot of blood?"

You squeezed your eyes tight, not wanting to relive the memory, before nodding again.

I took a deep breath. *Okay*, I thought. *That's something.* I was relieved to gain some insight into what you saw, even though it sounded grim.

"And what happened after I started bleeding?" I asked. When you didn't answer, I added, "What did I do?"

You thought it over.

"Nothing," you said, wiping tears out of your eyes with a sleeve.

"Nothing?"

"Yes. Nothing."

I frowned, trying to ascertain your meaning.

"I don't understand," I said, and then a thought hit me. "Can you show me what I did after the man hurt me?" You showed no sign of responding, which compelled me to add, "Please, Quince. It's important."

"Umm," you muttered, processing what I was asking of you.

At first you didn't move, and I wondered whether you simply didn't understand my request. But then you lowered yourself to the ground, laying on your back with one arm sprawled to the side and the other pressed against your hip. Upon settling in that position, you didn't move—you laid as still as a statue. As troubling as that was, it wasn't the worst of it. No, it was what you did with your eyes that made my heart race even faster than it already was.

As you lay on the ground, recreating what you saw me do in your vision, you didn't blink at all. Instead, your eyes remained open, unfocused and lifeless, blind to the blue sky above. I observed you, waiting for you to reveal some hint of life as you pantomimed your vision of my future.

But you didn't.

# PART III

*The Choices I Made*

# 14

I had no reason to fear death before you entered my life.

I'd met spiritual or religious people who seemed downright giddy at the prospect of death. Others to cross my path have been open about their deep-seated dread of their inevitable demise. But I didn't fall into either camp—I'd largely been apathetic to the question of what would happen to me after I died. If I had to guess, I suspected the afterlife was probably just a lot of nothing, but that didn't trouble me, since my primary goal in life before meeting your mother was simply avoiding pain or annoyance.

In that light, nothingness suited me just fine.

Things changed once you were born. One night, a week or two after I took you home, I found myself unable to sleep, and I lay at your side for hours with random thoughts shooting through my mind. As I watched you in my exhausted but sleepless state, an errant memory surfaced about a musician I admired who unexpectedly passed away in his sleep at the age of forty-one —roughly the same age I was at the time. I couldn't avoid envisioning what would happen to you if I were also to die in my sleep. How long would it take until someone even noticed that I was gone? What would happen to you, a newborn baby, if your *sole caretaker were to suddenly perish? Those questions were too terrifying to explore, yet I couldn't push them aside, and fear kept me from sleeping at all that night.*

*The next day I called my in-laws—your mother's parents— who lived in the area, and I explained that out of an abundance of caution, I wanted to text them every morning to confirm I survived the night. If there ever came a morning when I failed to check in, I asked them to follow up and, if necessary, take steps to ensure you were safe. I'm sure they thought I was being overly paranoid, but they readily agreed, if only to give me one less thing to worry about. That routine was enough of a safety mechanism to allow me to sleep again, and those morning texts to the in-laws became a habit I continued until you were over three years old.*

*That was the only time in my life I had occasion to worry about death, even though that fear was more linked to ensuring your safety than any self-preservation concerns. Thankfully, that worry faded over time until it was nothing but a distant memory. At least, it was, until I learned about your vision at our town's community center. Because at that point, my fear not only found renewed life.*

*It became all-consuming.*

"WHAT ARE YOU GOING TO DO?" Nora asked.

We were at our Saturday session with Nora, a few days after the incident at the community center, and I had just finished recapping that fiasco to her while you sat on the floor with your pooping puppy. You weren't nearly as engaged with the toy as you had been in the past, and I wasn't sure whether that was because you were tiring of it or if you were still working through the trauma of what you'd seen a few days earlier.

I had hoped Nora might have some advice for dealing with our latest dilemma. She had a knack for offering simple but practical advice, or at least seeing problems in a different way than I did. But Nora didn't spring forth with any clear guidance after I got her up to speed. Instead, she looked as stupefied as I'd felt over the past few days.

"What do you mean?" I asked, confused by her question.

"I mean, what are you going to do about what Quince saw relating to you?" she said. When I didn't answer, she added, "You can drive hundreds of miles south this afternoon and set up a new life, and make a point of never again setting foot in New York state, let alone that community center. And you would be safe."

"True," I admitted, speaking as softly as I could manage so you wouldn't overhear us. "But that would render Quince's vision a lie. And I believe that would kill him."

"I know you don't want to hurt him," Nora said, "but he survived last time and—"

"He was in a coma for over twenty-four hours last time," I interrupted. "And I saw firsthand how dicey things were—trust me when I say he nearly died. I don't think he could survive another one of those."

"But he might," Nora pressed, albeit with little conviction. I shook my head.

"What odds would you give that?" I pressed. "What odds would you need in order to risk your child's life to save your own?"

Nora let out a deep breath, collecting her thoughts.

"Of course you want to keep Quince safe," she said in a measured tone. "But what do you think will happen if you allow what he saw to come to pass? There's more to protecting Quince than keeping him safe from physical harm. He's already lost his mother. How do you think—"

"I know, Nora!" The words erupted out of me, and I was taken aback by how harsh I sounded. After forcing myself to take a deep calming breath, I added in a softer voice, "Do you really think I don't know this?"

Nora didn't seem upset by my outburst—she only looked uncharacteristically helpless. And sad. I had never seen her look so sad.

"I'm sorry," I said. "It's just—"

"Yeah, I know," she said. "I'm sorry, too. And all things considered, you're handling this much better than I would if I were in your shoes."

"It's funny," I said, even though I felt nothing close to humor. "For most of my life, if I'd been told my death was imminent, I don't think I would've been that bothered. There were times I might've even welcomed the news, as messed up as that is. But at this point, I very much would prefer not to die anytime soon. And it's because of him." I jerked my head toward you on the floor, where you were halfheartedly pushing the pooping puppy around. "He's already lost his mother—it kills me to believe he's destined to be an orphan sooner than later. But even putting Quince aside, I don't want to die. Despite all the adversity we've faced over the course of these past few months, I no longer wake up looking forward to nothing, other than going back to bed at the end of the day. I'm legitimately enjoying life. Or, at least, I was until a few days ago."

Nora remained silent and attentive, inviting me to say more.

"But you said I'm handling this well," I added. "If that's true, it's because I'm at peace with the choice I've made. It looks like it's either me or Quince. And that's no choice at all."

Nora opened her mouth to speak and paused, choosing her words carefully.

"What if it's not that simple?" she finally said.

"What do you mean?" I asked. But I knew what she was getting at.

"You weren't the only thing Quince saw at that center Whenever this happens, it sounds like it's something big Something bigger than just you. What if—"

I cut her off.

"Whatever hypothetical you throw at me, I promise you I already went through it myself." I grimaced—the one area where my imagination seemed to be boundless was in conjuring worst-case scenarios. "I ran through all of them in my head multiple times. And the bottom line is, I can't hurt Quince again. Whatever that takes."

That sharp truth was a harsh position to articulate, and I had to look away from Nora out of fear of what the judgment in her eyes might convey. Desperate to change the subject, I continued.

"Two days ago, I reached out to my sister-in-law, Ronnie. I didn't get into the details, but I told her I'd been thinking about what would happen to Quince in the event of my unexpected passing, and I asked if she'd be willing to take him on in that scenario. She readily agreed, although she has no idea how soon I'm planning to cash in that check. It's a huge ask of her, but Ronnie has three children of her own, so I know she can handle it. Her kids are much wilder than Quince, or at least they were the last time I saw them, but Quince should be okay with that arrangement. He's resilient."

I didn't mention the rest of my conversation with Ronnie, in which she lamented she hadn't seen Quince in such a long time and that I'd been rejecting all of her invitations to get together over the past year. She was absolutely right, of course, although I had enough on my plate without worrying about scheduling a family get-together. I put her off with a vague promise to meet up sometime soon, and she seemed satisfied enough.

"I'm seeing a lawyer next week to formalize that plan in a will," I added. "But beyond that, there's something else I need to take care of. And only you can do it for me."

"What's that, Will?" Nora asked. I handed her a sealed envelope labeled, "For Ronnie."

"I wrote down everything I've gone through with Quince over the past few months concerning his visions. Everything we've learned. Ronnie will have to understand all of this if she's taking care of him, but I don't want her to know until it's absolutely necessary. So when the time comes, I need you to give this envelope to her and make sure she takes it seriously. Do whatever you can to make her believe it."

"I can do that," Nora said, before quickly adding, "if it becomes necessary." I nodded my thanks.

"There may come a time you'll need to talk to Quince yourself," I added. "Because one day Quince will be old enough to act on his visions. He's going to see some glimpses of the future and want to change things for the better. That's just who he is. So if you have the sense that Ronnie isn't buying into this, I need you to find Quince before he can hurt himself and explain all of this to him directly. Let him know the cost that comes with changing what he sees of the future and convince him he has to leave those visions alone. Can you promise me that, Nora?"

Nora stared at me, and I knew what was running through her mind. She wanted to reassure me that those precautions were unnecessary. She longed to tell me my efforts to protect Quince posthumously were unwarranted. She wished she could tell me everything would be just fine.

But she couldn't.

"I'll do that," she finally said. "I swear it."

Nora's promise removed at least one of the many weights I'd been carrying, and I mouthed a silent "thank you" to her. It was an important burden to lay at her feet, but I was confident she'd be able to offer you whatever guidance you needed when the time was right.

"How's he taking it?" Nora asked, tilting her head in your direction.

"It's hard to tell. His sleep hasn't been great the past few days. He's waking up a few times a night and calling out for me. And I've tried on several occasions to talk to him about what he saw, but he just shuts down. Quince seemed traumatized in many ways when he first started dealing with these visions, but he worked through that as he gained a better understanding of what he was seeing. But this thing he saw with me... it seems to have set him back."

"Did you get any more information out of him?" Nora asked. "Anything at all?"

"No. But I didn't press him that hard."

Nora shifted in her seat and grabbed a legal pad and pen from her desk.

"Okay," she said. "Let's go through what we know and don't know. For example, do you have any hints about when whatever Quince saw will come to pass?"

"Well, his teacher mentioned the class has a couple of functions at the community center throughout the year that I would attend in the ordinary course. Some sort of holiday recital in December and an art show in the spring."

Nora jotted a few notes and then lowered her pen to look at me.

"Quince is still in that class?" she asked. "There were no issues after his teacher saw that whole incident?"

"I called her later, and the drama unsettled her, to be sure. But I believe I convinced her that Quince's outburst was an aberration, although she made a point of warning me that she had to release some students from the program in prior years because she couldn't address their special behavioral needs. Perhaps she's hedging her bets with us? But I'm sure everything will be fine once Quince starts school and goes a few days with no issues."

"Okay." Nora picked up her pen again and studied her notes. "So we are looking at a recital in December or an art show in spring, most likely. Is there any way to narrow it down further?"

I thought it over, trying to remember everything Michelle told me when we met a few days earlier.

"I believe the recital will be held in the evening. Well, late afternoon, but effectively night since we're talking about mid-December. The art show takes place during the day— probably in the morning, since that is when their class meets. But I don't know if Quince could tell if what he saw was happening during daylight or at night."

Nora jotted down a few more notes.

"Okay, we'll come back to that. Now, you said he saw you injured and, apparently, killed. Do you have any idea how that goes down?"

I shook my head. "Not really. I was assuming a gunshot wound, but that's just an educated guess."

"Based on what?"

"Well, not much more than the fact we live in America. But no, I didn't get into those specifics with Quince."

Nora rolled her eyes, and I wasn't sure if she felt frustrated with me or the overall situation.

"Do you know anything about the person who hurt you?"

"No."

"Do you know if you were the only person hurt?"

"Not really, although Quince was clearly seeing some things in the lobby before getting to the hallway where he started yelling about me. Again, he shut down when I tried to ask him about those other visions."

Nora continued to take notes while I awaited her next question, but then we were interrupted.

"Are you talking about me?"

You stood between me and Nora, head swiveling as you looked for either of us to answer your question. I had no idea how long you'd been listening. My eyes flicked to Nora, who gave a subtle tilt of her head, conveying I should respond to you.

"Well, yes," I said. "We were talking about the thing you saw the other day, where you saw me get hurt."

Your face darkened, and I could tell you were on the verge of shutting down again. I threw a pleading glance at Nora, silently begging for her to intervene, and she picked up on my unspoken request.

"Quince," she said, getting out of her seat and kneeling next to you to place a reassuring hand on your shoulder. "Your daddy told me you saw something very scary, and I'm so sorry that happened to you. We were talking about that to make sure what you saw never actually happens to your daddy. Because that would be very sad, right?"

Some of the anger left your face, and you nodded, although you still looked uncomfortable with the topic of conversation.

"One thing we were talking about was trying to learn *when* the thing you saw might happen. That will help us keep your daddy safe. I know this isn't easy for you to talk about, but do you know if the scary things you saw happened during the day, or at night?"

You looked down, and I could sense you didn't want to answer.

"Please, Quince," Nora said in a soft voice. "If you know, I promise it will be a big help to your daddy."

You continued to look down as you muttered, "I don't know."

I shrugged at Nora, but she remained focused on you.

"Think, Quince," she pleaded. "When you saw that stuff, did you happen to look out a window? Was it dark outside?"

You closed your eyes, deep in thought. "Yes, it was dark outside."

*It was bright and sunny when we were at the community center*, I recalled. *If he saw darkness, that was part of the vision.*

"Was there anything else you saw that made you think it was night? For example, could you see stars? Or the moon?" Nora asked, prompting you to close your eyes again and think.

"Yes!" you said after a moment. You sounded excited to have a helpful answer, finally. "I did! I did see the moon!"

"Are you sure?" Nora pressed.

"Yes," you said. "I remember seeing the moon out the window."

You sounded confident, and I thought we had managed to at least possibly pinpoint the day your vision would become reality: the holiday recital in December, which was less than four months away. *That's not far off*, I thought. *At least in the context of how much longer I have to live.*

"Can I ask you another question?" Nora asked, and you gave a reluctant nod.

"Do you know the person who hurt your daddy?" Nora

continued. You winced, struck by the memory of your vision, and you emphatically shook your head "no."

"Did you see that man hurt anyone else?" Nora said, and again you grimaced at the question.

"No!" you burst out, although it wasn't clear if you were answering her or simply voicing your objection to the entire line of questioning. "No more questions! I don't want to talk about this anymore." You turned to me, a pleading expression on your face. "I don't want to do this anymore, Daddy. Can we go home?"

Nora and I shared a look, and I could see we'd reached the same conclusion: we would not make any more progress with you that day, so we should just move on.

"We don't have to talk about that anymore," I told you. "How about if you just play with Ms. Nora for a bit, and then we'll go home?" You took a moment to think over that proposal.

"Okay," you finally said.

*Maybe one day we can talk about this again*, I thought. It was frustrating, knowing so much more information about my ultimate fate was just out of reach. *I have four months* I reminded myself. *There will be other opportunities to discuss this. I have to be patient.*

I stood up to leave the office so you and Nora could get to work, and on my way out, I leaned close to Nora's ear.

"Thank you for that," I whispered to her. "That's more information than I started with, so it was some progress, at least."

"He just needs time to process what he saw," Nora said. "I'm sure we'll get more out of him when he's ready."

I nodded, but Nora grabbed my arm before I could walk away.

"We should also keep in mind that we may be

completely misunderstanding what he saw. We're assuming the worst, but we could be wrong." She forced a small smile, as if trying to lend weight to her fanciful optimism.

I shrugged a "maybe."

"It's possible," I admitted. "And if that's the case, then in a few months we'll be looking back and laughing at all of this worrying we're doing right now. So, of course, I hope we're wrong."

I didn't bother to finish the rest of that thought.

*But I don't think we are.*

# 15

*You were always a cautious kid.*

*As an infant you were slow to crawl, and even once you did, it was still many months later, well after your first birthday, before you attempted your first steps. I was initially concerned about those possible developmental delays until I noticed something: while other children your age may have been quicker to get up and run around, they were constantly falling or otherwise crashing into obstacles. By contrast, when you decided you were ready to try ambulating on your feet, after those first few wobbly steps, you were remarkably sure-footed. I can probably count on one hand the number of times you fell while you were learning to walk, and I don't think I ever had to bandage a skinned knee. Not even once.*

*My takeaway was that it simply wasn't your nature to rush headlong into new endeavors—you were more than comfortable taking your time to study and reflect upon an unfamiliar pursuit before trying it yourself, which more often than not allowed you, both literally and figuratively, to hit the ground running.*

*As a result, your developmental milestones manifested in spurts. You had a tendency to avoid a new activity—whether it was riding a tricycle, jumping on a trampoline, or going down a playground slide—for prolonged periods, taking the time to mentally prepare, only to one day suddenly exhibit a new skill with surprising dexterity. There were very few instances of watching you learn something through trial and error—most of the preparatory work seemed to happen internally.*

*Over time, I learned to stop worrying about when you reached those developmental milestones. Even on those occasions when other children your age were doing things you didn't seem close to pulling off, there would inevitably come a day when your own abilities burst out with no hint of any delays whatsoever. Like all children, you were constantly growing—you simply kept most of that growth bottled up inside until it was ready to be revealed.*

*That's why, with the gift of hindsight, I realize I should've known your speech would follow a similar pattern.*

∾

Because it did.

Enrolling you in Tiny Toes felt like the smartest thing I had ever done. In early September, during those first few days of school, Michelle reported that you kept mostly to yourself and were quietly taking it all in, content to sit on the sidelines and watch the other children play. But your comfort grew as time went on, undoubtedly assisted by Michelle, who was eager to jump into the play herself and facilitate relationships amongst the students. She gently encouraged you to join the fun, rather than be a passive observer, and it wasn't long before she was telling me you regularly sought out certain children during playtime—typically those who were likewise on the quiet side.

Michelle also communicated that you were eager to

please and would excitedly raise your hand whenever she sought a volunteer to help with putting away toys or erasing the whiteboard. As I expected—or at least hoped—any concerns Michelle had about you following the incident at the community center were quickly laid to rest, and it was plain to see that she saw you as a welcome addition to her program.

While your development at school was slow and steady, the strides you made at home appeared to manifest overnight. After a few days of getting acclimated to your new preschool, language poured out of you as soon as I picked you up at lunchtime. You simply couldn't wait to tell me about everything you saw at school that morning, which was something you never did while at your old preschool.

"You know what?" you would typically ask on our drive home, as an introduction before launching into a story.

"What?" I would say in response, giving you the green light to regale me with a tale.

"Ms. Michelle yelled at Bobby today," you told me on one occasion. I doubted whether there was any actual "yelling" involved—Michelle didn't seem the sort, and you were always overly sensitive to any sort of corrective messaging. "He was jumping up and down on the couch and Ms. Michelle said, 'Stop it!' but he didn't listen, so Ms. Michelle said, 'If you don't listen, I will have to call your mommy!' But Bobby didn't listen, so Ms. Michelle said, 'Okay, I'm calling your mommy!'"

"What happened then?" I asked. "Did Bobby's mommy have to come get him?"

"Umm." You thought it over. "Yes. Bobby's mommy came and said, 'That's it! You're in trouble now, Bobby!'"

I suspected you may have embellished some details in

your stories, but I was thrilled to have actual conversations with you.

"You know what?" you asked on another occasion.

"What?"

"Today Ellie and Brandon were playing with the train, and Brandon went, 'Arrrgh!' and destroyed the train tracks and Ellie started to cry. And then Brandon threw a train at Ellie's head and Ellie said, 'Ouch!'"

"Whoa! What did Ms. Michelle do?"

"She said, 'Brandon! You don't do that!' And then she put him in jail."

"In jail?"

"Yes. Brandon is still in jail."

"He's in jail?"

"Yes. He's going to be in jail forever."

It was surprisingly fun trying to divine the truth from your fanciful stories. I wasn't all that concerned about any anecdotes you were making up, which I understood to be a standard phase children go through. Even if it was something you should have gotten over at your age, I figured your language delays possibly contributed to you not getting those tall tales out of your system just yet.

What a relief it was to hear language pour out of you like that! Nora and I had suspected for some time that you were squirreling away most of your speech-related abilities, only showing us the tip of the iceberg because of your shyness, and your chatterbox phase—even if confined to me—seemed to confirm our theory. Still, I didn't feel tempted to cut off your twice-a-week sessions with Nora. You remained extremely shy around anyone other than me and her, and I thought your work with Nora remained beneficial. Plus, Nora had fallen into the additional role of being my advisor with the rest of the adversity we faced. That, in and of itself, justified you continuing to see her for at least a while longer, as far as I was concerned.

Of course, I remained concerned about the apparent expiration date on my life that was approaching. There were plenty of times I'd mentally wrestle with the dilemma only to accomplish nothing other than stirring myself into a state of high anxiety. But if I couldn't solve the problem, at the very least I could make the most of the months I had left, and that's exactly what I did. I was as good of a father to you during that time as I'd ever been, and it was unfortunate it took a countdown on my life to draw the best out of me.

One evening, toward the end of September, I was putting you to bed when you announced, "You know what?"

"What?" I responded as I tucked you in.

"Sloane's mommy and daddy were in school today."

"Oh?" Sloane's parents were a pair of fairly famous actors who had settled in the Hudson Valley, presumably seeking a quiet lifestyle. Despite their celebrity status, they were generally hands-on as far as dropping off and picking up their daughter from school, and they were always polite enough whenever I shyly mumbled a greeting to them.

"What were they doing in school?" I asked.

"I don't know. I think they were talking about work."

"Do you mean what they do for work?" I asked, and you nodded in response. I had a vague recollection of Ms. Michelle saying at the beginning of the school year that she'd periodically invite parents in to talk about their careers. *God, I hope she doesn't ask me*, I thought—even thinking about how I would try to explain to a bunch of four-year-olds what I did every day as an in-house attorney was enough to give me agita.

"Oh, that's cool," I said. "Were they nice?"

"Umm, yes." You paused, thoughtful. "Sloane's mommy gave everybody a book, but I forgot it at school."

"That's okay, you can get it tomorrow. And that was very kind of Sloane's mommy to give you that."

"Yes, it was," you agreed, before adding, "Is my mommy dead?"

I was caught off guard, and it took me a moment to respond.

"Yes," I finally said. "Yes, she is."

It wasn't the first time you had brought up the topic of your mother, although it had been a while since you last did so. I was never really sure what to tell you in response to those questions, and when you raised the issue in the past, I thought you were too young to fully understand my answers, in any event. But you had grown a lot over the past few months, and I thought you might finally be of an age to have an actual conversation about it. In fact, having a heart-to-heart with you about your mother was on my list of things to do with you before December, when it appeared my time was likely up, so I was grateful you had been the one to broach the topic.

"Why did she die?" you asked. I sensed your mother was something you wanted to talk about, even if it was hard for you to ask the right questions.

"You came into this world after living inside your mother for nine months," I said. "And then you were born. That's never a simple process, but usually mommies are okay afterwards. Tired, but otherwise fine. But it was very hard for your mother to give birth to you. I think it was all too much for her, for whatever reason. She was so exhausted. Too exhausted. And she passed away a few minutes after you were born."

You processed this in silence, and I didn't know what was going through your head.

"Are you mad at me?" you finally asked, and I was surprised to see you looked nervous.

"What? No! Not even a little bit." I shook my head, thrown off by your question, before adding, "And your mother absolutely loved you. She was full of joy the entire time you were living inside her belly. And she loved you right away after you were born. In fact...."

I dug out my phone and swiped through my pictures, going back several years until I found what I was looking for, before handing the phone to you.

"That's a picture of you with your mommy right after you were born," I explained, as you studied the photo of you as a newborn. "Look at how you're touching your mommy's face. And do you see how happy she looks?"

"I see it," you murmured without taking your eyes off the phone. I didn't rush you as you stared at it, your face unreadable.

"What happens after a person dies?" you finally asked, looking up at me but keeping a hold of the phone.

*These questions are getting deep*, I thought. I took a seat at the foot of your bed, weighing my response.

"Many people think that a person's spirit—which is the part of them inside their body—lives on and goes to a new place after they die," I said. "Some people think the place the spirit goes to is called heaven."

"Is my mommy in heaven?" you asked.

"I'm not sure exactly what happens to us when we die," I admitted. "Because I'm still alive. But I do think your mother is somewhere watching you, and she's very proud."

You reflected on that, and I could see the gears in your head turn as you tried to come up with another question.

"My mommy's spirit left her body?" you asked.

"Yeah, I think so. I think the spirit lives forever, but our bodies are just what we use while we are on this earth."

"What happens to our bodies when we die?"

I wasn't entirely comfortable with this line of questioning, but I understood your curiosity and wanted to indulge it.

"Our bodies just tend to... shut down. It's like a very long sleep. And a lot of times, we will bury the bodies in the ground so they can rest forever. That's usually done in what's called a cemetery."

"Is my mommy's body in the ground?"

"Yes, she was buried after she passed away."

"In a 'cemetery?'" You struggled in pronouncing that new word.

"Yes."

You didn't respond, and I thought you'd finally reached the end of your questions. I stood up and turned out the lights, but before I could leave, you asked one more thing.

"Can I see my mommy's cemetery?"

"You want to see where your mother is buried?"

"Yes."

I tried to think about what I had on the calendar the next day work-wise and came up with nothing. As far as I knew, I was perfectly positioned to take a day off.

"Okay," I said. "We can do that."

THE NEXT MORNING, we departed for a four-hour drive to eastern Long Island. The weather was cool when we left—cold enough for the two of us to be wearing jackets—but it was otherwise a sunny day. You fell asleep partway through the ride and only woke up once we slowed to a stop upon hitting traffic in the Bronx.

"Are we there yet?" you asked in a sleepy voice from the back seat.

"No, we still have almost another two hours to go."

Traffic remained bad after we crossed the Throgs Neck Bridge into Queens, but it opened up as New York City transitioned to Nassau County, only to let up completely upon reaching Suffolk County—the easternmost part of Long Island. Despite the long drive, you seemed content enough in the back seat. If you had been paying attention, visions of car accidents along the way would have undoubtedly distracted you, but you were too lost in your own thoughts to notice as you stared at the back of the seat in front of you.

At one point, I pulled off an exit of the Long Island Expressway and you snapped out of your reverie.

"Are we there?" you asked.

"No," I said. "I just want to pick up some flowers."

"Why?"

"You'll see."

A few more minutes of driving and I located a florist where I purchased a bouquet of sunflowers, which were your mother's favorite. Then we were back in the car, heading further east. After we passed a dozen cars with their flashers on, trailing a hearse as a funeral procession, I knew we were close to the cemetery.

Minutes later, we reached our exit and finally exited the expressway. It then took another fifteen minutes of driving along various back roads until we reached our destination.

"Is *this* it?" you asked in a weary tone as we drove through the gated entrance.

"It is," I said. "I just have to drive a little further to get to the area where your mother is buried." It had been years since I visited her site, but the night before I had pulled up directions to her burial stone from the cemetery's website.

You looked around in amazement as we drove through the cemetery, which was empty other than a scattered person or two paying their respects.

"Look," you marveled, looking around. "There are so many people!"

"What do you—" I stopped, thinking about all the emotions the surrounding land had absorbed over the course of its existence as a cemetery. All the tearful burials it had hosted. "Oh. Right."

Soon I reached a curve that I understood to be close to where your mother was buried. I parked on the grass next to the road and took the sunflowers from the passenger seat before exiting.

"There are so many people!" you said again, looking around in wonder, after I let you out of the car. While you marveled at the crowd only you could see, I spotted a container full of metallic burial vases and grabbed one.

"Come." I extended a hand. "It's this way."

You took my hand and allowed me to lead you through the rows of engraved stones. I took care, out of respect, to avoid stepping on any areas of land covering the deceased, and you followed my lead in that regard. As we approached your mother's stone, you shook off my hand, looking straight ahead.

"Daddy!" you cried.

"Yes?" I asked.

But as you ran off toward your mother's stone, I realized you weren't actually talking to me.

You sprinted twenty yards ahead to the headstone identifying your mother's burial site and stopped, looking in amazement at the area directly in front of the grave marker.

*He sees me,* I realized with a start. *He sees me standing in that exact spot nearly five years ago.*

"What are you doing, Daddy?" you asked, and I wasn't sure if you were talking to me or the vision in front of you.

"What do you see, Quince?"

"It's you. You're just standing there. You're wearing fancy clothes."

I tried to remember the moment you were witnessing, but aside from a general recollection of burying your mother, I couldn't recall any details. Those days remained a chaotic blur in my mind. A sad, chaotic blur.

"Oh, you moved!" you suddenly exclaimed.

"What did I do?"

"You touched the stone. You look sad, even though you're not crying. But I can tell when you're feeling sad."

"I was very sad," I admitted, although I'm sure you were correct in noting my grief wasn't necessarily obvious to see.

I often thought of myself as being dead on the inside, but your vision compelled me to rethink that self-diagnosis. Being demonstrative isn't in my nature, so it didn't surprise me at all that you didn't see me wailing and drenching the ground with my tears. To the untrained eye, there was probably no sign on my face of the loss I had experienced. But it was there. And it was strong enough to leave its imprint, waiting for you to revisit it years later.

*Maybe there's more life in me than I've given myself credit for.* It was an oddly comforting thought.

I arranged the bouquet of sunflowers in the memorial vase I had snatched earlier and set it on the ground near your mother's gravestone.

"What is that for?" you asked, curious.

"Your mother always loved flowers. Especially sunflowers. So I wanted to bring her some. I haven't had a chance to really bring her any flowers since she passed away."

"Why not?"

"Because I was busy watching you!" I tussled your hair to make it clear I harbored no resentment for it. "But that's okay. There were days I thought about coming down here to visit your mother, but every time I considered it, I could imagine your mother saying, 'Don't worry about me. Just take care of Quince.' And I knew that's what she'd want me to do, so that's what I did. I always think about your mother —every single day—but I haven't been here in years. It's not because I didn't want to visit her, but because doing so would have pulled me away from you. At least, until today."

You moved to stand off to the side of your mother's engraved stone, and I realized with a jolt you had positioned yourself directly between me and the vision of me from nearly five years earlier. I put a hand on your shoulder, and you and I—along with the vision of me from the past— stood together in a respectful silence. The stillness was only disturbed when a monarch butterfly found us and fluttered around your face, causing you to giggle before it flew away.

"Was my mommy nice?" you asked as you watched the butterfly weave across the cemetery.

"She was the nicest. Much nicer than me. She cared so much about everyone, even animals. She's the reason you and I are vegetarians today—she convinced me years ago that animals weren't for eating. But she was also great with kids. Did you know she was a teacher?"

"Like Ms. Michelle?" you asked.

"Yes. Except your mom taught fourth grade, so she was teaching kids that were about nine or ten years old. She was amazing at it, but she was thinking of stopping—at least for a while—so she could raise you. Her decision to do that surprised me, but I was more than okay with it. She would've been a fabulous mother to you."

"Was she ever mean?" you asked. "Did she ever get mad?"

"She was never *mean*, but everyone gets mad sometimes. Your mother included."

"Why did she get mad?"

"It was usually because of something silly I did. I can be difficult to live with at times." I chuckled, remembering my long history of inadvertent transgressions with your mother. "There was one time before we got married when she was showing me something for our wedding—maybe it was picking out flowers for the tables. She presented me with two choices and asked which one I liked better. I wanted your mother to pick whatever made her happier, but I'm terrible with words sometimes. So all I said was 'I don't care.' And your mother was very upset with me about that for a while."

"Was it mean for you to say 'I don't care?'" you asked.

"It... it wasn't nice. People don't like to hear 'I don't care' if they are asking you about something important to them. What I should have said is something like, 'Both choices are great, so whichever one you prefer is fine with me.' But my words were clumsy, and it hurt your mother's feelings. At least for a while. She was understanding when I explained what I was trying to say to her, and she forgave me. After a while, she even learned to laugh about the whole thing. Your mother loved to laugh. She laughed at me when I did silly things, but she also laughed at herself. One time she tripped on a rug and fell on her bottom, and she just sat on the floor hysterically laughing for five minutes."

You smiled at the image but remained silent while you

processed this information, mentally putting together some of the pieces constituting the puzzle that was your mother.

"Maybe every night before bed, after I read you a story, I can tell you a story about your mother?" I asked. "Would you like that?"

You considered my proposal. "Yes," you said. "I would like that."

"Alright. Then we'll do that." I looked around, but no one was near us. "We can stay here as long as you like. You just let me know when you're ready to go."

"Okay," you said, turning to study the stone in front of you. As you reached out a hand to feel its engraved lettering, you asked, "What does this say?"

I took half a step back to read the stone. "It says: 'A beautiful soul. Anne Backman. November 3, 1980 to December 4, 2017. Beloved wife, mother, sister, daughter, and friend.'" I took a moment to reflect on the inscription, and then added, "Your mother's name was Anne Backman. She kept her last name when we got married—she liked Backman more than Banfield. I couldn't blame her."

You ran your hand across the engravings on the stone and stopped at "December," tracing the letters of the word with an index finger.

"December 4," you read aloud. "That's my birthday!"

"Yes, it is." I paused and then added, "Are you glad we came here?"

You nodded.

"I'm glad," you said. "I just wish I could see her."

"I have some videos of her on my phone," I said. "We can watch them together after we get home later."

"Okay," you said. But I could tell that you yearned for something deeper than that. *I'm sorry, Quince*, I thought. *I wish I had more to offer you.*

After a few minutes, you stepped away and looked back toward our parked car.

"I think I'm done," you announced.

"Okay. That's fine." I looked back at the stone and placed a hand on it, trying to think of something profound to say to your mother before I departed. Nothing came to mind, but that felt oddly appropriate. Your mother never doubted my love for her, even when I struggled to find the words to convey it.

As we walked back to the car, my phone vibrated. The displayed number looked vaguely familiar, so I took the call.

"Will?" a man's voice said. "It's Doug Nichols. Your attorney."

*Oh, that guy.* Doug was my attorney in my lawsuit relating to your mother's death. I instantly regretted answering.

"Listen," he added, "I wanted to see if you can come into the office this week. We have that mediation on Friday, but I wanted to talk to you beforehand."

"Oh, right. The mediation. I keep forgetting about that."

"Yes." Doug sounded impatient and annoyed. "It was originally scheduled for this past summer, but you had to reschedule—"

"I had to reschedule because my son was in the hospital in a coma."

"Right, right." Doug paused. "Anyway, the hospital made a pre-mediation settlement offer of fifty thousand, so the ball is in our court. We need to talk about where we want to go with this thing. I think we can easily get them up to high-six figures, if not a million, but we should definitely talk about our next move. I suggest lowering our demand to three million, which would target a midpoint of about one and a half million. But we can discuss it. Can you come in Thursday at ten?"

"Yeah, sure. See you then." I hung up, feeling disgusted. I continued to feel uncomfortable with that litigation—I firmly believed it had simply been your mother's time, with no fault on the part of the hospital or doctors, regardless of what our medical experts were willing to argue on the stand. Spending a day in a conference room mediation was the last thing I felt like doing, particularly since my remaining days were likely down to double-digits. There were times I tried to convince myself that the litigation was a means for you to have financial protection after my death, but I already had a sizable life insurance policy in place. I couldn't imagine how any settlement proceeds from the lawsuit would have a material impact on your well-being down the road.

Then an idea struck me—a notion that was completely out of the box. But it felt right, so I called back Doug, who answered on the first ring.

"Hey, this is Will again," I said. "Look, we don't have to meet this week after all. I want to accept the fifty thousand dollar offer."

"What?" Doug stammered. "Are you kidding? That's their opening offer, in response to our four million demand. I'm sure we can get them past a million if we push hard enough. It would be crazy to—"

"Doug," I interrupted. "Our case stinks. I know it and you know it. I want to be done with it. We're going to settle for the fifty thousand."

"You're making a mistake," Doug growled into the phone, his contingency fee clearly on his mind, but I was unintimidated.

"No. I'm not," I said. "But there's something else. I'll accept the fifty thousand—but only if the hospital also agrees to one other non-monetary settlement term...."

**16**

As pleased as I was to hear you wanted to learn everything possible about your mother, it was a surprisingly difficult topic for me to discuss.

It took some time before I could pinpoint the source of that unease. Of course, I wanted you to know and understand her, at least, as well as you could under the circumstances, and our new arrangement where I told you a story about your mother each night undoubtedly furthered that goal. It had long been our practice that I would read you a book you selected before putting you to bed, even though, more often than not, you struggled to pay attention through the duration of the story. But after we added to that routine my telling an anecdote about your mother, you always snapped to attention once I started discussing her and sat rapt as I shared some innocuous tale to help flesh out the picture of her that was developing in your mind.

There was no shortage of stories, as you were satisfied by hearing anything new about her, however mundane. One evening I told you about the time she and I vacationed in Iceland and swam together in subzero temperatures in a heated pool outside of Reykjavík. At one point, I dove under a floating *plastic divider to access a new area of the pool before waiting for your mother to follow. She was not a strong swimmer, but she dunked her head underwater, kicking and flailing for some time in a crude approximation of swimming, before reemerging, only to knock her head on the divider she had been trying to swim under. It was a bizarre sight—even though she had been underwater for close to a minute, she had somehow moved only about three feet. But your mother's poor swimming skills weren't the point of that story. No, it was her reaction that made me consider that tale worth telling, because when she came up for air and hit her head, she didn't cry out in pain or sulk. She laughed and continued to laugh at herself, to the point where I worried about her drowning in a fit of hysteria. The reserved Europeans in the pool with us threw her odd looks, wondering if she had lost her mind, but that only caused her to laugh even harder.*

*Your mother's laughter was my favorite sound in the world.*

*When I told you that story, you giggled as well, repeating "bonk!" as you pretended to knock your own head into the wall. And for a moment, it felt as if time had dissolved and you and your mother were laughing together.*

*My trepidation about telling you stories of your mother was solely based on a lack of confidence in myself. I wasn't sure I could tell you about your mother with the skill needed to fully convey the essence of who she was. To the extent you ended up with an incomplete or inaccurate picture of her, the fault would lie exclusively with me. Still, I pressed on, knowing I was the only resource available to you just then. I was grateful that after my death, your Aunt Ronnie—your mother's sister—would be entrusted with your care and could share her own stories of your mother, allowing you to see her in an entirely different light. Until then, you were stuck with me, and I was determined to do the best I could while knowing full well my efforts would be imperfect. But photographs, videos, and memories were all I could offer in furtherance of you getting to know your mother.*

*Or so one might think.*

TWO WEEKS after we visited the cemetery, my settlement agreement with the hospital was finalized, and you and I once again returned to Long Island. Only this time we weren't venturing far out onto the island—we were heading to a hospital located just over the border between Queens and Nassau County.

Specifically, the hospital where you were born.

"Where are we going?" you asked from the back seat, even though I had explained that to you before we left.

"We're going to a hospital," I answered, yet again.

"Why?"

"I want to show you something." I was intentionally vague, in case things didn't work out the way I hoped they would.

We arrived at the hospital shortly before lunchtime, and I had to ascend many levels in the parking garage before I could find an open spot. After parking, you held my hand as we made our way to the main building, and I could sense your excitement when we got closer to the entrance. There's an undeniable energy to a hospital—a hustle and bustle you picked up on—and there was a bounce in your step as we entered the building.

We found an elevator to take us to the fifth floor, which was dedicated to labor and delivery and was, as we learned upon getting there, a bit of a chaotic mess. Nurses and doctors scurried about like ants around a disturbed anthill, punctuated by the occasional pregnant woman being pushed in a wheelchair down the hallway. I wasn't sure where to go and I paused, waiting for someone to point me in the right direction, until I realized I'd have to bother someone in order to be helped.

Looking around, I located a bearded nurse sitting at a desk, studiously reading something on a computer. As I approached him, I noticed the man was actually engrossed in a fantasy football roster displayed on the monitor, which he quickly minimized.

"Hello, my name is Will Banfield," I said. The man stared at me blankly.

"Okay..." the nurse finally said.

"I was told to come up here and ask for a woman named Maureen?"

The man frowned, and I suspected he wasn't comfortable summoning whoever this Maureen was.

"May I ask why?" he asked.

"It concerns a lawsuit I just settled. Maureen should know about it."

The nurse pursed his lips, trying to hide his frustration with my lack of details, before turning around and assessing the area. After spotting a large woman in scrubs walking a few yards away, he wordlessly stood and strode toward her. The woman, who I assumed to be Maureen, threw me an annoyed look as the man spoke with her, and I had a greater understanding of why the man appeared to be afraid of her.

Maureen beelined over to me once the nurse had finished speaking with her.

"You're Will?" she asked bluntly.

"Yes. Are you Maureen? I was told to ask for you."

"You're the guy who wants to look at an OR?" she asked.

"Yes. And it's not just *any* operating room—there's a specific one we have to see. And it's not just that I *want* to look at it so much as it was a part of a settlement agreement that I—"

"You're early," she said, looking at a clock on the wall. "I was told you were coming at noon."

"Right. Well, we came down from upstate, so it was hard for us to time exactly when we'd arrive. I'm happy to wait if you—"

"Alright," she interrupted again. "Let's get this over with." Her eyes flicked to you. "Is he coming, too?"

I tried not to sigh.

"Yes. That was all part of the agreement. He has to come as well." I waited, wondering if an argument was inevitable. She frowned as she studied the two of us, clearly unhappy with being assigned this menial task.

"You'll both have to wear scrubs if you come into the OR," she finally said.

"Fair enough," I replied, sounding as agreeable as I could muster. *Whatever gets us in there.*

You'd been watching this exchange with wide eyes, and you jumped when I gently prodded you to follow Maureen as she took us to another area to put on scrubs. You laughed at me after I was dressed, and your excitement grew when you realized you would have your own smaller set to wear.

"Looks busy here today," I said to Maureen, as she watched me struggle to dress you in your set of scrubs. Small talk was something I usually tried to avoid, but her silent stares were making me uncomfortable.

"It is," she replied. "And it doesn't help that I'm being pulled away from my work to babysit you guys."

I closed my mouth, deciding her angry looks were preferable to what small talk might offer.

Once we were both dressed, Maureen led us down a

busy corridor. Everything looked unfamiliar to me, even though I'd been there nearly five years earlier.

"Why do you need to see this OR, anyway?" Maureen asked while we walked.

"His mother passed away in that operating room just after he was born," I explained, hoping you couldn't hear me over the commotion in the corridor. "I think seeing the room where she died will help him process that loss."

I thought Maureen rolled her eyes, but she had just enough sensitivity not to voice how stupid she thought my explanation was. In fairness, her cynicism was probably warranted, based on my vague answer alone. But, of course, she didn't know the entire story.

We finally reached a set of double doors and Maureen stopped.

"This is it," she said.

"Okay, thank you." I started to guide you in, but paused when I realized Maureen was accompanying us inside.

"Oh, I'm sorry," I said to Maureen, stopping in my tracks. "But I'd prefer if you waited out here. The settlement agreement states—"

Maureen's nostrils flared, and I clammed up. She pointed inside the operating room at a security camera mounted in a corner by the ceiling.

"Fine, go in by yourselves," she spat at me. "But don't touch anything in there. I'll be watching."

"Yes, ma'am," I mumbled, taking you by the hand to escort you into the OR.

I let out a long breath once we were inside with the doors closed, separating us from Maureen on the other side. "Wow, that was frightening," I muttered under my breath, before crouching down to be at your eye level.

"Quince," I said, looking directly at you. "This is the

room where you were born and where your mother died. They use this room for surgeries, which is when doctors have to cut people open to help fix something inside their bodies. And that can be scary, so it's possible you may see some things in here. But try not to let anything bother you, okay? Because whatever you see won't be something that's happening right now, and nothing in here can hurt you."

You gave a solemn nod, and I could only hope you understood.

"Ready?" I asked, looking into your eyes.

"Ready," you replied.

I bobbed my head and stood up. Then the two of us walked deeper into the room.

I recalled little of the hospital from the last time I was there, but the operating room looked almost familiar. I remembered walking through those same doors nearly five years earlier and immediately seeing your mother laying on the far side of the room with a team of physicians and nurses clustered around her, and a curtain bifurcating her head from the rest of her body. But in its present state, the room was empty other than some random medical equipment.

"Can you see anything?" I asked as you looked around the room. But you shook your head, looking frustrated.

"There are too many people," you said. "It's too crowded."

*Damn it*, I thought with a grimace—I feared that might be the case. Given the number of surgeries and deliveries that took place in the room, it was small wonder it was a hotspot for your visions. But then an idea came to me.

"Can you see *me*?" I asked. You looked up at my face, and I added, "Not this me. Another me. In the middle of all the people."

You looked back at the room and squinted your eyes, struggling to focus.

"Yes!" you suddenly exclaimed. "I do! I see another you!" You pointed at the far side of the room, which is where I remembered being stationed during the C-section procedure.

"Okay, try to focus on that other me," I said. For a long time, I'd wondered if you had the ability to filter out certain visions, and it seemed like that might be possible after all. *Maybe that's a skill he'll develop as he gets older*, I thought, but that was speculation for later.

"Okay," you said. "I'm looking at you now. The other you."

"Is everything clear? Nothing is blocking me?"

"Yes," you replied. "I can see the other you."

"Who else do you see? Besides me?"

"Umm...." You studied the room. "I see two people walking around. And there are more over there," you added, pointing.

"Are they all standing up?" I asked.

"Yes. They are dressed like this." You touched the scrubs you were wearing.

"Then those are probably the nurses and doctors. Do you see a woman laying down?"

You frowned and walked deeper into the room.

"Yes! I see her! You're standing next to her."

*Oh, thank God*, I thought with a sense of relief. *This actually worked.*

"That woman is your mother," I said. You looked up at me, seeking confirmation I was being serious, before looking back to the area where your mother would have been laying. You took a tentative step forward, peering intently, and then you reached out a hand as if to touch her, only to pull it back with a disappointed look. As you settled in to study your mother, I tried to imagine what you were seeing: your mother with a respirator in her nostrils and her hair covered by a medical cap, looking exhausted, but I couldn't conjure any details beyond that.

"Oh!" you suddenly cried out. "Look!"

"I can't see anything, Quince," I reminded you. "What are you seeing?"

"It's a baby!" you cried out. "It's so cute!"

"Guess who that is?" I asked.

"Who?"

"That's you!"

"That's me?"

You advanced a few steps and leaned forward to look, apparently admiring yourself as a baby. Looking entranced, you wandered to a corner of the room, which I vaguely recalled was the area where the pediatrician conducted his initial assessment, and continued to study your younger self, fascinated.

I wasn't sure how long your vision would last. When we arrived, I was hopeful your mother's joy would have been enough to leave an emotional imprint for you to view, and that appeared to be the case. The effort of getting into this room seemed to be worth it, as you were transfixed at seeing your mother come alive in front of you and witnessing your own first moments in this world.

"What's going on now, Quince?" I asked.

"Umm." You wandered back to the area where your mother had been laying. "You and a woman are bringing the baby over to my mommy."

"Oh, right. I remember walking with a nurse as she carried you over so your mother could meet you. That's when I took that picture of you and your mommy that I showed you a few weeks ago."

"Yes, I see you taking a picture now. My mommy is looking at baby me. I think she loves me."

"She does," I said. "Absolutely."

You stared into space, looking thoughtful. "Oh, they just took the baby away." A brief pause, and then you added, "And now you are leaving with a woman, Daddy." You frowned, confused. "Why are you leaving?"

*Oh God.* I had hoped this wouldn't be part of what you saw, but of course I had no way of knowing for sure. The positives of you seeing your mother come alive, in my mind, outweighed the downside of seeing the post-birth complications, but I was unprepared for the wave of emotions that hit me at being reminded of the moment things went awry.

*Why are you leaving?* It was a question I had asked myself for years, and the simple answer was because I was told to. Utterly useless in that situation, I allowed myself to be escorted out of the room, hoping others, more competent than me, could save your mother. But they couldn't, and I was left with the guilt of your mother dying alone and knowing that if nothing else, I could've helped ease her passing had I stayed at her side.

"They are all doing things to my mommy," you reported. "What are they doing?"

"This is the part where your mommy passes away," I gently told you. "They are trying to save her, but—" I trailed off. "Do you want to leave?"

"No," you murmured, continuing to watch the scene that was invisible to me. "I want to stay."

"Okay." I put a hand on your shoulder and waited. "Try to ignore the doctors and just watch your mommy."

We stood for some time, and although I wondered what you were seeing, I didn't ask.

"She's looking at me," you said after a few moments of silence.

"Who's looking at you?"

"My mommy. She's looking at me. And smiling."

"She is?"

You took a few steps to your left and then squealed with delight.

"She's still looking at me!" You darted back to your right before quickly sidestepping back to your left. "And now she's laughing at me!"

*Could it be? Could she actually be seeing Quince?*

You seemed to think so. While you had acted as a passive observer throughout your time in the operating room, you showed renewed vigor upon discovering that your mother could somehow see through time to interact with you. You bounced in place, delighted at whatever expressions your mother was radiating in your direction.

I tried to make sense of it. *Could your mother have had some ability to see visions of the future herself?* She never mentioned anything like that during our time together, but it would provide some explanation for where your own abilities came from. *Did she have a latent gift that she passed along to Quince genetically?*

"What should I do, Daddy?" you asked, cutting into my thoughts. "My mommy is still looking at me."

"I think your mother will pass away soon," I said, thinking fast. "I don't think you can touch her, but maybe you can give her a wave?"

"Okay."

You waved at the air and turned to me, beaming.

"She's smiling!" you reported. "And blinking her eyes at me."

*Her hands would have been pinned at her sides—she is waving back in the only way she can.* My throat tightened, and I struggled to hold back tears.

"You can also tell her you love her," I suggested in a choked whisper.

"Okay," you said. And then, to the open air in front of you, you shouted, "I love you, Mommy!"

You turned back to me, smiling from ear to ear.

"She looks very happy!" you said.

I didn't know how much time we had left. Your visions tended to jump around at times, and the connection you had established with your mother could end without warning. But I wondered: if your mother was truly seeing you then, in her final moments, could she see me as well? And if so, what could I say to comfort her before she was gone? I had a propensity for blurting out the wrong things during our relationship, but I couldn't waste the opportunity.

One step forward and I was next to you. I placed a hand on your shoulder and hugged you tight against my hip.

"Don't worry, Anne," I said to the air in front of us, tilting my head down toward you, pressed against my side. "I got this."

I stood there, left to wonder whether your mother had received my message. But then you turned your head up toward me, looking serene.

"She closed her eyes after you said that," you whispered. "But she looks happy. She's still smiling."

I gave you a small hug of thanks, and we stood together as you watched the rest of the scene play out. After a few moments, I felt your shoulders sag beneath my arm, as if the shot of adrenaline you experienced at seeing your mother had dissipated.

"Oh," you said. "She is gone now."

I released the breath I'd been holding with a long exhale. Your vision had to end at some point, of course, but it was an emotional blow hearing it had concluded. You didn't seem troubled by what you had seen, or even because your connection with your mother had been severed. Instead, you mostly looked reflective, as if appreciating the restoration of a piece of yourself you hadn't even realized was missing all of your life.

It would take me some time to sort through my own emotions, but I could already sense the lifting of a weight I had been carrying for years. I had long speculated about what your mother had gone through in the minutes after I left her, until the moment she slipped away, and I always imagined the worst: her dying alone, with her final thoughts being a fervent wish that I was there at her side. But that bleak scenario appeared not to be the case, and I was grateful for it. Beyond grateful.

You were certain that your mother could see you in her last moments and that she was filled with joy upon seeing you as a young boy. I had no reason to doubt you, although I could only guess how that connection came to be. Perhaps your mother had a dormant ability to see the future—one that she passed along to you—that awakened at the very end. Maybe it was simply her imminent departure from this world that granted your mother some degree of clairvoyance. In any event, it was a tremendous relief knowing that she'd spent her ultimate moments gifted with a vision of you, warming her with a smile full of love and comforting her with a wave that was equal parts "hello" and "goodbye."

**17**

"I got this."

I didn't go into that operating room expecting to get an opportunity to communicate with your mother, yet somehow I came out of that experience having made a deathbed promise to her. The words fell out of me, but I knew as soon as I said them that they were just what your mother needed to hear to be at peace as she departed from this world. While those three words seemed to have achieved the desired effect, I was left pondering exactly what my promise meant.

Was I a good father? It was easy to be my own worst critic, and there were many ways in which I undoubtedly failed you as a parent. I knew that regardless of how much time I had left, I'd continue to have my share of failures. Focusing on those missteps helped sustain a belief you wouldn't be much worse off without me. You were resilient and your inherent goodness would not be extinguished regardless of who assumed the task of raising you after I was gone.

And yet....

Could I have been selling myself short? I had dedicated my entire existence to your well-being, even if my execution was *often clumsy. Still, I didn't question the effort I put in for your benefit. That labor stemmed, at first, from a perceived obligation to your mother, but as I grew into the role of a father, it evolved from being a duty to an act of love. There were unquestionably more skilled parents out there, but I couldn't imagine anyone being able to match my love for you. Your mother surely would, if she was around. But she wasn't.*

*There was only me.*

*While I was fully prepared to die if it meant you would be safe, I started to accept you'd be worse off in my absence, and so I felt my resignation to the prospect of expiring in the near future waver. I wanted to live, and not just because of my newfound appreciation for life.*

*I wanted to live because I believed, maybe for the first time, that you truly needed me.*

~

"Is something on your mind?" Nora finally asked me.

"What makes you say that?"

"Well, usually when you linger at the beginning of a session, it's because there's something you want to discuss," Nora said. "Otherwise, you excuse yourself so I can get to work with Quince. But you've just been sitting there silent for five minutes."

It was the Saturday morning after the incident at the hospital, and Nora was correct in ascertaining there was plenty on my mind. You were happily playing by yourself as I struggled to get my thoughts together. Even though you'd finally tired of the pooping puppy, you were perfectly content building a castle made of Lego blocks that Nora had dug out of a closet on our arrival.

I hadn't told Nora about the incident in the operating

room. That impromptu family reunion felt like it should stay in the family, at least for the moment, and I was still trying to process what happened that day. While I wanted to work through some of my issues with Nora, I didn't know how to articulate my specific concerns.

"Do you think I'm doing a good job with Quince?" I finally asked.

Nora rolled her eyes, as if I had said something profoundly stupid.

"Is *that* what's bothering you?" she asked. "I'm not normally inclined to take the bait when people are fishing for a compliment, but I'll make an exception in your case. Yes, I think you're doing a good job. He's very lucky to have you."

"What makes you say that?"

"What makes me say that?" Nora muttered to herself in rhetorical fashion. "Well, let's see—you changed your entire routine to spend more time with Quince. You don't seem to have any life of your own outside of caring for him. He clearly adores you, so I can tell you're not just putting on a show when you're around me. And he talks about you all the time: all the play you do together at home and the excursions you both go on after school. But most of all, the proof is in the pudding."

"What does that mean?"

"It means he's a great kid, and you're his sole caretaker. If a child has behavioral issues, it doesn't necessarily mean the parents are doing a poor job. But when a child is as great as Quince, well, it's hard to imagine that being the case with a terrible parent at home. So yes, I think you're doing a wonderful job of parenting." Nora squinted at me, trying to read my face. "Now I know you're not just looking for me to say nice things about you. So what's really on your mind?"

"The same thing that's been on my mind for the past two months," I said. "That vision Quince saw of me dying."

"*Possibly* dying," Nora was quick to add. I acknowledged her correction, if only to appease her.

"Okay, sure," I said. "But assuming the worst, I made peace with the idea of dying because it seemed like the only way to protect Quince and ensure his vision of the future was preserved. Only, that's starting to feel like something of a cop-out. I guess I'm only beginning to fully appreciate that Quince and I are a team, and if I die, I think a part of him might, too. When I was first confronted with this dilemma, I thought all I had to do to 'win' was to make sure Quince survived whatever's going to happen. But I'm no longer certain that's the case."

*I got this.*

The promise I made to your mother bubbled up again, as it had so often done over the past few days. That vow was the source of my sense of unease. It felt like I'd be breaking that pledge if I were to bow out of your story only a few years into it. You had a lot of growing up left to do, and I wanted to be there to see it. I *needed* to be there.

"So you want to find a way for you both to live," Nora summarized. It seemed so obvious when she put it like that.

"I will not risk Quince," I stressed. "No matter what. But... I guess I'm not willing to accept that he's destined to be an orphan in a matter of months. Not without a fight."

"Fair enough," Nora said. Then her face suddenly lit up, and she added, "And I'd be lying if I told you I hadn't been giving this some thought. I didn't want to butt in with my ideas if you didn't want to hear them, but since it sounds like you're open to talking about this again...."

I gave a quick nod of my head, and Nora smiled outright.

"Alright. Let's do this!" She grabbed a legal pad and pen and turned back to face me, looking determined.

"Are there any movies you feel compelled to watch whenever you stumble across them on TV?" she asked, and I blinked at her non sequitur.

"Not that I can think of," I said slowly, not understanding where she was going with that. "It's been a while since I've seen a movie. Maybe *The Shawshank Redemption* back in the day?"

"Oh, that's a good one," she conceded. "But for me it's the *Back to the Future* trilogy. When that comes on, I'm with it until the end. The first movie was on TV over the weekend, and I made my kids sit with me to watch. And it led me to think about you and your dilemma."

"How so?"

"Well, at the beginning of the movie, Marty sees Doc gunned down by the Libyans, remember? Then Marty goes back in time and comes back at the end of the movie to see that same scene from a different angle, where it's revealed that Doc was protected by a bulletproof vest."

Nora paused, waiting for me to seize on her point. But I remained at a loss.

"Are you saying I should just make a point of wearing a bulletproof vest?" I asked, confused, but Nora shook her head.

"No. Well, maybe. But that's not my point. All I'm saying is Marty saw the same scene twice, and each version appeared to have a very different outcome because of a factor Marty couldn't appreciate the first time around."

Nora stopped again, looking impatient at my inability to grasp whatever point she was trying to make.

"I'm sorry," I said. "I don't—"

"You're concerned about taking any sort of action that

would contradict what Quince saw, right?" Nora asked. At my nod, she added, "You told me a few months ago that causing any of his visions to become untrue would hurt him. But how much of this problematic vision do you really understand? Is there any wiggle room there for you to save yourself without contradicting his vision?"

"I don't know," I admitted. "What he told me about that vision was vague. He said he saw me bleeding, though, so I don't think it's as simple as me throwing on a bulletproof vest like Doc did."

"I'm not saying it has to be a bulletproof vest," Nora pressed. "I'm just saying that without a comprehensive understanding of what Quince saw, we have no way of knowing what steps we can take to protect you while maintaining the integrity of his vision."

"Quince couldn't give many details the last time we discussed this with him," I reminded her. "Either because he didn't remember or he wasn't comfortable talking about it."

"That was months ago," Nora said. "He's grown leaps and bounds since then. I think it's worth revisiting. The strides in his language alone may allow us to get more information than we did back in August."

Nora's plan was vague and undefined, but it was more than anything I had come up with. It was *something*.

"Okay," I said. "We can talk to him about it. I don't know what we'll get, but—"

I trailed off with a small shrug. Nora ignored me and called you over to join us. You were initially reluctant to put down your Lego bricks, but after some back-and-forth, Nora coaxed you over. I gave her a small nod to convey my blessing for her to speak with you.

"Quince," she said. "We need your help with something. And it is something scary, so I need you to be brave, okay?"

You glanced at me before nodding.

"It's about that time you saw your daddy get hurt," Nora continued. "Do you remember that?"

You grimaced and gave a quick nod.

"We really want to make sure what you saw never actually happens. And I know it isn't easy for you to talk about but it will be easier for us to keep your daddy safe if we know exactly what you saw. Do you understand?"

You didn't respond at first. Instead, you looked down studying your feet, and I feared you were shutting down once again. But then you raised your head.

"Yes." You sounded wary, but resigned. "I understand."

"Good," Nora said, picking up her pad and pen. "So, can you please tell us again what you saw that day?"

"Umm." You thought hard. "I remember Daddy was hurt and fell down, and he was bleeding." Your face scrunched as you tried to summon more details, but you added nothing further.

"Do you remember the person who hurt your daddy? It was a man, right?"

"I think it was a man," you said. "But I don't remember."

"Okay," Nora said. "Did this person hurt anyone else?"

"I don't remember," you said, before turning to me, tears in your eyes. "I'm sorry, Daddy. I really don't remember. Are you mad?"

"Of course not, Quince," I said. "It was a long time ago. It's okay if you can't remember everything."

I exchanged a look with Nora, who seemed frustrated by her lack of success in questioning you. You likewise looked chagrined at your inability to offer any meaningful details.

But before Nora could ask anything further, you said, "I think I can remember if I see it again. Can I look at it again?"

Nora and I turned toward you, each of us stunned by

your offer. You were scared—you clearly had no desire to go back to the community center and revisit the nightmares you had seen there. But you understood the gravity of the situation, and in making that suggestion, it was plain your desire to keep me safe trumped your terror at returning to that building.

"You want to go there again?" I asked.

Your eyes screamed "no," but you nodded your head, looking resolute. "I can look again," you said. "I want to help you."

I took a hard look at you, assessing whether this was something you could handle. The last thing I wanted was to subject you to further trauma, but going back to the community center was clearly a lesser evil than losing your only remaining parent. You held my gaze as I peered for some sign that we were asking too much of you, and I made my decision.

"Okay," I said. "We can go."

Nora frowned and gestured for me to come closer to her.

"I don't think that's a good idea, Will," she whispered. "You should stay clear of that place out of an abundance of caution. I can take him myself and meet up with you afterward."

Nora had been trying to keep her voice down, but you must have heard because you then pulled me over for your own sidebar.

"I don't want to go with Ms. Nora, Daddy," you said, trying to emulate Nora's whisper but speaking loud enough for everyone to hear. "I want you to come."

"You want me to go with you?"

"Yes," you said. "I have to keep you safe."

*Ah, the logic of a four-year-old*, I thought. Your concern touched me, although I saw Nora's point—assuming your vision held true, the only place where I was even theoretically at risk was the community center, and it made sense for me to stay clear. But given that the incident happened at night, I thought venturing there well before sunset was a reasonably safe proposition. And, of course, there was another consideration.

"I think Quince is tapping into every ounce of courage he has in offering to go back there," I whispered to Nora. "And if he feels even a little bit braver having me in his line of sight, that might make all the difference."

I pulled away from Nora and added, "I think it will be fine. One thing we know—the only thing we know, really— is that whatever we're dealing with goes down at night. And if we leave now, we can get there by noon. We'll be gone hours before sunset."

Nora looked troubled but didn't object.

"You're planning on heading there right now?" she asked.

"Might as well. Get it over with before anyone changes their mind." I gave a subtle nod toward you, and then added, "And if this thing is really happening in December like we suspect, we'll need as much time as possible to come up with a game plan before then. That's only two months away at this point."

"Okay," Nora said. "If you're leaving now, I'm just going to take a few minutes to finish up some reports I've been working on and then head home myself. So I'll be up your way soon. Why don't you call me when you're finished, and we can meet up at a diner to talk it through?"

"Sounds like a plan," I said.

Nora's eyes narrowed, as if struck by a thought.

"Will you even be able to access the community center today?" she asked. "It's a Saturday, after all."

"Yeah, they've been having an autumn festival there throughout October," I said. "We'll be able to get on the grounds and into the building."

"Okay." Nora turned and gave you a hug, which you were happy to return. "You're very brave for helping your daddy like this, Quince. You keep him safe, okay?"

She said it with a twinkle in her eye, but you responded with a somber nod.

"Yes. I will."

I regretted cutting your session with Nora short, but it felt important to strike while the iron was hot, so to speak. Besides, given your advances in speech over the past few weeks, I didn't see how the loss of a single session with Nora would be that detrimental to you. What we had to work on was much more important. For the both of us.

After saying our goodbyes to Nora, we drove north in silence. I didn't want to spend any more time at the community center than was strictly necessary, so I mentally prepared for the task ahead of us by assessing what areas of inquiry we had to cover once we arrived. You stared out the window on the drive, and I assumed you were bracing yourself for the visions you knew you'd have to confront once again.

"Quince," I said once we were about five minutes away from the community center. "We're almost there. You're going to see some scary stuff again. But keep in mind that's not real. None of it is real. We're going to find a way to make sure that bad stuff doesn't happen. So we'll talk about what you see, but the things you'll see can't actually hurt us. Okay?"

"Okay," you murmured, your face a mix of dread and resolve.

And then, a few minutes later, we were on the block of

your preschool. And slightly beyond the school, on the opposite side of the road, sat the community center.

I ventured down that road nearly every day to get you to and from preschool, but I always made a point of coming in from the west to avoid driving past the community center. The structure was an uncomfortable reminder of my own impending death, and I took great pains to steer clear of it to the extent possible. But avoiding it wasn't a luxury I had at that moment.

The parking lot of the center had been mostly empty the last time we were there, but it didn't take long after pulling into the lot to realize it was filled to capacity with the cars of families attending the autumn festival. After circling the lot once on the off chance a spot had opened up, I gave up and drove further down the street, parking on the side of the road.

"It's crowded because there's a festival," I told you as I let you out of the car. You accepted my explanation with a nod, and numbly took my hand as we walked back toward the community center.

We made our way through the crowded parking lot and came across an open gate on the side of the building. Just inside the gate was a foldout table where two teenage girls sat together, a money box on the table between them. A sign next to the table read, "Admission: Adults $10, Children 5–18 $5, Children under 5 free."

"Guess it's our lucky day," I said to you. "You get in for free." I fished a ten-dollar bill out of my wallet and handed it to one of the girls.

"Thank you," the girl replied, stuffing the bill into the box in front of her and marking each of our hands with a pumpkin stamp. 'But just to warn you, they're saying a storm may hit later today, so we might be closing early."

"That's okay," I replied, while you studied the pumpkin stamp on the back of your hand. "We don't plan on staying here that long." *Not a second longer than necessary.*

There had only been a few people milling about in front of the community center when we drove by earlier, but the packed parking lot made sense once we made our way to the area behind the building. Families filled the green field, and children of all ages ran about freely in clusters, their warm breath vaporizing into small clouds in the cool fall air.

*Looks like a fun set up*, I thought. One station in the area was selling coffee and cider donuts, and if we hadn't had a pressing assignment, I would've been tempted to stop there. There was also a fenced area containing several lambs and goats—an impromptu petting zoo—and my heart went out to those animals. Toward the back of the lot, I noticed corn fields where someone had constructed what looked to be a fairly elaborate corn maze.

They had set up an orange Halloween-themed bouncy castle near the building, and it was overflowing with children. One girl, about three years old, emerged from the castle in tears, her hands pressed to the side of her head as she ran to her father, a uniformed police officer. The father immediately started yelling at a boy perched at the top of an inflatable slide protruding out of the castle, and I assumed there'd been some sort of altercation between the two children.

*It's chaos in there*, I marveled, grateful you usually eschewed attractions with that degree of pandemonium.

"Can you see anything?" I asked, gesturing around the outside area and trusting you to know what I meant. But you shook your head.

"I can't," you said, sounding pained. "There are too many people here. Except I see a girl crying to her daddy. He's a policeman." You looked up at me, hopeful you had passed along at least a small bit of useful intel.

"Thank you. But I see that girl, too," I said with a smile. I contemplated wandering around the outside in the hope you'd be able to see something noteworthy from a different angle but decided against it. The important stuff, as far as I knew, happened inside—we could always come back later to revisit the back area.

I led you inside the community center through its back doors. The lobby area was mostly empty, notwithstanding the sizable crowd outside. *Most people probably don't realize this building is open and there are clean bathrooms here,* I thought. *How many people are needlessly subjecting themselves to the porta-potties?* Still, a few people wandered about, and I spotted some men and women going in and out of the restrooms.

Your eyes were wide as you surveyed the area.

"Do you see something, Quince?" I asked.

"Yes," you said, looking around the lobby. "The man is hurting people, and they are falling down. I think they're dead." Your voice was neutral, as if you were purposefully holding your emotions at arm's length.

I let out a deep breath.

"Can you count how many people are hurt?" I asked. You wordlessly pointed your finger around the area, stabbing the air with each tick.

"Four," you finally said.

*Four people dead? Jesus....*

I couldn't accept letting those deaths happen, and I made a mental note to work through that problem with Nora. But that was an issue for later.

"How did the man hurt them?" I asked. "Is he using a gun?" I always tried to keep you away from violent media, but I figured you'd come across the concept of a gun at some point in your life.

"I think so," you said.

I didn't want to spend too much time there since I wasn't sure how long you could handle being subjected to that imagery, and I didn't want to skip the visions involving me.

"Can we go look in that hallway?" I asked you, as gently as I could, pointing to the corridor running along the side of the community center. You assessed that area of the building with a look of dread on your face, but you gave a taut nod.

As we walked toward the narrow hallway, a man and his wife came in from the outside area, with the man carrying a crying five-year-old girl.

"It's going to start pouring soon," the man was explaining to the girl. "We want to get home before the rain."

But the girl wasn't satisfied with that reason for leaving and continued wailing. You gave her a brief sympathetic look before walking with me to the hallway.

Once there, you stopped, looking distraught but otherwise in control.

"Are you seeing it again?" I asked.

"Yes. You and the man are looking at each other, and you said something."

"What did I say?"

"I... I don't know. I think you called him a bad name. You called him *ilsh*."

"*Ilsh*?"

"I think so."

I didn't know what that meant, but I made a note of it on my phone.

"Can you see the man hurting me?"

You looked too pained to speak, but you gave a tight nod.

"He hurts me with the gun?"

Another quick nod.

"And then you fall over there," you said, on the verge of tears, pointing down the hall. "Then you move over there," you repositioned your finger slightly, aiming at a spot marginally closer to where we were standing, "and you lay there with your eyes open. You aren't moving."

I winced at the imagery. "How do I move from one spot to the other? Do I walk? Did someone carry me?" I asked.

"I don't know." You shrugged. "You fall there and then you are over there."

Your description wasn't making complete sense to me, but the picture of what appeared fated to happen was clearing up somewhat. *Nora is better at this than me*, I thought. *Hopefully, she can make sense of some of this.* I considered calling her to see if she had any ideas about anything else I should inquire about while we were in the hallway, but there was one thing I wanted to nail down first.

"Now, you told us before this all happens at night. Do you remember that?"

You blinked, confused.

"The last time you saw this," I said, "you said it was dark outside and you could see the moon."

"Oh. Yes." You arched your head to look past me out the large glass windows at the end of the hall facing the rear of the building. "Yes, it is dark. And I see the moon."

"Okay. Good."

Satisfied with that confirmation, I took out my phone to call Nora, turning away from you. Through the window you had just looked out, I could see storm clouds rolling in, and it occurred to me that the family we'd passed earlier had been smart for clearing out when they did. Other families, finally realizing a storm was imminent, were trying to coax their children out of the bounce castle, positioned a few yards away from the building.

I held the phone up to my ear, waiting for Nora to answer, and absently gazed at the drama unfolding in and around the bounce castle, with some parents even taking off their shoes to go in themselves to drag out their children. As I chuckled at the chaos, my eyes wandered upwards and stopped.

My mind was racing as I lowered my phone, my thumb absently moving to end the call.

*Oh.*

*Oh God.*

The bounce castle was Halloween-themed—I realized that much when I spotted it outside. But I hadn't gotten a good look at the top of it, which was plainly visible from our vantage point inside the community center. From inside the building, I could see at the apex of the castle a silhouette of a witch riding a broomstick.

And the witch was flying over the backdrop of a full moon.

*That can't be it.* My mouth went dry.

"Is that the moon you saw?" I asked, dreading your answer.

You followed where I was pointing.

"Yes," you said. "That's it."

Black clouds continued to roll in, obscuring the sun and plunging the back area into darkness. A deluge of rain seemed imminent. But that wasn't what I feared.

"We have to get you out of here," I said, and you were taken aback by the urgency in my voice. "Now!"

But before I could take a step, a loud crash from outside caused the entire building to reverberate. I paused, not knowing where was safe to go. Moments later, I heard a piercing crack, and then another, coming from somewhere out in front of the building. Those noises sounded vaguely like fireworks, or maybe even thunder. But I knew they were neither.

It was gunfire.

*No.*

It was the only thought I could generate in my desperate state.

*Not yet.*

Even though you hated being carried, I lifted you up, trying to decide on a course of action. You were likewise stunned and didn't resist my hold. The sound of another few cracks from somewhere outside kept me rooted to the spot. I heard a woman scream in the distance, only to go silent after yet another pop.

Fear had left me incapable of action, so I simply stood there with you in my arms, trying to will my brain or my body into doing something other than perseverating on the obvious.

*It's starting.*

*And I'm not ready.*

**18**

*Others in my shoes might have been consumed by questioning what mistakes led to the miscalculation regarding when the dreaded incident would occur. Whether it was failing to ask you the right questions, or miscommunications causing Nora and I to believe the incident would occur at night, or my willingness to step back on the grounds of the community center at all, there were plenty of options when it came to identifying where I went wrong. But I didn't feel tempted to go down that road because I immediately realized it didn't matter.*

*Fate had dictated I be there, at that precise spot and at that precise time. No trick or manipulation on my part could have avoided that outcome. Not without hurting you, at least.*

*Optimism had permeated my defenses and allowed me to buy into the possibility there might be a way to save us both, but upon realizing the attack was beginning, I saw those notions for what they were: nothing more than wishful thinking. In my gut, I had known the truth for some time, but my desire to live had kept it buried.*

*But in that moment, the truth revealed itself and I could perceive what remained of my existence with startling clarity. I saw that my life had been reduced to a to-do list comprising two items, which I had to address in order.*

*The first was getting you to safety, and my mind immediately zeroed in on the logistics of accomplishing that all-important objective. Those details dominated my thinking, which was just as well since the second item on my list required less planning and was, in any event, something I didn't want to think about until it was absolutely necessary.*

*I simply had to die.*

I LISTENED, trying to ascertain where the danger lay. After those first few fits of gunfire coming from somewhere outside, there was silence, and I could only guess at what was happening. I heard an uproar behind the building where the festival was taking place, but that noise suggested confusion more than terror. I didn't believe the assailant, or assailants, had gone that way.

Which meant they were coming through the building itself.

The far end of the hallway we were waiting in had a door leading to the outside, which appeared to only be an exit—we could leave, but no one could come in that way. It was unlikely the unknown assailant would even attempt to use that door, but I still hesitated. Any mistiming on my part could cause us to rush directly into the arms of the perpetrator out front.

*Or perpetrators*, I reminded myself again, but then I recalled what you reported seeing: a man. Not men. I didn't want to assume too much—that could be even more disastrous, and it was very possible you simply hadn't viewed the complete picture of what was transpiring—but it seemed more likely we had a single person to worry about. But that was plenty.

It felt unsafe to move from our location without having a better idea of where the assailant was, so I forced myself to continue to wait. You started asking a question, but I shushed you with a finger to my lips. Your fear had driven you to a state of compliance, and you nodded in understanding.

"See that door?" I whispered to you, pointing at the exit. "Very soon, we're going to run out that way and get somewhere safe. But I think the bad man you saw is here, so I want to make sure he isn't outside when we go. That's why we're waiting right now."

You didn't respond—I couldn't even be sure you were paying attention to me at all. Still, you seemed to have placed your complete trust in me to deal with this crisis, and you allowed me to hold you as we waited.

The silence continued, and I wondered whether I should call 911. *Hopefully, multiple people have already made that call*, I thought, but it felt wrong to stand there doing nothing. I took out my phone, but before I could dial, I heard the cracks of gunfire again, only much louder as they echoed deafeningly through the hallway.

The man was inside the building.

"Let's go," I whispered, pushing open the exit door with my hip. It was unnaturally dark outside—the commencement of the storm seemed imminent—and it took me a second to get my bearings. A tall fence separated the back area from our exit, but a rough pathway made of loose stones led from the door toward the front of the building, and I knew that was the way we had to go.

But I was already thinking several moves ahead, and I didn't leave right away. Instead, I reached down and searched with my hand until I found a round stone, roughly the size and shape of a softball. While maintaining my hold of you in my left arm, I held the door open a crack with my foot and positioned the rock to keep the door from fully closing behind us. I thought that setup would be enough to keep the exit from shutting and locking, at least for a few minutes, but those hopes were dashed almost immediately when the rock started vibrating under the weight of the door trying to close. I was on the verge of adjusting the stone when it squeezed out of the door's hold, falling into the hallway inside with a loud *bang.*

Lunging, I caught the door with the fingernails of my right hand as it was about to fully close and then struggled to pry it open again, all while maintaining my hold of you. *I need something else,* I realized once I had the door opened again, feeling increasingly anxious about how long this was all taking. I knew the assailant could show up any second, only to find me puttering about by the side exit.

With the door once again propped open by my foot, I awkwardly bent over and found a thin piece of slate, which I inserted between the door's hinges. Again, the door tried to shut, but the stone operated as an effective wedge to keep it from fully closing and locking. The end result was subtle— to any casual observer, the door appeared shut, which worked out even better than my original plan.

Finally satisfied that I'd be able to reopen the door from the outside, I crept toward the front of the building but stopped before reaching the front lawn. The street was about ten yards away from us, but I knew going further at that point would leave us exposed to gunfire coming from the main doors if the shooter happened to be looking our way. I stuck my head out for a peek and spotted some people running away through the parking lot beyond the opposite end of the building. The amount of people fleeing was a small fraction of the crowd in the back, and I wondered why so few had made their escape. But there was no sign of the assailant near the main set of doors.

Another burst of gunfire from inside the building led to a fresh round of screams from everyone in the back. I knew that now was our best chance to make a run for the street.

"We're going for it," I whispered to you, and I didn't wait for a response before darting out as fast as I could.

Despite my best instincts, I glanced back as I ran, looking for movement to reveal we'd been spotted and were under fire. But no such attack came in our direction.

Upon reaching the street, I crossed diagonally, away from the community center, and finally slowed to a walk once I reached your preschool. We weren't completely out of danger, but we were, at least, out of all lines of sight from the building we had just vacated. Winded from the effort of carrying you at a full run, I placed you back on the ground to lead you toward the back of your school.

"Where are we going, Daddy?" you finally asked. Your eyes were wide, and I worried you might be in some state of shock.

"We have to find someplace safe for you," I said. Reaching into my pocket, I dug out my phone and made a call.

Nora picked up immediately.

"Hey Will, I'm in the car and about ten minutes away. How did it—"

"It's happening now," I cut in. My head swiveled about as I spoke, searching for an adequate place to hide you. "It seems like a mass shooter, but I have no details. I got Quince out and I'm taking him behind his preschool to hide. It should be safe, but I don't have time to get him anywhere more secure. I'm sorry, Nora, but I need you to come get him —his school is called Tiny Toes Preschool. Please."

A crack of lightning and the dark clouds above us opened, drenching us in rain. You winced at the outbreak of the downpour but didn't speak. I didn't want to leave you exposed to the elements, but I couldn't see a way to get into the school itself, and I certainly didn't have time to break in.

There weren't many options. I spotted an empty dumpster, but it seemed too risky to leave you in there during a lightning storm, even under the circumstances. There were also stairs leading to a back entrance to the school I hadn't realized existed until then, with a small landing area at the top of the steps, but there was nowhere for you to hide on that tiny porch.

*But under it....*

"Why do you need me?" Nora demanded. "Where are *you* going, Will?" But I ignored her questions.

"Quince will be hiding under a porch behind his school. I'll tell him to stay there until you find him. Please get him as soon as you can and call the police on your way."

"What are you doing?" Nora screamed, sounding panicked. "You can't—"

"Tiny Toes Preschool," I said again, cutting her off. "And I'm sorry, Nora."

I ended the call.

"Quince," I said to you, shoving my phone back into my pocket and leading you toward the side of the porch. "I need you to hide in here." I pointed at a small opening through which you could gain entry to the area under the stairs. "You have to stay quiet and hide until Ms. Nora comes for you, okay? She'll be here in about ten minutes."

You glanced at the small, dark area under the porch but didn't move.

"Where are you going, Daddy?" you asked in a small voice that was barely audible over the sound of the pounding rain.

"I'm... I have to go back and help those people," I said, trying not to wince at my lie. "I have to go now. So please—can you hide here?"

Again, you didn't move. You simply stared at me, your wet hair plastered across your forehead. I felt my throat constrict.

"Look, Quince, I really have to go."

I was trying to mask my terror, although I recognized the emotions surging through me were undoubtedly strong enough to leave an imprint. Something you might revisit one day.

"You're too young to understand this," I said, "but if you come back to this exact spot when you're older, I think you'll hear what I'm saying now, and it will all make sense to you. I'm sorry. I wish I could have found another way, and I'm so sorry I couldn't. I don't want to do this, but I have to. And it's all because I love you. Please know that. Okay?"

My rambling probably made little sense to you, but something in my tone must have registered because you nodded in acquiescence.

"Okay, Daddy." You clambered through a small opening and crouched under the porch, peering out at me from under a step. "Be careful."

"I will," I said. *Another lie.* I reached through a gap in the steps to touch your face, just for a moment, before pulling my hand back and walking away. It was beyond reckless to leave you alone under these circumstances, but the alternative was undoubtedly worse. Resisting the urge to look back, I jogged toward the street and faced the community center once again.

Now that I was alone, I could get a better look at what was happening. Some people were evacuating the area through the parking lot, but it remained a trickle—not nearly as many people as I would've thought. But then, through the pouring rain, I spotted a truck at the main entrance to the back area. It appeared to be a large moving truck, purposefully driven directly into the building and blocking the opening in the fence entirely. I could make out some escaping the back area by climbing other sections of that tall fence, but that was just a smattering of the crowd. Hundreds undoubtedly remained in the festival area, unless they had somehow found another direction in which to escape.

*That truck was the loud crash we heard earlier*, I realized. I thought I could make out a couple of bodies on the ground in front of the community center, but it was impossible to see any details through the torrent of rain. There were sparse lights inside the building, as if the main power had gone out and the emergency backup had kicked in, providing just enough illumination to keep the interior from plunging into complete darkness. I didn't know if the storm had knocked the power out or whether the assailant had purposefully cut it, but regardless, things appeared ominous inside.

*How long have I been gone?* I wondered. It probably took less than a minute to get you to the back of the school, another minute or two to call Nora and get you settled, and another minute to get back to the community center. *Four minutes, at most.* There was still no sign of the police, but I knew the station was over five minutes away, plus whatever time it took to alert them of this attack. I assumed they'd arrive shortly, and I didn't know what would happen at that point.

But I knew what part I had to play.

*How far could this guy have gotten in four minutes?* The answer really depended on what he was doing inside. Was he going through each area of the building, methodically killing anyone in his path, or was his intention to cut straight to the back area where throngs of families remained? Both options were bleak, and I tried to put them out of mind.

Regardless of where the man was, I thought it would be a mistake to try to reenter through the main doors of the building. Even if they were unlocked—which I figured was far from certain since the assailant could have locked them to keep anyone from sneaking in behind him—the lobby wasn't where I had to be. Thankful for my foresight in rigging the side door to remain unlocked, I headed off in that direction.

Through the pouring rain, I ran back across the front lawn area, nearly slipping on the wet grass, before making my way to the right side of the building—the opposite side from the parking lot. Once I hit the stony path, I slowed my stride until I was walking up to the exit that we'd traversed only minutes earlier. After a few deep breaths to calm myself, I opened the door and stepped back into the hallway.

It took a moment for my eyes to adjust to the dark. While the sky outside had been nearly black because of the storm, there had been at least some visibility. Once I was back inside the community center, however, I couldn't see anything other than the dim lighting supplied by the building's backup power system. The large window at the far end of the corridor was a translucent gray, offering a nominal amount of light but not revealing what was happening in the back. I listened carefully for any hint of where the shooter might be, but all was still for the moment.

*Where the hell is this guy?* I took a step forward and stopped, horrified, at the squeak my wet sneaker made after stepping onto the tiled floor. There was no logical reason for me to be concerned about the noise given my objective, but I nonetheless turned quickly to wipe my feet, as quietly as I could manage, on a mat by the exit door. Once I was satisfied that the bottoms of my shoes had adequately dried, I turned and headed down the hallway to find the gunman.

Only this time, when I started down the hall, I could make out a silhouette standing at the back of the building, framed by the dim gray light of the window behind him. The shadow appeared to be facing me.

And it looked to be holding an AR-15 rifle.

The shadow took a casual step toward me, and then another—it did not appear to be in any hurry at all. I was prepared for this moment—at least as much as I could've been—and I didn't run. It continued to walk toward me, unhurried, until it was close enough for me to make out the man behind the shadow.

He was young—perhaps a few years older than twenty —with a wiry frame. His light blond hair was styled in a bizarre mushroom cut, with long hair on the top and the sides shaved down to the skin. It looked as if he had prepared for the darkness caused by the storm by dressing in black from head to toe: black combat boots and black pants, with a black bulletproof vest over a black thermal. But his most disturbing feature was his eyes.

In the past, I had often referred to myself as being dead on the inside—an expression I'd abandoned in recent months—but coming face-to-face with that man made me truly appreciate how off I had been in my self-assessment.

Even if I wasn't demonstrative by nature, I regularly felt emotions operating deep within, confirmed by some visions you had seen of me. But in seeing that man's eyes, I learned for the first time what it truly meant when a person was dead on the inside. Because there was nothing in that man's eyes. Nothing at all.

Only a desire to make others as dead as he was.

The man slowly raised his rifle, taking aim at me, but he didn't move. Likewise, I stood frozen in place, with no desire to run from my fate, despite the terror pouring out of me. But there was more than fear. I felt profound sadness. I was consumed by despair at the thought that this person was on the verge of taking me from you, and you from me. But that despair wasn't powerful enough to compel me to move and put you at risk.

And so I remained in place.

The man continued to stare at me, and my thoughts went back to you standing in that hallway two months earlier, shrieking, "Stop it! Stop it!" But the man couldn't hear those screams from the past, nor would he have heeded them, regardless.

*What is he waiting for?* I wondered. *Does he want me to run?* I imagine everyone else he encountered up to that point had put up some sort of resistance, and my acceptance of my fate may have confused him at some level. Or perhaps he was feeling some version of disappointment at my nonresponse. For whatever reason, he didn't seem content merely pulling the trigger and putting me down.

As we stared at each other, the man's eyes flicked to his left before settling back on me. Having nothing to lose, I followed his glance and noticed he was eyeing the exit. *He wants me to make a run for it*, I realized. *He's toying with me. Trying to trick me into believing I might escape before he takes me out.* But I had no inclination to go along with his sick game.

"Hey, zilch!" I called out, my voice sounding calmer than I felt. "Can we get this over with?"

A hint of a smile touched the man's lips, and he removed his left hand from the rifle's hand-guard. For a brief moment, I worried he wouldn't shoot me at all, and that through my taunt, I had inadvertently turned your prior vision into a lie. But all the man did with that free hand was flip me off, brandishing his middle finger as he squeezed the trigger with his right hand multiple times in quick succession.

I didn't flinch as the bullets from that rifle tore through my body.

## 19

*I was dying.*

*I was dying, and I realized it almost immediately upon hitting the floor, agony pulsating from the left side of my body. I couldn't pinpoint every area where I'd been hit, but I felt the pain concentrated around my upper left leg and the left side of my abdomen. In the aftermath of absorbing those bullets, screams surely poured out of me, but I have no memory of them, as my cries were not volitional—they were a purely physiological response to punishment that a human body isn't designed to endure.*

*I was dying even as I regained some control over my thoughts while I lay prone on the ground, struggling to modulate the torture through gritted teeth and sharp breaths. My vision was blurry due to the tears in my eyes, but I could see my assailant walk closer to study me, bleeding and helpless, to assess whether his errant shots—a byproduct of cockily firing his rifle with a single hand—were sufficient for his purposes, even if he did not attain the instant kill that he was going for. He eyed me on the ground and seemingly agreed with my prognosis that the wounds were fatal, because after a moment he pivoted to walk away, leaving me to die alone on the tiled floor.*

I was dying, and I felt my strength departing with alarming rapidness as I laid in an expanding pool of my blood, desperate for anything to distract me from my suffering. While every other part of my body shut down, my hearing somehow became more attuned, and through the glass window at the end of the hallway I could make out muffled voices outside, which had reignited in terror at the sound of renewed gunfire in the building.

A woman's desperate cry: "Stacey? Stacey?"

A young girl's pleading voice: "Daddy? Where's my daddy?"

A teenage boy, trying to hide his fear: "I can't find her, Mom! I can't find her!"

I was dying and left to wonder why so many people remained in the back area. Was the moving truck blockage truly that effective at penning everyone in? Surely there were other means of egress, even if it involved fleeing into the cornfield maze on the far side of the clearing. Was it that difficult to corral a family to escape a dangerous area? Or perhaps it was simply a case of deer in the headlights, with most people too shaken to realize the basic steps they had to take to remove themselves from harm's way.

I was dying, and my nearness to death bestowed clarity upon me, and I could see the next moments play out as clearly as if I had been gifted one of your visions: the assailant, with the building now completely secured, was free to head out back where families would be nothing more than helpless lambs, doomed to slaughter. Even if most of those at the festival had made it out somehow, that still left dozens behind to face that monster's mindless bloodlust. Fathers and mothers would be gunned down as they shielded their children behind them, and then those children would not expect or receive any mercy.

I was dying, and I had been so focused on carrying out my

*role and maintaining the integrity of your vision that I hadn't looked beyond this moment, but as I lay writhing in pain, I could finally see the larger picture: children, not all that different from you, dying for no reason whatsoever. Parents, like me, willing to give anything to protect those children, but coming face-to-face with the harsh reality that sometimes even "anything" is insufficient. I was resigned to my own death, but the additional injustices the next few moments would bring filled me with a rage eclipsing even my physical torment. I grit my teeth and steeled myself.*

*I was dying...*

∾

BUT I WASN'T dead yet.

The assailant walked away at a normal pace, but through my racing thoughts, I perceived him as moving in slow motion. I grew weaker with every second that passed, and I suspected my life was down to its last minutes, if not seconds. But I was still alive for the moment, and I could either lie there and wait for my end, or do something—even if I didn't know what I could accomplish with the meager reserves left to me.

And then, a moment of clarity: *get up.*

Anything I attempted to do involved the same first step, which was getting back on my feet. I moaned as I struggled to roll onto my right side in order to keep weight off the areas of my body that had received the brunt of the gunfire. The agony I felt upon getting shot, which was beyond anything I'd ever experienced, somehow increased when I moved, and it was difficult to fight off the urge to remain still solely to minimize the misery. But I successfully rejected that instinct and was amazed when I fought through that excruciating pain and rolled over, face down to the ground and ready to lift myself back onto my feet.

Moving as quickly and as silently as I could, I pushed down on the ground, raising myself up....

Only to be slammed back to the floor by an unseen force.

Panic set in. *I'm changing something*, I realized with horror. *Something Quince saw. The universe doesn't want me to stand up.* And even if I could force through that resistance in my weakened state....

*Quince.* I thought of you alone, hiding under a porch in the midst of a storm, waiting in vain for my return. *Oh God, Quince. I can't hurt you again.*

*I can't alter your vision.*

But what was the alternative? Lie there, complicit, as families were decimated outside? I had only come to know you—to truly know you—over the past several months, and one thing was clear to me, even though you hadn't yet turned five: you wouldn't want me to let that man hurt anyone else.

*Even if....*

I discarded the thought as I tried to rise again, shutting down my emotions and refusing to think about the consequences of my actions. Because if I gave even a moment of thought to what I was doing to you, I would assuredly fail.

My left hand slipped in a puddle of blood as I tried to push myself back to my feet, and it knocked into something as I caught myself. *A rock*, I realized. Specifically, the stone that had been squeezed into the hallway during my first botched attempt to prop the door open earlier. I closed my fingers around it and, ignoring the resultant stab of pain, pushed myself up again. Gravity's hold was unusually strong, and every inch I lifted myself felt as if I was defying the rules of physics. But I slowly moved upwards with all of my mental energies focused on that single task. When my arms reached full extension, I yanked my right leg under me with a painful grunt and steadied that foot on the ground.

One more push with everything I had, and I was on my feet once again. I was shaky and tilting left to accommodate my severe injuries, but I was standing.

By that time, the assailant had nearly reached the end of the hallway and I focused on the one task left to me before I could rest. *I'll have to run*, I realized, tightening my grip on the stone. *Somehow catch up to him and brain him. Or at least knock him out.* It seemed impossible, but so did getting up at all. Without thinking, I pushed off my right foot to break into a run...

...only to fall immediately after putting weight back onto my damaged left leg.

I stumbled forward and my elbow struck the ground, causing me to lose my grip on the stone I had planned to use as my improvised weapon. All I could do was watch helplessly as the rock jumped out of my hand, skittering across the floor until it gently bumped up against the boot of the gunman, who was on the verge of turning out of the hallway toward the building's rear exit. He glanced down at the rock before looking back at me, laying defenseless on my side. The corners of his mouth twitched as he let out a small noise—a scolding "tsk-tsk"—and then raised his weapon once again, this time taking careful aim with both hands on the rifle. Lightning flashed outside, briefly illuminating the corridor before plunging it back into near darkness.

There was nothing I could do while he targeted me in the scope's crosshairs. I closed my eyes, defeated, and tried not to think about the ramifications of my failure.

A shot rang out, and I rolled onto my back, the side of my head slamming on the hard tile beneath me. It took a moment to register that something was amiss.

Somehow, I still wasn't dead.

I tilted my head enough to look down the hall, but the assailant was no longer standing there. Stretching my neck even further, I located him sprawled on the ground, motionless, with his rifle laying at his side a few inches from his hand. Through the resulting silence, I could make out muffled voices coming through the glass window at the end of the hallway.

"Did you get him, Frank?" someone yelled.

"I don't know," another man called out in response, and I could hear the uncertainty in his voice. "I can't see shit! I thought I saw him for a second, but...." the voice trailed off.

I arched my neck again and observed a rough circle of blood expanding on the tiles around the assailant's head. Focusing on the window beyond the man, I could just make out a small hole in the glass. A tiny bullet hole that somehow didn't shatter the entire window.

"You got him!" I tried to call out, but those words turned into a gurgled cough. Once that cough subsided, I said it again. "You got him." But I couldn't generate any force behind the words, and all that emerged was a raspy whisper.

I tried to stand up once again, but it had been a minor miracle that I was able to do so at all earlier, given the severity of my wounds. I was too far gone to have any hope of replicating the feat. It wasn't a question of effort—it was a downright physical impossibility. All I could do was lie on my back, struggling to formulate thoughts through the pain.

*Quince.* Now that the threat was extinguished, I was free to think of you once again, and I let out a groan as the emotions I had pushed away earlier flooded back. *Oh God,*

*Quince, what did I do?* I hadn't accomplished much through my efforts—I merely distracted the assailant for a few seconds to allow someone else to take him out—but it had been enough. He wouldn't hurt anyone else. But I thought back to the battle in getting to my feet earlier—a struggle that, against all odds, I overcame. My efforts had surely saved many lives, but I didn't dwell on those.

All I could think about was the life I likely sacrificed in doing so.

*I turned part of Quince's vision into a lie.* And I knew the penalty for diverting reality in that fashion.

I blindly reached for my phone in my front pocket, hoping to check in with Nora, but all I felt was shattered glass and blood. One of the bullets I had absorbed had also destroyed my phone, leaving me to wonder what was happening to you right then.

*Someone will come in soon. And I can tell them where Quince is, and that he'll need help....*

I continued waiting for the sound of footsteps as people ran into the building to investigate, but there was nothing but silence and the muffled noise of panicked voices outside. And then I realized what was happening: *they don't realize they got him. They think he might still be in here... and they're afraid to come in.*

At some point, once the police arrived in full, I imagined they would storm the building and figure out what had transpired. Of course, by that point, I would be long gone.

And, I knew in my heart, you would be as well.

I laid on the ground, face up and staring into nothing, as the full import of what I'd done hit me. For the past few months, I had mentally prepared for my death. There were even times when I lost control of my thoughts and envisioned what a worst-case scenario would look like, where I failed in my task, leaving you to die in my place. But what ultimately happened hadn't been on my radar at all.

*I've killed us both.*

I gazed at the ceiling through unseeing eyes, struggling to process the events of the past few minutes. The choice presented to me was impossible, but that offered no comfort whatsoever. I was on the verge of death, and I imagined you were in a similar state under a porch in the rain, alone until Nora found you. We were across the street from one another, probably less than a hundred yards apart, and it broke my heart that we'd be deprived of the small comfort of each other's company as we departed from this life.

*Maybe this was our destiny all along?* I wondered. *If there is an afterlife, our family should be reunited shortly.* I felt a tear fall out of the corner of my eye and slide down my temple toward the floor beneath me.

The way things had ended was more painful than my wounds, but I had no option but to endure it all as I lay there unmoving and helpless, with nothing to do but reflect on the choices that had brought us to that endpoint. *I hope I have the chance in the afterlife to explain everything to Quince,* I thought. *Explain and apologize.* But I couldn't dwell on that thought for long.

Because that was the moment I heard your voice.

"Daddy?"

I blinked, confused. *Am I hallucinating?* But then a different possibility struck me: *am I experiencing my own vision? Is this the same experience Anne went through at the hospital while she was on the verge of death?* Curious whether there was a visual component to what I was hearing, I found the strength to move my head a few degrees and waited for my eyes to refocus.

I saw you standing at my side, your wet hair dripping and concern written across your face as you looked down at me. You appeared to be solid, as if you were physically there, and doubt crept in about what I was seeing.

"Quince?" I asked in a barely audible voice. "Is that really you?"

"Yes," you said. And then, sounding nervous, you added, "I came to help you. Are you mad?"

*Mad?* I tried to make sense of it all. *Quince wasn't hurt!* was my first exultant thought. It made no sense, but I was too relieved to care.

"Not mad," I muttered, trying to smile through my pain.

*He must have come back through that side door*, I thought. *The one I propped open earlier. If he had arrived even a minute or two earlier, he would have walked right into....*

But you hadn't. You were there—unharmed and safe. That was all that mattered.

"Are you hurt, Daddy?" you asked. It was clear you were merely stating the obvious from the way you eyeballed my wounds with a mix of curiosity and horror.

"A little bit," I croaked. My mind was foggy, and it was growing harder to think.

You shuffled your feet, nervous. "You were just doing the thing I saw. The thing with your eyes open."

"What?" I breathed, struggling to process what you said. *His vision of me*, I realized through my stupor. *I had been staring at the ceiling for some time, emotions pouring out of me. Quince didn't see me dead when we were here months ago. He saw me dying.* Although given the circumstances, it seemed like a distinction without a difference.

"You're... okay?" I asked, laboring for each syllable, and you nodded.

"I'm okay." You looked scared, but otherwise unharmed. I lifted my right arm, reaching for you, and you grabbed my hand and held it as tightly as you could.

"I'm... sorry... Quince...."

We were together, and that was something. It was everything. I knew I was close to the end, but it was bearable with you at my side. I gripped your hand, determined to hold it for as long as I could summon the strength, and you didn't let go. We waited in silence, content being together again, even under those circumstances.

But after a few moments, I felt my last reserves of strength fade, and my hand slipped out of yours, falling to the floor.

I closed my eyes, waiting for whatever was to come. The pain at my side was fading, and I knew my body was shutting down. I barely registered the sound of your footsteps walking away from me, cautious and tentative, as if you were looking for something.

*What is it, Quince?* I thought. *What are you trying to find?*

I couldn't see what you were doing, but then I heard a noise that not only told me what you were looking for, but confirmed you had found it.

"Help!"

It was the sound of you finding your voice.

"Help!" you shrieked again, your cries echoing through the corridor. It sounded as if you were down the hallway near the window facing the back area, close to the spot where the assailant was lying dead. "My daddy is hurt! Help! Help!"

I was powerless to do anything but listen.

"Please help!" I heard you cry out again in a high-pitched voice. "Help! Help!"

You abruptly stopped yelling, and there was once again silence. I didn't know if anyone had heard your plea for help, and if they did, whether it would be enough to spur anyone to come inside.

But then, moments later, I heard a new sound: footsteps running through the hallway, squeaking on the tiles with each step. A sharp intake of breath, and then the sound of a man's voice, sounding overwhelmed by whatever he saw: "Holy shit."

A few more steps, and the voice was directly above me. "Jesus Christ. Hang in there buddy—I'll be right back." Squeaky footsteps running away again, as the man called out, "I need Joan in here! Where is Joan Regan?"

And then your voice again, floating above me. "You'll be okay, Daddy. The people will help you."

I couldn't respond, and a few moments later, I heard a cacophony of footsteps running into the hallway.

"Forget *him*." The voice of the man from moments earlier, coming from down the hall. "That's the shooter, and he's gone. But that one over there's alive. Help him, if you can—I'm going to look around the rest of the building to see if there's anyone else."

And then more footsteps, some getting louder while others faded in the distance, until a woman's voice, directly above me, barked out commands with authority: "Put pressure on the abdomen. Yes, right there."

I felt someone push down on my midriff, and I grunted through the pain.

"We'll need a tourniquet for that thigh," the woman added, hurried but confident. "We have to slow that blood loss. Can you take care of that?"

Another woman's voice: "I'm on it, Mom."

"What are you doing to my daddy?" It was your voice, sounding worried.

"I'm Dr. Regan, and this is my daughter Kate," the woman with the authoritative voice said. "We're going to try to help your father. But we need room, so please stand back. Thank you."

I felt pressure on my leg, and the resultant pain forced my eyes open. Unable to focus my vision, I could barely make out the blurry outline of two women hovering above.

"You're going to be okay," the younger-sounding woman said, placing a comforting hand on my forehead. "You just need to hold on for a little longer. Can you do that?"

Movement beyond the two women caught my attention, but I still couldn't focus my eyes. All I could register was the vague outline of you, anxiously rocking from side to side as you struggled to keep me in your line of sight. You stood a small distance away, not wanting to interfere, although it seemed, from the way you bounced in place, that you were fighting against the desire to get closer. As I gazed at that foggy image of you, I breathed my response. I was too weak to push those words beyond the confines of my lips, but my answer reverberated inside my head. I could only hope it was a vow I'd be able to keep.

*I will try.*

## 20

*And try I did.*

*All my life I've heard stories of someone "being a fighter" in challenging some illness or malady, and it never made much sense to me. How could one consciously fight against something inside of them? I couldn't get my head around the notion of a person steering their own fate regarding an ailment through willpower alone.*

*But then I was shot multiple times, and I finally understood what it meant to fight for your life.*

*As they wheeled me off in an ambulance, I drifted in and out of consciousness, unable to track what was reality and what was a dream, but through that journey, I held onto three intertwined thoughts: you were alive, you were unharmed, and you were waiting for me. At the hospital, I didn't register the transfusions I received to restore the vast amounts of blood I had lost or the surgeries I underwent to remove bullets from my abdomen and repair my damaged organs, but even in my unconscious state I maintained a will to live, and that carried me. No one would have realized it by merely looking at me, laying still in my battered state, but I was fighting as hard as I ever did in my life. And I can say with absolute certainty that I wouldn't have made it but for the fact I knew you were okay and that you needed me to pull through.*

*It was just another example of the many ways in which you saved me.*

I FULLY REGAINED consciousness the day after the attack, opening my eyes to the sight of various medical professionals hovering over me while I lay in a hospital bed. They talked amongst each other, occasionally examining me and whispering findings amongst themselves.

My mouth was dry, and it took some time to regain control of it.

"My son...." I whispered.

"Your son is fine," a bearded doctor told me. "He's worried about you, but he's otherwise safe. So let's just worry about you for now, okay?"

The examinations continued, and I was informed of the surgeries I'd undergone to that point and the additional procedures to come once I had regained adequate strength. Although I was repeatedly told I wasn't out of the woods yet, the doctors' tones seemed to suggest the worst was behind me. Then, once they were collectively satisfied with my condition, the doctors and nurses exited the room en masse, promising to check back on me shortly.

Moments later, you ran in.

"Daddy!" you squealed, running to the bed. Your Aunt Ronnie, who I hadn't seen in years, trailed behind and caught you just before you jumped on me. You didn't push back against your aunt's restraint and instead satisfied yourself by hugging my arm, which I dangled over the side to touch you.

"Quince!" I'd been on the verge of death the last time I had seen you, and it was overwhelming being reunited with you in a peaceful environment. I fought the tears that were threatening to surface and asked, "Are you okay?"

"I'm okay," you said. "Are *you* okay?"

"Basically everything hurts," I admitted. "But I think I'll be okay." I turned to your aunt. "Hey, Ronnie."

"Will," Ronnie said, shaking her head at me. "You scared us!"

"I'm sorry," I muttered. "When did you—"

"I got a call asking me to come up and keep an eye on this guy while you were out of commission," she said, cutting me off. "He's been worried sick about you! He refused to leave until he saw you awake again."

Ronnie looked tired, and I imagined she had a rough night watching you in the hospital waiting room.

"Thank you for taking care of that," I said. "I'm sorry you had to step away from your life for this." Ronnie had three kids of her own who were a few years older than you, so I knew it wasn't a simple thing for her to leave them on short notice.

Ronnie waved me off. "Of course. We're family." She leaned in close to whisper, "And to be honest, this guy is easier to manage than my three demons! But they are Grandma and Grandpa's problem right now."

I smiled and glanced at you.

"Say Ronnie, do you mind if I have a minute with Quince? I'd like to talk to him real quick."

"Of course." Ronnie turned to you and said, "Quince, your daddy is still very hurt, so you promise you won't jump on him if I leave? Or climb up on the bed?"

"I promise," you replied, sounding shy. Ronnie tussled your hair and exited, and you seemed to loosen up immediately once she left the room.

"Can we go home, Daddy?" you asked, sounding anxious.

"Not yet," I said. "I think they have more work to do to fix me up first. And then it may take some time for me to get strong again. So I may be stuck here for a while."

You bit your bottom lip, looking disheartened by that news.

"But, Quince," I quickly added. "I thought for a long time I was going to *die*. But, somehow, I didn't. I'll be back on my feet eventually, and we'll be together again. So I understand if you're sad, but please don't be *too* sad. Because this could have been much, much worse. Do you understand?"

You nodded and held out your hand for me to hold.

"You were so brave during all of that scary stuff," I told you. "So, so brave. I just need you to be brave for a little longer. Okay?"

I felt a small squeeze of my hand, and you nodded again.

"Yes, Daddy, I can be brave," you said. "But you have to be brave, too."

"Okay," I said. "I can do that."

SEVERAL DAYS LATER, the doctors got to work on fixing the damage to my left leg. They knocked me out before undertaking to remove additional bullets from that limb and repair my frayed muscles. Once I awoke again, the lingering effects of the anesthesia kept me from feeling the full impact of the pain, but I knew that was a temporary reprieve. The doctors then reported that the surgeries had been successful across the board, and the work ahead was focused on rehab and regaining my strength. It remained to be seen what the long-term physical toll would be, but I couldn't get too upset about it. The impossible had happened:

I emerged from that nightmare with my life. We both did.

There wasn't much for me to do in the immediate aftermath of my final surgery. You had previously left with your aunt, albeit reluctantly, to stay with your cousins on Long Island while I recuperated in the hospital, and you were only willing to leave once Ronnie reassured you she'd drive you up to visit me as often as she could manage. With nothing else to do than carry out the doctors' vague orders to rest, I contented myself with half-watching television while drifting in and out of sleep.

While watching "The Price Is Right" the morning after the operation on my leg, I was startled by a familiar voice in the room.

"Under the circumstances, I'm willing to forgive you for hanging up on me."

With a smile, I turned off the television and pressed a button to further prop up my mattress so I could get a better look at Nora, who had snuck in without me noticing her. She came over to give me a gentle hug and whispered in my ear, "It's good to see you, Will. Things looked dicey there for a bit."

"It's good to see you, too," I said once she released her embrace and settled into a chair on the side of the bed. "And I'm sorry about all of that. It was... it was chaotic."

"I can't imagine," Nora said with a shake of her head. "And I guess I owe you an apology as well. You probably figured out I didn't get there in time to grab Quince?"

"Yeah, I put that together. But it's okay. It all worked out for the best." I realized my phrasing was atrocious and tried to correct myself. "I meant the best as relates to me and Quince. Not that—"

"I knew what you meant."

"How bad was it?" I asked, dreading the answer. "The rest of it?"

Nora frowned as she contemplated what to tell me.

"How much do you know?" she finally asked.

"Not much. Everyone here has been reluctant to discuss it, and I haven't had an opportunity to look up anything about it on the internet. So please tell me everything and assume I know nothing."

"Okay." Nora paused, trying to figure out the best place to start. "To state the obvious, a gunman started a shooting spree at your community center, and he went through some effort at the outset to pen in as many people as he could into the fenced area behind the building. He had some sort of manifesto that he published online, but I don't know much about that. I can't remember the guy's name—do you want me to look it up?"

"No," I said. "It doesn't matter."

"It doesn't," Nora agreed. "Anyway, he positioned a truck to make it difficult for everyone at the fall festival to exit the grounds. It also started pouring right after his attack started, and the rain and darkness only added to the confusion. It wasn't clear if he purposefully timed his attack to coincide with the storm or if it was just bad luck, but either way it ended up being a perfect recipe for chaos."

"How many?" I asked, and Nora took a deep breath before answering.

"Five," she said. "And two wounded, yourself included.

But the other woman who was injured is also expected to survive."

"Five," I repeated in a soft voice. The death total seemed off to me, and after a moment I could place why. "Before that all started, Quince told me he saw four bodies inside."

"A couple was killed outside, on the lawn in front of the building," Nora explained. "They probably didn't even realize what was happening at the time, which would explain why Quince didn't see them in his visions. Four others were shot inside, and three of those people died."

"Did he.... Were any of the victims...." I trailed off, but Nora understood my question.

"They were all adults," Nora said. "No children were hurt. One woman and four men. Don't get me wrong, Will, it was awful. But it could have been *so* much worse."

I looked away, processing these numbers. *Five deaths. How many children lost a parent that day? Did the couple who was killed have children who are now orphans?* But I wasn't ready to ask those questions.

"What else can you tell me?" was all I asked.

"The guy made his way around the inside of the building, shooting anyone he came across. Including you. Shortly after you were injured, a police officer out back, who had been attending the festival with his daughter, took a desperate shot through the window after he thought he glimpsed the gunman aiming his rifle at someone. The cop had no idea if he hit the guy, and he was waiting for backup before going inside to investigate. But then he heard a boy calling through the window, and that prompted the officer to check things out on his own. Was that child—"

"Yes," I interjected. "It was Quince." *Thank God for that kid.*

Nora nodded. "I figured, but the news didn't have that

kind of detail. Anyway, the cop found you, ran back outside, and quickly found a doctor he knew who he'd run into earlier in the day. One of the benefits of living in a small town is that everyone knows each other, I suppose. That doctor went inside with her daughter, who I heard is currently enrolled in med school, and they somehow kept you alive until the ambulances arrived."

"That was Dr. Joan Regan and her daughter Kate who saved me," I said. 'They stopped by earlier in the week to check on me. They're very nice. I should really send them flowers or something for saving my life."

"Yes, flowers would be a good start," Nora agreed. "But anyway, while you were wheeled away in an ambulance, I worked with the police to get Quince into his aunt's care. And here we are."

"And here we are," I repeated, although it was far from a comforting thought. *Here* was a scary place where gun violence could erupt unprompted and without warning at any time. *I'm alive*, I reminded myself. *Better alive and afraid than the alternative.*

"Can I ask you something?" Nora said. "I don't want to force you to relive any of that, but—"

"Go ahead," I said. "You answered my questions. Fair is fair."

"What *happened* in there? I mean, how are you even alive? I'm so thankful you are, of course, but that guy was only a few yards away from you when he fired, right?"

"Yeah, he was maybe ten yards away. But he was firing his rifle with only one hand, and I think that messed up his aim somewhat."

Nora frowned. "Why was he only using one hand?"

I shrugged, and even that subtle movement triggered a stabbing pain on my left side. "He was flipping me off with his left hand because I called him 'a zilch.' That really seemed to push his buttons."

"A *zilch*?" Nora asked.

"Yes, a zilch. I was going to call him something harsher, but I remember thinking that Quince was watching—or had watched—that scene playing out, so I took care to mind my language. And maybe that guy would have aimed with both hands and killed me outright if I had simply called him an asshole. Who knows?"

"It's funny," Nora said, "the way the smallest things can have huge implications. It boggles the mind."

"It does," I agreed. After a moment, I asked, "Can I tell you something? It's an issue I can only talk to you about, and it's bothering me."

Nora looked around to confirm we were still alone. "Of course."

"After I was shot, I tried to get up to stop that guy before he made his way outside and had access to the families who were still there. But it was so hard to get back on my feet. It felt *exactly* like those other times I tried to alter one of Quince's visions, and I thought I couldn't stand because reality was holding me down."

Nora scoffed. "Of *course* it was hard to get up! You had just been shot five times!"

"I realize that *now*, although I was confused at the time. My point is I *thought* the universe was pinning me down and that if I stood up and stopped that guy somehow, I would kill Quince by altering what he saw in his vision. And despite knowing that, I could still steel my heart, avoid thinking about the repercussions of my actions, and get back on my feet. In the end, I didn't do anything particularly useful—all I accomplished was breaking the guy's stride by distracting him for a second—but that was enough for that cop to put him down. And once I realized what had happened, I thought I had knowingly killed my son. That was a choice I willingly made. How do I live with that, Nora?"

"He's alive, Will. And so are you. That's all that matters."

"Is it?" I shook my head. "Then why do I feel such guilt?"

"You had an impossible choice," Nora said in a forceful tone. "What was the alternative? Lie back and allow other families to be massacred? Is that really what you think Quince would have wanted out of you right then? No matter what you did there, you'd be hating yourself afterwards. So just be thankful things worked out for you and your son. How do you live with that? I don't know, but you better find a way. Because that boy needs you, and you feeling guilty for the rest of your life won't help either of you."

I didn't respond, and Nora must've known I remained troubled because she let out a long exhale before she continued in a softer tone.

"Alright, you feel guilty," she said. "I get that. And the only person who can forgive you, to the extent you need forgiving, is Quince. But he's not old enough to understand what you did, and why you did it. So if this is truly something that is going to eat away at you, this is what I suggest: write down everything that happened. Not just at the community center, but all of it. How you learned about Quince's visions and what they meant. The sacrifices you made to help him. That you put your life on the line without hesitation to keep him safe. You write all that down and soon, while it's still fresh in your head, but don't rush too much because it's going to be a while before Quince is old enough to understand it. Once he is, you share this story with him and accept his judgment. Because I already know what he'll say. But if that's something you need to hear out of his own mouth to come to terms with the path you took and the choices you made, that's the way to do it."

"That's... that's actually good advice," I said. *Write it all down, as honestly as I can.* It would mean I'd have to live for years with my guilt, but Nora was right in saying that was simply a burden I'd have to learn to bear. There would come a time you'd be old enough to understand everything and, hopefully, forgive me for my failings. And at least there would be a hope of that emotional baggage being relieved down the road at some point, even if my physical injuries never fully healed.

"*Actually* good advice?" Nora asked with a raised eyebrow, and I smiled.

"You're right. It's your standard good advice. You've been full of that since I met you. I don't know where I'd be if you hadn't been around to steer me in the right direction when I was going askew. Which was often."

Nora tilted her head, accepting the compliment, and stood up to leave.

"Just try not to let guilt weigh you down too much while you're waiting for Quince to grow up, okay?" she said. "Because I know what he'll tell you, even though it's something you stubbornly refuse to admit to yourself."

"What's that?" I asked.

Nora threw me a withering look, as if I was missing the obvious, and then softened as she answered my question.

"You're a good father."

## 21

*The next several weeks were bittersweet for me. I was mostly alone in the hospital, working toward regaining my strength, while you stayed with your aunt's family on Long Island. True to her word, Ronnie brought you up to visit me at least once a week, and although you appeared happy to see me on each occasion, I knew I wasn't a ton of fun in my bedridden state. My rehab was challenging—even the most basic tasks, such as walking, were extremely taxing, and I soon discovered the damage to my hip made ambulating without a cane all but impossible. I maintained hope that the day would come when I would once again be able to walk entirely on my own, but deep down I accepted that the cane would likely become my permanent companion. But even with those bumps in the road, it was hard to remain down for long for one simple reason: I was still alive.*

*My boss, Andrew, surprised me one day when he popped in to check on me at the hospital. It was rare for the two of us to be together in person, and we were both somewhat awkward at seeing each other in the flesh. Andrew reassured me that in my absence, our company had hired another attorney to handle the day-to-day responsibilities that had been neglected while I was recuperating.* "*But this new guy strikes me as a bit of a dope,*" *Andrew told me.* "*So once you're back on your feet, he's officially your responsibility. I figured we've grown to the point that it was worth doubling the size of our legal department.*"

*On his way out, Andrew asked me, as he so often did, what was going on in my wrongful death litigation against the hospital, and I explained we'd recently settled the case.* "*Attaboy!*" *Andrew exclaimed.* "*What did you get out of them?*"

*I contemplated the question and answered truthfully:* "*More than I could have ever hoped for.*"

*I understand there had been a frenzy of news coverage in the wake of the attack, with the police officer who fatally shot the assailant briefly rising to the level of national hero, but several days later there was another shooting in the Midwest, giving rise to an even greater number of casualties, prompting the media to pivot to that new incident. Even our local journalists didn't seem to have any interest in me or my recovery—as far as they were concerned, the fact that I didn't die only meant the death total wouldn't tick up to six. No one other than Nora knew of my role in ending the carnage. And that was perfectly fine with me.*

*By mid-November, I had finally regained enough strength to be discharged. I would require a part-time nurse for some time, and there remained months of additional rehab ahead of me, but those were mere hiccups, as far as I was concerned. I was alive.*

*And I was going home.*

∼

I WAS SITTING on the couch when I spotted the car pulling into the driveway.

With a pained groan, I got to my feet and limped with the help of my cane to the front door. It was frosty outside, but I ignored the brisk winds while I stood on the porch, waiting for the car to park.

Moments later, your Aunt Ronnie emerged from the vehicle and opened the rear door. Seconds later you bounded out, darting down the walkway, up the porch steps, and into my arms.

"Quince!" I exclaimed, and you pulled back to look up at me.

"Am I home forever?" you asked out of the blue.

"That's the plan, buddy," I said. "It's freezing out. Why don't you run inside and get warm?"

You sprinted into the house while I waited in the cold for your aunt, who was slowly making her way to me as she dragged a suitcase behind her.

"Thanks so much for driving him up, Ronnie," I said once she was near the porch. "I know the roads are brutal these days."

"Of course," she said, waving me off as she plodded up the steps. "It'd be crazy to make you drive three hours and back in your condition."

We went inside, and Ronnie deposited your suitcase on the floor.

"Can I get you anything?" I asked. "Coffee? Lunch?" But Ronnie shook her head.

"Thank you, but no. My kids were especially wild this morning—maybe just nerves at Quince leaving us—so I feel obligated to get home as soon as I can to help reign them in. I'll just use your bathroom and be on my way, if it's alright with you."

"Of course," I said, gesturing down the hall toward our first-floor bathroom. Ronnie scurried off in that direction and reemerged shortly thereafter.

"Hey, Ronnie?" I asked while she gathered herself to leave.

"Yes?" she asked absently.

"Was everything normal with Quince while he was with you? Did he act strange in any way?"

Ronnie stopped what she was doing to consider my question before shaking her head.

"No. He missed you, obviously, but nothing out of sorts as far as I could see. Why do you ask?"

"Oh, no reason." I had often wondered over the previous month whether you had revealed any hints of your visions to Ronnie or her family while you were staying with them. Ronnie never alluded to anything in that regard when the two of you visited me in the hospital, and her confused response seemed to confirm that she remained in the dark on that front, whether because you had been hiding your visions from her or simply because you didn't have occasion to see anything of note while you were there.

Ronnie threw her winter coat back on. You were working on a puzzle at our kitchen table, but you detected Ronnie's imminent departure and hopped up to join us.

"I have to go now, Quince," she said. "Is it okay if I give you a hug?"

After a moment's thought, you nodded and extended your arms. Ronnie pulled you in a tight embrace with her face split in a wide smile.

"It was wonderful having you stay with us these past few weeks!" she said as she rocked you back and forth with her eyes closed, savoring the moment. "But your daddy will need you to help take care of him now, okay?"

"Okay," you said.

Ronnie let go of you and stood, giving me a quick hug.

"Don't hesitate to call if you need anything, okay?" she asked.

"I won't. And again, I can't thank you enough for everything."

"Of course. It was my pleasure." Ronnie opened the door to leave and stopped, deep in thought. After a moment, she turned back to me.

"I hope you don't mind, but Quince was asking me a lot about Anne while he was with us, so I told him some stories about her. Mostly stories about me beating her up when we were young, but he seemed to enjoy learning anything new about her. I just wanted you to know that Quince has been asking about his mother."

"Thank you," I said. "That's something we had started getting into before we were sidetracked with this." I held up my cane with a flourish. "But I appreciate you talking to him about Anne. I know that's important for him."

Ronnie nodded her agreement, but remained rooted on the spot.

"And for what it's worth, Quince really enjoyed getting to know his cousins," she finally added. "And we loved spending some time with him. I hope we'll have other opportunities in the future to see him, under better circumstances. And you, of course."

"You're right," I said, feeling guilty. "We aren't *that* far from each other. I shouldn't have been such a recluse all these years. I'll do better." Ronnie gave me a skeptical look, so I added, "I promise. We'll make definitive plans to get together for the holidays."

Ronnie gave me a thumbs-up and threw me a toothy grin to show there were no hard feelings before heading outside. Moments later, I heard her car start up and back out of our driveway, leaving just the two of us again.

You had settled back at the kitchen table with your puzzle, and you laughed at the sight of me hobbling in to join you.

"Daddy!" you exclaimed. "You look like an old man!" You stood up and imitated a decrepit man, hunched over as he walked with a cane.

"Thanks, Quince," I said drily.

You didn't catch my sarcasm, and you continued to mock, giggling all the while. You kept up those theatrics while I looked on, pretending to be insulted with an exaggerated glare, until I could no longer maintain the facade and allowed myself to be drawn into your laughter.

You and I thrived under established routines, but we were both thrown off after my stint in the hospital. It didn't help that the temperature had plummeted since mid-October, making it all but impossible to spend time outside for prolonged periods of time. We largely spent those first few days after our reunion focused on sedentary indoor activities: building Lego sets, working on puzzles, or making art. I looked forward to the day where I could comfortably walk around with you again, exploring some new area, but in the short-term I was thrilled that I could participate in any activities with you, even if they mostly involved me sitting around like a lump.

Still, I felt some relief when Saturday rolled around and we had an excuse to go out together. It was our first appointment with Nora since the shooting incident, and I hadn't seen her other than that one occasion where she visited me in the hospital. You were excited to see her as well, and you bounced around the house all morning until it was finally time to drive down to her office.

"Did you enjoy your time with your cousins?" I asked as we drove. It wasn't the first time I'd tried to discuss the weeks you spent with them, but you hadn't provided much intel in response to those earlier inquiries.

You nodded in response, before quickly adding, "Are we going back to them?"

"What? No! We're going to Ms. Nora, remember? But would you like to see your cousins again?"

"Umm, yes," you said, sounding cautious. "But not now. Maybe in one hundred days."

I laughed at your announced timetable.

"Fair enough. But I don't know about one hundred days —I'm working on plans to see them soon."

I watched you when we reached the location of the car accident memorialized by the cross on the side of the road— the cross that had kicked off that strange chapter of our lives.

Your head swiveled as we passed the cross, engrossed in that vision you had already witnessed multiple times, but you said nothing. It was a bitter reminder that even though our biggest crisis was behind us, there remained unnatural obstacles we'd have to face together. Still, I was determined to keep that a problem for another day—I simply wanted to focus on enjoying being out of the house with you again.

Once we arrived at Nora's office, you squealed at the sight of her and gave her an enthusiastic hug, which she was happy to return. Nora then looked at me, and I saw her eyes flicker toward my cane with a hint of sympathy written across her face. She gave me a gentle hug as well, careful not to knock me over, before taking a seat. I remained standing, and Nora stared at me as if she was expecting something more. But after that moment of awkwardness, Nora broke out into laughter.

"You know," she said, "I'm so used to you starting off these meetings with some sort of crisis to discuss, I just assumed you'd sit down to rant about something."

"Sorry," I said with a grin. "No rants today! But I reserve the right to change my mind later."

I exited the office to let you get to work with Nora. Even though it was a chilly day, I contemplated going out for a stroll, but decided against it. Walking was still uncomfortable for me, and I was content simply to rest on the wooden bench and wait for the two of you to finish.

After nearly an hour, Nora called me back into the office and surprised me by asking me to take a seat. You were playing with a Rubik's Cube, and I wasn't sure whether you were paying us any mind. After a mild struggle, I plopped myself onto a chair and waited for Nora to speak.

"I wanted to talk to you about a couple of things," she said, sounding serious. "The first is that I don't think Quince needs me anymore. His language has blossomed, and I have no reason to believe that his speech is delayed at this point. In fact, I suspect his language may actually qualify as above average as compared to that of his peers in many ways."

"Oh," I said. It was good news, and yet…. *Nora helped us get through that impossible stretch*, I thought. It was disheartening to think her time in our lives might be coming to an end, and Nora seemed to pick up on what I was feeling.

"Don't get me wrong," she added. "I'll miss working with Quince, and with you, tremendously. But I don't think you—either of you—really need me at this juncture. And that brings me to my second point."

Nora glanced at you, and I could see pain reflected in her eyes.

"I told you some time ago that my husband and I have been discussing him taking a new position at a different college," she continued. "We've reached a decision on that front, and we'll be moving to Chicago next month so that he can be settled by the start of the spring semester."

"Oh," I said again. That news also caught me off guard, but I quickly recovered. "Congratulations! Assuming, of course, that's something you want. Because when we last spoke—"

"I know, I know," Nora said, shaking her head. "I was against it at first, if only for our kids' sake. But I talked to them about the possibility of moving, and their openness to it surprised me. There's anxiety there, of course, but.... Well, I'm often surprised at how resilient kids can be when they receive the love they need."

We both looked at you after she said that, and I'm sure we were thinking the same thing.

"So I'll be ending services with all of my clients here in New York, giving referrals to new SLPs as warranted, but I meant it when I said Quince doesn't need services anymore. He's a shy kid, but he's doing great. And I know he'll continue to do great. As will you."

"Thank you. Best of luck to you with all of that. And thank you so much for everything. For being a friend when I absolutely needed one. At some point I'll write you a long letter that adequately conveys my gratitude. But I really couldn't have done any of this without you." I paused and chuckled. "Not that I completely understand what I did."

But Nora didn't crack a smile—she looked serious. And stern.

"What you did?" Nora asked rhetorically, holding out a hand to count on her fingers. "You raised a great kid," she said, ticking off a finger, before continuing, "The two of you saved God only knows how many lives along the way. You kept Quince safe, and you kept yourself alive in the process. Don't discount any of that!"

"Well, sure. But through all of that, I was floundering. There was no method to the madness at all." A thought struck me, and I added, "Although I can't imagine how anyone could have come up with a plan to deal with that mess. You told me once that sometimes there's nothing to be done but love your child and hope for the best."

"Yup," Nora said with a solemn nod. "And that's what you did, alright. Fortunately for you, it was enough. Be grateful."

Of course, she was right. Not only did I realize I should be thankful for how things turned out, but I was actually overflowing with gratitude. That appreciation intertwined with the guilt I had felt since the incident at the community center, but it was undeniably there. I hoped to hold onto it as long as I could.

With nothing more to say, I called you over to bid farewell to Nora.

"Quince," I said gently. "We have to say goodbye to Nora. She just told me she's moving with her family to another state soon."

Your face scrunched as you tried to process the implications of that news. You glanced up at Nora for confirmation, and she offered you a sad nod in response.

"Nora is going away?" you asked in a small voice.

"I'm afraid so," I said. "But we should thank her for all of her help. Can you do that?"

You paused before erupting to give Nora a fierce hug.

"Thank you, Nora," you murmured into her shoulder. Pulling back, you looked at me and asked, "We'll see her again, right?"

I didn't answer, but Nora jumped in.

"I'm sure we will see each other again, Quince," she said, and you nodded, looking appeased, and the hope I saw in your eyes broke my heart.

You were simply too young to realize a promise to see someone again is all too often a lie adults tell each other to make parting less painful.

THE FOLLOWING THURSDAY, you woke me up at 3:30 in the morning.

I was confused and disoriented when you called out for me in the dark. After taking a moment to locate my cane, I staggered bleary-eyed into your room and turned on a light.

"What is it, Quince?" I asked. "Nightmare?"

But you shook your head. You didn't look scared at all—in fact, you looked awake and alert.

I was confused, and not just because I was still partially asleep. You had always been an early riser, but for months you consistently woke up around dawn. That day's 3:30 a.m. wake-up call reminded me of your toddler days, when you would go through some sort of sleep regression every few months and snap awake, fully alert, at bizarre times in the middle of the night.

"Alright," I said with a yawn. "Let's go downstairs." Then I remembered what day it was, and added, "Oh, and happy Thanksgiving." *God, I hope this wake-up time is an aberration and not the start of a new pattern.*

I made a pot of coffee while you ate some cereal at the kitchen table. Once I was adequately caffeinated, I dug out a new Lego set for us to build, and we worked on that for some time. The sun finally came up after four hours of us assembling Lego blocks, and I looked up the outside temperature on my phone: thirty-three degrees. Cold, but not cold enough to keep us inside all day. I was feeling antsy after being cooped up for hours and longed to go out in the world, if only for a bit.

"Should we go somewhere?" I asked.

"Where?" you responded. It was a good question—it was still early, and most businesses were still closed. I wasn't even sure if any of them would open later in light of the holiday.

We had no big holiday plans ourselves. Earlier in the week, you informed me that all you wanted for Thanksgiving dinner was buttered spaghetti with crescent rolls, and I was happy to accommodate that simple request later that afternoon.

"How about the churches in town?" I suggested. "We haven't looked at churches in a while."

You thought it over, and let out a long, dramatic sigh.

"Fine," you moaned reluctantly, sounding remarkably like an angsty teenager. I assumed that was something you picked up during your stay with your cousins.

We bundled up the best we could and drove into town. The roads were quiet and, except for a handful of people filtering in and out of the solitary coffee shop in the village, there was no action on the streets.

I parked in front of the white Catholic church on the far side of town and let you out of the car. It was unclear whether it would have any services later in the day—I couldn't remember if churches made a point of holding Mass on Thanksgiving—but there was no activity when we arrived.

You walked toward the church, arching backwards and

looking up to admire its tall steeple before lowering your head and surveying the area.

"Where are all the people?" you suddenly asked.

"It's really early in the morning," I explained. "And no one is here yet. Maybe later there'll be—"

I stopped once I realized what you were *really* asking.

"You... you don't see anyone else here?"

You shook your head, looking more puzzled than anything else, and asked, "Where did they go?"

We had last visited that church a few months earlier, over the summer, and during that visit, you saw throngs of people celebrating various weddings. This was one of the churches I had used to test your abilities in those early days, and I remembered cracking you up as I danced through your visions of weddings.

The visions that inexplicably seemed to be gone.

"I don't know where they went," I admitted. I studied you carefully, trying to find out whether this development bothered you, but your face was unreadable.

*What changed?* I wondered, replaying the last day in my head. There was nothing particularly noteworthy, other than your early wake-up that morning. But I didn't see how a poor night of sleep could cause the loss of your abilities.

And then I recalled something the administrator of your old school, Ms. Leona, told me back in April during my meeting to address your speech delays:

*"I've read that sleep regressions can be a side effect of children's brains developing as they grow, but aren't our brains still developing into adulthood? It never made much sense to me that the experts claim sleep regressions stop so early in childhood."*

Was that it? Had your brain continued to grow in a way that resulted in your visions being turned off—a rewiring so substantial that it triggered another sleep regression? You were on the verge of turning five—well beyond the age children typically experience those types of regressions. But you were an atypical kid, and I remained in the dark about what rules applied to you.

As I was pondering the possibilities, a door to the church opened, and a priest emerged, looking surprised at our presence.

"I'm sorry to scare you, Father," I said. "We were just looking at the church. My son loves them." I didn't add that your interest in churches wasn't particularly pious in nature.

"No need to apologize!" the priest boomed. "And feel free to take a look at the inside, if you like. It is a beautiful church, if I do say so myself." An icy wind hit us, and the priest shivered. "Plus, it's much warmer inside."

I looked down at you.

"Do you want to see the inside, Quince?"

"Yes, please."

I thanked the priest and went in with you. The church wasn't all that large, at least as far as churches go, but you were amazed as you studied the imagery in the stained glass windows, the carved wooden pews, and the ornate altar at the front of the chapel. You seemed to appreciate the sanctity of the space, and you walked around in a slow and respectful manner, taking care not to make any noise.

"Can you see anyone else in here, Quince?" I whispered to you.

"No. I can't." You tried to whisper as well, but your voice still emerged loud enough to echo throughout the church.

We walked deeper into the building, and you stopped to gaze at a statue of Mary set against the wall. You appeared to be taken by the sculpture, and I wondered if you were remembering your own brief interaction with your mother from several weeks earlier. It occurred to me that the peace and quiet of an empty church was probably a new experience for you, although I was unsure whether you were enjoying it.

"Are you sad?" I asked, and you looked at me, confused. I added, "You used to be in the middle of a big party whenever you went to a church, but now it's quiet. Are you sad because everyone is gone?"

You wordlessly looked back at the statue, and at first, I thought you were ignoring my question. But then you turned back to me and answered.

"I'm not sad," you said. "Because everyone isn't gone."

And then you reached up and your hand found mine.

# EPILOGUE

Mistakes are often easy to see with the gift of hindsight, and mine were no different. Throughout our ordeal, I failed to comprehend the true nature of our adversity. I assumed your visions were a problem in search of a solution, but I couldn't have been more wrong. Now I see they were a storm that simply had to be endured.

Yet, somehow, endure we did, which was miraculous. But we did more than weather that tempest—we actually emerged from that experience stronger than ever. Perhaps not in a physical sense—I've long accepted that I'll spend the rest of my life tied to my cane. But you and I each came out of that episode transformed at a fundamental level. And, more importantly, we solidified and strengthened our small family of two.

Over the course of less than a year, you found your voice —a noteworthy achievement in and of itself. But your voice is more than just the projection of words. It's a channel through which you can release the good in you, gifting it to the world at large. And it's a gift we sorely need. Darkness threatens to overwhelm us all, at times. We can't afford to squander any sources of light.

I had called this "the story of you," but that characterization didn't stem from the unique challenges you faced when you were four years old, since we aren't defined by what happens to us. I view this as your story, or at least the beginning of your story, because of how you responded to those obstacles. We're more than the scars we carry—we are the marks we leave upon the world. And viewed under that lens, I couldn't be prouder of what your story represents.

For nearly a year, you endured a bombardment of images depicting the worst that life has to offer, but you never allowed those visions to diminish your light. Rather than wilt under the parade of nightmares that assaulted you on the regular, your spirit was strong enough to brighten the lives of all you touched.

Including me.

You taught me how to be a father. You helped me find the beauty in the world and taught me how to restore it when it's lacking. You simply made me a better person.

And yet even with my growth, I'm well aware that I remain far from perfect. In sharing this story, I laid out the choices I was forced to make and the reasons underlying my decisions, and I accept your judgment on those fronts. And, if it is warranted, I beg your forgiveness for all of the ways in which I misstepped. But I can tell you this: everything I did as your father was with you in mind, and in consideration of what the good in you represents. My failures may have been failures of judgment, but not once did they stem from a lack of love.

At the risk of stating the obvious, my love for you continued, and continues, beyond the end of this specific story. Even after the experience of your visions receded into our collective memories, your inherent goodness never stopped radiating as you grew, injecting light into a world that tends to fall prey to the darkness. The story I shared was in many ways your beginning—an unorthodox origin, to be sure, but a clear arrow pointing in the direction your life would take.

Yours is a story that will continue, God willing, long after my own reaches its end. Like all stories, there will be times of conflict and times of drama. There will be moments of joy, moments of humor, and moments of sadness. There will be points where the story is so terrifying that I'll want to look away. But I won't. Because I know in my heart that whatever challenges you face, you'll live your story to its full potential.

I'm overjoyed at being fortunate enough to witness it.

# ACKNOWLEDGMENTS

I put everything I have into this book, yet I still couldn't have managed to bring it to the finish line without the substantial support I received from many directions.

My first and loudest thank you, as always, goes to my incredible wife, Lynne, who has encouraged me to write and "put my work out there" for as long as she has been in my life. She is always my first reader, and her enjoyment of my stories is all that I need for them to feel like a success. It's impossible to list all of the reasons I'm profoundly grateful for her presence in my life, but that gratitude is something I feel each and every day.

This book is dedicated to our son, Patrick, whose kindness and sense of wonder inspired much of this story in the nearly four years it took to write it. The greatest motivation I had in the course of writing this novel was crafting a story that might one day make Patrick as proud of me as we are of him.

Thank you once again to all of the members of my family who enthusiastically jumped at the chance to read early (and occasionally messy) drafts of this work and generously shared their encouraging feedback: my mother, Barbara Lush, as well as my in-laws, Walter and Patricia Anderson and Tracey Kappenberg.

I also owe a huge thank you to Emylie Zollo and Green Crow Publishing for the opportunity to publish this story and for the countless hours they devoted to polishing and promoting this novel. It was a wonderful experience working with a partner that shares my passion for this story, and I am beyond grateful for their efforts in helping this book reach its full potential.

My heartfelt thanks also go out to Sasha Shapiro for her vigilant work as the first copyeditor of this novel. Her thoughtful edits and suggestions went a long way towards bringing this story to where I dreamed it could be.

Much appreciation as well to Erica Ball (and specifically, her impressive eagle eye) for her diligent work in proofreading this novel as it approached completion.

I am very fortunate to have partnered myself with an artist who always manages to surprise me with designing covers I adore, and this one is no exception. So, many thanks, once again, to Stephanie Ciccotta, for patiently listening to my bland suggestions for a cover and disregarding pretty much everything I said in order to create something exponentially more beautiful, interesting, and touching than I could have ever imagined.

I am grateful yet again for the assistance of my friends Dr. John Reagan and super-nurse Nick Montella for thoughtfully answering all of the strange, out-of-context medical questions I threw at them in the course of writing this story (and generously never billing me for their time in responding to these bizarre inquiries).

This book touches upon some serious topics that required a good amount of research in order to do them justice, and I would be remiss if I did not acknowledge two works that served as the foundation for much of my education in that regard. *Trauma Through a Child's Eyes*, by Peter A. Levine and Maggie Kline (2006); and *Childhood Speech, Language & Listening Problems*, by Patricia McAleer

Hamaguchi (2010) are excellent resources for those inclined to learn more about these topics.

Finally, if you are reading these words, please know that I am grateful to you for picking up this book. Whether you are a reader who has been along for my writing journey from the outset, or a brave soul willing to try out a new book from an unfamiliar author, I am immensely thankful for your support.

## ABOUT THE AUTHOR

 When he isn't writing or otherwise dreaming up stories, Daniel Maunz works as in-house counsel for a major insurance company. He has spent the past few years bouncing back and forth between New York and South Carolina along with his wife, Lynne; their son, Patrick; and their two cats, Admiral and Captain, and they currently reside in Norwalk, Connecticut. *The Story of You* is Daniel's third novel.

www.danielmaunz.com